SENDING A MESSAGE

Rolling back his right sleeve beyond his elbow, to keep the material clear of the blood, the tall man rested the point of the dagger gently on the man's chest, feeling for one of the spaces between the ribs, then began slowly increasing the pressure on the handle of the weapon. As the point pierced his skin, the captive cried out, a muffled grunt lost in the folds of the rudimentary gag.

The tall man pressed harder still and the front of his captive's *jellaba* suddenly turned a deep red as blood spurted from the wound. The tall man worked the knife in slowly, his gaze never leaving the dying man's face. When he estimated that the point of the weapon was about to touch the heart, he paused for a few seconds, changed his grip on the knife and twisted it sideways, the tip of the blade ripping his victim's heart virtually in half.

"Spread the word," he said, as he and his men headed back toward the *souk*. "Make sure everyone knows that Hassan al-Qalaa died because of what he did; ensure that everyone knows that if they talk to the police, they will suffer the same fate. And offer a reward for the recovery of the tablet. We *must* find it, whatever it takes."

ALSO BY JAMES BECKER

The First Apostle

THE
MOSES STONE

James Becker

AN ONYX BOOK

ONYX
Published by New American Library, a division of
Penguin Group (USA) Inc., 375 Hudson Street,
New York, New York 10014, USA
Penguin Group (Canada), 90 Eglinton Avenue East, Suite 700, Toronto,
Ontario M4P 2Y3, Canada (a division of Pearson Penguin Canada Inc.)
Penguin Books Ltd., 80 Strand, London WC2R 0RL, England
Penguin Ireland, 25 St. Stephen's Green, Dublin 2,
Ireland (a division of Penguin Books Ltd.)
Penguin Group (Australia), 250 Camberwell Road, Camberwell, Victoria 3124,
Australia (a division of Pearson Australia Group Pty. Ltd.)
Penguin Books India Pvt. Ltd., 11 Community Center, Panchsheel Park,
New Delhi - 110 017, India
Penguin Group (NZ), 67 Apollo Drive, Rosedale, North Shore 0632,
New Zealand (a division of Pearson New Zealand Ltd.)
Penguin Books (South Africa) (Pty.) Ltd., 24 Sturdee Avenue,
Rosebank, Johannesburg 2196, South Africa

Penguin Books Ltd., Registered Offices:
80 Strand, London WC2R 0RL, England

Published by Onyx, an imprint of New American Library, a division of Penguin
Group (USA) Inc. Previously published in a Transworld Publishers edition.
For further information contact Transworld Publishers, a division of Random
House, Ltd., 61–63 Uxbridge Road, London W5 5SA, England.

First Onyx Printing, March 2010
10 9 8 7 6 5 4 3 2 1

PROLOGUE

"We can wait no longer."

Elazar Ben Ya'ir stood on a heavy wooden table almost in the center of the fortress and looked down at the faces of the men and women who surrounded him.

Outside the massive stone walls, a torrent of sound—shouted orders, the noise of digging, and of stone falling on stone—formed a loud and continuous backdrop to his words. The racket was interspersed with the occasional thud and crack, as a missile from one of the *ballistae*, the massive Roman siege engines, crashed into the fortress walls.

Ben Ya'ir had led the Jewish Sicarii rebels for the last seven years, ever since they'd seized Masada from the resident Roman garrison. The Sicarii were radical Zealots. They were so radical, in fact, that they now numbered even the Zealots themselves, as well as almost everyone else in Judea, among their enemies. For over two years they'd used the hilltop fortress as a base for raiding both Roman and Jewish settlements throughout the country.

The previous year, Lucius Flavius Silva, the Roman governor of Judea, had finally lost patience with the Sicarii and attacked Masada with the *Fretensis* legion—some five thousand battle-hardened soldiers. But Masada was a tough nut to crack, and all the Romans' initial attempts to breach its defenses had failed. As a last resort, they had built a containing wall—a *circumvallation*—around part of the fortress and had then begun creating a ramp that could reach high enough to use a battering ram on the massive wall that surrounded the citadel.

"You've all seen the rampart that is now touching our walls," Elazar Ben Ya'ir said, his voice strong but tinged with resignation. "Tomorrow, or the day after at the latest, the rams will breach our defenses. We can no longer prevent that, and when they break through the Romans will overrun us. We number less than a thousand—men, women and children. Outside the walls, our enemies can muster five times that number. Make no mistake about this, the Romans *will* prevail, no matter how fiercely or bravely we fight."

Elazar Ben Ya'ir paused and looked around. A salvo of arrows flew through the air from beyond the battlements, whistling over the heads of the assembled defenders, but hardly any of them so much as glanced up.

"If we fight," Ben Ya'ir continued, "most of us—the lucky ones—will be killed. Any who survive will be either executed, probably by crucifixion, or sold in the slave markets on the coast."

An angry murmuring rose and fell in the crowd in response to the words of their leader. The Romans had employed a refinement that had severely restricted the ability of the Sicarii to retaliate: they had forced slaves to construct the ramp, just as they would no doubt use slaves to drive the battering rams. And to attack a fortress held by Jews, the Romans had used Jewish slaves. To protect themselves, the Sicarii would have had to kill their own enslaved countrymen—something that even they, who were not noted for their compassion or tolerance toward anyone—found distasteful.

That was why they hadn't been able to stop the building of the ramp; and it was also why they would not be able to stop the rams.

"Our choice is simple," Ben Ya'ir concluded. "If we fight, and if we aren't killed in battle, we will either die nailed to crosses in the valley below us or become slaves of the Romans."

The crowd looked at him, their murmurs silenced.

"And if we surrender?" an angry voice asked.

"That's your choice, my brother," Elazar Ben Ya'ir replied, looking down at the young man who had spoken. "But you'll still face slavery or crucifixion."

"So what can we do if we can't fight and we can't surrender? What other choices do we have?"

"There is one way," Ben Ya'ir said, "just one way, that we can achieve a victory here that will resound for all time."

"We can defeat the Romans?"

"We can beat them, yes, but not in the way you mean."

"Then how?"

Elazar Ben Ya'ir paused for a few moments, looking round at the people with whom he'd shared his life and the fortress for the last seven years. Then he told them.

As night fell, the sound of construction work outside the ramparts died away. Inside the citadel, teams of men made preparations for what would be the final act in the drama of Masada.

They stacked wood and containers of flammable oil in all the storerooms at the northern end of the fortress, except one group of rooms that Elazar Ben Ya'ir specifically told them to leave untouched. Then, as the last rays of the sun vanished from the peaks of the surrounding mountains, they built a large fire in the center of the main square of the fortress and lit it. Finally, they set fire to the wood piles in the storerooms.

Their preparations complete, Elazar Ben Ya'ir summoned four men and gave them explicit instructions.

The creation of the ramp had focused the attention of the Romans on the western side of the citadel; that was where the majority of the legionaries had gathered, ready for the final assault. There were guards posted around the rest of the fortress, on the desert floor far below the rocky outcrop, but far fewer than in previous days and weeks.

At the eastern edge of Masada, the cliffs fell some thirteen hundred feet. It was not a sheer drop, but such a difficult and dangerous descent that the Romans clearly didn't think any of the Sicarii would be foolhardy enough to attempt it, and so the number of sentries they'd posted there was small. And until that night, they'd been right.

Ben Ya'ir led the men to the foot of the massive wall

that guarded the edge of the Masada plateau. He handed over two cylindrical objects, each well-wrapped in linen cloth and securely bound with cord, and two heavy stone tablets, again wrapped and padded with linen. Then he embraced each of the men for a few moments before turning and walking away. Like ghosts in the night, the four men climbed the wall and vanished silently into the tumble of boulders that marked the start of their perilous descent.

The assembled Sicarii, nine hundred and thirty-six men, women and children, knelt in prayer for what they knew would be the last time, then formed a line at a table set against one wall of the fortress to draw lots. When the last person had taken his straw, ten of them moved forward from the multitude, returning to the table where Elazar Ben Ya'ir stood waiting. He ordered that the names of the ten men be recorded, along with the name of their leader, and a scribe faithfully wrote them down, on eleven shards of pottery, one name on each.

Then Ben Ya'ir led the way to the northern palace, the building that had been erected by Herod over a hundred years earlier as his personal fortress when he was appointed King of Judea by his Roman masters. There, he directed that the fragments of pottery be carefully buried, to act as a kind of a record of the end of the siege.

Finally he walked back to the center of the fortress, and issued a single command, a shout that ran out across the citadel.

Around him, all the fighting men, except the ten chosen by lot, unbuckled their weapons, their swords and daggers, and dropped them on the ground. The clattering sound made by hundreds of weapons tumbling onto the dusty soil echoed thunderously off the surrounding walls.

He issued a second order, and the ten men prepared themselves, each standing directly in front of one of their unarmed companions. Ben Ya'ir watched as one of the first victims moved forward to embrace the man chosen to be his executioner.

"Strike quickly and sure, my brother," the man said, as he moved back.

Two of his companions gripped the unarmed man's arms and held him steady. The armed man unsheathed his sword, leaned forward, gently pulled aside the victim's tunic to expose his chest, then drew back his right arm.

"Go in peace, my friend," he said, his voice choking slightly, and then with a single strong blow he drove the blade of his sword straight into the other man's heart. The victim grunted with the sudden impact, but no cry of pain escaped his lips.

Gently, with reverence, the two men laid his lifeless body on the ground.

In the small clusters of men around the square, the same sequence of actions was repeated, until ten of the defenders lay dead on the ground.

Elazar Ben Ya'ir issued the order again, and once more the swords hit home, this time one of them felling Ben Ya'ir himself.

About half an hour later, all but two of the Sicarii lay dead on the ground. Solemnly, the last two men drew lots, and again a short, powerful thrust of a sword ended another life. The remaining warrior, tears streaming down his face, walked around the fortress, checking every motionless body to ensure that none of his companions still lived.

He took one last look around the citadel, now deserted by the living. He muttered a final prayer to his god asking for forgiveness for what he was about to do, reversed his sword and placed the point against his chest, then threw himself forward onto the blade.

The following morning, the battering ram began its work on the wall at the western side of Masada, and quickly broke through. The Romans were immediately confronted with another bulwark, clearly raised by the Sicarii as a desperate last-ditch defense, but smashed their way through that as well in a matter of minutes. Moments later the soldiers began pouring into the fortress.

An hour after the wall was finally breached, Lucius Flavius Silva walked up the approach ramp, past lines of legionaries, and through the gaping hole in the wall. Once inside, he looked around in disbelief.

Bodies lay everywhere, men, women and children, the blood that caked their chests already blackened and solid. Flies swarmed, feeding greedily in the afternoon sun. Carrion birds pecked at the soft tissues of the corpses and rats ran over the bodies.

"All dead?" Silva demanded of a centurion.

"This is how we found them, sir. But there were seven survivors—two women and five children. We found them hiding in a cistern at the southern end of the plateau."

"What do they say happened here? Did these men kill themselves?"

"Not exactly, sir, because their religion prohibits it. They drew lots and killed each other. The last man"—the centurion pointed at one of the bodies lying facedown, the tip of a sword-blade sticking out of the man's back—"threw himself on his blade, so he was the only one who actually committed suicide."

"But why?" Silva asked, almost a rhetorical question.

"According to the women, their leader—Elazar Ben Ya'ir—told them that if they took their own lives, at a time and in a manner that they chose for themselves, they would deny us victory." The centurion pointed to the northern end of the citadel. "They could have fought on. The storerooms—those that they deliberately didn't set on fire—are full of food, and the cisterns have plenty of fresh water."

"If *they've* won, it's a very strange kind of victory," Silva grunted, still looking at the hundreds of bodies that surrounded him. "We have possession of Masada, the filthy Sicarii are all dead, at last, and we haven't lost a single legionary in the assault. I could do with a lot more *defeats* like this!"

The centurion smiled politely. "The women and children, General. What are your orders?"

"Have the children taken to the nearest slave market, and give the women to the troops. If they're still alive when the men have finished with them, let them go."

Just outside Masada, the four Sicarii waited, hidden behind a rocky outcrop a few hundred feet above the desert floor. Once the Roman troops breached the wall and entered the citadel, orders were sent down to the other sentries to leave their posts. But even after the legionaries had moved away, the four men still waited for darkness to fall before they completed their descent.

Three days later they reached Ir-Tzadok B'Succaca, the hilltop community that two millennia later would become famous as Qumran. The four Sicarii remained on the plateau for a day, then resumed their journey.

They followed the west shore of the Dead Sea for about five miles before striking north. They passed through the towns of Cyprus, Taurus and Jericho, before stopping for the night at Phasaelis. On the second day they turned northwest for Shiloh, but the going was much more difficult once they left the town and trudged north along the eastern slopes of Mount Gerizim, and they only made it as far as Mahnayim as dusk fell. The next day they walked as far as Sychar, where they stopped to rest for a further day, because the most arduous part of their journey was about to begin, a ten-mile hike over very difficult terrain to the west of Mount Ebal to the town of Bemesilis.

That trek took them the whole of the following day, and again they rested for twenty-four hours before resuming their journey further north to Ginae. They reached the town almost two weeks after leaving the fortress of Masada and there purchased additional provisions in preparation for the final section of their journey.

They set off the following morning, trekking northwest through the date-palm forests carpeting the fertile lowlands that stretched from the Sea of Galilee down to the shores of the Dead Sea, heading up into the Plain of Esdraelon. The track they were following meandered left and right, skirting obstacles and avoiding the higher ground that lay between them and their destination. It made for very slow going, and was all the more exhausting because of the relentless heat of the sun, their constant companion.

It was midafternoon before they saw their objective, and almost dusk before they reached the foot of the hill. Rather than attempt to climb the slope and carry out the task they'd been given by Elazar Ben Ya'ir in the dark, they decided to rest for the night.

When the sun rose the following morning, the four men were already on the plateau. Only one of them had been to the place before, and it took them over eight hours to complete their task.

It was late afternoon before they were able to descend the steep path to the plain below and almost midnight before they reached Nain, their journey made slightly easier because now they were no longer carrying either of the two cylindrical objects or the stone tablets.

The following morning, they sought out a local potter. They offered him just sufficient gold that he would ask no questions, then took possession of his workshop for the remainder of the day. They remained in there, with the door barred shut, until late into the evening, working by the flickering light of a number of animal-fat lamps.

The next day the four men went their separate ways, each with a single further task to perform.

They never saw each other again.

PART ONE

Morocco

1

Margaret O'Connor loved the *medina*, and she simply adored the *souk*.

She'd been told that the word "*medina*" meant "city" in Arabic but in Rabat, as in many places in Morocco, it was a generic term applied to the old town, a labyrinth of winding streets, most far too narrow to accommodate cars. Indeed, in many of them two people walking side by side would find it a bit of a squeeze. And in the *souk* itself, although there were large open areas surrounded by stalls and open-fronted shops, some of the passageways were even more restricted and—to Margaret—even more charming in their eccentricity. The streets meandered around ancient plastered houses, their walls cracked and crazed with age, the paint flaking and discolored by the sun.

Every time she and Ralph visited the area, they were surrounded by hordes of people. At first, she'd been slightly disappointed that most of the locals seemed to favor Western-style clothing—jeans and T-shirts were much in evidence—rather than the traditional Arab *jellabas* she'd been expecting. The guidebook they'd bought from the reception desk of their hotel helped to explain why.

Although Morocco was an Islamic nation, the population of the country was only about one-quarter Arab; the bulk of the inhabitants were Berbers, more properly called Imazighen, the original non-Arab people of North Africa. The Berbers had formed the original population of Morocco and initially resisted the Arab invasion of their country, but over time most of them converted to Islam and began speaking Arabic. This gradual assimilation of the Berbers into the Arab community had resulted in a colorful mixture of dress, culture and language, with both Arabic and the Berber tongue—Tamazight—being widely spoken, as well as French, Spanish and even English.

Margaret O'Connor loved the sounds and the smells and the bustle. She could even put up with the seemingly endless numbers of small boys running through the narrow passageways, pleading for money or offering to act as guides for the obvious tourists wandering about.

It was her first visit to Morocco with her husband Ralph who was—it has to be said—rather less enamored with the country than his wife. He found the crowds of people that thronged the *souk* claustrophobic, and the myriad and unfamiliar smells bothered him. He much preferred the foreign—but infinitely more familiar— seaside resorts that lined the Spanish *costas*, their usual holiday destination. But this year Margaret had wanted to try something more exotic, somewhere different, and Morocco had seemed a good compromise.

It was on a different continent—Africa—but still close

enough to avoid having to endure a long-haul flight. They'd rejected Casablanca, because everybody had told them it was just a typically dirty and noisy seaport—a far cry from the classic romantic image created by Hollywood. So they'd settled on a budget flight to Casablanca and hired a car for the drive north to the midpriced hotel they'd booked in Rabat.

And early that evening, their last in Morocco, they were walking toward the *souk* once more, Margaret excited, Ralph with a resigned expression on his face.

"What, exactly, do you want to buy in there?"

"Nothing. Everything. I don't know." Margaret stopped and looked at her husband. "There's no romance in your soul, is there?" It was a statement more than a question. "Look, we leave here tomorrow, and I just wanted to walk through the *souk* again and take some more photographs, something to help us remember this holiday. After all, I doubt if we'll be coming back here again, will we?"

"Not if I've got anything to do with it," Ralph muttered, as his wife turned back toward the *medina*, but not quite *sotto voce* enough to prevent Margaret hearing him.

"Next year," she said, "we'll go back to Spain, OK? So just stop complaining, smile, and at least *pretend* you're enjoying yourself."

As on every previous occasion since they'd arrived in Rabat, they approached the *medina* from the *Kasbah des Oudaïas*, simply because it was, for Margaret, the most attractive and picturesque route. The *kasbah* itself was a twelfth-century fortress erected on a cliff-top, its crenellated battlements and solid stone ramparts overlooking what was originally the pirate town of Sale, and within its walls the place was a delight. The whitewashed houses all sported a band of sky-blue paint, the color identical on every property, that ran around their bases, from ground level up to, usually, about three feet in height, though on some it reached as high as eight or ten feet. Though the color had clearly not been applied recently, it nevertheless gave the area the feeling of having been newly painted.

It was a strangely attractive decorative feature that neither Margaret nor her husband had ever seen before and, though they'd asked several people, nobody appeared to have any idea why it had been done. Their requests for elucidation had been met with puzzled faces and elaborate shrugs. The houses within the *kasbah*, it seemed, had always been decorated like that.

From the *kasbah*, they wound their way steadily down a wide walkway, flat sections of the sloping path broken by individual groups of three steps, obviously constructed to cope with the gradient, toward the *medina*. The river ran beside them on their left, while to the right lay an open grassy area, a popular spot for people who wanted to sit and admire the view, or simply to lie there and watch the world go by.

The entrance to the *medina* looked dark and uninviting, partly because of the brilliance of the late-afternoon sunlight outside, but mainly because of the curved metalwork that formed an elegant semicircular roof over this part of the old town. The metal panels were geometric in design and didn't seem to allow much light to penetrate, but imparted a kind of opaque and shimmering iridescence to the sky above, almost giving it the appearance of mother-of-pearl.

Once inside, the now-familiar smells reasserted themselves in the gloom—smoke, metallic dust, herbs and spices, newly cut wood, and a strange and pervasive odor that Margaret had finally identified as coming from the tanneries. The noise level rose markedly as they walked into the *souk*, the clatter of the metalworkers' hammers a constant counterpoint to the hum of conversation, of buyers haggling with traders, and the occasional shouts as voices were raised in excitement or anger.

And, as usual, it was full of both people and cats.

The first time Margaret had visited the *medina* and *souk*, she'd been appalled at the sheer number of feral cats they'd seen. But her concern was allayed almost immediately when she realized how healthy they looked and saw the first of several feeding areas, where noticeably well-fed cats and kittens lolled about, and where plates of food were left out for the market's feline residents. She presumed that the traders welcomed their presence because they would ensure that the number of rats and mice were kept under control, though the look of some of the larger cats sleeping in the sun suggested it had been quite a long time since they'd had to hunt for their own dinners.

The sheer range of products and skills on offer in the *souk* was, as always, amazing. They passed stalls selling black metal lanterns; blue and green glass bottles that could be made to order; leather goods, including chairs; exquisite boxes fashioned from cedar; shoes; clothes hanging on racks and poles that extended out into the narrow streets, forcing passersby to duck and weave their way around them; clocks; spices sold from open sacks; carpets; blankets, and silver trinkets. Margaret always stopped at one particular stall and watched, fascinated, as sheets of silver were hammered flat and then cut, shaped, molded and soldered to form teapots, bowls and utensils.

And everywhere she looked there were food stalls, selling everything from sandwiches to lamb cooked in traditional Moroccan tajines, the peculiarly shaped earthenware pots that look something like inverted funnels. The first time they had walked through the *souk*, Margaret had wanted to try some of the local "fast food," but Ralph had cautioned her against it.

"Just look at the condition of those stalls," he'd said. "A British health inspector would have a fit if he saw them. These people have no idea about hygiene."

Margaret had been tempted to point out that everybody they'd seen looked notably healthy on their diet of local food, prepared without the "benefit" of flavorings, colorings, preservatives and all the other assorted chemical compounds that seemed increasingly essential in the British diet, but bit her lip. So they had, predictably enough, eaten every meal in their hotel since they'd arrived in the city. Ralph had even been suspicious of some of the dishes served in the hotel dining room, but they had to eat somewhere, and it seemed to him to be the safest option.

Taking pictures in the *souk* hadn't proved to be quite as easy as Margaret had expected, because most of the traders and shoppers appeared very reluctant to be photographed, even by a tourist. And, obviously, what she had been hoping to capture on her pocket-sized Olympus were the people there—they were what she wanted to remember.

When yet another tall Moroccan swerved away from her as she raised the camera, she muttered in irritation. "Oh, for God's sake."

Margaret lowered the Olympus and held it at chest height, partially concealed by her handbag. She'd altered the length of the bag's strap, looped it over her shoulder and was holding it against her body with her left hand because they were in an area where pickpockets were known to operate. She would take a scatter-gun approach to her photographic mission, she decided, and just click the shutter as they walked through the *souk*, not bothering to aim the camera properly. That was one advantage of digital photography—the memory card was big enough to hold well over a hundred pictures. She'd be able to delete those that were no good when she got back home to Kent, and she had a spare data card with her if she filled up the one in the camera.

"OK, Ralph," Margaret said, "you can walk on my right side. That'll help keep the camera out of sight. We'll go all the way through to the other end. And then," she added, "we'll walk back to the hotel and enjoy our last dinner here in Morocco."

"Good idea." Ralph O'Connor sounded relieved at the prospect of getting out of the *souk*. He moved across the narrow passageway to stand where his wife had instructed. Then, pursued by a small group of boys clamoring for their attention, they began to walk slowly, their progress punctuated by a succession of faint clicks as Margaret snapped away.

About halfway through the *souk* there was a sudden commotion at one of the stalls almost directly in front of them. Some half a dozen men, all of them wearing traditional Arab clothing, were shouting and jostling each other, their voices loud and—though Margaret understood barely a word of Arabic—clearly very angry. The focus of their attention seemed to be a small, shabbily dressed man standing beside one of the stalls. The men confronting him appeared to be gesturing toward the wares on display, which puzzled Margaret as it looked as if the stall offered only a collection of grubby clay tablets and potsherds, the kind of rubbish that could be dug up in almost any ancient site in Morocco. Perhaps, she thought, the Arabs were officials and some of the goods on display were stolen or looted from an archaeological site. Whatever the cause of the dispute, it was a lot more dramatic than anything they'd seen before in the *souk*.

Margaret did her best to aim the camera straight at the group and began clicking the shutter release.

"What are you doing?" Ralph hissed.

"Just getting a bit of local color, that's all," Margaret replied. "Much more interesting if I can take pictures of a fight rather than some old stall-holders flogging brass coffeepots."

"Come on. Let's go." Ralph tugged at his wife's sleeve, urging her to leave the scene. "I don't trust these people."

"God, Ralph, you can be such a wimp sometimes."

But the argument they were witnessing did seem to be turning nasty, so Margaret took a final couple of pictures and then turned away, heading back toward the entrance to the *souk*, her husband striding along beside her.

Before they'd gone fifty yards, the commotion behind them flared into still angrier shouts and yells, and moments later they were aware of the sound of running feet, rapidly approaching.

Quickly Ralph pulled Margaret into one of the narrow side alleys of the *souk* and, almost as soon as they'd moved out of the main thoroughfare, the small and shabby man they'd seen at the stall raced past. A few seconds behind him, the other men who'd been arguing followed, yelling something at their quarry.

"I wonder what he's done," Margaret said, as she stepped out of the alley.

"Whatever it is, it's nothing to do with us," Ralph said. "I'll feel a lot happier when we're back inside the hotel."

They threaded their way through the crowds, but before they reached the main gateway, as they were walking past another of the short side alleys beside a spice-seller, they heard another outburst. Moments later, the little Arab ran past them again, his breath coming in short, urgent gasps as he desperately sought sanctuary. Behind him, Margaret could clearly hear his pursuers, now much closer than they'd been before.

And as he ran past, a small beige object fell from one of the pockets of his *jellaba* and tumbled toward the ground, its fall interrupted by an open sack of light-colored spice. The object landed virtually in the center of the sack, and almost immediately became invisible, its color blending with the spice around it.

The man clearly had no idea that he'd dropped any-thing, and continued in his headlong flight. Seconds later, half a dozen men pounded past, their pace increas-ing as they caught sight of their prey, now only about thirty yards in front of them.

Margaret glanced down at the object, then looked up at the stall-holder, who had turned in the direction of the retreating men. Swiftly, she bent down, plucked the beige object out of the bag of spice and slipped it into one of the pockets of her light jacket.

"What on earth are you doing?"

"Shut up, Ralph," Margaret hissed, as the stall-holder looked at them. She smiled pleasantly, linked arms with her husband, and began to walk away, heading for the closest exit from the *souk*.

"That doesn't belong to you," Ralph muttered, as they walked out of the *souk* and turned toward their hotel. "You shouldn't have taken it."

"It's only a bit of clay," Margaret responded, "and I doubt if it's worth anything. Anyway, I'm not stealing it. We know which stall that little man runs, so tomorrow I'll come back into the *souk* and return it to him."

"But you don't *know* he was anything to do with that stall. He might just have been standing beside it. You shouldn't have got involved."

"I'm *not* 'involved,' as you put it. If I hadn't picked it up, somebody else would have, and there would be no chance of making sure it was returned to its rightful owner. I'll take it back tomorrow, I promise. And then we need never think about it again."

2

The pursuers finally caught up with the fleeing man in the open area that lies between Rabat's walls and the *Chellah*, the ancient necropolis that is now a popular picnic spot for tourists during the day, but is largely deserted in the evening. He'd ducked down among the wild flowers that covered the area, but unfortunately one of the men chasing him had seen exactly where he'd gone to ground, and within seconds they had him, slamming him back against a rock.

The rest of the pursuers quickly gathered around the captive, and a tall, thin man with a pronounced hook nose stepped forward from the group. He'd suffered from untreated Bell's Palsy as a child, and the right side of his face was frozen. The condition had also robbed him of the sight of his right eye and left him with a milky-white cornea that contrasted dramatically with his dark brown skin.

"Where is it, Hassan?" he asked, his voice calm and measured.

The captive shook his head, and was rewarded by a vicious blow to the stomach from one of the men holding him. He bent forward, gasping and retching.

"I'll ask you once more. Where is it?"

"My pocket," Hassan al-Qalaa muttered.

At a gesture from the tall man, the two guards allowed the captive to reach into one of his pockets, then another, despair replacing exhaustion on his face as it slowly dawned on him that the object he'd grabbed when he ran was no longer in his possession.

"I must have dropped it," he stammered, "somewhere in the *souk*."

The tall man gazed at him impassively. "Search him," he snapped.

One of his men pinned the captive down against the rock while another rummaged through his clothing.

"Nothing," the man said.

"You four," the tall man snapped, "go back and search the *souk*. Follow the route we took, and question the stall-holders."

The four men left the group and ran swiftly back toward the entrance to the *souk*.

"Now, Hassan," the tall man said, leaning closer to the captive. "You may have dropped it, or you may have given it to somebody, but it doesn't matter. It will surface somewhere, sometime, and when it does I'll get it back." He paused and looked down at the pinioned man, then bent closer still. "Do you know who I am?" he said, his voice barely more than a whisper.

The captive shook his head, his terrified gaze fixed

upon the tall man's ruined face and unblinking sightless eye.

"Then I'll tell you," he said, and muttered a few words into his ear.

Immediately the captive began shaking his head, sheer naked terror in his eyes.

"No, no," he shouted, struggling violently. "It was only a clay tablet. I'll pay you. Anything."

"This is nothing to do with money, you fool, and it wasn't *only* a clay tablet. You have no idea—no idea at all—what you held in your hands."

The tall man made another gesture and one of his men roughly ripped the captive's clothing aside to expose his chest, then shoved a piece of cloth into the man's mouth and tied it behind his head as a gag. They held him firmly against the boulder, arms outstretched, his writhing and twisting achieving nothing.

The captive kicked out violently—his legs were all he was able to move—and caught the tall man a glancing blow on the thigh.

"For that," the tall man hissed, "you will suffer longer."

Reaching into his *jellaba*, he withdrew a curved dagger with a vicious double-edged blade from a hidden sheath. Rolling back his right sleeve beyond his elbow, to keep the material clear of the blood, he stepped slightly closer. He rested the point of the dagger gently on the man's chest, feeling for one of the spaces between the ribs, then began slowly increasing the pressure on the handle of the weapon. As the point pierced his skin, the captive cried out, a muffled grunt lost in the folds of the rudimentary gag.

The tall man pressed harder still and the front of his captive's *jellaba* suddenly turned a deep red as blood spurted from the wound. The tall man worked the knife in slowly, his gaze never leaving the dying man's face. When he estimated that the point of the weapon was about to touch the heart, he paused for a few seconds, changed his grip on the knife, then rammed the point home and twisted it sideways, the tip of the blade ripping his victim's heart virtually in half.

"Do you want us to bury him? Or dump him somewhere?" one of the men asked, as the captive slumped onto the ground.

The tall man shook his head. "No, just drag him over there," he instructed, pointing toward a clump of slightly denser undergrowth before bending down to clean the blood off the blade of his knife on the dead man's clothing. "Somebody will find him tomorrow or the next day.

"Spread the word," he said, as he and his men headed back toward the *souk*. "Make sure everyone knows that Hassan al-Qalaa died because of what he did; ensure that everyone knows that if they talk to the police, they will suffer the same fate. And offer a reward for the recovery of the tablet. We *must* find it, whatever it takes."

3

Just after ten the following morning, Margaret walked back into the *souk* with the clay tablet secreted in her handbag. She'd examined it carefully in their hotel room the previous evening, and taken several photographs of it.

The tablet was actually remarkably dull. Perhaps five inches by three, and maybe half an inch thick, it was a light gray-brown, almost beige, in color. The back and sides were smooth and unblemished, and the front surface covered with a series of marks that Margaret assumed was some kind of writing, but not one that she recognized. It certainly wasn't any form of European language, and it didn't even look much like the Arabic words and characters she'd seen on various signs and in newspapers since they'd arrived in Rabat.

In exchange for her promise that she'd simply go back to the stall, hand over the object and come straight back to the hotel, Ralph had agreed not to come with her.

But when Margaret stepped into the *souk* and walked through the twisting passageways to the stall, there was an obvious problem. Neither the small Moroccan nor the collection of ancient relics she'd observed the previous day was there. Instead, two men she'd never seen before were standing behind a trestle table on which were displayed rows of typical tourist souvenirs—brass coffeepots, metal boxes and other ornaments.

For a few seconds she stood there, irresolute, then stepped forward and spoke to the men.

"Do you understand English?" she began, speaking slowly and clearly.

One of the men nodded.

"There was a different stall here yesterday," she said, her words again slow and measured, "run by a small man." She made a gesture to indicate the approximate height of the Moroccan she'd seen previously. "I wanted to buy some of his goods."

The two men looked at her in silence for a few seconds before exchanging a couple of sentences in rapid-fire Arabic. Then one of them looked back at her.

"He not here today," he said. "You buy souvenirs from us, yes?"

"No. No, thank you." Margaret shook her head firmly. At least she'd tried, she thought as she walked away, but if the man who'd dropped the clay tablet wasn't there, there obviously wasn't any way she could return it to him. She'd just take it with her, back home to Kent, as a strange souvenir of their first holiday outside Europe, and a reminder of what they'd seen.

What she didn't notice, as she walked away from the stall, was one of the stall-holders taking out his mobile phone.

*   *   *

Margaret decided to take one last look around before she returned to the hotel. She was quite sure Ralph would never agree to return to Morocco, because he really hadn't enjoyed his time in Rabat. This would be her last opportunity to take in the sights and get a few final pictures.

She wandered through the *souk*, snapping away whenever she could, and then walked outside. She hadn't, she remembered, managed to persuade Ralph to visit the *Chellah*, and she really ought to walk around the gardens, even if she didn't visit the sanctuary itself.

But as she headed toward the old walls of the necropolis, she saw several police officers and other people milling about directly in front of her. For a moment, she wondered if she should simply call it a day and go straight back to the hotel.

Then she shrugged her shoulders—whatever the problem was that had attracted the small crowd, it had nothing to do with her—and pressed on. Curiosity had always been one of her virtues, or her faults in Ralph's view, and so as she walked past the handful of men she looked closely at what was going on.

At first, all she could see were their backs, but then a couple of them stepped slightly to one side and she could see exactly what they were all staring at. Fairly close to a large boulder, a slight figure lay on the ground, the front of his *jellaba* sodden with blood. That was startling enough, but what stunned Margaret was that she immediately recognized the dead man's face. She was so surprised that she stopped in her tracks.

Suddenly, she knew exactly why the small Arab wasn't behind the stall in the *souk*. She also guessed that the clay tablet in her bag—the object he'd dropped as he ran past them—might be more important and valuable than she'd ever thought.

One of the policemen noticed her standing there, her mouth open as she stared at the body on the ground, and irritably waved her away.

She turned back toward the *souk*, lost in thought. She wouldn't, she decided, follow her original plan and simply leave the clay tablet in her handbag when they left for the airport. She'd have to think of a way of getting it out of Morocco without it being detected.

And there was one obvious way to do that.

4

"I won't be sorry to get back home," Ralph O'Connor said as he steered their hired Renault Megane out of Rabat toward Casablanca and their flight to London.

"I know," Margaret replied shortly. "You've made it perfectly clear that Morocco is right at the bottom of your list of desirable places to revisit. I suppose you'll want to go back to Benidorm or Marbella next year?"

"Well, at least I feel at home in Spain. This country's just too *foreign*, somehow, and I don't like it. And I still think you should have just thrown away that blasted stone you picked up."

"Look, what I did was the best option in the circumstances, and I'm not going to discuss it any further."

They drove for some minutes in silence. She'd not told Ralph what she'd seen near the *Chellah* that morning, though she had sent her daughter a hasty e-mail about it just before they left the hotel.

About five miles out of Rabat, the traffic died away almost to nothing, and they had the road virtually to themselves. The only vehicle Ralph could see in his mirrors was a large dark-colored four-by-four jeep some distance behind them. Oncoming traffic grew less frequent as they got further away from the city.

When they reached a stretch of road fairly near the Atlantic coast, the driver of the jeep accelerated. Ralph O'Connor was a careful driver, and began switching his attention between the road ahead and the jeep, which was gaining on them very rapidly.

Then he saw an old white Peugeot sedan coming in the opposite direction. He eased his foot slightly off the accelerator to allow the driver of the jeep to overtake before the Peugeot reached them.

"Why have you slowed down?" Margaret demanded.

"There's a jeep coming up on us fast, and a fairly sharp bend in front. I'd rather he overtook us before we reach it."

But the jeep showed no signs of overtaking, just closed up to about twenty yards behind the O'Connors' Renault and matched its speed.

Then everything happened very quickly. As they approached the left-hand bend in the road, the Peugeot suddenly swerved toward them. Ralph braked hard, and looked to his left. The jeep—a Toyota Land Cruiser with tinted windows and a massive bull bar on the front—was right beside him.

But the driver of the Toyota still seemed to have no intention of overtaking. He just held the heavy vehicle in position. Ralph slowed down even more. Then the Toyota driver swung the wheel to the right and drove the right-hand side of the bull bar into the Renault.

There was a terrifying bang and Ralph felt his car lurch sideways.

"Christ!" He hit the brakes hard.

The tires screamed and smoked, leaving parallel skid marks across the road. The Renault was forced to the right, toward the apex of the bend.

Ralph's efforts were never going to be enough. The speed of the Renault, and the power of the two-ton Toyota, forced the lighter car inexorably toward the edge of the tarmac.

"Ralph!" Margaret screamed, as their car slid sideways toward the sheer drop on the right-hand side of the road.

Then the Toyota hit the Renault again. This time the impact triggered Ralph's air bag, forcing his hands off the steering wheel. He was now helpless. The Renault smashed into a line of low rocks cemented into the verge at the edge of the road.

As Margaret screamed in terror, the left-hand side of their car lifted and began to topple sideways. It rolled over the edge and began an uncontrolled tumble down the near-vertical drop to the bottom of a dried-up riverbed some thirty feet below.

The comforting noise of the engine was instantly replaced by a thunderous crashing, thumping and jolting as the car left the road.

Margaret screamed again as the world span in front of her eyes, her terror the more acute because she was utterly helpless to do anything about it. Ralph still had his foot hard on the brake pedal, and was again grasping the steering wheel, both instinctive and utterly pointless actions.

In that moment, their world turned into a maelstrom of noise and violence. Their bodies were flung around in their seats as the window glass shattered and panels buckled with the repeated impacts. The belts held them in their seats, and the remaining air bags deployed, but neither action helped.

Margaret reached out for Ralph's hand, but never found it as the crashing and tumbling intensified. She opened her mouth to scream again as the violence suddenly, catastrophically, stopped. She felt an immense blow on the top of her head, a sudden agonizing pain and then the blackness supervened.

On the road above, the Toyota and Peugeot stopped and the drivers climbed out. They walked to the edge of the road and peered down into the *wadi*.

The driver of the Toyota nodded in satisfaction, pulled on a pair of rubber gloves and scrambled swiftly down the slope to the wreckage. The trunk of the Renault had burst open, and the luggage was strewn about. He opened the suitcases and picked through their contents. Then he walked to the passenger side of the car, knelt down and pulled out Margaret O'Connor's handbag. Reaching inside, he extracted a small digital camera. He put this in one of his pockets, then continued rifling through the bag. His fingers closed around a small plastic sachet containing a high-capacity memory card for a camera and a USB card-reader. He pocketed that as well.

But there was obviously something else, something that he hadn't found. Looking increasingly irritated, he searched the suitcases again, then the handbag and, his nose wrinkling in distaste, even checked inside the O'Connors' pockets. The glove box of the Renault had jammed shut, but after a few seconds the lock yielded to the long blade of a flick-knife that the man produced from his pocket. But even this compartment was empty.

The man slammed the glove box closed, kicked the side of the car in annoyance, and climbed back up to the road.

There, he spoke briefly to the other man before making a call on his mobile. Clambering down the slope again, he jogged back to the remains of the car, pulled Margaret's handbag out of the wreckage, searched through the contents once more and took out her driving license. Then he tossed the handbag inside the Renault and climbed back up to the road.

Three minutes later, the Toyota had vanished, heading toward Rabat, but the old white Peugeot was still parked on the side of the road above the accident site. The driver was leaning casually against the door of his vehicle and dialing the number of the emergency services on his mobile phone.

5

"So what do you expect me to do when I get there?" Chris Bronson asked, his irritation obvious. He'd been summoned to his superior's office at the Maidstone police station as soon as he arrived that morning. "And why do you want *me* to go? Surely you should be briefing one of the DIs for something like this?"

Detective Chief Inspector Reginald "Dickie" Byrd sighed. "Look, there are other factors to consider here, not just the rank of the officer we send. We've been tasked with this simply because the dead couple's family lives in Kent, and I've chosen you because you can do something none of the DIs here can; you speak French."

"I speak Italian," Bronson pointed out, "and my French is good, but it's not fluent. And didn't you say the Moroccans were going to provide an interpreter?"

"They are, but you know as well as I do that sometimes things get lost in translation. I want a man out there who can understand what they're really saying, not just what some translator tells you they're saying. All you have to do is check that what they're claiming is accurate, then come back here and write it up."

"Why do you think their report *won't* be accurate?"

Byrd closed his eyes. "I don't. My own view is that this is just another bloody British driver forgetting which side of the road he was supposed to be on and losing it in a big way. But I need you to confirm this or see if there's any contributing factor—maybe there was a fault with the hire car, the brakes or the steering, say? Or perhaps another vehicle was involved, and the Moroccan authorities are glossing this over?

"The family—it's just the daughter and her husband— live in Canterbury. They were told about the accident first thing this morning and I understand from the local force that they'll be going out to Casablanca themselves to arrange the repatriation of the bodies. But I'd like you to get out there before them and run some checks. If they haven't left here by the time you get back, I'd also like you to go and see them, just to answer any questions they might have. I know it's a shitty job, but—"

"Yeah, I know, someone's got to do it." Bronson looked at his watch and stood up, running his hand through his unruly dark hair. "Right, I'll go and pack a weekend case, and I'll need to make a few phone calls."

In fact, Bronson would only have to make one call. His plan to take his ex-wife Angela out for a meal the next evening—an event that had already been postponed twice because of the pressure of his work—would have to be put on hold yet again.

Byrd slid the file across the desk. "The ticket is for Casablanca, because all the Rabat flights were full, and you're flying economy." He paused for a few seconds. "You could always try smiling at the girl on the check-in desk, Chris. She might decide to upgrade you."

6

"Is that it?" David Philips demanded, staring at the image on the screen of his wife's laptop. They were sitting side by side in the third bedroom-cum-study in their modest semidetached in Canterbury.

Kirsty nodded. Her eyes were red-rimmed and streaks of tears marred the smoothness of her cheeks.

"It doesn't look like much. Are you certain that's what your mother picked up?"

His wife nodded again, but this time she found her voice. "That's what she found in the *souk*. She said that was what the man dropped."

"It looks like a piece of junk to me."

"Look, David, all I can tell you is what she told me. This is what fell out of the man's pocket as he ran past them."

Philips leaned back from the screen and sat in thought for a few moments. Then he stuck a blank CD into the disk drive and clicked the touchpad button a couple of times.

"What are you doing?" Kirsty asked.

"There's one easy way to find out what this tablet is," Philips said. "I'll give this photograph to Richard and tell him what happened out there. He can write a story about it and do the research for us."

"Is that really a good idea, David? We've got to get out to Rabat tomorrow morning, and I've not even packed anything yet."

"I'll call him right now," Philips insisted. "It'll take me ten minutes to drop off the CD at his office. I'll pick up something for lunch while I'm out, and you can start sorting the stuff we'll need in Morocco so we're ready to leave first thing tomorrow. We should only be out there for a couple of days—can't we manage with a couple of carry-on bags?"

Kirsty dabbed at her eyes with a tissue, and her husband wrapped his arms around her. "Look, my love," he said, "I'll be out for maybe twenty minutes. Then we'll have lunch and do our packing. We'll get to Rabat tomorrow and sort everything out. And I'm still happy to go there on my own if you'd rather stay at home. I know how hard this must be for you."

"No." Kirsty shook her head. "I don't want to be left here by myself. I don't want to go to Morocco either, but I know that we have to." She paused and her eyes filled with tears again. "I just can't believe they've gone and that I'll never see them again. Mum seemed so happy in her e-mail, and really excited by what she'd found. And then this happens to them. How could everything have gone so wrong, so quickly?"

7

"I'd like to see the vehicle, please, and the place where the accident happened."

Bronson looked across the table at the two men facing him and spoke slowly, in English. Then he sat back and waited for the police interpreter to translate his request into French.

He was sitting in an upright and fairly uncomfortable chair in a small interview room at the police station in Rabat. The building was square, white-painted and distinguished from its neighbors only by the large parking area for police vehicles at its rear, and by the signs—in Arabic and French—that graced its façade. Bronson had arrived in Rabat about an hour earlier, having rented a car at Casablanca airport and checked into his hotel. He'd then driven straight to the police station.

The capital of Morocco was smaller than he'd expected, with lots of elegant squares and open spaces linked by generally wide roads. Stately palm trees lined many of the boulevards, and the city exuded an air of cosmopolitan sophistication and gentility. It felt, in fact, almost more European than Moroccan. And it was hot: a kind of dusty, dry, baking heat redolent with the unfamiliar smells of Africa.

Bronson had decided that if DCI Byrd was right, and there was something about the fatal accident that the Moroccan police were trying to conceal, the easiest way to catch them out was to pretend he spoke no French whatsoever and just listen to exactly what they said.

So far, his plan had worked brilliantly, except that the local police had answered all of his questions without so much as a hint of evasion and, as far as he could tell, the translations had been exceptionally accurate. And he was lucky that all the police officers he'd met so far had tended to converse in French. The first language of Morocco was Arabic, French the second, and his plan would have failed at the first hurdle if the Rabat police had decided to speak Arabic.

"We expected that, Sergeant Bronson," Jalal Talabani, the senior police officer from Rabat—Bronson thought he was probably the equivalent of a British inspector—replied, through the interpreter. About six feet tall and slim, with tanned skin, black hair and brown eyes, he was immaculately dressed in a dark, Western-style suit. "We've had the vehicle transferred to one of our garages here in Rabat, and we can drive out to the accident site on the road whenever you want."

"Thank you. Perhaps we could start now, with the car?"

"As you wish."

Talabani stood up, then dismissed the interpreter with

a gesture. "I think we can manage without him now," he said, as the man left the room. His English was fluent, and he spoke with a slight American accent.

"Ou, si vous voulez, nous pouvons continuer en Français," he added, with a slight smile. "I think your French is probably good enough for that too, Sergeant Bronson."

There were clearly no flies on Jalal Talabani. "I do speak the language a little," Bronson admitted. "That's why my people sent me out here."

"I guessed. You seemed to be following our conversation before the interpreter provided a translation. You can usually tell if somebody can understand what's being said, even if they don't actually speak. Anyway, let's stick to English."

Five minutes later Bronson and Talabani were sitting in the back of a Moroccan police patrol car and speeding through the light midafternoon traffic, red and blue lights flashing and the siren blaring away. To Bronson, used to the slightly more discreet activities of the British police, this seemed a little unnecessary. They were, after all, only driving to a garage to look at a car that had been involved in a fatal crash, a task that could hardly be classed as urgent.

"I'm not in this much of a hurry," he said, smiling.

Talabani looked across at him. "No, perhaps *you're* not," he said, "but *we* are in the middle of a murder investigation, and I have a lot to do."

Bronson sat forward, interested. "What happened?"

"A couple of tourists found the body of a man in some gardens near the *Chellah*—that's an ancient necropolis just outside the city walls—with a stab wound in his chest," Talabani said. "We can't find a witness or a motive, but robbery's an obvious possibility. All we've got at the moment is the corpse itself, and not even a name for the man yet. I'm under a lot of pressure from my boss to solve the case as quickly as possible. Tourists," he added, as the police car swung off the road to the right and into a garage, the noise of the siren dying away in midbellow, "don't normally want to visit a city where there are unsolved murders."

At one side of the cracked concrete parking area was a Renault Megane, though the only way Bronson could be that certain about the identification was because he could see part of the badge on the remains of the trunk lid. The roof of the car had been crushed down virtually to the level of the hood, and it was immediately obvious that the accident had not been survivable.

"As I told you, the car was going too fast around a bend in the road a few kilometers outside Rabat," Talabani explained. "It drifted wide, hit some rocks at the side of the road and flipped over. There was a drop of about thirty feet into a dried-up riverbed, and it rolled down the bank and landed there on its roof. Both the driver and passenger were killed instantly."

Bronson peered inside the wrecked vehicle. The windscreen and all the other windows were smashed and the steering wheel buckled. Partially deflated air bags obscured his view of the interior. He pushed them aside and checked behind them. The heavy bloodstains on the front seats and on the roof lining told their own story. The two front doors had been ripped off, presumably by the rescue crews to allow them to remove the bodies, and had later been tossed onto the back seat of the car. It was, by any standards, a mess.

Talabani peered into the wreck from the other side. "The two people in the car were clearly dead long before the ambulance arrived on the scene," he said, "but they were taken to the local hospital anyway. Their bodies are still there, in the mortuary. Do you know who will be making the arrangements for their repatriation?"

Bronson nodded. "I've been told the O'Connors' daughter and son-in-law will be coming out to organize it through the British Embassy. What about their belongings?"

"We found nothing in their hotel room—they'd already checked out—but we recovered two suitcases and a small carry-on bag from the scene of the accident. The trunk of the car burst open with the impact, and the cases were thrown clear of the wreckage. Their locks had given way and the contents were scattered about, but we collected everything we could find. We also found a woman's handbag in the car itself. That wasn't badly damaged, but it was covered in blood, we presume from Mrs. O'Connor. We're holding all of those items at the police station for safekeeping, until the next of kin can arrange to collect or dispose of them. You can inspect them if you wish. We've already completed a full inventory of their contents for you."

"Thanks—I'll need that. Was there anything significant in their bags?"

Talabani shook his head. "Nothing that you wouldn't expect to find in the luggage of a middle-aged couple taking a week's vacation. There were mainly clothes and toiletries, plus a couple of novels and quite a large supply of travel medicines, most of them unopened. In the pockets of the clothes they were wearing and the woman's handbag we found their passports, car hire documents, return air tickets, an international driving license in the husband's name, plus the usual credit cards and money. Were you expecting anything else?"

"Not really, no."

Bronson sighed, convinced he was just wasting his time. Everything he'd seen and heard so far made him more and more certain that Ralph O'Connor had been fatally incompetent, and had lost control of an unfamiliar car on a road he'd never driven before. And he was itching to get back to London to reschedule his much-delayed dinner date with Angela. The two of them had recently spent some time together, and Bronson was starting to entertain hopes that they might be able to give their failed relationship another try. He just wasn't sure that his ex-wife felt quite the same way.

He stood up. "Thank you for that, Jalal," he said. "I'll take a look at the O'Connors' possessions, if I may, and the place where the accident happened, and then I'll get out of your way."

8

Bronson stood on the dusty, unmade verge of a road about ten miles outside Rabat.

Above him, the sun marched across a solid blue sky, not the slightest wisp of cloud anywhere, the air still and heavy. The heat was brutal after the air-conditioned cool of the police car, now parked some twenty yards down the road. He'd discarded his jacket, which had helped a little, but already he could feel the sweat starting to run down his body inside his shirt, an uncomfortable and unfamiliar feeling. He knew he didn't want to be out there any longer than absolutely necessary.

It was, Bronson reflected, looking up and down the road, a pretty desolate place to meet one's maker. The ribbon of tarmac stretched arrow-straight in both directions from the bend beside the *wadi*. On both sides of the road, the sandy desert floor, studded with rocks, stretched out in uneven ripples and waves, devoid of any kind of vegetation apart from the occasional stunted bush. Below the road, the narrow chasm of the dried-up riverbed looked as if it hadn't seen a drop of moisture in decades.

Bronson was hot and irritated, but he was also puzzled. Although the bend *was* quite sharp, it was nothing that a reasonably competent driver couldn't have coped with. And the road was clear and open. Despite the bend, visibility was excellent, so any driver approaching the spot should have been able to see the curve well in advance and been able to anticipate it. But the two parallel skid marks that marred the smooth tarmac, their course heading straight for the point where the Renault had left the road, showed clearly that Ralph O'Connor *hadn't* done so.

Down below the road, the place where the Megane had finally stopped rolling was obvious. A collection of bits and pieces of the vehicle—glass, plastic, twisted pieces of metal and torn sections of ruined panels—lay scattered in a rough circle around a patch of discolored sand.

Apart from its location, some thirty feet below the edge of the road, it was typical of dozens of accident sites Bronson had been called to over the years, a sad reminder of how a moment's inattention could reduce a perfectly functioning vehicle to nothing more than a pile of scrap metal. Yet something about this accident site didn't quite ring true.

He bent down and looked at the line of rocks, roughly cemented into the very edge of the tarmac, which, according to Talabani, the O'Connors' car had hit. The Renault, he'd noted back at the garage, was a silver-gray color, and he could clearly see flakes and scrapes of gray paint on the rocks. Two of them had been dislodged from their concrete bases, presumably by the impact of the car as it slid sideways off the road.

It all seemed to make sense—yet why had the accident happened? Had Ralph O'Connor been drunk? Had he fallen asleep at the wheel? It was, he noted again, glancing up and down the road, a sharp bend, but it wasn't *that* sharp.

"You've explained what you think happened here," he said to Talabani, but the Moroccan police officer interrupted him.

"Not so, Sergeant Bronson. We know *exactly* what happened. There was a witness."

"Really? Who?"

"A local man was driving along this road in the opposite direction, toward Rabat. He saw the Renault come around that corner, much too fast, but he was far enough away to avoid being involved in the accident. He was the first on the scene and summoned the emergency services on his mobile phone."

"Could I speak to him?" Bronson asked.

"Of course. He has an address in Rabat. I'll call my people and tell him to come to the station this evening."

"Thanks. It might help when I have to explain what happened to the O'Connors' family." Breaking the kind of news that irrevocably wrecks lives was, Bronson knew, one of the worst things a police officer ever had to do.

He looked again at the stones and the road at the apex of the bend, and noticed something else. There it was—a scattering of small black flakes, at the very edge of the road and barely visible against the dark of the tarmac.

He glanced around, but Talabani was again talking

to the police driver, and both men were facing the other way. Kneeling down, Bronson picked up a couple of the flakes from the verge and slipped them into a small plastic evidence bag.

"You've found something?" Talabani asked, moving away from the police car and coming back toward him.

"No," Bronson replied, slipping the bag into his pocket and standing up. "Nothing important."

Back in Rabat, he stood by himself in the parking area of the police garage and stared again at the wreck of the O'Connors' Renault Megane, wondering if he was seeing things that simply weren't there.

Bronson had asked Talabani to drop him at the garage so he could get some photographs of the remains of the vehicle, and the Moroccan had agreed. Bronson used his digital camera to take a dozen or so pictures, paying particular attention to the left-hand-side rear of the car, and the driver's door, which he pulled out of the wreck and photographed separately.

The vehicle's impact with the rock-strewn floor of the dried-up riverbed—the *wadi*—had been so massive that every panel on the Renault was warped and dented, with huge scrape marks caused either by the accident itself or by the subsequent recovery operation.

Talabani had explained the sequence of events. Because it was perfectly obvious to everyone that the two occupants of the car were dead, the Moroccan police officer sent to the accident site had ordered the ambulance crew to wait, and had instructed a photographer to record the scene with his digital Nikon, while he and his men had examined the vehicle and the road above the crash site. Talabani had already supplied copies of all these pictures to Bronson.

Once the bodies had been cut out of the wreck and taken away, the recovery operation had started. No crane had been available at the time, and so they'd been forced to use a tow-truck. The *wadi* was inaccessible to vehicles anywhere along that stretch of highway, so they'd parked the tow-truck at the very edge of the road and used the power of its winch to pull the car over onto its wheels. Then they'd dragged the Renault up the steeply sloping bank of the *wadi* to the road, and finally hauled it onto the back of the low-loader.

Bronson had no idea what damage had been caused by the crash itself, and what by the subsequent recovery. Without specialist examination—and that would mean shipping the car to Britain for a forensic vehicle examiner to check it, and God knows how much that would cost or how long it would take—he couldn't be certain of his conclusions. But there were a number of dents in the Renault's left-hand-side doors and rear wing that looked to him as if they could have been caused by a sideways impact, and that didn't square with what Talabani had told him, and what the witness had apparently reported seeing.

Bronson reached into his pocket and pulled out the evidence bag containing the flakes of very dark paint he'd picked up at the bend in the road. They looked fresh but that, he realized, meant nothing. There might have been a dozen fender-benders along that stretch of road, and the paint flecks could have come from any accident.

In Britain, the rain would have washed them away in a matter of hours or days but, in Morocco, rain was an infrequent event.

But in just one place on the driver's door of the Renault he'd found a dark scrape, possibly blue, perhaps black.

Bronson was just walking into his hotel when his mobile rang.

"Have you got a fax machine out there?" DCI Byrd asked, his voice loud and clearly irritated.

"This hotel has, I suppose. Hang on, and I'll get you the number."

Ten minutes later, Bronson was looking at a poor-quality fax that showed an article printed in a Canterbury local paper, with a dateline of the previous day. Before he could read it, his mobile rang again.

"You've got it?" Byrd demanded. "One of the officers at Canterbury spotted it."

Bronson looked again at the headline: KILLED FOR A LUMP OF CLAY? Underneath the bold type were two pictures. The first showed Ralph and Margaret O'Connor at some kind of function, smiling into the camera. Below that was a slightly fuzzy image of an oblong beige object with incised markings on it.

"Did you know anything about this?"

Bronson sighed. "No. What else does the article say?"

"You can read it yourself, and then go and talk to Kirsty Philips and ask her what the hell she and her husband think they're playing at."

"You mean, when I get back to Britain?"

"No, I mean today or tomorrow. They should have arrived in Rabat about the same time you did. I've got her mobile number for you."

Byrd ended the call as abruptly as he'd started it, and Bronson read the article in its entirety. The story was simple enough.

The O'Connors, the reporter suggested, had witnessed a violent argument in the *souk* in Rabat. Immediately afterward, Margaret O'Connor had picked up a small clay tablet dropped by a man who was being pursued through the narrow streets and alleyways. The following day, on their way back to the airport at Casablanca, the couple was ambushed on the road near Rabat and killed.

"This was no accident," David Philips was quoted as saying. "My parents-in-law were hunted down and killed out of hand by a gang of ruthless criminals intent on recovering this priceless relic." And what, the article demanded in conclusion, were the British and Moroccan police going to do about it?

"Not a lot, probably," Bronson muttered, as he reached for the phone to call Kirsty Philips' mobile. "And how do they know the tablet's worth anything at all?" he wondered.

9

The Canterbury copper wasn't the only person to read the brief article in the local paper with interest. A fair-haired young man saw the picture of the clay tablet and immediately reached for a pair of scissors. Snipping around the story, he put it aside and turned his attention to the rest of the newspaper. Beside him in his modest apartment on the outskirts of Enfield was a pile that contained a copy of every British national daily newspaper, a selection of news magazines and most of the larger-circulation provincial papers.

Going through every one of them and extracting all the articles of interest—a task he performed every day—had taken him all the morning and a couple of hours after lunch, but his work still wasn't finished. He bundled the mutilated newspapers and magazines into a black rubbish bag, then carried the pile of stories that he'd clipped over to a large A3-size scanner attached to a powerful desktop computer.

He placed them on the scanner's flatbed one by one,

and copied each onto the computer's hard drive, ensuring that every image was accompanied by the name of the publication in which it had appeared, and storing them in a folder that bore the current date.

When he'd finished, he put all the clippings in the rubbish bag with the discarded newspapers, then prepared an e-mail that contained no text at all, but to which he attached copies of all the scanned images. Some days the sheer number and size of the attachments meant he had to divide them up and send two or even three e-mails to dispatch them. The destination e-mail was a numerical Yahoo web-based address that gave no clue as to the identity of the owner. When the account had been set up, five separate e-mail addresses had been created to form a chain that would obscure the identity of the originating e-mail. Once the account was up and running, all those other addresses had been canceled, ending any possible attempt to trace the source.

Of course, he knew exactly who the recipient was. Or, to be absolutely accurate, he knew precisely *where* his message would be read, but not exactly *who* would read it.

He had been stationed in Britain for almost two years, steadily building a name and establishing himself as a journalist specializing in writing for foreign magazines and newspapers. He could even produce copies of various continental journals that included articles he'd written—or which appeared over his byline. If anyone had bothered to check the original copies of those publications, they'd have seen the articles reproduced word for word, but with an entirely different byline. In fact, the copied pages had been carefully prepared in a secure basement in an unmarked and equally secure building in a town named Glilot in Israel, just outside Tel Aviv, for the sole purpose of helping to establish his cover.

He wasn't a spy—or not yet, at any rate—but he *was* an employee of the Mossad, the Israeli intelligence service. One of his tasks as a support agent was to copy any and every article that related, however obliquely, to the British government and to all branches of the armed forces, including the special forces, and to the United Kingdom intelligence and counterintelligence agencies. But like all agents in the employ of the Mossad, he had also been given an additional list of topics that were in no way connected with any of these subjects. Ancient tablets, whether made of clay or any other material, had been accorded a very high priority in the list.

Once he'd dispatched the e-mail, there was usually nothing else for him to do until the following day, but on that afternoon, within minutes of sending the message, his computer emitted a double-tone that showed an e-mail had been received. When he opened his inbox, the coded name of the sender jumped out at him, as did the priority. He scanned the message quickly, then read it again.

Whatever the importance of that old clay tablet, it looked as if the article he'd sent had stirred up a hornets' nest in Tel Aviv, and the new instructions he'd been given clearly emphasized this. He glanced at his watch, weighing his options, then grabbed his jacket from the hook in the hall, left his apartment and headed for the stairs leading to the small parking lot at the back of the building.

With any luck, he should reach Canterbury in just over an hour.

10

"This," Talabani said in English, "is Hafez Aziz, and he's the man who saw the accident. He only speaks Tamazight, so I'll have to translate for you."

Bronson was in another interview room at the Rabat police station. On the other side of the table was a short, slim Moroccan wearing faded blue jeans and a white shirt.

For the next few minutes, Jalal Talabani translated what Aziz said, sentence by sentence, and at the end of it Bronson knew no more than he had before. Aziz patiently repeated exactly the same story that Talabani had told him earlier, and what he said sounded to Bronson like a statement made by an honest man.

He said he'd seen the Renault approaching the bend, traveling very quickly. He'd watched the car start to make the turn, but then swing wide and hit the rocks at the side of the road. He'd seen it fly into the air, tumble sideways over the edge and vanish from sight. He'd stopped his car at the scene and called the police, then scrambled down into the *wadi* to try to help the occupants, but it was already too late.

There was only one question Bronson really wanted to ask, but he kept his mouth shut and just thanked Aziz for coming to the police station.

When the Moroccan had left the interview room, Bronson turned to Talabani.

"I'm very grateful for all your help," he said, "and for arranging that interview. I think I've seen almost all that I needed to. The last thing is the suitcases and stuff you recovered from the car. And I think you said you'd already prepared an inventory?"

Talabani nodded and stood up. "Stay here and I'll have the cases brought in," he said, and left the interview room.

Twenty minutes later, Bronson acknowledged that the Moroccan had been right. There was nothing at all in the O'Connors' luggage that was in any way unusual, not that he had expected that there would be. It was just one last check he'd needed to make. In fact, the only unusual thing about the inventory was not what *was* on the list, but what *wasn't*. One item he was certain he would see—the O'Connors' camera—simply wasn't there.

"One last thing, Jalal," he said. "There wasn't any sign of an old clay tablet in the car when you recovered it, was there?"

The Moroccan looked puzzled. "A clay tablet?" he asked. "No, not that I remember. Why?"

"Just something I heard. No matter. Thanks for everything. I'll be in touch if I need anything more."

Bronson's last appointment was to see the O'Connors'

daughter and her husband at their hotel the following morning. He folded up the printed inventory, slipped it into his pocket, and glanced at his watch. He should, he hoped, be able to catch a flight out of Casablanca the following day and be back home by late afternoon.

When Jalal Talabani left the police station in Rabat that evening, he didn't follow his usual routine and walk to the parking lot to collect his car and drive to his home on the northern outskirts of the city. Instead, he visited a local café for a drink and a light meal. Then he followed a circuitous route around the nearby streets, varying his pace and stopping frequently to check behind him. Only when he was quite certain that he was unobserved did he walk to a public telephone and dial a number from memory.

"I have some information you might find useful."

"Go ahead."

"There's a British policeman named Bronson here in Rabat looking into the deaths of the O'Connors. He's also interested in finding an old clay tablet. Do you know anything about that?"

"I might," the man replied. "Where's he staying?"

Talabani told him the name of Bronson's hotel.

"Thank you, I'll take care of him," said the man, and ended the call.

11

Early that morning, in a conference room in one of the numerous Israeli government buildings near the center of Jerusalem, three men met by appointment. No secretaries were present; no notes were taken.

In front of each man were two large photographs, one in color and the other monochrome, depicting a gray-brown clay tablet in considerable detail. There was also a photocopy of the article from the British regional newspaper, together with a translation of the text into Hebrew.

"That report appeared yesterday in a British newspaper," Eli Nahman began. He was elderly, thin and stooped, with a white beard and a mane of white hair topped with a black embroidered yarmulke, but his eyes were a clear and piercing blue, and sparkled with intelligence. He was a senior professor at the Israel Museum in Jerusalem, and an authority on pre-Christian relics.

"The story was spotted by one of the Mossad's assets in London and forwarded to Glilot," he continued, gesturing to the younger man sitting at the head of the table.

Levi Barak was in his late thirties, with black hair and a tanned complexion, his otherwise regular features dominated by a large nose that would forever stop him being described as handsome. He was wearing a light tan suit, but had hung the jacket over the back of his chair to reveal the shoulder holster under his left armpit, from which the black butt of a semiautomatic pistol protruded.

"As you know, we have standing instructions to inform Professor Nahman when any such reports are received, and I called him yesterday afternoon as soon as I saw this article," Barak said. "What you see is all the information we have at present. We've instructed our asset to monitor the British press for any further information about this story. He's also been ordered to drive over to Canterbury—that's the city in Kent where these people lived—and obtain copies of all newspapers printed there. He will forward to us any other reports and articles he can find."

Barak paused and glanced at the two other men.

"The problem we have is that there's very little hard data here. All we really know is that two elderly English people died a couple of days ago in a road accident in Morocco, and that at some point prior to this they came into possession of an old clay tablet. What we have to do today is decide what action, if any, we should take."

"Agreed," Nahman said. "The first step, obviously, is to decide if this clay tablet is a part of the set, but that's not going to be easy. The picture printed in the paper is so blurred as to be almost useless, and the report gives no indication as to where the relic is now. To help us make a decision, I've supplied photographs of the tablet we already possess, so we can at least compare the appearance of the two of them."

He paused and looked across the table at the young man sitting opposite him. "So, Yosef, what's your opinion?"

Yosef Ben Halevi stared down at the photocopied picture of the newspaper article for a few seconds before he replied. "There's not much to go on here. Without a ruler or something else in this picture to provide scale, we can't do more than estimate its size. It could be anything from about five to twenty or thirty centimeters long. That's the first problem. If we're to determine if this *is* one of the set, the size is critical. Is there any way of finding out the dimensions of this relic?"

"Not that I can think of, no," Nahman said. "The newspaper report describes the object as a 'small clay tablet,' so the chances are that we're looking at something no more than, say, ten or perhaps fifteen centimeters in length. Any bigger than that and I doubt if the word 'small' would have been used. And that, of course, *is* about the right size."

Ben Halevi nodded. "The second point of comparison must obviously be the inscriptions. Looking at the pictures of the two relics, it appears to me that both are superficially similar, and both have the diagonal mark in one corner that I'd expect. The lines of characters are different lengths, and that's not a normal characteristic of Aramaic script, but the newspaper photograph is too poor to allow me to do more than try to translate a couple of words."

Like Nahman, Ben Halevi worked for the Israel Museum, and was an ancient language specialist and an expert on Jewish history.

"Which words *can* you decipher?" Nahman asked.

Ben Halevi pointed at the newspaper article. "Here, along the bottom line. That word could be 'altar,' and I think the second word from the right is 'scroll' or perhaps 'scrolls.' But the image is very blurred."

Nahman regarded his friend and colleague keenly. "How confident are you, Yosef?"

"You mean, do I think this tablet *is* one of the four? Perhaps sixty or seventy percent, no higher. We need to see a high-quality picture of the inscription or, better still, actually recover the tablet. Only then can we be certain."

"That's my view exactly." Eli Nahman nodded. "We have to get our hands on that tablet."

Levi Barak looked at the two academics. "It really *is* that important?"

Nahman nodded. "If it's what we think it is, then it's vital we recover it. Make no mistake about this, Levi. What's written on that tablet could be the final clue we need to locate the Testimony. It could mark the end of a search that's been running for the last two millennia. Take that to your masters at Glilot and ensure they know just how serious this is."

"It won't be easy, and it might not be possible," Barak pointed out. "Even for the Mossad."

"Look," Nahman said, "that tablet exists, and we simply have to find it before anyone else does."

"Like who?"

"Anyone. Treasure-hunters, obviously, but we can deal with people whose only motivation is money. What worries me are the others—the ones who would be desperate to find the relic so they can destroy it."

"Muslims?" Barak suggested.

"Yes, but perhaps radical Christians as well. We've always been a persecuted minority, but if we could find the lost Testimony it would validate our religion in a way that nothing else ever could. That's why we simply *must* recover that clay tablet and decipher the text."

Barak nodded. "We have assets in Rabat and Casablanca. I'll instruct them to start looking."

"Not just in Morocco," Nahman emphasized. "The couple who found it were English, so you should search there as well. Spread your net as wide as possible. Thanks to that newspaper, a lot of people will now know about that clay tablet. Your men are likely to find they're not the only ones hunting for it."

"We can take care of ourselves."

"No doubt. Just make sure you also take care of the tablet. Whatever happens, it mustn't get damaged or destroyed."

12

"Thank you for meeting us out here," Kirsty Philips said, shaking Bronson's hand. They were sitting in the lounge bar of the Rabat hotel where she and her husband had booked a room. Kirsty's brown eyes were red-rimmed and her dark hair disheveled, but she seemed to be more or less under control.

"David's gone over to the British Embassy to sort things out," she said, "but he shouldn't be too long. Have a seat here and I'll order some coffee."

"Thank you," Bronson said, though he really didn't need anything to drink. "That would be very welcome."

A few minutes later a waiter appeared carrying a tray bearing two cups and saucers, a cafetière, milk and sugar.

"I'm very sorry about the circumstances," Bronson began, as the waiter walked away.

Kirsty nodded, her lower lip quivering slightly.

"I've been discussing what happened with the police out here," Bronson hurried on, "and it looks as though it was simply a tragic accident. I know it won't be much consolation, but both your parents died instantly. They didn't suffer at all." He paused for a few seconds, looking at the attractive young woman in front of him. "Do you want me to explain what happened?" he asked softly.

Kirsty nodded. "I suppose I'd better know," she replied, a sob in her voice, "otherwise I'll always wonder about it."

Bronson sketched out the circumstances. When he'd finished, Kirsty shook her head.

"I still don't understand it," she said. "Dad was such a good driver. He was always cautious, always careful. As far as I know, he'd never even had a parking ticket."

"But he was driving an unfamiliar car on a road he didn't know," Bronson suggested. "We think he failed to anticipate how sharp the bend in the road really was, and unfortunately there were no crash barriers." Even as he said the words, he knew he didn't really believe them either.

"Now," he said, opening his briefcase, "this is a copy of the inventory of your parents' possessions."

He passed Kirsty the typed sheets of paper prepared by the Rabat police, and then sat back in his chair.

Kirsty put the papers down on the table in front of her, barely glancing at them. She took another sip of her coffee, then looked across at Bronson.

"It's such a stupid waste," she said. "I mean, they'd only recently decided to take proper holidays, to actually start enjoying themselves. They usually went to Spain for a couple of weeks. This was the first time they'd done anything even slightly adventurous. And now this happens." Her voice broke on the last word, and she began to cry softly.

"They were having a good time out here," she continued after a minute, blowing her nose. "Or at least my mother was. I don't think Dad was all that fond of Morocco, but Mum simply loved it."

"She sent you postcards, I suppose?" Bronson suggested, though he already knew the answer to that question.

Because the Canterbury paper had printed a picture of the tablet, either Margaret or Ralph O'Connor must have had a camera and have e-mailed a copy of the photograph to their daughter. But he also knew that no camera was listed in the inventory the police had given him. And he certainly hadn't seen one when he'd examined the O'Connors' possessions.

Talabani had told him that the suitcases had burst open in the accident, so maybe the camera had been flung so far away that the police hadn't found it when they recovered everything. Or maybe Aziz or somebody else at the scene had picked it up and decided to keep it? On the other hand, modern digital cameras were both tiny and expensive, and he would have expected Margaret O'Connor to have kept hers in her handbag or perhaps in one of her pockets.

Kirsty shook her head. "No. My mother had started using computers when she was still working, and she was heavily into e-mail and the Internet. Their hotel had Internet access, and she would send me a message every evening, telling me what they'd been up to that day." She tapped the black bag on the ground beside her chair.

"I've got them all here on my laptop. I was going to print all her messages and give them to her when she came home, and do decent copies of the pictures she'd sent."

Bronson sat up a little straighter. "Did she take a lot of photographs?" he asked.

"Yes. She had a small digital camera, one of the latest models, and one of those memory stick things that could read the data card. I think she plugged that into one of the hotel computers."

"May I see the pictures your mother sent you? In fact, could you make me a copy of them? On a CD, perhaps?"

"Yes, of course," Kirsty said. She picked up the bag, pulled out a Compaq laptop and switched it on. Once the operating system had loaded, she inserted a blank CD into the DVD drive, selected the appropriate directory and started the copying process.

While the CD was being burned, Bronson moved his chair around beside Kirsty's and stared at the screen as she flipped through some of the pictures. He could see immediately that Margaret O'Connor had not been a photographer. She'd simply pointed the camera at anything that moved, and most things that didn't, and clicked the shutter release. The images were typical holiday snaps—Ralph at the airport, waiting for their luggage by the carousel; Margaret standing beside their hire car, before they set off on the drive to Rabat; the view through the windscreen as they drove out of Casablanca; that kind of thing—but the images were sharp and clear enough, the high-quality camera compensating for the inadequacies of the person holding it.

"This is the *souk* here in Rabat," Kirsty said, pointing at the screen. She extracted the CD as the copying process finished, slipped it into a plastic sleeve and passed it to Bronson. "Mum loved going in there. It was one of her favorite places. She said the smells were simply intoxicating, and the goods on display just amazing."

She clicked the mouse button, cycling through the pictures. Then, in contrast to the earlier footage, Bronson saw a succession of clear but very poorly angled shots, apparently taken almost at random.

"What happened with these?" he asked.

Kirsty smiled slightly. "That was the day before they left Rabat. She told me she was trying to take pictures in the *souk*, but a lot of the traders weren't keen on being photographed. So she hid the camera beside her handbag and clicked away, hoping that some of the pictures would come out."

"What's this?" Bronson pointed to one of the photographs.

"There was some sort of an argument in the *souk* while they were there, and Mum took about a dozen pictures of it."

"Ah, yes. The story in the Canterbury newspaper. I wish you'd talked to someone about this before you went to the press, Mrs. Philips."

Kirsty colored slightly, and explained that her husband David had a contact on the local paper and that he'd asked him to write the story.

As she told him what had happened, Bronson realized that not only were Margaret O'Connor's digital camera and memory stick missing, along with the clay tablet—the finding of which she'd described to her daughter in such breathy and exciting detail in her last but one e-mail—but also her spare data card and card reader.

"My husband's convinced it wasn't just a road accident," Kirsty said. "Of course, if the clay tablet was still in the car after the accident, then obviously he's got it all wrong." She looked at Bronson keenly. "So was it?"

"No, it wasn't," he admitted, pointing to the inventory on the table in front of them. "I asked the police officer in charge about it myself. I should also tell you that your mother's camera and one or two other bits are also missing. But they could have been stolen by a pickpocket on their last day here, and perhaps she decided not to bother bringing the tablet back with her. We're not necessarily looking at a conspiracy here."

"I know," Kirsty Philips sounded resigned, "but I haven't been able to change David's mind. Oh, and there's probably going to be some more press coverage. David's contact on the Canterbury paper told a *Daily Mail* reporter about the story, and he phoned us here yesterday afternoon to talk about it. I think he's doing a story on it in today's edition."

At that moment a tall, well-built young man with brown curly hair appeared in the lounge and strode straight across to them.

Kirsty stood up to make the introductions. "David, this is Detective Sergeant Bronson."

Bronson stood up and shook hands. There was a kind of tension in the man in front of him, a sense of suppressed energy, of forces barely contained.

"Let me guess, Sergeant," Philips said, as he sat down

on the sofa, his voice low and angry. "A road accident, right? Just one of those things? A British driver in a foreign country and he just makes a Horlicks of steering his car round a gentle bend? Or maybe he was driving on the wrong side of the road? Something like that?"

"David, please don't do this." Kirsty looked close to tears again.

"It wasn't a gentle bend, actually," Bronson pointed out. "It was quite sharp, and on a road your father-in-law probably wasn't familiar with."

"You've been there, right? You've seen the place where the accident happened?" Philips demanded.

Bronson nodded.

"Well, so have I. Do you think *you* could have steered a car around that bend without driving into the ravine?"

"Yes, of course."

"Then why do you suppose my father-in-law, who had an unblemished driving record, who was a member of the Institute of Advanced Motorists, and who I think was one of the safest and most competent drivers I've ever known, couldn't manage to do the same?"

Bronson felt torn. He agreed with David—the circumstances of the accident didn't make sense. But he also knew he had to toe the official line.

"The thing is," he said, "we have an eyewitness who observed the whole thing. He says he saw the car swerve off the road, hit some rocks and then crash into the ravine, and his testimony has been accepted by the Moroccan police. I sympathize with your misgivings, but there's really no evidence to suggest that what he described didn't happen."

"Well, I don't believe a single word any of them are saying. Look, I know you're only doing your job, but there just has to be more to it. I *know* my parents-in-law didn't die in a simple road accident. And nothing you say will convince me otherwise."

13

When Bronson left the Philipses' hotel, he stopped a few hundred yards down the road at a pavement café and ordered a coffee while he tried to decide what he should do. If he called DCI Byrd and told him he was satisfied the O'Connors had been killed in a freak accident, he knew he could just walk away. But if he voiced his suspicions—and that was really all they were—he guessed he'd be stuck in Rabat for far longer than he wanted.

Not that the city was unpleasant—far from it, in fact. Bronson lifted the cup to his lips and glanced round. The café's tables and chairs were spread across a wide pavement on one side of a spacious boulevard, lined with palm trees. Most of the tables were occupied, and Bronson could hear the slightly guttural sounds of conversation in Arabic alternating with the softer and more melodic accents of French speakers. No, the beautiful weather, café society and relaxed lifestyle of Rabat were undeniably attractive—or would have been if Bronson had been there with Angela. And that thought made the decision for him.

"Sod it," he muttered to himself. "I'll just wrap it up."

He drained the last of his coffee, stood up and walked away from the table, then realized he'd forgotten to pick up his briefcase and turned back. And found himself looking straight at two men wearing traditional *jellabas* who had just stood up from their table on the far side of the café and were themselves staring directly at him.

Bronson was used to being stared at in Morocco—he was a stranger in a foreign land and more or less expected it—but he had the uncomfortable sensation that these men weren't just looking at him with idle curiosity. Something about their gaze bothered him. But he gave no sign of even noticing them. He simply picked up his briefcase and walked away.

Fifty yards from the café, he stopped at the curb, waiting to cross the road, and looked in both directions. He wasn't entirely surprised to see the two men walking slowly toward him, and less surprised when they, too, crossed to the far side of the street. Within two hundred yards, he knew without any doubt that they were following him, and one was talking animatedly into a mobile phone. What Bronson didn't know was what he should do about it.

But that decision was taken out of his hands less than half a minute later. As well as the two men behind him, steadily getting closer, Bronson suddenly saw another three men closing on him from the front.

They might just have been three innocent men taking an afternoon stroll, but he doubted it, and he wasn't going to hang around and find out. Bronson took the next side-street, and started running, dodging through the scattering of pedestrians on the pavements. Behind him he heard shouts and the sound of running feet, and knew his instincts had been right.

He took the next turning on the left, then swung right, getting into a rhythm as he picked up the pace. He risked a quick glance behind him. The two men from the café were running hard to keep up with him, perhaps fifty yards back. Behind them, another running figure was visible.

Bronson dived round another corner and saw two men approaching from his left, trying to intercept him. It looked as if they'd guessed which streets he'd take and were trying to cut him off.

He accelerated, but headed directly toward them. He could see them hesitate and slow down, and then he was on them. One of them fumbled in his *jellaba*, perhaps looking for a weapon, but Bronson gave him no chance. He slammed his briefcase into the Moroccan's chest, knocking him violently to the ground, then turned to face his companion, just as the man swung a punch at him. Bronson ducked under the blow and rammed his fist into his attacker's stomach.

He didn't wait to see the man tumble to the ground; already he could hear the yells from behind as the other men closed up on him. Two down—at least for a short while—three to go.

Without a backward glance, Bronson took to his heels again, his breath rasping in his throat. He knew he had to finish this, and quickly. He was used to running, but the heat and humidity were getting to him, and he knew he couldn't go much further.

He ducked left, then right, but all the time his pursuers were slowly eroding his lead, catching him up. As Bronson reached a main road, he slowed slightly, scanning the traffic, looking for one particular kind of vehicle. Then he took off again, and ran into the road, weaving between slow-moving cars and trucks.

Perhaps a hundred yards in front of him, a taxi had stopped to let out two passengers, and the instant before the driver pulled away, Bronson wrenched open the back door and leaped inside. He met the man's startled gaze in the interior mirror.

"Airport," he gasped. "Quickly." For good measure he repeated the request in French.

The driver pulled out and accelerated, and Bronson slumped in the seat, sucking in great gulps of air, then looked back through the rear window. About forty yards behind, two figures were running along the pavement, but slowing down as the taxi gathered speed.

Then they started speeding up. Bronson looked through the windscreen to see half a dozen stationary vehicles blocking the road in front. If the taxi stopped, he knew the men would catch him.

"Take the next turning," Bronson said, pointing.

The driver glanced back at him. "That's not the way to the airport," he said, his English good but heavily accented.

"I've changed my mind."

The driver swung the wheel. The side-street was mercifully almost empty of other traffic, and as the taxi sped down it, Bronson saw his pursuers stop at the end of the road to stare at the retreating vehicle.

Ten minutes later, the taxi pulled to a halt in a street close to his hotel, and Bronson paid the fare, adding a generous tip.

About ninety minutes later, in the security of his room in another Rabat hotel—he'd decided to move just in case his pursuers had followed him from his original lodging—he picked up his mobile and rang Maidstone police station.

"What have you found, Chris?" Byrd asked, once Bronson was connected.

"I've just been chased through the streets of Rabat by a gang of thugs who definitely didn't just want my autograph."

"What? Why?"

"I didn't stop to ask. But I don't believe that the O'Connors' accident was quite as accidental as we thought it was."

"Oh, shit," Byrd said. "That's all we need."

Quickly, Bronson outlined his concerns about the accident and the damage to the Renault Megane, and then explained Margaret O'Connor's habit of snapping anything that moved.

"Kirsty Philips gave me copies of all the photographs her mother took here, and I spent an hour or so going through them. What really bothers me is that one of the men she photographed in the *souk* turned up as the only eyewitness to the accident on the road outside Rabat, and according to Kirsty another man in the same picture was found dead just outside the *medina* with a stab-wound in his chest. I think she photographed an argument in the *souk* that led to murder, which means the killer was almost certainly one of the people in the pictures she took.

"And that," Bronson finished, "is a pretty good motive for knocking off the two eyewitnesses and stealing the camera."

14

MYSTERY OF THE MISSING TABLET was the title of the short article on page thirteen of the *Daily Mail*. Bronson was able to read it thanks to Dickie Byrd and one of the fax machines at the Maidstone police station. Below the headline, the reporter asked the question: "Were British pensioners killed to recover priceless object?"

The story was pretty much a straight rehash of what had appeared in the Canterbury evening paper, with a single addition Bronson was sure had been carefully incorporated in the text to give it an importance it didn't deserve. Toward the end of the article, when the reporter was discussing the value of the clay tablet, he stated that a "British Museum expert" had been unavailable for comment, but managed to imply this was slightly sinister, as if the "expert" knew exactly what the tablet was, but had for some reason refused to divulge the information.

Well, that was something Bronson could check straightaway, and it gave him a perfect excuse to talk to Angela. He pulled out his mobile and dialed her direct-line number at the British Museum, where she worked as a ceramics conservator. Angela answered almost immediately.

"It's me," Bronson said. "Look, I'm really sorry about the other night—I didn't want to come tramping all the way out here to Morocco, but I had no choice."

"I know, Chris, but it's not a problem. You told me what happened."

"Well, I'm still sorry about it. Now, are you busy?"

Angela laughed shortly. "I'm always busy; you know that. It's eleven thirty in the morning. I've been at work for nearly three and a half hours and I've just had another three boxes of potsherds dumped on my desk. I haven't even had time to grab a cup of coffee this morning, so if you're calling just to pass the time of day, forget it. Or did you actually want something?"

"Just the answer to a question, really. There's an article on page thirteen of the *Mail* today about a clay tablet. Have you seen it?"

"Oddly enough, I have, yes. I read it on the way in to work this morning. It made me laugh because *I* was the so-called expert the reporter couldn't contact. He rang the museum yesterday afternoon, and the call was diverted to my office. Clay tablets aren't really my field, but I suppose the switchboard operator thought 'ceramics' was close enough. Anyway, I'd just slipped out for a cup of tea and by the time I got back, the *Mail* reporter had hung up. So it's quite true that I was 'unavailable' for comment, but only for something like three minutes. Typical of the bloody press."

"I thought it would be something like that," Bronson

said. "But could the report be correct? Could that clay tablet be really valuable?"

"Highly unlikely. Clay tablets are ten a penny—well, not literally, but you know what I mean. They're found all over the place, sometimes as fragments, but complete ones turn up very frequently. There are estimated to be about half a million locked in museum storerooms around the world that haven't yet been studied or deciphered, or even really looked at. They really are that abundant. They were used by most of the ancient races as short-term records, and they listed everything from property ownership details and accounts to recipes, and almost any other information you can think of in between. They've been found with inscriptions in Latin, Greek, Coptic, Hebrew and Aramaic, but the majority are cuneiform."

"Which is what, exactly?"

"It's an ancient written language. Cuneiform letters are wedge-shaped, and that kind of script is particularly easy to impress onto wet clay using a stylus. Clay tablets are just curiosities, really, that help us better appreciate daily life in whatever period they were made. They do have some value, obviously, but the only people who are usually interested in them are academics and museum staff."

"OK," Bronson said. "But two people have been killed out here in Morocco and the clay tablet we know the woman picked up in the *souk* is missing, along with her camera. And yesterday I was chased through the streets of Rabat by a gang of men who—"

"What? You mean some local thugs?"

"I've no idea," Bronson admitted. "I didn't hang

around to ask what they wanted. But if the tablet really is worthless, maybe the important thing is what's written on it. Is that possible?"

Angela was silent for a few moments. "Just about, I suppose, but it's extremely unlikely, simply because of the age of the object—most of them are between two and five thousand years old. But what happened to you is a worry, Chris. If you're right and the inscription on the tablet *is* significant, then anyone who's seen it might be in danger."

"I've got half a dozen pictures of it, but I haven't the slightest idea what the inscription means. I don't even know what language it's written in."

"Well, we can do something about that. E-mail a few of the photographs to me here at the museum and I'll get one of our ancient-language specialists to take a look at them. That way, at least we'll know what's on the tablet, and then you can see if you're right about the inscription."

"Good idea." That was exactly what Bronson had been hoping she'd suggest. "I'll do it right now. Look in your inbox in about five minutes."

15

A quarter of an hour later, Angela checked her messages and immediately spotted the one sent by her ex-husband. She glanced at the four pictures of the clay tablet on the screen of her desktop computer and printed a monochrome copy of each of them, because the definition would be slightly better in black and white than in color. Then she leaned back in her leather swivel chair and studied the images.

Angela had occupied the same office ever since she'd first arrived at the museum. It was small, square and organized, dominated by a large L-shaped desk, on the short arm of which stood her computer and a color laser printer. In the center of the larger section of the desk was a collection of potsherds—part of her current workload—and several files and notebooks. In one corner of the office was the wooden bench where she carried out the mechanical aspects of her conservation duties, working with a collection of precision stainless-steel tools, cleaning fluids, various types of adhesive and other chemicals.

Beside that was a row of filing cabinets and above them a couple of shelves lined with reference books.

The British Museum is simply huge: it has to be to accommodate the one thousand permanent staff who work there and the five *million* visitors who pass through the doors every year. The structure covers about seventy-five thousand square meters—that's four times larger than the Colosseum in Rome, or the equivalent of nine football pitches—and contains three thousand five hundred doors. It's one of the most spectacular public buildings in London, or anywhere else, for that matter.

Angela stared at the photographs she'd printed, then shook her head. The quality of the images was nothing like as good as she'd hoped and expected. The object in the pictures was clearly some kind of clay tablet, and she was reasonably sure she could identify the language used, but transcribing it was going to be difficult because all four photographs were so badly blurred.

After a minute or so, she replaced the pictures on her desk and sat in thought for a few seconds. Looking at the images had inevitably started her thinking about Chris and that, as usual, revived all the confusion and uncertainty she felt about him. Their marriage had been brief but it hadn't been entirely unsuccessful. They had at least remained friends, which was more than a lot of divorced couples could say. The problem had always been the unacknowledged third person in their relationship—the shadowy presence of Jackie Hampton, the wife of Bronson's best friend. And that was almost a cliché, she realized, a wry smile playing across her lips.

Bronson's problem had been his unrequited desire for

Jackie, a desire that she knew he had never expressed, and that Jackie had been blissfully unaware of. There had never been any question of his being unfaithful to her—Bronson was far too loyal and decent for anything like that—and in one way the failure of the marriage had been Angela's fault. Once she'd realized where his real affections lay, she had found she simply couldn't cope with playing second fiddle to anyone.

But now Jackie was dead and Bronson's feelings had inevitably changed. He'd been trying—trying hard—to get closer to her, to spend more time with her, and so far Angela had done her best to keep him at arm's length. Before she would allow him to reenter her life, she had to be absolutely sure that what had happened before would never be repeated, with anyone. And so far, she didn't feel she had that assurance.

She shook her head and looked back at the photographs. "I was right," she muttered to herself. "It *is* Aramaic."

Angela could understand a little of the language, but there were several people working at the museum who were far better qualified than her to translate the ancient text. The obvious choice was Tony Baverstock, a senior member of staff and an ancient-language specialist, but he was far from being Angela's favorite colleague. She shrugged, picked up two of the printed photographs, and walked down the corridor to his office.

"What do you want?" Baverstock demanded, as Angela knocked, walked in and stood in front of his extremely cluttered desk. He was a stocky, grizzled, bearlike individual in his late forties, who had the indefinably scruffy appearance common to bachelors everywhere.

"And good morning to you, too, Tony," Angela said sweetly. "I'd like you to look at these two pictures."

"Why? What are they? I'm busy."

"This will only take you a few minutes. These are a couple of pretty poor photographs of a clay tablet. They're not good quality, and don't show the text—which is Aramaic, by the way—in enough detail to be fully translated. All I need from you is an indication of what the inscription is about. And if you could hazard a guess at its date, that could be useful."

Angela passed the pictures across the desk and, as Baverstock glanced at them, she thought she detected a glint of recognition in his eyes.

"Have you seen it before?" she asked.

"No," he snapped, glancing up at her and then quickly dropping his gaze back to one of the images. "You're right," he said grudgingly. "The text is a form of Aramaic. Leave these with me and I'll see what I can do."

Angela nodded and left the office.

For a few minutes Baverstock just sat at his desk, staring at the two photographs. Then he glanced at his watch, opened a locked drawer and pulled out a small black notebook. He slipped it into his jacket pocket, left his office and walked out of the museum and down Great Russell Street until he came to a phone box.

His call was answered on the fifth ring.

"This is Tony," Baverstock said. "Another tablet's turned up."

16

Alexander Dexter was reading a magazine article about antique clocks and didn't bother looking at his phone when the text came in. When he finally read it, he sat back and muttered a curse. It read: CH DML 13 CALL ME NOW.

He noted the originating number, grabbed his car keys, bolted the shop door and spun round the sign so that "CLOSED" was displayed. Then he took a pay-as-you-go mobile phone and its battery—he always removed the battery when he wasn't using it—from his desk drawer and walked out of the back door of his shop.

Dexter ran a perfectly legitimate antiques business, one of several in the small Surrey town of Petworth, which had become known as something of a Mecca for antique dealers and buyers. He specialized in early clocks and chronometers, and small pieces of good furniture, though he would buy anything he thought he could make a profit on. His turnover was faithfully reported to the Inland Revenue on his tax return every year. His VAT returns were similarly accurate and he kept his books impeccably, recording every transaction, every purchase and every sale. The result of his meticulous care and attention to detail was that he'd never been audited by the Inland Revenue, and only once by a VAT inspector, and he didn't expect to receive a second visit any time soon.

But Dexter had a second business, one that most of his customers—and certainly the tax authorities and the police—knew absolutely nothing about. He had assiduously built up an impressive list of wealthy clients who were always on the lookout for "special" items, and who were unconcerned about their source, cost or provenance. These clients always paid in cash and never expected a receipt.

He called himself a "finder," although in truth Dexter was a handler of up-market stolen property. Granted, the property was usually looted from unrecorded tombs and other rich sources of antiquities in Egypt, Africa, Asia and South America, rather than stolen from an individual, a private collection or a museum, but he was happy to handle those goods as well, if the price was right and the risk was sufficiently low.

He walked round to the rear of his building, climbed into his 3-series BMW sedan and drove away. He stopped at a garage on the outskirts of Petworth, filled the tank and bought a copy of the *Daily Mail*, then drove about ten miles out of the town and pulled over in a turnout.

Dexter flipped through the newspaper until he reached page thirteen. He glanced at the slightly fuzzy picture and immediately began reading the article. Clay tablets were neither particularly rare nor very desirable, but that wasn't why he read what the *Mail* reporter had written with increasing excitement.

He finished the article and shook his head. Clearly the family of the dead couple had been badly misinformed—or, more likely, not informed at all—about the likely value of the artifact. But this left one very obvious question: if the theory suggested by David Philips—the son-in-law—*was* correct, and the couple had been murdered as part of a robbery, why would the thieves leave such obviously juicy pickings as their cash and credit cards behind and just take an old clay tablet? It very much looked, Dexter mused, as if his client—a man named Charlie Hoxton, a brutal East End villain with a surprisingly sophisticated taste in antiques who had frankly terrified Dexter from the moment they'd first met—wasn't the only person who had recognized the possible significance of the tablet.

He slipped the battery into place, switched on the mobile phone and dialed the number he'd written down.

"You took your time."

"Sorry," Dexter replied shortly. "So what do you want me to do?"

"You read the article?" Hoxton asked.

"Yes."

"Then it should be obvious. Get that tablet for me."

"That could be difficult, but I might be able to get a picture of the inscription for you."

"Do that anyway, but I want the tablet itself. There might be something on the back or the sides, something the photographs don't show. You told me you had good contacts in Morocco, Dexter. Now's your chance to prove it."

"It'll be expensive."

"I don't care what it costs. Just do it."

Dexter switched off the mobile, started the BMW's engine, drove about five miles south to a pub and stopped in the far corner of the large parking lot. From his jacket pocket he removed a small notebook containing telephone numbers and the first names of people he occasionally employed, specialists in various fields. None of these numbers would ever have been found in any trade directory and all were disposable mobiles, their owners regularly updating him with their new numbers.

He switched on the mobile again and opened his notebook. The moment he had a good signal, he dialed one of the numbers.

"Yup."

"I've got a job for you," Dexter said.

"Keep talking."

"David and Kirsty Philips. They live somewhere in Canterbury, and they should be on the electoral roll or in the phone book. I need their computer."

"OK. How soon?"

"As quickly as you can. Today, if possible. You're happy with the usual terms?"

"Rates have gone up a bit," the gruff voice at the other end said. "It'll cost you a grand."

"Agreed," Dexter said, "and make it look good, will you?"

Once he'd ended that call, Dexter drove another couple of miles before stopping the car and again consulting his notebook. He switched on the mobile and dialed another number, this one with a "212" prefix.

"As-Salaam alaykum, Izzat. Kef halak?"

Dexter's Arabic was workable, though not fluent, and his greeting was formal—"peace be upon you"—followed by a more conversational "how are you?" He'd learned the language mainly because a lot of his "special" customers wanted the kind of relics that were most often found in the Arab world, and it helped to be able to converse with sellers in their own tongue.

"What do you want, Dexter?" The voice was deep and heavily accented, but the man's English was fluent.

"How did you know it was me?"

"Only one person in Britain knows this telephone number."

"Right. Listen, I've got a job for you."

For just over three minutes Dexter explained to Izzat Zebari what had happened and what he wanted him to do.

"It won't be easy," Zebari said.

His reply was almost precisely what Dexter had anticipated. In fact, every job he could ever remember giving the man had produced exactly the same response from him.

"I know. But can you do it?"

"Well," Zebari sounded doubtful, "I suppose I could try my police contacts, see if they have any information."

"Izzat, I don't need to know how you're going to do it, only whether or not you can do it. I'll call you tonight, OK?"

"Very well."

"Ma'a Salaama."

"Alla ysalmak. Goodbye."

　　　　　*　　*　　*

On the way back to Petworth, Dexter worked out what he would have to do next. He'd need to close his shop and fly out to Morocco as soon as he could. Zebari was fairly competent, but Dexter trusted almost nobody, and if the Moroccan did manage to find and recover the tablet, he wanted to be right there when it happened.

To Dexter, the slightly blurred picture in the *Mail* was very familiar, because he'd sold an almost identical tablet to Charlie Hoxton about two years before. That tablet, if his recollection was correct, had been part of a box of relics one of his suppliers had "liberated" from the storeroom of a museum in Cairo. Hoxton, he remembered, had been very keen to acquire any other tablets of the same type, because he believed that the tablet he had purchased had been part of a set.

And it looked as if Hoxton had been right.

17

The two men in the scruffy white Ford Transit looked pretty much like delivery men anywhere. They were casually dressed in jeans, T-shirts and leather jackets, with grubby trainers on their feet, and they both looked fit and quite strong. In fact, they actually *were* deliverymen for a small Kent company, but they had a second line of employment that provided the bulk of their income.

In front of the driver, a satnav unit was attached to the windscreen with a sucker, which made the town plan that the man in the passenger seat was studying largely redundant. But while their first job was finding the right address in Canterbury, they also needed to identify their best route out of the housing estate and back onto a main road, and both men preferred to see the layout of the roads on a map rather than rely only on the satnav's small color screen.

"That's it," the passenger said, pointing. "The one on the left, with the Golf parked outside."

The driver pulled the van in to the side of the road

and stopped about a hundred yards short of the property. "Call the number again," he instructed.

The passenger pulled out a mobile phone, keyed a number and pressed a button. He listened for perhaps twenty seconds, then ended the call. "Still no answer," he said.

"Right. We'll do it now."

The driver slipped the van into gear and pulled away from the curb. A few seconds later, he stopped directly outside the semidetached house on the left and switched off the Ford's engine. The two men pulled on baseball caps, walked round to the back of the vehicle, opened the doors and picked up a large cardboard box from inside.

They carried it between them up the path, past the Volkswagen in the drive, to the back door, and lowered it to the ground. Although a casual observer would have assumed the box was heavy, it was actually completely empty.

The two men looked back toward the road, then glanced all round them. There was no bell, so the driver rapped on the glass panel in the back door. As he expected, there was no sound from inside the house, just as there'd been no response to their telephone call a couple of minutes earlier. After a moment he slipped a jimmy out of his jacket pocket, inserted the point between the door and the jamb beside the lock and levered firmly. With a sharp cracking sound, the lock gave and the door swung open.

They picked up the cardboard box and stepped inside, then immediately split up, the driver going up the stairs while the other man began searching through the ground-floor rooms.

"Up here. Give me a hand."

The second man ran up the stairs as his companion walked out of the study carrying the system unit of a desktop computer. "Get the screen and keyboard and stuff," the driver instructed.

They placed the computer in the cardboard box, then trashed the place, ripping the covers off the beds, emptying all the wardrobes and drawers, and generally wrecking the house.

"That should do it," the driver said, looking around the chaos of the lounge.

The two men walked back down the driveway to the road, again carrying the large cardboard box between them. They slid it into the load compartment of the Transit and climbed back into the cab. They'd just earned a total of five hundred pounds. Not bad for less than ten minutes' work, thought the driver as he turned the key in the ignition.

Not bad at all.

18

"Angela? My office."

The summons from Tony Baverstock was, Angela thought, typical of the man: short to the point of being brusque, and completely lacking any of the usual social graces. When she went in, he was leaning comfortably back in his swivel chair, his feet up on one corner of the desk. The two photographs she'd given him were in front of him.

"Any progress?" Angela asked.

"Well, yes and no, really."

That was also typical Baverstock, Angela thought. He was an acknowledged expert at giving curved answers to straight questions.

"In English, please," she said, sitting down in one of his visitor's chairs.

Baverstock grunted and leaned forward. "Right. As you guessed, the text *is* Aramaic, which is slightly unusual in itself. As you ought to know"—Angela's hackles rose at his thinly veiled implication of her lack of knowledge—

"the use of this type of tablet declined after the sixth century BC, simply because it was a lot easier to write cursive Aramaic on papyrus or parchment than inscribe the individual characters into clay. The even more unusual feature is that it's gibberish."

"Oh, for heaven's sake, Tony. In English, please."

"That *is* English. The stupid woman—I presume it *was* a female behind the camera—who took these pictures was clearly incompetent as a photographer. She's somehow managed to take two photographs of the upper surface of the tablet without ever managing to get more than about half of one line of the inscription actually in focus. A translation of the whole tablet is absolutely impossible and, from what I *have* been able to decipher, it would probably be a waste of time."

"What do you mean?"

"What's on the tablet seems to be a series of Aramaic words. Their individual meanings are perfectly clear, but taken together they make no sense." He pointed at the second of the six lines of characters on one of the pictures. "This is the only line of the inscription that's anything like readable, and even then there's one word that's unclear. This word here—*'arəbə'āh*—is the number four, which is simple enough. The word after it means 'of,' and three of the words that precede it translate as 'tablets,' 'took' and 'perform,' so the sentence reads 'perform took' another word, then 'tablets four of.' That's what I mean by gibberish. The words make sense, but the sentence doesn't. It's almost as if this was a piece of homework for a child, just a list of words selected at random."

"Is that what you think it is?"

Baverstock shook his head. "I didn't say that. I've seen a lot of Aramaic texts, and this looks to me like an adult hand because the letters are formed with short, confident strokes. In my opinion, this was written by an educated adult male—don't forget, in this period women were usually illiterate, much like many of them are today," he added waspishly.

"Tony," Angela warned.

"Just a joke," Baverstock said, though Angela knew that there was always an edge to his remarks about women. In her opinion, he was arrogant and pompous but essentially harmless, a closet misogynist who made little secret of the fact that he resented high-achieving women, and especially high-achieving women who were inconsiderate enough to combine beauty with their brains. Angela remembered a couple of occasions when he'd even had a pop at her, though both times she'd verbally slapped him down.

Angela knew she wasn't beautiful in the classical sense, but her blonde hair and hazel eyes—and lips that Bronson always used to describe as "lucky"—gave her a striking appearance. She almost invariably made an impression on men, an impression that tended to linger, and she knew Baverstock had resented her from day one.

"What date are we talking about?" she asked.

"This is Old Aramaic, which covers the period between about 1100 BC and AD 200."

"Come on, Tony. That's well over a thousand years. Can't you narrow it down a bit more than that?"

Baverstock shook his head. "Do you know anything about Aramaic?" he asked.

"Not very much," Angela admitted. "I work with pottery and ceramics. I can recognize most ancient languages and read a few words in them but the only one I can translate or understand properly is Latin."

"Right, then. Let me give you a short lesson. Aramaic first appeared around 1200 BC when a people later known as the Aramaeans first settled in an area called Aram, in upper Mesopotamia and Syria. It was apparently derived from Phoenician, and, like that language, it was read from right to left. Phoenician didn't have any letters for vowels, but the Aramaeans began using certain letters—principally *'aleph*, *he*, *waw* and *yodh*—to indicate vowel sounds.

"Written examples of the language that became known as Aramaic started appearing about two hundred years later, and by the mid 700s BC, it was the official language of Assyria. Around 500 BC, after the conquest of Mesopotamia under the Persian king Darius I, the administrators of the so-called Achaemenid Empire started using Aramaic in all official written communications within their territory. There's some dispute about whether this was imperial policy, or if Aramaic was simply adopted as a convenient lingua franca."

"The Achaemenid Empire? Remind me."

"I thought even you would know that," Baverstock said, slightly testily. "It lasted from about 560 to 330 BC, and was the first of the various Persian Empires to govern the majority of the country we now call Iran. In terms of occupied territories, it was the biggest pre-Christian empire, covering nearly three million square miles on three continents. The countries subjugated by the Persians included

Afghanistan, Asia, Asia Minor, Egypt, Iran, Iraq, Israel, Jordan, Lebanon, Pakistan, Saudi Arabia, Syria and Thrace.

"The important point is that from about 500 BC, the language became known as Imperial or Achaemenid Aramaic and, because it had acquired official status, it showed remarkably little variation for the next seven hundred years or so. Usually the only way to find out where and when a particular text was written is to identify loaned words."

"Which are what?"

"Words describing objects or places, or expressing views or concepts, that didn't have an exact equivalent in Aramaic and were borrowed from the local language to ensure clarity or accuracy in a particular passage."

"And there's nothing like that in the text you've read?" Angela asked.

"In those half a dozen words, no. If I had to guess, I'd say the tablet's fairly late, probably no earlier than the start of the first millennium BC, but I can't be any more specific."

"Nothing else?"

"You know I hate speculating, Angela." Baverstock paused for a few seconds, looking down again at the pictures of the clay tablet. "Do you have any better photographs than these?" he asked. "And where did the tablet come from?"

Something in Baverstock's manner put Angela on her guard. She shook her head. "As far as I know these are the only ones," she said, "and I've no idea where the tablet was found. I was just sent the photographs for analysis."

Baverstock grunted. "Let me know if it turns up. With better pictures of the inscription I might be able to narrow down its origin for you. But there is," he added, "just a possibility it might have come from Judea."

"Why?"

Baverstock pointed at the single Aramaic word he hadn't translated in the second line of the text. "These pictures are so blurred they're almost useless," he said, "but it's possible that word is *Ir-Tzadok*."

"And that means what?"

"Nothing useful by itself, but it could be the first part of the proper name *Ir-Tzadok B'Succaca*. That's the Old Aramaic name for a settlement on the northwest coast of the Dead Sea. We know it rather better these days by its Arabic name, which means 'two moons.'"

Baverstock stopped and looked across his desk.

"Qumran?" Angela suggested.

"Got it in one. Khirbet Qumran, to give it its full name. Khirbet means 'a ruin.' The word comes from the Hebrew *horbah*, and you'll find the name used all over Judea to indicate ancient sites."

"I *do* know what khirbet means, thank you. So you believe the tablet came from Qumran?"

Baverstock shook his head. "No. I can't guarantee I'm reading it correctly and, even if I am, the word isn't conclusive—it could be a part of a different phrase. And if it *does* mean Qumran, it might be nothing more than a reference to the community."

"Qumran was started when—first century BC?"

"A little earlier. Late second century BC, and it was occupied until about AD 70, round about the time Jerusalem fell. That's the main reason I think the tablet's fairly late, simply because, if I'm right and the word *Ir-Tzadok* forms a part of *Ir-Tzadok B'Succaca*, then the tablet was most probably written while the Yishiyim—the tribe now commonly known as the Essenes—were supposedly in residence at Qumran, hence the rough date I suggested to you."

"So the tablet just refers to Qumran, but didn't come from the Essene community."

"No, I didn't say that. What I said was that the inscription *possibly* refers to Qumran and the tablet *probably* didn't come from the Essenes."

"So were there any other words you thought you could translate?"

"Here." Baverstock pointed at the bottom line of text. "That word could be 'cubit' or 'cubits,' but I wouldn't want to put any money on it. And I think this word here could mean 'place.'"

"And you've still no idea what the clay tablet itself is? Or if it's valuable?"

Baverstock shook his head. "It's certainly not valuable. As to what it is, my best guess is that it was used in a school environment. I think it was a teaching aid, something to show children how to write particular words. It's a curiosity, nothing more, and certainly of no value other than simple academic interest."

"OK, Tony," Angela said, standing up. "That was my conclusion, too. I just wanted to make sure."

Once she'd left, Baverstock sat in thought for a few minutes. He hoped he'd done the right thing in giving Angela Lewis an accurate translation of some of the sections of Aramaic script he'd been able to read. There were another half-dozen words he'd managed to decipher, but he'd decided to keep the meanings of those to himself. He would far rather have told her nothing at all, but he didn't want her running off to another translator who might take an interest in the possible implications of some of the words on the tablet.

And now, if she did decide to do any more digging, about the only place she'd be likely to turn up was Qumran, and he was quite certain that she'd find absolutely nothing there.

About two hours later Baverstock knocked on Angela Lewis's office door. There was no reply, as he'd hoped and expected, because he knew she normally went out to lunch at about that time. He knocked again, then opened the door and stepped inside.

Baverstock spent fifteen minutes carrying out a rapid but thorough search, checking all her drawers and cupboards, but without success. He'd hoped she might actually have had the clay tablet in her possession, but all he found were two other pictures of the relic, which he took. The last thing he did was try to check her e-mails, but her screen saver was protected by a password so he couldn't access her PC.

There was, he supposed, still a possibility Angela had the tablet in her possession, maybe at her apartment. It was time, he mused, as he walked back to his own office, to make another call.

19

Half of the ability to blend into a particular situation is having the right appearance, and the other half is confidence. When the dark-haired, brown-skinned man walked in through the doors of the Rabat hotel, wearing a Western-style suit and carrying a large briefcase, he looked pretty much like any other guest, and the receptionist didn't give him a second glance as he strode across the lobby and walked up the main staircase.

He reached the first floor, stopped and called an elevator. When it arrived, he pressed the button for the fourth floor. As the doors opened, he stepped out, glanced at the sign on the wall indicating the location of the rooms, and turned right. Outside number four zero three he stopped, put down his briefcase, pulled on a pair of thin rubber gloves, took a hard rubber cosh from his pocket and rapped sharply on the door with his other hand. He'd spotted the woman sitting with a drink in the bar just off the lobby as he'd walked through, but he hadn't seen her husband in the building. Hopefully he'd be out somewhere, in which case the man would use the lock-picking tools in the slim leather case in his jacket pocket; if her husband was up there in the room, that was his hard luck.

He heard movement from the other side of the door, took a firmer grip on his cosh and lifted a large white handkerchief up to his face, as if he was blowing his nose.

David Philips opened the door wide and peered out. "Yes?" he said.

Philips registered the presence of a dark-haired man directly in front of him, his face largely obscured by a white cloth, and then fell backward as a dark object whistled through the air and crashed into his forehead. For an instant he saw stars, bright flashes of white and red light that seemed to explode inside his skull, and then his consciousness fled.

His attacker glanced quickly up and down the corridor, but there was no one in sight. He picked up his briefcase again, stepped into the room, dragged the body of the unconscious man inside and then closed the door behind him.

It wasn't a big room, and his search took him under five minutes. When he left the room, his briefcase was significantly heavier than when he'd arrived and, just as when he'd walked in, nobody took the slightest notice of him as he left the hotel.

"I'm sorry to bother you with this as well," Bronson said, sitting down opposite Kirsty Philips.

Dickie Byrd had called him a few minutes earlier and

told him there had been a burglary at the Philipses' house—something that Bronson hadn't liked the sound of at all. The theft of their computer just had to be connected to what had happened in Morocco. The trouble was that Byrd wasn't convinced.

"What happened?" Kirsty asked, a mixture of irritation and concern clouding her voice. "I mean, didn't any of our neighbors see anything?"

"Actually," Bronson said, an apologetic smile on his face, "several of your neighbors saw *exactly* what was happening. They all thought you were back from Morocco and were having a fridge or something delivered. Two men arrived in a white van and carried a big cardboard box into your house. They were inside for about ten minutes, and then walked out with your desktop computer, presumably in the same box."

"And was that all they took?"

"Yes, according to your neighbor, a Mrs. Turnbull. She's looked round the house, and thinks that only the computer was taken. The good news is that although the place was ransacked—it looked as if every drawer had been emptied—nothing seems to have been damaged apart from the lock on the back door. Mrs. Turnbull has already arranged to have that replaced for you, and she's told us she'll tidy up the place before you get back."

Kirsty nodded. "She's always been good to us. A very competent woman."

"She sounds it. Where's your husband, by the way?"

"He nipped up to our room just before you arrived. He should be down any minute."

As she said this, Kirsty glanced toward the lobby, and

gave a sudden start. "David," she called out, and jumped to her feet.

David Philips was staggering across the lobby, a trickle of blood running unheeded down his cheek as he weaved from side to side.

Bronson and Kirsty reached him at almost the same moment. They grabbed his arms and led him across to a chair in the bar.

"What the hell happened? Did you fall or something?" Kirsty demanded, her fingers probing at the wound on his forehead.

"Ouch! That hurts, Kirsty," Philips muttered, pulling her hand away. "And no, I didn't fall. I was quite definitely pushed."

"I don't think you'll need stitches, but that's a very nasty bruise," Bronson said, looking closely at the wound.

The barman appeared beside them, clutching a handful of tissues. Bronson took them, and asked the man to bring a glass of water.

"I'd prefer something stronger," Philips muttered.

"It's not for you to drink," Bronson said.

"And a brandy," Kirsty called out to the man's retreating back.

When the barman returned, Philips sipped the brandy while Kirsty dampened the tissues in the water and gently cleaned away the blood from his face and the wound itself.

"The skin's broken, obviously," she said, looking at the injury, "but the cut's not big enough for stitches. That should help stop the bleeding," she said, folding another few tissues and placing the wad over the wound. "Just hold it in place. Now tell us what happened."

"I was in our room," Philips said, "and there was a knock on the door. I opened it and some guy hit me over the head, hard. He didn't say a word, just knocked me cold. When I came round, he'd gone and so had your laptop."

Kirsty looked at Bronson, clearly terrified. "They're after our computers, aren't they?" she demanded.

Bronson ignored her question. "I've just heard there's been a burglary at your home," he told David. "The thieves took your desktop machine."

"Oh, bloody hell."

"How old were your PCs?" Bronson asked.

"We bought them about three years ago," David Philips said. "Why?"

"That makes them antique," Bronson said flatly, turning back to face Kirsty. "A three-year-old computer's only worth a couple of hundred pounds at best. And that means whoever carried out these two burglaries wasn't after the computers, but what was on their hard disks— the e-mails your mother sent and the pictures she took."

"So do you still think the car crash was just a simple traffic accident?" David Philips asked.

Bronson shook his head. "Definitely not. It looks to me like you've been targeted, and that can only be because of the pictures your mother-in-law took out here in Rabat. Nothing else makes sense. Have you sorted out the repatriation?"

David Philips nodded.

"Right," Bronson said. "I think you should go back

home as soon as possible. And watch your backs while you're out here. Right now you've only got a headache. Next time, you might not be so lucky."

Bronson got up to leave, then looked back at the two of them. "I've got one other question. If I'm right and the thieves were after your data—the photographs and other stuff—did you have copies on the other machine?"

David Philips nodded. "Yes. The e-mails were only on Kirsty's laptop, but I copied the photographs my mother-in-law took onto the desktop. It's a belt-and-braces form of backup, really—we've always done that, regularly duplicated the data on both machines. So whoever stole the computers will now have pictures of the fight they witnessed in the *souk* and photographs of the clay tablet that Margaret picked up. And now the computers have been stolen, all our evidence has gone."

20

Angela stepped inside her apartment and closed the door behind her. She was carrying two bags of shopping, which she took into the kitchen, then walked through into her bedroom to get changed. She pulled on a pair of jeans and jumper, returned to the kitchen and put away her shopping, then made a coffee. She was on her way into the lounge when she heard a faint knock from outside the apartment.

Angela stopped and for a couple of seconds just stared at the door. It hadn't sounded like someone knocking, more like something knocking against it. She put down her drink on the hall table, walked across to the door and peered through the spy-hole.

Her view was distorted, but the bulky shapes of two men outside her door were clear enough. One of them was in the act of raising a jimmy or crowbar to insert between the door and the jamb. And the other man was holding what looked like a pistol.

"Dear God," Angela muttered, and stepped back, feeling her pulse starting to race.

With fingers made clumsy by nerves, she slipped the security chain into place, though she knew that wouldn't hold up the burglars for very long. If they'd brought a crowbar, they would probably have a bolt-cutter as well.

Her drink and almost everything else forgotten, she ran down the hall and into her bedroom, scooping up her handbag en route. She grabbed a warm jacket from her wardrobe, slipped her feet into a pair of trainers, picked up her laptop bag, checked that she had her passport, mobile and purse in her handbag, stuffed the phone charger in as well, and unlocked the back door of her flat, which gave access to the fire escape that ran down the back of the building.

She glanced down, checking that nobody was waiting at the bottom of the steel staircase, and pulled the door closed behind her. As she did so, she heard a cracking sound from inside her apartment, then a sharp snap that she guessed was the security chain being cut.

She didn't hesitate, just started running down the fire escape as fast as she could, glancing back up toward her apartment door every few steps. She was barely halfway to the street when two figures emerged. She saw them look straight at her, and then one of them started pounding down the fire escape, the impacts of his shoes making the metal staircase ring and shudder.

"Dear God," Angela murmured again, and moved even faster, jumping the last few steps to each of the steel platforms as she neared the ground. But she could almost feel that her pursuer was gaining on her.

She hit the ground running, dived around the side of

the building and headed for the street, where she hoped desperately she'd find crowds of people.

But as she reached the corner of her apartment block, a man stepped out from the front of the building, his arms stretched wide as he grabbed for her.

For one heart-stopping moment she felt his hand grasping at her jacket; then she spun round, swinging her laptop bag with all her strength. The heavy bag smashed into the side of his face and the man grunted with pain and staggered backward, almost losing his footing on the damp grass. Angela sprinted past him, through the open pedestrian gate and out onto the pavement.

A handful of people were walking down the street, and she immediately saw a single black cab cruising down the road, its light illuminated. Angela whistled and waved her arm frantically at the driver, then looked behind her. The two men were still running after her, now only about twenty yards back.

The cab pulled into the curb and stopped. Angela sprinted the last few yards, wrenched open the door and climbed in the back.

The driver had been watching through his window, and the instant the back door closed he powered the vehicle out into the traffic, directly in front of an approaching car whose driver had to hit the brakes hard to avoid a collision, and sounded a long indignant blast on his horn.

Angela glanced back. Her pursuers had stopped on the pavement, staring toward the taxi.

"Friends of yours?" the driver asked.

"God, no. And thank you. Thank you so much."

"Right, where to, love?"

"Heathrow airport," Angela said, taking her mobile phone out of her handbag.

For a few moments she looked back through the rear window at her apartment building as the cab accelerated down the road; then she dialed triple nine. When the operator answered, she asked for the police and told them that her flat was being burgled.

21

Dexter drove away from his shop in Petworth that afternoon and met a man in a café on the outskirts of Crowborough. Once they'd finished their drinks, he slid a sealed envelope across the table. In the parking lot outside, he removed a cardboard box from the back of the man's small white van and transferred it to the trunk of his BMW. Then he drove away.

In Petworth, he carried the box into his storeroom and lifted out the computer. He placed it on the bench that ran down the length of the room, plugged in the peripherals, and switched on. Fifteen minutes later, having connected one of his own printers, he was looking at half a dozen pictures that showed a grayish-brown oblong tablet, covered in a form of writing. They weren't particularly clear, and didn't show the inscription in anything like the detail he had hoped, but they were a lot better than the fuzzy image printed in the newspaper.

He had not the slightest idea what the text meant, or even which language it was written in. He slipped the pictures into a manila envelope, locked the storeroom and returned to his shop. In the office at the back he had a powerful computer of his own, with a massive hard disk that contained images and written descriptions of everything he'd bought and sold over the years through the shop and, in a hidden partition protected by an eight-digit alphanumeric password, full details of all his "unofficial" private sales as well.

Minutes later, he was comparing the pictures he'd just printed with images of the clay tablet he'd sold to Charlie Hoxton two years before.

He leaned back, satisfied. He'd been right. The tablet *was* part of a set, which made it very important indeed.

22

"So what's the verdict?" Chris Bronson asked, as he recognized Angela's voice.

"It's a virtually worthless clay tablet that probably dates from around the start of the first millennium," Angela said, "but that's not why I'm calling."

Something in her voice registered with Bronson. "What's wrong?"

She took a deep breath. "When I came back from lunch today I found someone had searched my office."

"Are you sure?"

"Quite sure. It wasn't ransacked, nothing like that, but some of the papers and stuff on my desk had definitely been moved and another couple of the photographs you sent me were missing. And my computer screen was on, showing the screen saver."

"Which means?"

"The screen saver starts after five minute's inactivity and then runs for fifteen minutes. After that, the screen goes blank. I was out of the office for just over an hour."

"So somebody must have used your computer between five and twenty minutes before you came back. What was on it? Anything confidential?"

"Nothing, as far as I know," Angela said, "but my screen saver's password-protected so whoever it was couldn't have accessed it anyway." She paused, and when she spoke again Bronson could hear the tension in her voice. "But that's not all."

"What else?"

"I had a few things to do this afternoon so I left the museum shortly after lunch. A few minutes after I got back to the flat I heard a noise outside the door. When I looked through the spy-hole there were two men standing in the corridor. One of them was holding a jimmy or something like that, and the other one was carrying a gun."

"Jesus, Angela. Are you OK? Did you call the police? Where are you now?"

"Yes, I called them, and I suppose there's some chance they'll send an officer around there sometime this week, but I wasn't going to hang around waiting for him to turn up. I ran out of the back door and down the fire escape. And right now I'm heading for Heathrow."

"Where are you going?" Bronson demanded.

"Casablanca. I'll let you know my flight details when I get to the airport. The flight goes through Paris with a stopover, so I'll be quite late. You *will* pick me up, won't you?"

"Of course. But why—"

"I'm just like you, Chris. I don't believe in coincidence. There's something about that clay tablet, or maybe what's written on it, that's dangerous. First my office, then my flat. I want to get out of the way until we find out what's going on. And I'll feel safer with you than I do here in London by myself."

"Thanks." For a moment Bronson was lost for words. "Call me when you know your flight details, Angela. I'll be at Casablanca waiting for you. You know I'll *always* be waiting for you."

23

Two men dressed entirely in black lay on the hillside, close to a clump of low bushes, both staring through compact binoculars at the house in the valley below them.

After Dexter had called him, Zebari had spent some time on his mobile, asking questions. The answers had led him here: the clay tablet had been stolen from a wealthy man, and this was where he was known to keep most of his collection. The house was two-story, with a large roof terrace at the rear overlooking the garden and with views to the hills beyond. At the front was a paved parking area, protected by a pair of large steel gates.

The property was surrounded by high walls—Zebari estimated their height at about three meters—but these wouldn't necessarily prove to be an obstacle. Solid walls could always be climbed. He was more worried about electronic alarms, and the dogs were a nuisance that he'd need to take care of. He could see two big black animals, possibly Dobermans or similar, prowling restlessly inside the compound and peering through the closed metal gates at the road outside. But they would sleep well with a piece of raw meat each, laced with a cocktail of barbiturates and tranquilizers.

Zebari looked around him, at the stunted bushes and shrubs that covered the top and sides of the sandy hillside he'd chosen as a vantage point. They were perhaps half a kilometer from the house, well out of sight of any guards, and he was quite certain they were unobserved.

He glanced toward the western horizon, where the sun was sinking in a blaze of pinks and blues and purples. Sunsets in Morocco were always spectacular, particularly close to the Atlantic coast, where the clear air and gentle curve of the ocean combined to create a daily kaleidoscopic display that never failed to move him.

"How long?" his companion asked, his voice barely above a whisper, though there was no possibility of them being overheard.

"Another hour," Zebari murmured. "We need to see how many people are in the house before we move."

A few minutes later, the light faded as the sky turned a blackish purple, and then entirely black. And above them the vast unchanging canopy of the universe, studded with the brilliant light of millions of stars, was slowly revealed.

24

Angela Lewis stepped into the arrivals hall at Casablanca's Mohammed V Airport, looked round and spotted Bronson almost immediately. He was a couple of inches taller than most of the locals milling about, but what made him stand out was his obvious European dress—gray slacks, white shirt and light-colored jacket—and comparatively pale face under his slightly unruly thatch of black hair. That, and his undeniable good looks, which always gave Angela a visceral thrill when she saw him.

A sudden feeling of relief flooded through her. She'd known he'd be there, because he'd told her so, and her ex-husband was nothing if not reliable, but there'd still been a slight nagging doubt at the back of her mind. Her biggest fear was that something might have happened to him, something that would leave her stranded in Casablanca by herself, and that was a prospect she'd been dreading.

She smiled broadly and started threading her way through the crowds toward him. Bronson spotted her approaching and gave a wave. Then he was right in front of her, his strong arms pulling her unresisting body toward him. For a few moments they hugged; then she stepped back.

"Good flight?" he asked, taking her suitcase and laptop bag.

"Pretty average," Angela replied, swallowing her pleasure at seeing him again. "Not enough leg-room, as usual, and the in-flight meal was rubbish. I'm starving."

"That we can rectify. The car's outside."

Twenty minutes later they were sitting in a restaurant on the southern outskirts of Casablanca, watching the waiter place a large dish of lamb tajine on the table in front of them.

The restaurant was under half full, but Bronson had been adamant that he didn't want one of the tables by the windows, or close to the door. Instead, he had chosen one right at the back, with a solid wall behind it. And although Angela preferred to sit where she could see the other diners—she'd always enjoyed people-watching—Bronson had insisted on taking the seat that offered a clear view of the door so he could see anyone coming in.

"You're worried about this, aren't you?" she asked.

"Damn right I am. I don't like what's been happening here in Morocco or in London," Bronson said. "Something's going on, and the people involved seem to be completely ruthless, so I'm watching our backs. I don't think anyone could have followed us here, but I'm not taking any chances. Now, tell me what happened at your apartment."

"Just a second." Angela's mobile had begun ringing inside her handbag, and she quickly fished it out and answered it.

"Thanks," she said, after a few moments. "I knew about it. Did the police turn up? I called them when I left the flat."

There was another pause as the caller explained something to her.

"Good. Thanks again, May. Listen, I'm out of the country for a few days, so could you get in a locksmith, please? I'll settle up with you when I get back."

Angela closed her mobile and looked at Bronson. "That was my neighbor in Ealing," she said. "No surprises, except that the police *did* turn up—I wasn't sure they'd bother. My apartment's been thoroughly trashed. Oddly enough, it doesn't look like much, or maybe anything, was taken. May said the TV and stereo are still there, but every drawer and cupboard has been emptied."

"That sounds familiar," Bronson said. "So you scrambled down the fire escape?"

Angela swallowed, and when she spoke again her voice was slightly unsteady. "Yes, that's right. All I had time to do was grab my handbag and laptop, and then I just ran for it. One of the men . . ." She paused and took a sip of water. "One of them chased me down it. The other one must have run down the stairs inside the building, because he was waiting for me when I got round to the front."

"God, Angela. I hadn't realized." Bronson reached over and took her hands, squeezing them gently. "How did you get away?"

"I hit him with my laptop bag. It caught the side of his head, and that gave me enough time to get out onto the road. There was a black cab passing, and I ran across and jumped in. The driver saw what was happening and just drove off before the two men could grab me."

"Thank God for London cabbies."

She nodded enthusiastically. "If he hadn't been there, they'd have caught me. There were people about, Chris, lots of pedestrians, but these guys just didn't care. I was terrified."

"Well, you're safe out here—I hope," he said.

Angela nodded and sat back in her seat. Explaining what had happened had been almost cathartic, and she felt herself regaining her normal composure.

"The good news is that my laptop seems to have survived the impact. And then I enjoyed a bit of retail therapy at Heathrow, hence the new suitcase and stuff."

"I hadn't noticed," Bronson admitted.

"I'm not surprised," Angela said. "You're only a man, after all."

Bronson grinned at her. "I'll ignore that. I'm really glad you're here, you know."

"Now, before we start," Angela said, her face suddenly serious, "we need to establish the ground rules. You and me, I mean. You're out here because you're trying to find out what happened to the O'Connors, and I'm here because I was frightened about what had happened in London."

"So what are you saying?"

"We've been getting along better these last few months, but I'm still not ready for the next step. I really don't want to get hurt all over again. So separate rooms—OK?"

Bronson nodded, although Angela could almost taste his disappointment.

"Whatever you want," he muttered. "I did book you a separate room at the hotel."

Angela leaned forward and reached for his hand. "Thank you," she said. "I want it to be right for us both."

Bronson nodded, but still looked concerned. "One thing you need to understand, Angela. Morocco might not be any safer for us than London," he said, and explained what had happened at the Philipses' hotel. "I told you about that gang of thugs who chased me. I've moved to a different hotel, just in case they'd managed to find out where I was staying, but we'll have to keep a low profile."

Angela smiled at him. "I expected that," she said. "How's David Philips?"

"He's OK—he didn't even need stitches. He's got a nasty bruise on his forehead, and I guess he's nursing a weapons-grade headache. Whoever attacked him used something like a cosh."

"And you don't think it was just a thief after the laptop?"

"No. I checked their room afterward, and it had obviously been thoroughly searched. The laptop was the only thing missing, and the thief ignored their passports, which were on the desk in the room, and didn't touch their money or the credit cards that David Philips had in his pocket. The theft was almost exactly the same, in fact, as the robbery at their home in Kent. In both cases, it looks as if the thieves were after their computers, nothing else."

"And that means?"

"Well, neither computer had much intrinsic value, so the thieves must have been after the data on the hard disks, and that means the pictures of the tablet. Can you trust your guy at the British Museum? Because no matter what he thinks about that lump of fired clay, somebody— apparently with international connections—obviously thinks it's important enough to mount almost simultaneous burglaries in two countries, *and* knock David Philips out cold when he got in their way."

Angela didn't look entirely convinced. "I asked Tony Baverstock to take a look at the pictures, and he's one of our most senior ancient-language specialists. You're not seriously suggesting that he's involved, are you?"

"Who else knew about the pictures of the clay tablet? At the museum, I mean?"

"I see what you're getting at. Nobody."

"So suspect number one has to be Baverstock. Which means he could even have been involved in your burglary as well. More to the point, it also means everything he told you about the tablet might be deliberate misdirection. What did he say, by the way?"

Angela shrugged. "He thinks the tablet was most likely used in a teaching environment, something like a basic textbook, and he was adamant that it's not valuable."

Bronson shook his head. "But it must have *some* value, because I still think it's likely the O'Connors were killed to recover it."

"But Margaret O'Connor took pictures of an argument in the *souk*. Couldn't the killers have wanted to silence her for that reason, and stole the camera to remove the hard evidence?"

"That might well be a part of it," Bronson conceded. "It would explain why the camera and memory stick weren't found in the wreckage. But unless Margaret O'Connor threw away the clay tablet before they left Rabat, somebody took that as well."

"And you don't think she just chucked it away?"

"No. Kirsty told me her mother was going back to the *souk* the next morning to return the tablet to the man—the Moroccan—who'd dropped it, and if she couldn't find him she was going to take it back home with her as a souvenir of their holiday. She put all that in the e-mail she sent to Kirsty the evening before she and Ralph left the hotel. But by then the Moroccan was lying dead outside the *medina* with a stab wound in his chest—Kirsty got a final message from her mother the following morning, telling her she'd actually seen the dead man. Talabani's confirmed that he *was* one of the people Margaret O'Connor photographed."

"Margaret didn't say what she was going to do with the tablet, though?"

"No. Her last message was very short, just a couple of lines, probably sent while her husband was paying the hotel bill or getting the car or something." Bronson paused and leaned forward. "Now, the tablet. What *did* you manage to find out about it?"

"As I told you on the phone," Angela replied, "it's a lump of clay of almost no value. The writing is Aramaic, but Baverstock told me he could only translate one line. And I think he was probably being honest in that at least, because he knows I can read a little Aramaic. If he was trying to mislead me, all I'd have to do to check that would be to compare his translation with the original."

"And have you?" Bronson asked.

"Yes. I looked at a couple of the lines on the photograph, and I came up with the same words."

"OK," Bronson said grudgingly, "for the moment, let's assume he *is* being accurate. Tell me what he said."

"On that single line of text, the words are clear but they don't make sense. I've got a translation of that line and another couple of words written out for you."

"Is there anything special about the tablet? I mean, anything that would make it worth stealing, let alone killing someone because of it?"

"Nothing. Baverstock found a part of a word that might refer to the Essene community at Qumran, but even that's not conclusive."

"Qumran? That's where they found the Dead Sea Scrolls, isn't it?"

"Yes, but that's probably irrelevant. As far as Baverstock could tell, the tablet didn't originate at Qumran, but simply mentions the place. What's interesting is that one of the few other words he translated was 'cubit.'"

"And a cubit was what?" Bronson asked.

"It was a unit of measurement equivalent to the length of a man's forearm, so it was pretty variable—there were at least a dozen different sizes, ranging from the Roman cubit of about seventeen inches up to the biggest, the Arabic Hashimi cubit of nearly twenty-six inches. But the fact that there's a mention of a cubit could mean that the tablet *is* written in a type of code, and it might be indicating the location of something that's been hidden. Maybe that's why it's important."

"Let's face it," Bronson said, "if Baverstock *was* being accurate, the inscription has to be a code of some sort. Nothing else makes sense."

"I agree. Here"—Angela opened her handbag and fished around inside it—"this is the translation of the Aramaic."

Bronson took the single sheet of A4 paper from her and quickly scanned the list of about half a dozen words.

"I see what you mean," he said, looking at the text more carefully. "Did Baverstock think this might be encrypted?"

"No, but his field of expertise is ancient languages, not ancient codes, and that's something I *do* know about. The good news is that we're dealing with an object that dates back around two millennia. And that's good because although there are very few known examples of codes and ciphers from that period of history, those that we do know about are very, very simple. The best-known was probably the Caesar Cipher, which was allegedly used by Julius Caesar in the first century BC to communicate with his generals. It's a really basic monoalphabetic substitution cipher."

Bronson sighed. He knew that Angela had done some research on cryptology as part of a project at the museum. "Don't forget I'm just a simple copper. You're the one with the brains."

Angela laughed. "Now why don't I quite believe

you?" She took a deep breath. "To use a Caesar Cipher, you write out the message as a plaintext, apply whatever shift you've selected to the alphabet, and then transcribe the enciphered message."

Bronson still looked blank, so Angela moved her empty plate to one side and took a piece of paper and ballpoint from her handbag.

"Let me give you an example. Say your message is 'move forward,'" she said, writing the words in capital letters on the paper, "and the shift is left three. You write out the alphabet, then write it out again underneath, but this time you move each letter three places to the left, a so-called left rotation of three. So you'd find 'A' directly above 'D,' 'B' above 'E' and so on. In this case, the enciphered message 'move forward' would read 'pryh iruzdug.' The obvious problem with this method is that every time a particular letter appears in the plaintext, the same enciphered letter will be in the coded message. So in this example, which is only two words in length, two letters the 'R' and 'U'—are repeated, and somebody trying to decrypt the message can use frequency analysis to crack it.

She looked hopefully at Bronson, who shook his head. "Sorry, you'll need to explain that as well."

"Right," Angela said. "Frequency analysis is a simple method of cracking a basic code. The twelve most common letters in the English language, in order, are 'E,' 'T,' 'A,' 'O,' 'I,' 'N,' 'S,' 'H,' 'R,' 'D,' 'L' and 'U.' I remember it as two words—'ETAOIN SHRDLU.' And you probably already know the most famous example of a Caesar Cipher."

"I do?" Bronson looked blank and shook his head. "Help me out here."

"*2001*," Angela said, and sat back in her chair. "*2001— A Space Odyssey*. The sci-fi film," she added.

Bronson frowned; then his expression cleared. "Got you," he said. "The filmmakers didn't want to use the acronym 'IBM' for the computer on the spaceship, so they came up with the name 'HAL,' which, if I've understood you correctly, is a Caesar Cipher with a right rotation of one."

"Exactly. There's another slightly bizarre example," Angela said. "The French '*oui*' becomes the English 'yes' if you apply a left rotation of ten."

"Do you think anything like that is probable in this case?"

"No," Angela replied, "and for one very simple reason: we can read the Aramaic words on the tablet. One of the obvious problems with a Caesar Cipher is that every word of the enciphered text is invariably gibberish, which is the biggest clue that the message is encrypted. That definitely isn't the case here."

"What about other kinds of ciphers?" Bronson asked.

"You've got the same problem with all of them. If the individual words are encrypted, they cease to be recognizable as words and end up as collections of letters. The Aramaic words on this tablet"—she tapped the paper in front of Bronson—"aren't encrypted. But that doesn't mean there isn't some kind of message hidden in the text."

"You need to explain that," he said, "but wait until we're back on the road."

*   *   *

"Just wait in here a second," Bronson said as they reached the door of the restaurant. "I want to check there's nobody waiting for us out there. Then I'll bring the car over."

Angela watched him walking around the handful of cars parked outside, glancing into each of them, then stepped through the door as Bronson pulled the hire car to a halt just outside.

"So if the words aren't encrypted, how can there be a message in the text?" he asked, as he pulled out onto the main road.

"Instead of an alphabetic substitution, you can use word substitution. You choose particular words to mean something completely different. The Islamic terrorist groups have been doing this for quite some time. Instead of saying something like 'We will plant the bomb at three this afternoon' they say 'We will deliver the fruit at three this afternoon.'"

"So the sentence still makes sense, but the apparent meaning is entirely different to its real meaning," Bronson said.

"Exactly. Shortly before the attack on the World Trade Center, the lead terrorist, Mohammed Atta, contacted his controller and passed him a message that made no sense to the American security forces at the time. He used a sentence that included a phrase something like 'plate with one stick down, two sticks.' With a bit of imagination, you can see that he meant the numbers '9' and '11.' He was actually telling his al-Qaeda contact the exact date when the attacks on America were going to take place."

"And on this tablet?"

Angela shook her head in the darkness of the car, the headlamps boring a tunnel of light down the almost empty road in front of them. "I don't think there's anything like that incorporated in the text, simply because the sentences don't make sense."

She paused as she looked through the side window at the clear night sky. Casablanca was now several miles behind them, and away from the light pollution of the city, the stars looked brighter and closer, and far more numerous, than she'd ever seen them. She glanced back at Bronson, glimpsing his strong profile in the faint light cast by the jade-green illumination of the dashboard instruments.

"But there's one possibility that we haven't even considered," she said.

25

Izzat Zebari waited until after one in the morning, when the lights in the house had been switched off for well over an hour, before he walked across to the double steel gates and lobbed two large raw steaks into the compound beyond. Melting back into the darkness, he heard a low growl and the swift patter of clawed feet as the two guard dogs ran out of their kennels to investigate the intrusion.

"How long before it works?" Hammad asked, as Zebari slid down into the passenger seat of the car they'd parked in a deserted side-street about a hundred meters away.

Hammad would deal with any burglar alarms or other electronic devices they encountered at the property. On the floor beside him was a small fabric case that held specialist tools and other equipment. Zebari knew that because Hammad had opened and checked the contents at least six times since they'd returned to the car. They'd cautiously walked down from the hillside just after darkness fell, and had been waiting in the vehicle ever since.

"Half an hour should do it," Zebari replied. "We just have to wait for the drugs to do their work. My chemist friend calculated the dose very carefully."

Zebari waited another forty-five minutes before he gave the order to move. They climbed out of the car, easing the doors closed as carefully and quietly as they could, then opened the trunk to remove the rest of their equipment. The biggest single item was a collapsible ladder long enough to reach the top of the boundary wall of the property.

Minutes later, they were crouched beside the wall, their all-black clothing making them almost invisible in the darkness. Swiftly Hammad and Zebari assembled the ladder, quietly slotting the sections together, then rested the base on the ground. The other end of the ladder was padded with cloth, and made no sound as Zebari leaned it against the top of the wall.

"OK, up you go," Zebari whispered.

Hammad climbed silently almost to the top, where he carefully examined the wall. He shone a pencil flashlight in both directions along it, the narrow beam barely visible. Next, he removed a spray can from his fabric bag and depressed the nozzle, aiming the jet at the area directly above the top of the wall, at the point where they would have to climb over it. Then he descended again.

"No wires or pressure pads on top of the wall, no infrared sensors and no lasers," he reported.

"Excellent," Zebari muttered. "They probably just rely on the dogs. Let's go."

The two men ascended the ladder and climbed onto the top of the wall to sit with their legs astride it. Then Hammad lifted the ladder up and lowered it to the ground inside the courtyard.

They descended swiftly, and Zebari jogged round to the front of the house to check that the two dogs were sleeping peacefully. Then they ran together toward the rear of the property.

In the center of the back wall of the house was a substantial ancient wooden door, decorated with a random pattern picked out in steel studs and fitted with a massive old lock. Zebari pointed at it, but Hammad shook his head decisively.

"Possibly alarmed," he said, and turned his attention to the windows on either side. Like those in many Moroccan houses, these were square and quite small, as a protection against the intense heat of the sun. Hammad stood on tiptoe and used his pencil flashlight to carefully inspect the frame, checking for wires or contacts that might be linked to an alarm system.

"There it is," he muttered. "A simple break-no-break contact if the window's opened, but there's no sensor on the glass. I'll go in that way so I can open the back door from the inside."

He stepped down from the window, took out a roll of sticky tape and plastered several lengths on the center of the pane, leaving a short length sticking out that he could hold on to. He ran a diamond-tipped glass cutter firmly around the very edge of the glass, as close to the window frame as possible, and then rapped on the edge of the pane with his fist. With a cracking sound, the entire pane of glass shifted inwards and Hammad was able to slide it out of the frame. No alarms sounded.

He placed the glass against the wall a safe distance away and then, with Zebari's help, he hoisted himself up and wriggled through the frame and into the property. Zebari passed him the fabric bag of tools, and waited.

Less than three minutes later, having disabled the alarm system, Hammad unlocked the back door of the house and swung it open just wide enough for Zebari to slip inside.

Zebari led the way down a short corridor, Hammad checking each door carefully for wires or any other sign of an alarm system before opening it, and using a flashlight to check the rooms. The third door he opened led into a long room with cabinets along all four walls: it looked like an exhibition room in a museum.

"Show me the picture again," he muttered, flashing the beam from his pencil flashlight over the rows of wooden cabinets, their glass fronts reflecting the light around the room.

Zebari pulled an A4-size color print from his pocket, unfolded it and passed it over. Dexter had sent him the picture by e-mail the previous evening.

For a few seconds, Hammad stared at the image on the paper, then nodded and stepped across to the first of the cabinets on his right. Zebari turned left and began his own search.

Four minutes later, it was clear to both of them that the tablet wasn't on display in any of the cabinets in the room.

"What now?" Hammad hissed.

"We keep on looking," Zebari told him, leading the way out of the room and further down the corridor.

At the very end was a set of double doors. Zebari opened them and stepped into the room.

"There," he breathed, and pointed.

The room was obviously used for meetings or perhaps social gatherings. Strewn across the floor were perhaps twenty large cushions, upon which guests could sit comfortably cross-legged in the traditional Arab fashion. Decorating the plain white walls were a number of rugs and tapestries, obviously old and very valuable. But what had caught Zebari's attention was a single glass-topped cabinet located at one end of the long room.

The two men hurried across to it and looked down. Inside the cabinet was a clear plastic plinth and beside it a card bearing a color photograph of a small oblong gray object and a text in Arabic.

"No tablet," Hammad whispered.

Zebari pulled out the photograph again and held it above the display case, flicking the beam of his flashlight from the image on the paper to that on the card in front of them.

"No, but I'll take that card anyway. Is there an alarm?" he asked.

Hammad carefully examined the back and sides of the display case. "I can't see any wires apart from the power cable for the light." He pointed at a short fluorescent tube mounted at the rear of the case. Then he turned his attention to the catch that secured the glass top. "Nothing there either," he said.

"Good," Zebari muttered. He reached down, unclipped the catch and lifted the lid. He gestured to Hammad to support it, then reached into the cabinet.

"Wait," Hammad whispered urgently, looking at the back of the cabinet, which was now revealed by the lifted lid. "I think that's an infrared sensor."

But it was too late. Immediately, security lights flared on around the outside of the property, most of the house lights came on and a siren began to wail.

"Out the back door," Zebari ordered, grabbing the card and sliding it into his pocket. "Run!"

They pelted down the corridor, wrenched open the back door of the house and ran for the ladder propped against the boundary wall. Zebari reached it first, Hammad right behind him.

Once on the top of the wall, Zebari grasped the rough stone with both hands and lowered himself as far as he could on the outside of the wall, then let go. He consciously bent his knees as he hit the ground, absorbing the shock of the impact with his legs. He toppled sideways and rolled once, then climbed to his feet, unhurt.

Then a volley of shots rang out from the other side of the wall.

From his precarious perch near the top of the ladder, Hammad looked back into the grounds of the property. Three men had appeared, two from around the front of the house and one from the back, and all of them were firing pistols.

He never stood a chance. Silhouetted in his dark clothing against the sheer white paint of the boundary wall,

Hammad was hit almost immediately. He tumbled sideways, screaming with pain as he crashed to the ground.

Outside the property, Zebari ran for his life, heading for the safety of the car. But even as he did so, he heard more shots echoing from behind him as one of his pursuers reached the top of the ladder and began firing.

26

"That's the wrong answer—again," the tall man with the paralyzed face snarled. He stepped forward and delivered a stinging backhand blow to the wounded man who sat directly in front of him, his arms and legs firmly bound to the upright chair, his battered head slumped down onto his chest.

Amer Hammad was dying, and he knew it. He just wasn't sure whether the tall man would finally lose patience with him and put a bullet through his head, or if he'd die before that from blood loss.

When the three guards had dragged him back to the house, the first thing they did was call their boss. Then they'd lashed his wrists together and roughly bandaged the gaping wound in his left thigh where the bullet had ripped through the muscles and torn a deep furrow. That had reduced—but hadn't stopped—the bleeding, and Hammad could see a slowly spreading pool of blood on the floor beneath him.

The interrogation was taking place in a small square

building in one corner of the compound. The dark stains that discolored the flaking concrete floor were mute evidence that the building had been used before, for similar purposes.

"I'll ask you once more," the tall man snapped. "Who were you with, and what were you looking for?"

Hammad shook his head and said nothing.

The tall man stared down at him for a long moment, then picked up a length of wood from the floor. One end of it had been sharpened to a point. His captive watched him through half-closed, bruised, bloody and terrified eyes.

The tall man rested the sharpened end of the wood quite gently on the blood-sodden bandage wrapped around Hammad's thigh and smiled, the paralyzed right side of his face barely moving.

"You probably think I've hurt you enough, my friend, but the truth is I've hardly started. Before I've finished with you, you'll be begging for death."

As he spoke, he steadily increased the pressure on the length of wood, twisting and driving the end of it through the bandages and deep into the open wound.

Blood spurted and Hammad howled, the incredible pain adding a new dimension to his agony.

"Stop, stop," he yelled, his voice a blubbering wail. "Please stop. I'll tell you anything you want to know."

"I know you will," the tall man said, pushing still harder.

Hammad's head flew back as a flood of pain overwhelmed his senses, and then he slumped forward, unconscious.

"Put another bandage on his leg," the tall man ordered, "then we'll wake him up."

Ten minutes later, a bucket of cold water and a couple of slaps brought Hammad round. The tall man sat down on a chair in front of him and prodded his captive sharply in the stomach with the sharpened length of wood.

"Right," he said, "start at the beginning, and leave nothing out."

27

"Does this hotel have wi-fi?" Angela asked, pushing her coffee cup toward Bronson and nodding for him to re-fill it.

They were sitting at a small table in Bronson's hotel room on the outskirts of Rabat, because he was still concerned about being seen by the wrong people, and breakfasting in his room had seemed a safer option than going down to the hotel dining room. Angela was still wearing her nightdress under the large white dressing gown she'd found in her bedroom next door. It was a gesture of intimacy he appreciated—it showed that she was comfortable enough in his company—but he was frustrated because she'd insisted on sleeping in the ad-joining room.

Bronson sighed. "You want to do some research?"

"Yes. If I'm right about the words on the tablet, there must be others like it—it has to be part of a set—and the logical place to start looking for them is museums. There's a kind of museum intranet that I can use to carry out a search. It allows people with the right access—and that includes me, obviously—to check both the exhibits and the relics that are in storage in most museums around the world. It's an ideal tool for researchers, because you can study particular objects without having to travel to the museum itself to do so."

Bronson cleared a space on the table, opened up his laptop and switched it on, then waited a couple of minutes for the Sony to access the hotel's wi-fi network.

"How does the system work?" he asked, turning the Vaio to face Angela and watching as she input her username and password to log in to the museum intranet.

"It's fairly simple. First, I have to fill in various fields to approximately identify what I'm looking for."

As she spoke, she was ticking a series of boxes and inserting brief details in text fields on the search form. When she'd completed the page, she turned the laptop so that Bronson could see the screen as well as her.

"We still don't know too much about this tablet, so I've had to be fairly flexible in the search. For the date I've suggested between the start of the first century BC and the end of the second century AD—that's a period of three hundred years, which should cover it. Baverstock thought the tablet was probably first century AD, based on what he could translate of the inscription, but he couldn't be sure. For the origin I've been just as vague: I've specified the Middle East."

"What about the object itself?"

"I've been fairly accurate with that, because we do have a pretty good idea what we're looking for. Here"—she pointed at two fields at the bottom of the screen—"I've listed the material it's made from and the fact that it bears an inscription in Aramaic."

"So now you just start the search?"

"Exactly." Angela moved the mouse pointer over a button labeled "Search" and gave it a single click.

The wi-fi network at the hotel was obviously quite fast, because the first results appeared on the screen within a few seconds.

"It looks like there are hundreds of them," Bronson muttered.

"Thousands, more likely," Angela said. "I told you clay tablets were really common. I'll have to do a bit of filtering or we'll never get anywhere."

She scanned the listings that were scrolling down the screen. "A lot of these are quite early," she said, "so if I reduce the date range that will eliminate a large percentage. And if we don't find what we're looking for, I can always expand it again."

She changed the search parameters and restricted the date to the first and second centuries AD, but that still produced several hundred results, far too many to trawl through quickly.

"Right," she muttered, "clay tablets were found in all sorts of shapes and sizes—square, oblong, round. There were even tablets shaped like drums or cones, with the inscription running around the outside. I've restricted the search to flat tablets, but it would help if I could put in the approximate dimensions of the one Margaret O'Connor acquired."

Bronson handed her the CD that Kirsty had prepared for him, and she flipped through the images on the laptop's screen until she found the first one showing the clay tablet. Margaret O'Connor had obviously placed the tablet on a chest of drawers in her hotel room, and had then photographed it from several different angles. In most of the pictures, the tablet was quite badly out of focus, probably caused by the camera's autofocus facility choosing a different object in the frame. In three photographs a part of a telephone was visible, including a section of the keypad.

"That'll do," Angela said. "I can work out the rough size from that."

She studied the best of the pictures closely, then jotted down a couple of figures.

"I reckon it's about six inches by four," she said, and typed those numbers into the correct box on the search screen.

This time, with the much tighter parameters, there were only twenty-three results of the search on the museum intranet, and they both leaned closer to the laptop to study each in turn.

The first dozen or so were clearly very different to the picture of the tablet Margaret O'Connor had picked up, but the fifteenth picture showed one that was remarkably similar.

"That looks just like it," Angela said.

"What about the inscription?" Bronson asked.

Angela studied the image carefully and saved a copy onto the hard disk of her laptop. "It could be Aramaic," she said. "I'll check the description."

She clicked one of the options on the screen, and a

half page of text appeared, replacing the photograph of the tablet.

Angela took one look at it, turned the laptop further to face Bronson and leaned back. "It's in French," she announced. "Over to you, Chris."

"OK. The tablet's in a museum in France, so no surprise there. It's in Paris, in fact. It was bought from a dealer of antiquities in Jerusalem as part of a job lot of relics about twenty years ago. The inscription *is* Aramaic, and the tablet's labeled as a curio, because the text is just a series of apparently random words—so you're right, Angela. This is another one."

"Does it say what the museum thinks the tablet was used for?"

Bronson nodded. "This description suggests it might have been used for teaching people how to write Aramaic or possibly was somebody's homework, which is pretty much the same as Baverstock thought, isn't it? In either case, the museum suggests that the tablet was fired accidentally, either because it was mixed up with tablets that *were* being fired deliberately or because there was an actual fire in the building where it was kept."

"That makes sense. Clay tablets were intended to be reused many times. Once an inscription had served its purpose, the tablet could be wiped just by running a knife blade or something similar over its surface to obliterate the existing inscription. The only tablets that would normally be fired were those recording something of real importance—financial accounts, property details, that kind of thing. And a fired clay tablet is virtually indestructible, unless it's broken up with a hammer or something."

"There's something else." Bronson looked at the bottom of the entry on the screen. He reached over and clicked on another link. "This is the original Aramaic inscription," he said, as the screen changed to show two blocks of text, "and below that is the French translation of what it says. We should make a copy of this."

"Absolutely," Angela replied, and swiftly copied an image of the web page onto her hard drive. "What does the French translation say? A lot of those words look like they're repeated to me."

"They are. There are some duplicates, and the words look as if they've been selected almost at random. It has to be part of the same set. Is it worth going to the museum to see it?"

"Hang on a second," Angela said, and clicked the mouse button to return to the "description" page. "Let's see if it's actually on display. What does that say?"

Bronson peered at the screen. "It says: 'In storage. May be accessed by accredited and approved researchers upon submission of written requests giving a minimum of two weeks notice.' Then it tells you who to write to if you're interested and what credentials are acceptable to the museum." He sighed. "Well, that's it then, isn't it? I guess we won't be going to Paris any time soon."

28

The calm, measured voice on his mobile was instantly recognizable to Jalal Talabani.

"How can I help you?" he asked, checking that none of his colleagues in the Rabat police station were within earshot.

"Two of my men followed the English detective—the man Bronson—to Casablanca airport yesterday evening. He met a woman who had arrived on a flight from London. We assumed she might be his wife, but one of my associates ran a check on her and her name is Angela Lewis. But she *is* staying with him at his new hotel in Rabat. Find out who she is and get back to me."

There was a pause, and Talabani waited. He knew his caller didn't like to be hurried.

"You have three hours," the voice said, and the line went dead.

Bronson had had enough. They'd spent the last hour and a half staring at drawings and translations and pictures of tablets from museums around the world. Some of the images were sharp and clear, some were so blurred and out of focus as to be almost useless, but after ninety minutes of looking at the never-ending sequence of pictures on the computer screen, he was about ready to quit.

"God, I need a drink," he muttered, leaning back and stretching his arms above his head. "I really don't know how you do it, Angela. Doesn't this just bore you rigid?"

She glanced at him and grinned. "This is how I spend my life. I'm not bored—I'm fascinated. And particularly by this tablet," she added.

"What?" Bronson said, returning his gaze to the Vaio's screen.

The picture showed a tablet that looked almost identical to the one Margaret O'Connor had picked up in the *souk*. But this one was listed as being stolen, along with a number of other relics, from a storeroom at a museum in Cairo. There'd been no trace of it since then. The tablet had been photographed as a matter of routine when the museum had acquired it, but no translation of the inscription—again a piece of Aramaic text—had been attempted either at the time or since.

"I wonder if that's the tablet Margaret O'Connor found in the *souk*," Bronson muttered, rubbing his eyes and sitting up straighter. "If it *was* stolen, that might explain why the owner—whoever it is—was so keen to get it back."

"Hang on a second," Angela said. She selected one of the pictures from the CD Bronson had given her, and then displayed the photograph of the stolen tablet right beside it on the screen.

"It's different," Bronson said. "I don't read Aramaic—obviously—but even I can see that the top lines are different lengths on those two tablets."

Angela nodded agreement. "Yes," she said, "and there's something else I've just noticed. I think there are only four tablets in the set."

"How do you work that out?"

"Here," Angela pointed at the right-hand image. "See that short diagonal line, right at the corner of the tablet?"

Bronson nodded.

"Now look at the other photograph. There's a similar line in the corner of that one as well." She flicked rapidly back to the picture of the tablet held in the Paris museum. "And on this one, just there."

Angela sat back from the laptop and looked at Bronson with a kind of triumph. "I still don't know what the hell this is all about, but I think I can tell you how these tablets were made. Whoever prepared these inscribed a small diagonal cross in the center of an oblong block of clay. Then they cut that block into four quarters and fired them. What we've been looking at are three of those four quarters. Each of the lines in the corners of the tablets is one arm of that original cross."

"And the idea of the cross is to tell us exactly how the four tablets are supposed to line up," Bronson said, "so that we can read the words in the correct order."

Discovering Angela Lewis's identity took less time than Jalal Talabani had expected. First, he called the hotel where the two English guests were staying and talked to the manager. The man had actually been behind the reception desk both when Bronson made the booking for her, and when Angela Lewis had checked in the previous evening.

"She's his former wife," the manager said, "and I think she works in London at a museum."

"Which one?" Talabani asked.

"I don't know," the manager replied. "It was just that when she checked in she was talking to Mr. Bronson about her work and mentioned a museum. Is it important?"

"No, not really. Thank you for that," Talabani said, and ended the call.

He turned to his computer, input a search string into Google and opened the "Britain Express" Web site's list of the museums of London. The sheer number both surprised and dismayed him, but he printed the list and started at the top. He put a line through the details of the small and highly specialized establishments, but began calling each of the others in turn and asking to speak to Angela Lewis.

The seventh number he tried was the switchboard at the British Museum. Two minutes later he not only knew that Angela Lewis was employed there, but also which department she worked in, and that she was away on leave.

And five minutes after that, the man with the calm, measured voice knew this too.

29

Tony Baverstock had been at work for a little over an hour when he took a call from the switchboard. A member of the public had telephoned the museum with a question about a piece of pottery he'd found, apparently bearing part of an inscription.

It was the kind of call the museum got all the time, and almost invariably the object turned out to be completely worthless. Baverstock vividly remembered one elderly lady from Kent who'd actually brought along the alleged relic for inspection. It was the grubby remains of a small china cup she'd dug up in her garden, and had borne the partial inscription "1066" and "le of Hastin" in a kind of Gothic script on one side.

The woman had been convinced she'd found something of national importance, a relic dating from nearly a thousand years earlier and a crucial reminder of one of the most significant events in England's turbulent past, and refused to believe it when Baverstock told her it was rubbish. It was only when he turned the cup over, cleaned the dirt off it and pointed to the other, complete, inscription on the base of the vessel that he'd been able to convince her that she was mistaken. That piece of text, in very small letters, had read "Dishwasher safe."

"Not my field," Baverstock snapped, when the switchboard girl described what the caller had apparently found. "Try Angela Lewis."

"I already have," the telephonist replied, just as irritated, "but she's taken some leave."

Five minutes later he had convinced the caller, who lived in Suffolk, that the best place to have his find examined was the local museum in Bury St. Edmunds. Let somebody else have their time wasted, Baverstock thought. Then he placed an internal call to Angela Lewis's superior.

"Roger, it's Tony. I was just looking for Angela, but she doesn't seem to be at work. Any idea where she is?"

"Yes." Roger Halliwell sounded somewhat harassed. "She's taken some leave. At pretty short notice, actually. She rang yesterday afternoon—some domestic crisis, I gather."

"When will she be back?"

"She didn't say—which is all pretty inconvenient. Anything I can help you with?"

Baverstock thanked him and replaced the receiver. Now that's interesting, he thought. Very interesting indeed.

30

"So there were originally four tablets, and together they formed a larger oblong?"

"Exactly," Angela said. "And we've identified three of them, but we've only got a clear photographic image of one—an image clear enough to read the inscription on it, I mean. The other problem is that we don't have the fourth tablet, and that means we're completely missing a quarter of the inscription."

"You can't do anything with the three we've located?"

"Not a lot," Angela replied. "We'll need to buy or maybe download an Aramaic-English dictionary before we can even start doing any work on the inscriptions. The bigger problem is that the pictures of these two tablets"—she pointed—"simply aren't good enough to allow us to translate more than the odd word. Most of them are blurred and out of focus, and to translate Aramaic you need a clear image of the original, because several of the letters are very similar in appearance."

"But it's still worth trying, especially as we've got a complete translation of the Paris tablet."

Angela nodded. "Yes, assuming I can find a suitable dictionary. Let's see what the web can offer."

She opened Google, typed "Aramaic dictionary" in the search field and hit the return key.

The two of them leaned forward and peered at the screen of Angela's laptop.

"Over a hundred thousand hits," Bronson muttered. "*Somewhere* in that lot there must be a dictionary that we can use."

"There is," Angela said. "The very first entry, in fact." She double-clicked the listing in Google and checked the screen. "This site offers translations both ways—to and from Aramaic—for single words. It even includes a downloadable font that we'll need to use for the Aramaic text. Aramaic is an *abjad*, a consonantal alphabet, with only twenty-two letters, and in appearance it's very similar to Hebrew. So we need a font like this one—this is called Estrangelo—to display it, so that the dictionary can recognize the words."

Angela downloaded and installed the font, then opened a new document in her word processor, selected the Estrangelo font and carefully wrote out one of the words from the clay tablet Margaret O'Connor had found in the *souk*.

"This is one of the words Tony couldn't translate," she said. "He told me it wasn't clear enough."

When she was satisfied that she'd got it as accurate as possible, she copied the word into the on-line dictionary and pressed the "search" button.

"That's not a good start," she muttered, looking at the screen. The message "word not recognized" was displayed under the search field. "It looks like Tony was right about this word, at least."

"Maybe one of the characters you've used isn't exactly right," Bronson suggested. "It *is* pretty blurred in that photograph. Why don't you try a different word?"

"OK. This is what Tony translated as 'tablet,' and it's one of the words I checked earlier. Let's see what the system makes of this."

She prepared the Aramaic characters ܪܘܠܒ and copied the word into the search field. Immediately the system returned the English translation as "tablet."

"That worked," she said. "Let's try this one."

She carefully composed a different set of characters— ܠܡܟ —and input that. The system correctly translated the Aramaic word as "cubit."

"OK, now we're cooking," she looked up at Bronson and smiled. "Let's make a start on the Cairo tablet."

31

"Did you get it?" Alexander Dexter asked, as Izzat Zebari—now wearing Western-style clothes instead of his usual *jellaba*—sat down opposite him in the lounge of the midpriced hotel near the center of Casablanca. It was early evening. Dexter had flown from London to Rabat that morning, and then driven down to the city in response to Zebari's summons.

It had been a blisteringly hot day and the evening wasn't much cooler. Dexter wished he'd thought to bring even lighter-weight clothes than the jacket and slacks he was wearing.

Zebari glanced around the room at the handful of other residents and guests. Then he looked back at Dexter.

"No, my friend, I did not get it."

Apart from the unwelcome news that he had failed to achieve his objective, something else in Zebari's voice and manner bothered Dexter.

"There's a 'but,' isn't there?" he asked.

Zebari nodded. "Yes, there is a 'but,' as you put it. A big 'but.' The cost of trying to recover the object was much higher than I had expected."

"How much higher?" Dexter asked, guessing that Zebari might be trying a serious shake-down, even though he'd failed in his mission.

"Probably more than you can afford. The man with me was shot down and captured as we tried to escape. I think we can assume that his subsequent death—and I've no doubt that he is dead—was neither quick nor painless."

"Oh, Jesus," Dexter muttered. He knew the world of stolen and smuggled antiques was pretty rough, but he hadn't expected anything like that. "All you had to do was steal a bloody clay tablet. How could you possibly screw that up so badly?"

Zebari's voice was ice cold. "One of the problems we faced, Dexter, was that the man who possessed the tablet pretends to be a businessman, but in reality he's nothing more than a gangster. His house was fitted with alarms, which we disabled, but he'd installed an infrared sensor inside the display cabinet, and we didn't see that until I reached inside it. And by then, of course, the alarms had gone off. I managed to scramble over the wall and get away, but my companion wasn't so lucky. His name, should you be interested, was Amer Hammad. He was a man I've known and worked with for over ten years, and I called him a friend."

"But you didn't get the tablet? You know I don't pay for failure."

"You're not listening, Dexter. I told you that I didn't

get it, simply because it wasn't there. And there are other . . . complications. Quite apart from Hammad's death, that is."

"Like what?" Dexter demanded.

"The man who owned the tablet has very good contacts inside the Moroccan police force. A number of officers are believed to be on his payroll."

"So?"

"So it probably won't take him too long to discover Hammad's identity."

"What will happen to his body?" Dexter asked.

"He'll probably stick it in the back of a Jeep, drive a few miles out into the desert and dump it. The jackals and the vultures will take care of it. But whatever method of disposal he chooses, Hammad's corpse will simply vanish. The point is that if this man manages to identify me as the other burglar, I've got real problems."

"So that's why we're meeting here in Casablanca instead of up in Rabat?"

"Exactly. I need to get out of Morocco, quickly, and for at least a year. And that costs money, serious money."

"OK, I understand the position you're in, and I'm sorry. But I told you I don't pay for failure."

Dexter shifted slightly in his seat, as if preparing to stand up and leave, but Zebari stilled him with a gesture.

"We did get something," he said. "A piece of card."

"Is that all?"

"Yes, but it has a good picture of the tablet on it, and the story of its origins. Does your client want the tablet itself, or just a copy of the inscription that's on it?"

Dexter looked at him appraisingly. "What do you mean?"

"What I say. Some people talk, other people listen. The word is that this clay tablet is worthless, but the inscription on it is priceless. It's a kind of treasure map, or a part of one, anyway. Now, if your client really just wants this lump of fired clay for his collection of relics, our conversation here is probably over. But if all he wants is a picture of the inscription—a much better picture than the one you sent me—then I hope he has deep pockets, because it's going to cost him plenty to get his hands on the card."

Dexter sighed. "OK, let's cut to the chase. How much do you want?"

Zebari took a slip of paper out of his pocket and passed it across the table.

Dexter picked it up and looked at the number written on it. "Ten thousand? Ten thousand pounds?" he asked, keeping his voice low, and Zebari nodded. "You have just *got* to be joking. Ten grand for a picture of a clay tablet? My client will never agree."

"Then neither you nor your client will ever see the card. It's your choice, Dexter. I've given you my first, last and totally nonnegotiable offer. If you don't agree, I'll walk out of here and you'll never see me again. I have friends who'll help me."

For a few seconds the two men stared at each other; then Dexter nodded. "Wait here. I'll call my client and see what he wants to do. I'll need a few minutes."

"Make it quick, Dexter. I'm running out of time."

Dexter left the hotel, walked a short distance down

the street, then pulled out his mobile phone. He relayed to Charlie Hoxton what Zebari had told him, and finished by telling him the price the Moroccan was demanding. Or, to be completely accurate, he told him Zebari wanted fifteen thousand pounds for the card—he had his commission to think of, after all.

When he told Hoxton the price, Dexter held the phone away from his ear, which was just as well. The stream of invective being emitted at full volume from the earpiece might have damaged his hearing. When the tirade had diminished, he cautiously replaced the phone.

"So I'll tell him it's no deal then?"

"I didn't say that, Dexter. Will he negotiate?"

"He told me he wouldn't, and I believe him. He's deep in the shit because of what happened, and selling this picture of the tablet is about the only way he has of getting out. And he wants to know right now. When I go back into the hotel, either it's a deal at fifteen or he walks. Those are our choices."

"Thieving bastard," Hoxton said angrily. "He does know the price he's demanding is totally bloody extortionate, doesn't he?"

"Oh, yes, definitely. He also told me that the inscription on the tablet appeared to be part of a treasure map."

Hoxton was quiet for a few seconds, then spoke again. "OK. Tell him it's a deal. I've already wired money to the account we arranged in Rabat. I'll authorize you to draw fifteen grand from it tomorrow."

Slightly surprised by Hoxton's response, Dexter slipped the phone into his pocket and walked back into the hotel lounge.

"Will you take eight?" he asked. There was no harm in trying a little haggling.

Zebari shook his head and stood up.

"OK, OK," Dexter said. "We'll buy the card for ten. The money will be in Rabat tomorrow. I presume you'll want it in cash? In dirhams?"

"Of course I want it in dirhams. Do you think I'm some kind of idiot? Call me on this after nine tomorrow"—he wrote a mobile number on the piece of paper he'd given to Dexter—"when you've got the money. Then we'll meet somewhere and do the exchange."

Without another word, Zebari stood up and walked out of the hotel.

32

At eight thirty the next morning Dexter walked through the doors of the Bank Al-Maghrib on Avenue Mohammed V in Rabat. Fifteen minutes later he left the premises, his transactions concluded. Five thousand pounds of the money Charlie Hoxton had wired to Morocco was on its way to a numbered account in a small and discreet bank in Lichtenstein, where it would earn minimal interest for him but be entirely safe.

The previously smooth line of Dexter's tweed jacket was now marred by two bulges. The wads of dirham notes in his inside pockets—each the equivalent of five thousand pounds sterling—were bulky, and he wanted to get the meeting with Zebari over with as quickly as possible and get home to the calm and safety of his antique shop in Petworth. He'd never liked Morocco as a country; he liked its inhabitants even less.

He walked briskly along Avenue Mohammed V until he found a café that looked reasonably clean, pulled out a chair from a vacant table and ordered mint tea—Arabic coffee was far too strong and bitter for his taste. He checked his watch: eight fifty.

At nine exactly he pulled out his mobile and dialed the number Zebari had given him.

The Moroccan answered almost at once. "Dexter?"

"Yes. I've got what you wanted."

"You're in Rabat?"

"Yes."

"Get yourself onto Avenue Hassan 2 and go east along it, heading toward the estuary. When you get almost to the end, just before it bends to the southeast, turn right into the Rue de Sebta. Walk down there and take a seat in the first café you come to on the right-hand side of the road. Sit outside, where I'll be able to see you. Got that?"

"Yes." Dexter studied his street map of Rabat. Avenue Hassan 2 actually crossed Avenue Mohammed V, and the rendezvous Zebari had specified was only about a mile away. "I'll be there in twenty minutes," he said.

Half a mile away, Izzat Zebari snapped his mobile closed and nodded to himself in satisfaction. He trusted Dexter about as far as he could throw him, but he had the Englishman over a barrel, and both of them knew it. Dexter's client was obviously desperate to get his hands on anything relating to the clay tablet and Zebari was fairly sure he wouldn't try anything underhand. But if Dexter did try to gain possession of the card without handing over the money, Zebari guessed that his Walther PPK automatic pistol would provide all the additional persuasion he'd need to complete the transaction.

Zebari glanced around him as he stood up in the hotel lobby where he'd been waiting. Satisfied, he walked out of the building, squinting in the sudden glare of the sunshine. He glanced up and down Rue Abd el Myumen before pulling a pair of sunglasses out of his jacket pocket and striding away toward the Rue de Sebta.

About fifty yards behind Zebari, two men dressed in jeans and T-shirts stood up from the café table where they'd been sitting and began to follow him, chatting to each other as they walked. One man held a small mobile phone close to his right ear.

In the back seat of a black Mercedes sedan that was even then cutting through the traffic toward the Rue Abd el Myumen from the south side of Rabat, the tall man with the frozen face was urging his driver to go ever faster. He listened on his own phone to the reports from his two men. It wouldn't be long now before he recovered what was rightfully his.

The traffic along Avenue Hassan 2, which was also the main N1 road that laterally bisected Rabat, wasn't anything like as bad as Dexter had anticipated. That, and the fact that he managed to flag down a cab within seconds of leaving the café, meant it took him less than ten minutes to reach the rendezvous.

He wasn't sure whether Zebari had chosen the café deliberately, or whether he'd just picked a fairly busy road and assumed that there would be a café somewhere along it. Either way, once he paid off the cab and turned into Rue de Sebta, he saw the white awning and collection of tables and chairs only twenty or so yards in front of him. Dexter glanced round when he reached the café but saw no sign of the man he was meeting. He ordered yet another mint tea and prepared to wait.

Five minutes later Izzat Zebari pulled out the chair opposite Dexter and sat down. He looked furtive and harassed, glancing all around him before he spoke, but at that hour there were few people in the café and only a handful of pedestrians. Two young men who'd been walking along the street behind Zebari carried on past the café without a backward glance, deep in conversation.

"You've got the money?" Zebari demanded, as the waiter placed a cup of thick black coffee in front of him and moved away.

Dexter nodded. "And you've brought the card?" he asked.

Zebari nodded in turn.

Dexter reached inside his jacket, pulled out two thick envelopes secured with elastic bands and slid them across the table. "Ten thousand, in dirhams, as we agreed."

Zebari mirrored Dexter's action, producing an envelope and placing it on the table. Each man reached out and took what the other had offered. Zebari opened the envelopes and ran the end of his thumb over the crisp banknotes they contained, riffling them like two packs of cards, then swiftly slid them into the pockets of his jacket. Dexter unsealed the brown envelope and slid out the piece of card. He stared at what was printed on it.

"Jesus," Decker said after a few moments. "This is nothing like as good as I was expecting. The picture's a lot smaller than I'd hoped, and the inscription's still not very clear." He tossed the card across the table. "I'm not satisfied. The deal's off. Give me back the money."

Zebari shook his head. "This Walther in my pocket says the deal is still on, Dexter." He pulled the butt of a small semi-automatic pistol into view. "Think about it. I've really got nothing to lose." He stood up, tossed a few dirhams on the table, and walked away, back down the street.

There's a slight kink in the Rue de Sebta, where a side-street links it with the Rue de Bured. The black Mercedes reached that point at almost precisely the same moment as Zebari.

The heavy car squealed to a halt half on the pavement, its long hood blocking Zebari's way forward as two other men closed in on him from behind.

Zebari saw the car swing toward him and immediately guessed the identity of the vehicle's owner. Right then he knew he was in trouble, deep trouble. He swung round, turning to run, but two men were right in front of him, the same two who'd walked past the café only minutes earlier. Both were clearly ready to intercept him no matter which way he went. Behind him he heard the unmistakable sounds of car doors opening.

Pulling the Walther from his pocket, Zebari snapped

off a quick and barely aimed shot at the men in front of him, forcing them to duck. But they too were drawing weapons. Zebari's only escape route was across the road, through the traffic—and that's where he ran.

He dodged around a slow-moving truck and sprinted for the pavement on the opposite side of the road. He'd almost reached it when he felt a tremendous punch in the center of his back. The echo of the shot reverberated from the buildings all around, and he tumbled to the ground, all feeling gone from his legs. He dropped the pistol, which landed with a clatter well out of his reach.

Almost casually, the tall man and one of his men jogged across the road to where Zebari lay. Numbers of people began to gather on both sides of the road, attracted by the drama, but none showed any inclination to become involved.

"You stole something from me. Where is it?" the tall man demanded, as his associate picked up Zebari's Walther.

The wounded man lay half on the pavement, crumpled and barely moving, a pool of blood spreading around him. He stared up at the tall Arab. Oddly enough, he felt very little pain, just a growing numbness.

"I haven't got it," he said, his voice barely audible.

The tall man gestured and his colleague roughly searched the recumbent figure. He didn't find the card, but pulled out the two envelopes stuffed with banknotes, which he passed to his boss.

"Have you sold the card?" he demanded, looking down.

"Yes," Zebari gasped, a sudden wave of agony coursing though his body.

"Not a bad deal, Zebari. All this money just for a small piece of card," the tall man said, his voice quiet and controlled. "You know me, or at least you must know my reputation. When you broke into my house to try to steal my tablet, you must have guessed what would happen to you. So why did you do it?"

"It was just a job," Zebari muttered, the pain now starting to bite. He coughed, and a spray of blood showered the front of his jacket. "An order from a British collector."

The tall man looked interested. "Does he have a name, this collector?"

"I was dealing with an intermediary, an agent."

"And what is *his* name?"

Zebari said nothing, and the tall man leaned closer. "Tell me his name," he said, "and we might walk away and you might live."

Zebari stared up, his gaze fixed with a kind of horrified fascination at the tall man's milky-white, unseeing and unblinking right eye.

"Dexter. Everybody just calls him Dexter."

"And where would I find him?"

"He's here in Rabat. He was right there. I've just sold the card to him."

"Good," the tall man said, straightening up. "We'll find him. Right, Ahmed, finish it."

"I told you what I knew," Zebari said, his voice rising in terror. "You said you'd walk away."

"I lied," the tall man muttered, the left side of his face

lifting in a travesty of a smile. He nodded to the other man.

The echo of the second shot was just as loud as the first. Another pool of blood began to spread from Zebari's shattered skull to mingle with the congealing puddle that had already covered a large area of both the road surface and the pavement.

33

Alexander Dexter guessed he'd broken every speed limit imposed in Morocco as he drove south in his hired Citroën toward Casablanca, but even he was surprised by how short a time it had taken him to cover the sixty-odd miles to the international airport.

As he'd walked away from Rue de Sebta, he'd made an instant—and actually very easy—decision.

He'd just witnessed Zebari's murder. The man had been tracked down and killed in broad daylight in the middle of Rabat, despite whatever precautions he had taken to ensure his own safety.

But even more terrifying was the ruthlessness of the man who had killed him, the man with the milky-white eye whose frozen face he would not forget—the man, Dexter knew, who would now certainly be after him.

He had his passport, wallet and keys for the hire car in his pocket; all that he'd left in his hotel room were a few clothes and his washing kit, nothing important. Given Zebari's killer's very obvious capability, Dexter suspected that even if he went back to his hotel immediately, there was a good chance that a couple of men would already be there waiting for him.

So he'd changed his mind and told the taxi driver to drop him on a corner a short distance from the building, and had then walked straight over to the Citroën that he'd left parked on the street, got in and driven away.

When Dexter had flown out to Morocco, he'd taken an Air France flight to Rabat from Heathrow. The return half of that ticket was still in his jacket pocket, but there was no way he was going to use it. That, he guessed, would be far too obvious—and too obviously dangerous. He was sure Zebari's murderer would already have men on the way to the Rabat-Sale airport some five miles north of the city. Dexter's decision to drive to Casablanca was an attempt to put some distance between himself and his pursuers, and hopefully to throw them off the scent.

At the Mohammed V airport in Casablanca, he didn't bother returning the car to the Hertz desk. He just parked it, locked the doors and tossed the keys underneath it. When—if—he got back to England, he'd tell the local Hertz office where it was, but that was the least of his concerns right then.

As soon as he walked into the departure hall, Dexter checked the boards. He rejected all Royal Air Maroc flights, irrespective of their destination, because he wanted to use a non-Moroccan carrier, but he had just enough time to catch the Air France/KLM flight to Paris. A running man in an airport—and anywhere else, for that matter—always attracts attention, so Dexter walked briskly to the Air France ticket desk and paid cash for a return flight to Paris. He wanted to avoid any credit card charges appearing in his name.

He knew enough about the threat of terrorism to realize that paying cash for an airline ticket was unusual, but buying a single ticket for cash would certainly raise eyebrows and might result in him being delayed and questioned, which he was keen to avoid. So the return ticket was essential.

The flight was due to start boarding imminently, but before he walked to the departure gate Dexter nipped into one of the airport shops and bought a cheap carry-on bag. In another he purchased half a dozen items of clothing, in a third a traveler's wash bag, then added a couple of novels. He actually needed none of the items that he'd bought, but he knew that *everybody* boarding an aircraft carried a bag of some sort, and he was desperate not to stand out or attract attention in any way. He now hoped he looked like a businessman just nipping up to Paris for a conference or meeting for a day or two, and not like a man on the run from a bunch of hired killers.

The Moroccan customs officers opened his bag and checked it, as they did for almost every traveler, but that was the only delay. Half an hour after arriving at the airport, Dexter was at the departure gate, standing in a line of people waiting to board the Airbus 319. Twenty minutes after that he was finally able to relax in his seat with the stiffest drink Air France could offer as the jet headed north toward Paris. And he'd seen nobody and nothing to suggest that Zebari's killer or his men had the slightest idea where he was.

In Paris, he took time out to grab a meal before he

flew back to Heathrow. He'd had very little to eat that day, and he found his appetite improved dramatically once he knew he was, at least for the moment, safe. By early evening he was back at home in Petworth, the small oblong card on the desk in front of him, and a large whiskey in the glass at his elbow.

He would, he decided, wait an hour or so before he called Charlie Hoxton. First, he would take several photocopies of the card and try to work out just why his client had been so desperate to get hold of the clay tablet.

34

Night was drawing in, and up in Bronson's hotel room he and Angela seemed to have reached a stalemate.

The tablet held in the Paris museum had yielded its secrets easily enough. In just a few minutes Bronson had translated the French words into English and written them out. But the Cairo tablet proved to be much more difficult because of the poor clarity and definition of the single photograph they'd managed to find in the museum archives.

They'd spent hours trying to match the letters from the downloaded font with the characters in the photograph, but it was a long and tiresome process and they hadn't had very much success.

"I think," Angela said, staring at the image on her laptop screen, "that this picture was only ever intended for basic identification purposes. Somebody must have been told to photograph each of the objects the museum had acquired, purely so they would have a visual record of the relics. Pictures that could be used for research and translation would presumably have been taken later on, with a higher-resolution camera and much better lighting."

"Can you get anything at all from it?" Bronson asked.

"Yes, but probably only about half the words in the top three lines. The others are so blurred and out of focus that they could be almost anything."

For over an hour Angela and Bronson studied the image, trying to interpret and copy onto paper the unfamiliar marks that comprised the written Aramaic script. Then Angela fed the results into the on-line Aramaic-English dictionary.

"So what have we got?" she asked, finally leaning back from the computer and stretching her aching muscles.

"Why don't I go and get us some drinks?" Bronson suggested. "Of the alcoholic variety, obviously."

"A gin and tonic would be just perfect. Preferably a long one, with lots of ice."

Bronson left the room and returned a few minutes later, carrying a tray with two tall glasses in which ice chinked agreeably. He put the drinks down on the small dressing table and then returned to his perch on the side of the bed.

"Thanks," Angela said. She raised the glass to her lips and took a long swallow. "That's better. Now, where are we?"

"I've written out every word that we've managed to translate, and I've done a kind of drawing of each tablet," Bronson said. "I've included blanks for the words we haven't deciphered so that we know which words are missing."

He placed a sheet of A4 paper on the table in front of Angela and they both looked at what he'd written on it.

He'd drawn three rectangles of roughly the same size, and in each of them he'd put the English meaning of the words Angela had translated from the Aramaic, in the same position as the original word on the tablet. The result wasn't encouraging.

"This first one"—Bronson pointed at one of the boxed outlines—"is the Cairo tablet. That's the top left of the four if you're right about the meaning of the cross in the center."

As they'd both expected, there were far more blanks than words:

> *our* ----- ----- *end*----- *the by*
> *and*----- ----- *the*----- ----- -----
> ----- *the temple scroll* ----- *task*
> ----- *a*----- ----- ----- -----
> ----- ----- ----- ----- ----- -----
> ----- ----- ----- ----- -----

"Now," Bronson said, handing another sheet to Angela, "as Aramaic is read from right to left, the words we've managed to translate should appear in this order."

On the new page, he had just written the words in sequence, including all the blanks, except for the last two lines on which they'd so far failed to decipher even a single word:

> *by the* ----- *end* ----- ----- *our*
> ----- ----- ----- *the* ----- ----- *and*
> *task* ----- *scroll temple the* -----
> ----- ----- ----- ----- *a* -----

"That's not a hell of a lot to go on," Angela muttered, then turned her attention back to the paper.

"This is the O'Connor tablet," Bronson said.

"There were only eight words in this text that Baverstock managed to translate," Angela said, "and that complete second line definitely makes no sense to me."

> ----- ----- ----- ----- ----- ----- -----
> *of four tablets Ir-Tzadok took perform*
> ----- ----- ----- ----- ----- -----
> ----- ----- ----- ----- ----- -----
> ----- ----- ----- ----- ----- -----
> ----- *cubit* ----- *place* ----- -----

"Nor to me," Bronson said. "This is the correct order of the words."

> ----- ----- ----- ----- ----- ----- -----
> *perform took Ir-Tzadok tablets four of*
> ----- ----- ----- ----- ----- -----
> ----- ----- ----- ----- ----- -----
> ----- ----- ----- ----- ----- -----
> ----- ----- *place* ----- ----- *cubit* -----

The final oblong, containing the text of the tablet held in the Paris museum, read:

> *within a days settlement scroll ben*
> *our stones of B'Succaca from the*
> *now side Jerusalem silver have the*
> *we of the we cave completed*
> *our height concealed cistern place now*
> *invaders to of of of last*

"And this is the list of words in the right order."

> *ben scroll settlement days a within*
> *the from B'Succaca of stones our*
> *the have silver Jerusalem side now*
> *completed cave we the of we*
> *now place cistern concealed height our*
> *last of of of to invaders*

"When Baverstock described this as gibberish, he wasn't kidding," Bronson added. "Can you make any sense of it?"

Angela groaned. "No," she said, "but whatever system of encryption the author of these tablets used, it must have been something fairly simple. I mean, at this period of history there *were* no sophisticated ciphers. We must be missing something, something pretty basic. The only thing that's fairly obvious is that Baverstock was right about Qumran."

She pointed at the two lower oblongs Bronson had drawn. "He said that this word here—*Ir-Tzadok*—might refer to Qumran. The full Aramaic name for the place was *Ir-Tzadok B'Succaca*, and the second part of that is right here on the Paris tablet. But," she added, "not even that makes much sense."

"Why?"

"Because Aramaic text is read from right to left, not left to right, but the word *Ir-Tzadok* is on the left-hand tablet and *B'Succaca* is on the right. So if I'm right about the cross that was inscribed in the middle of the slab of clay before the tablets were cut out of it, then we should read the right-hand tablet first, then the left-hand one. So that would make those two words read *B'Succaca Ir-Tzadok*, which is nonsense, quite meaningless."

"I see what you mean," Bronson said slowly. He leaned back in the chair and stretched. "Look, we seem to have been stuck in this hotel room all day trying to work this out. Why don't we have a bite to eat downstairs? It might clear our thoughts, and we might even have a flash of inspiration."

35

"I tell you, Charlie, I was lucky to get out of Morocco in one piece. If that bastard had guessed I was standing in the crowd, I really believe he'd have killed me right there."

"And this was out in the open?" Charlie Hoxton was hearing for the first time about the events Dexter had witnessed in Rabat. The two men had met in a noisy pub near Petworth, and Dexter had just handed over the card that he'd obtained from Zebari. "In broad daylight?" Hoxton persisted.

Dexter nodded. "It was just after nine this morning, and there were plenty of people about. He didn't care at all. One of his men shot Zebari in the head; then they got back in the car and drove away. I just legged it, straight to the airport. I didn't even stop to pick up my clothes."

Hoxton nodded and looked again at the piece of card he was holding, turning it over in his hands. "And all he was interested in doing was getting this back," he said to himself. "That's good. Very good indeed."

"What do you mean 'good?'" Dexter demanded.

"I mean that if Zebari's killer is so desperate to recover the tablet, he must know it's genuine. But where the hell is it?"

Dexter ignored the question. "He's bloody dangerous, Charlie, and he knows my name. He might be over here already, looking for me, and maybe for you as well."

"I'm bloody dangerous too, Dexter, and don't you forget it."

Across the table, Dexter could see the unmistakable bulge of a shoulder holster under Hoxton's left arm.

"And I'm not very impressed with this bloody card," Hoxton snapped. "The picture's not much better than the ones we've already got, and it's certainly not worth fifteen grand. Couldn't you have canceled the deal once you saw it?"

"I tried," Dexter said, "but he pulled a gun on me."

Hoxton grunted in displeasure. "And what the bloody hell does this bit here say? Is that a copy of the Aramaic text?"

Dexter shook his head. "No. That's just an explanation of where the tablet came from. It's in Arabic, but I've written out a rough translation for you."

Hoxton dropped the card on the table and took the sheet of paper Dexter offered. He unfolded it and read the English text.

"Is this accurate?" he demanded.

"It's probably not an exact translation—my Arabic isn't good enough for that—but it's close enough, I think."

Hoxton didn't reply, just scanned the words on the page.

"It doesn't tell us much, does it?" he said. "It's like an exhibit card in a museum."

Dexter nodded. "Zebari told me the tablet had been displayed in a case in one of the public rooms in the owner's house, with the card beside it."

Hoxton read out the first few lines from Dexter's translation. "'Ancient clay tablet recovered from the ruins of Pirathon or Pharaton (Greek), today the site of the Arab village of Farata in Israel. The inscription is in Aramaic but is garbled and the meaning is unclear. Possibly a part of a set.' So where was this Pirathon or Pharaton?"

"I checked. It was a small town in what used to be called Samaria, not far from Mount Gerizim and about twenty miles north of Jerusalem. It was never a very important place, and there's pretty much nothing left of the original settlement now."

"So how come this tablet finished up there?"

"We don't know that it did," Dexter replied. "What's on that card might just be the version that was offered for public consumption. After all, it's hardly likely to state it's been looted from some museum, is it? Don't forget that *your* clay tablet was once the property of a museum in Cairo, but I bet that's not what you tell people when you show them the relic."

"You'd better believe that."

Dexter gestured toward the paper Hoxton was still holding. "You've already got one of the tablets and now a few blurred photographs of another one. What are you going to do next?"

"*I'm* not going to do anything," Hoxton said. "*We* are going to do our best to find the missing relic."

"But you've only got one tablet, Charlie, and we've already worked out that there must be four in the set. How the hell are you going to find anything with well over half the text missing?"

"I've got Baverstock doing a trawl through every museum's database that he can access, looking for any other tablets that might have been recovered over the years. If he can get a decent picture of another tablet, I reckon we can crack this with two of them plus the partial translation of this tablet from Rabat. Whether he can or can't, we'll go out to the Middle East anyway. The picture on this card's better than any of the other pictures I've seen of this tablet, and Baverstock should be able to decipher at least half of it. This is probably the best chance we're ever going to have."

"Surely you don't want me to come along as well?"

"Yes, I do. You're coming because I need your contacts, Dexter, and Baverstock's coming because we'll need his language skills—unless you've added Imperial Aramaic translation to your other skills."

Dexter frowned, but after a moment he realized that getting out of Britain for a week or so might not be such a bad idea. If Zebari's killer had sent some of his men to track him down, they'd presumably be looking for him in Morocco and the United Kingdom, not in Israel or wherever else Hoxton had in mind.

He sighed and leaned back in his seat. It wasn't as though he had any choice in the matter in any case. "No," he said, "I still can't read Aramaic, Charlie. So when do we leave?"

36

"You know," Bronson said, as he and Angela strolled along a street near their hotel, enjoying the cooler night air, "there's one thing we haven't really talked about, and that's the purpose of the tablets. I mean, exactly *what* did the people who made these tablets hide? What *was* their treasure?"

They had finished their dinner, and Angela had insisted that she needed to stretch her legs before going back to her room. She'd told Bronson that if he was still concerned about the armed men who had chased him before, she would go out on her own—after all, nobody even knew she was in Morocco. Bronson hadn't liked it, but he'd agreed to go outside with her. If something happened to Angela, he knew he'd never forgive himself.

"Whatever it was, it had to have been really important to them because of all the trouble they took. They enciphered the message on the tablets and then, presumably, hid them in separate locations so that the hiding place of their treasure could only be found when all four tablets had been recovered. And there are some clues in what we've found already. About half a dozen words in particular seem to me to be significant."

"Let me take a guess. Those would be 'scroll,' 'tablets,' 'temple,' 'silver,' 'concealed' and 'Jerusalem'?"

Angela nodded. "Precisely. Any kind of ancient scrolls are of interest to historians and archaeologists today, but if a scroll was hidden two millennia ago, that suggests it was believed to be really important even then. And if you prefix the word 'scroll' with 'silver,' it raises a very interesting possibility—" She broke off as Bronson reached out and seized her arm, pulling her to a stop.

"What is it?" she demanded.

"I don't like—" Bronson started, looking first up the street, then back the way they'd come.

About twenty yards in front of them, a white van had just pulled into the curb and was sitting there, engine idling. Perhaps fifty yards behind them, a black Mercedes sedan was approaching slowly, keeping close to the curb, and closer—much closer—a handful of men in flowing *jellabas* were walking quickly toward them.

It could all be entirely innocent, just a series of separate and unconnected events, but to Bronson's trained eyes it looked like an ambush. He paused for under a second, then reacted.

"Run!" he whispered urgently to Angela. "Run. Get away from here." He pointed toward a side-street. "Down there, as fast as you can."

Angela glanced behind her, saw the approaching men for the first time and took to her heels.

Bronson span round to face the group, but tried to

stand his ground, walking steadily backward to provide a measure of protection for Angela. He looked behind him, and saw that she had reached the corner of the side-street and was starting to run down it. He turned on his heels to follow her, but at that moment the approaching men themselves began to run, and in seconds they had caught up with him.

He felt a sudden tug on his shoulder as somebody grabbed at him, and tried to spin round to face his attackers. Then two blows crashed into the back of his head. He lost his balance and fell forward, his body collapsing limply to the potholed pavement.

The last thing he heard before his consciousness fled was a single distant scream from Angela as she called out his name.

PART TWO

ENGLAND

37

One of the first things Kirsty Philips did when she arrived back in Britain and had finished unpacking was to drive round to her parents' house. While they'd been away in Morocco, she'd been doing that once every couple of days to check the house, make sure the indoor plants were watered, pick up the mail, check their answerphone messages and generally ensure that the place was in good order.

That morning, she parked her Volkswagen Golf in the driveway of the small detached house in a quiet street on the western outskirts of the city, took out her keys and opened the front door. As usual, there was a pile of envelopes lying on the mat, most of them clearly junk mail of various sorts. She picked them up and carried them through to the kitchen, where she placed them with others that had accumulated since her parents had left the house for what she now knew had been the last time. Her eyes misted at that thought, but she pushed her sorrow aside and began her usual walk-round of the property, inspecting all the rooms one after the other. The last thing she did was go into the lounge and check the answer-phone, but there were no messages on it.

She pulled open the door to the hall and immediately came face-to-face with a man she'd never seen before.

He had a dark-brown complexion and was tall and slim, but strongly built. In his right hand he was carrying a long black tool of some kind, perhaps a crowbar. He looked almost as surprised to see her as she was to confront him.

The intruder recovered first. He swung the crowbar round in a short, vicious arc, the tempered steel bar smashing into the left side of Kirsty's face, fracturing her cheek-bone and cracking the side of her skull. It was a killing blow. She felt an instant of shocking, numbing pain, then tumbled sideways, knocked unconscious by the force of the impact. She fell limply onto the car-pet, blood pouring from the side of her face where the skin had been brutally torn apart. But that wasn't what killed her.

The major damage was internal, half a dozen blood vessels in her brain ripped apart by the splinters of broken bone. Shards of the same fractured bone had been driven deep into her cerebrum, causing irreparable damage. She was still breathing as she lay there, but effectively she was already dead.

The man looked down at her for a long moment, then stepped over her body and continued walking toward the front door. He'd heard no noise from inside the house before he'd forced the side door, and had assumed that the car he'd seen parked on the drive had belonged to the O'Connors—an assumption he now realized had been erroneous.

He glanced round, saw no sign of any mail, and retraced his steps to the kitchen. He'd have to check each room in turn until he found the package.

On the kitchen table, he saw the post stacked neatly on one side and began searching through it. But there was no sign of the envelope he was looking for, so perhaps his boss's deduction had been wrong.

For perhaps a minute he stood irresolute, wondering what he should do next. Who the young woman was he had no idea—a neighbor, or a cleaner, perhaps—and already he was beginning to regret hitting her quite so hard. Should he try to shift the body, get it out of the house and dump it somewhere? Then he rejected that idea. He didn't know the area very well, and the risk of being seen carrying her out of the house—or being stopped by a police officer with her corpse in the car—was too great.

He opened the door, glanced around him, and walked away.

38

Bronson was aware of a throbbing ache at the back of his skull as consciousness returned slowly. Instinctively he raised his hand to his head. Or rather he tried to, but his arm wouldn't move. He couldn't move either arm, in fact, which puzzled him. Nor his feet. There were stabbing pains in his wrists and ankles, and a dull ache down the left side of his chest. He opened his eyes, but could see nothing in front of him. Everything was completely black. For a few seconds he had no recollection of what had happened to him, and then he slowly started to remember.

"Oh, shit," he muttered.

"Chris? Thank God." The voice came from out of the darkness, somewhere over to his left.

"Angela? Where the hell are we? Are you OK?"

"I don't know. Where we are, I mean. And I'm fine, apart from being tied up in this bloody chair, that is."

"Why can't I see anything?"

"We're in a cellar and the bastards turned the lights out once they'd tied us up."

"But what happened? All I can remember is something hitting me on the back of the head."

"I was running down the street and I turned back to see what was happening just as one of the men grabbed you and another swung a cosh or something. You dropped like a stone and for a few seconds I was certain you were dead. I ran back to—"

"You should have run on, Angela. There was nothing you could have done."

"I know, I know." Angela sighed. "And it's my fault we're here. I shouldn't have insisted we go outside. And then when I saw you were hurt, all I wanted to do was try to help."

"Well, thanks for trying, but it would have been better if you'd got away, because then you could have called the police. Then what did they do?"

"It was very slick. Two of the men grabbed me and stuck a gag over my mouth—I was yelling my head off—and then they bundled me into the back of the white van that had stopped a few yards up the road. They tied my wrists and ankles with some kind of thin plastic device—"

"Probably cable ties," Bronson interrupted. "They're virtually unbreakable."

"Then three more men picked you up and dragged you over to the van and tossed you inside."

That probably explained the ache in his chest, Bronson thought.

"They all climbed into the back of the van and tied you up the same as me as soon as it started moving. It drove for maybe fifteen or twenty minutes, then stopped and reversed. When the doors opened, all I could see was the whitewashed wall of a house, and then I was carried out, through a doorway and down a set of steps into this bloody cellar. There were two upright chairs down here. They tied me to one of them, while another couple of men dragged you down here and repeated the process. Then they turned out the lights and buggered off. I've been sitting here in the dark ever since. It's been hours." There was a pause. "I'm so sorry, Chris."

Bronson wasn't surprised to hear a quaver in her voice. Angela was tough—he knew that only too well—but he could understand how traumatized she must have been by the events of the evening, especially if she was blaming herself for what had happened.

"It wasn't your fault," he said, his voice gentle.

"Yes, it was. And do you know what I found most un-nerving about all this?"

"What?"

"During the whole process—the kidnapping, the drive in the van and when they tied us up down here in this cellar—none of the men said a single word. Nobody issued any orders; none of them asked any questions, or even made a comment. They all knew exactly what they were doing. That worries me, Chris. We weren't just snatched off the street at random by some gang of thugs. Whoever was responsible for this took us for a reason, and it was a really well-planned operation."

That worried Bronson as well, but he wasn't going to admit it.

"Well, I don't think we should stick around to find out what they want. We've got to find a way to get out of here."

But as he tugged ineffectually at the plastic ties securing his wrists and ankles, Bronson knew that wasn't going to be easy. With a blade of some kind, it would have been the work of a few seconds to free himself, but nothing he did had any effect.

Still, he tried, and it was only when he felt blood running down his hands from the cuts he'd opened on his wrists that he gave up and accepted the reality of the situation. He was held fast, and there was nothing he could do about it.

It was several hours before the cellar lights finally flared into life. Bronson closed his eyes tight against the glare, then cautiously opened them, squinting as he took in their surroundings.

Angela was sitting about ten feet away from him in an upright wooden chair, her wrists and ankles lashed to the frame with plastic cable ties. Her clothes were in disarray, but her expression was defiant.

The cellar was a small, more or less square concrete box with white-painted but grubby walls and ceiling, and a flagstoned floor. It was almost empty apart from the two chairs they were sitting on. A short flight of steps led from the cellar up to a solid wooden door directly opposite where they were sitting.

Bronson looked back at Angela, whose eyes were now fixed on that door. It had just creaked open to reveal a whitewashed passageway on the level above them. They heard a faint murmur of voices, then the sound of approaching footsteps.

Moments later, two dark-skinned men wearing *jella-*

bas strode down the steps into the cellar and stopped in front of Bronson.

He looked up at them, committing their faces to memory. One was unremarkable—dark skin, black hair, brown eyes, with regular features—but the other man had a face Bronson knew he'd never forget. He was a full head taller than his companion, and his right cheek drooped slightly, giving his wide mouth a lopsided twist, almost turning it into an S-shape, and his right eye was sightless, a milky-white abomination in his dark-brown skin. But he had an air of confidence, of suppressed power, about him, and Bronson knew instinctively that this man had to be the leader of the group.

"You're Christopher Bronson," the tall man said, his voice calm and measured.

It wasn't a question, but Bronson nodded.

The tall man turned slightly to look at Angela. "And you're Angela Lewis, the former Mrs. Bronson," he continued, his English fluent but strongly accented.

"Are these friends of yours, Chris?" Angela asked tightly.

"Absolutely not," Bronson snapped, his gaze never shifting from the figure standing in front of him, as his mind raced. How, he wondered, did this man—whom he was certain he'd never seen before—know so much about them? His own name, yes. That wouldn't be difficult to find out from the hotel register, say, or airline records, and even Angela's name from the same sources, but how could he possibly know that she was his former wife?

"You know our names," Bronson said. "Who the hell are you and what do you want?"

The tall man didn't reply, just nodded to his colleague, who walked over to one corner and picked up a collapsible chair. He placed it on the floor close to the concrete steps, then waited while his boss sat down.

"It's time we talked. I think one of you has something that belongs to me," the tall man said.

Bronson shook his head. "I don't think so," he replied. "And what, exactly, are you talking about?"

The tall man with the frozen face stared at him for a few moments. "The idea," he said, "is that I'll ask the questions and you'll give me the answers that I want." He turned and nodded to the second man, still standing beside his chair.

Unhurriedly, the man stepped forward, stopped directly in front of Bronson and without warning slammed his fist into his stomach.

Bronson slumped forward, retching and straining against his bonds.

"You bastard," Angela shouted. "Leave him alone."

"Ahmed," the tall man said softly.

Ahmed walked behind Bronson's writhing body to Angela's chair, stepped in front of it and slapped her hard across the face.

She reeled sideways with the shock. The chair teetered momentarily on two legs, then crashed backward.

Ahmed stepped forward, seized the back of the chair and levered it upright again. Without so much as a glance at Angela, he walked back to stand beside his boss once more.

"Now, we'll start again. I believe you've acquired something that belongs to me," the tall man said, his voice still calm and reasonable. He looked at Bronson. "We'll start with you, I think." He motioned for Ahmed to move over to one side of the bound man. "A small clay tablet was stolen from me. Do you have it?"

Bronson shook his head. "You mean the tablet Margaret O'Connor picked up in the *souk*?" he gasped, his breath still rasping in his throat.

The tall man nodded.

"We've no idea where it went," Bronson said. "Didn't you find it when your thugs drove their car off the road?"

"That's very good, Bronson," the tall man said approvingly. "At least you managed to work that out. No, we didn't find it in the car, and the police search didn't find it in the wreckage either."

"How do you know that?"

"I have contacts everywhere."

"So why the hell do you suppose we might have it?"

"Because you've been dealing with the daughter and her husband. It seems obvious that if the O'Connors didn't throw the tablet away—and I don't seriously believe they'd do that—they're the only other people who could have it."

"How?" Bronson asked simply. "How could the O'Connors have passed it to them?"

At a nod from the tall man, Ahmed stepped forward and smashed his fist into the left side of Bronson's face.

"You seem to be a slow learner, Bronson. I'm asking the questions, remember? Now, let's try again. Does the daughter have the tablet?"

Bronson spat a mouthful of blood onto the discolored

concrete floor in front of him. "No," he muttered, "she doesn't have it. And neither does her husband. You're looking in the wrong place."

For a few seconds the tall man didn't respond, just looked appraisingly at his two captives. "Now why don't I believe you?" he murmured. "I think it's time we asked your former wife."

"She's had nothing to do with this," Bronson said, his voice loud and urgent. "She's never even met the O'Connors' daughter."

"I know. I don't think she knows anything about the tablet either. But I think it might help *your* memory if we try a little gentle persuasion on *her*. Ahmed really enjoys this kind of thing," he added.

"Don't touch her," Bronson shouted.

Ahmed reached into the folds of his *jellaba*, pulled out a flick-knife and pressed the button to snap open the blade. Then he dug around in another pocket and extracted a small gray stone. He leaned casually against one wall of the cellar and began running the stone along the blade of the knife, sharpening it, each stroke accompanied by a sinister hissing sound. After a couple of minutes he tested the edge of the weapon with his thumb, and nodded his satisfaction.

"Kill her," the tall man instructed, as Ahmed walked toward Angela's chair, "but take your time. Just cut her up a little to begin with. Start with her cheeks and forehead."

Angela didn't say anything, but Bronson could see the naked terror on her face, and the effort she was making to hide her fear from their captors.

"You see, Bronson," the tall man said, his tone conversational, almost friendly, "I've always believed that my clay tablet was part of a set. Perhaps you've come to the same conclusion? I have a theory. I think the tablets, the complete set of tablets, I mean, reveal the location of the Silver Scroll, and perhaps even of the Mosaic Covenant, though that's probably a bit less likely. Both of those treasures are worth fighting for, even worth killing for, so you can see why I want the tablet returned."

Bronson was tugging desperately against the plastic cable ties that held him prisoner in the wooden chair, knowing his efforts were entirely futile, but determined to escape if he possibly could.

"But I don't have the bloody tablet. Haven't you listened to a single word I've said? I DON'T HAVE THE BLOODY TABLET. And neither of us has any idea where it is."

"We'll see," the tall man said, turning his seat slightly to face Angela's chair, the better to watch his henchman at work.

"Don't do this," Bronson pleaded. "Please don't do this."

"It won't take long," the tall man said. "And the sooner we get started, the sooner it'll be over for her."

Ahmed was standing beside Angela's chair, stroking his fingers gently down her cheek, a slight smile on his face.

Angela's eyes were wide, and she was gasping for breath as she strained against the ties that held her firmly in place.

"Wait," the tall man said, as Ahmed started to lift the

blade of his flick-knife toward Angela's face. "Gag her first, try to keep the noise down."

Ahmed nodded, clicked the knife closed and took a roll of thick black tape from his pocket. He tore off a piece about eight inches long, walked behind Angela's chair and positioned the tape over her mouth.

"Keep it clear of her nose. We don't want her to suffocate."

Ahmed ensured that the tape was securely in place, then stepped back beside the chair, snapping open his flick-knife again.

"Please, please stop," Bronson begged.

"It's too late now." The tall man nodded at Ahmed. "Get on with it."

39

"You have some news?" Eli Nahman asked, as he walked into the room in the ministry building in Jerusalem, Yosef Ben Halevi following close behind him.

"Yes," Levi Barak said, gesturing to the two academics to take seats at the table. "Through one of our operatives in Morocco," Barak began, "we do now have more information about this relic. But we still don't know where it is. Our best guess is that the English couple mailed it to their home."

"Can you send someone to check that?" Nahman asked.

Barak shook his head. "There's no need," he said. "Our people in London have already started investigating."

"And?"

"And we're not the only ones looking for it."

Nahman glanced at Ben Halevi. "Who?" he asked.

"There were two obvious addresses to cover in Britain," Barak began, not answering Nahman's question directly. "The O'Connors' own house and the one belonging to their daughter and son-in-law. Both are in a city called Canterbury, in Kent, in southeast England. We organized watchers at both properties. Yesterday, the team covering the O'Connors' property observed their daughter drive to the house and go inside. About ten minutes later an unknown male was seen at the side door of the house. He'd approached the property from the rear, across a stretch of waste ground, not down the street, which was why they didn't see him coming. Our team got several photographs of him."

Barak passed each man two pictures. They showed a dark-skinned, black-haired man, obviously filmed through a powerful telephoto lens, standing beside a house.

"He's holding a crowbar," Barak continued, "and he used it to force the side door. He was apparently unaware that anyone was inside the property. A few minutes later he came out of the house and ran away, using the same route as before, down the garden and over the waste ground.

"Several minutes after that, a neighbor entered the house—perhaps she'd seen the daughter's car parked in the driveway—and emerged seconds later screaming. Police cars and an ambulance appeared, and we now know that Kirsty Philips, the O'Connors' daughter, had been killed, obviously by this intruder."

"Who is he?" Nahman demanded.

"We don't know," Barak replied. "We've circulated an 'anything known' request through all the intelligence services with whom we have good relations but I don't expect this man's face will be on any of their databases. We believe he's probably a member of a Moroccan gang."

"And did he get the tablet?"

"We don't think so. Our watchers are still in place, and the same man has been seen in the vicinity again, but he didn't approach the house because of the large number of police there. Obviously, if he *had* got the tablet, he would be long gone."

"So where is it?" Ben Halevi demanded.

Barak shrugged. "We don't know. It could still be in the post system somewhere, or maybe the British police are sitting looking at it. If they are, we should find out today, through one of our contacts in the Metropolitan force."

"And if they're not?"

"The moment this man"—Barak gestured at the photographs on the table—"reappears after the police have left the house, I've given orders to our surveillance team to snatch him for interrogation."

An expression of distaste passed across Nahman's face. "But I haven't been consulted about any such action."

Barak shook his head. "I'm sorry, Eli, but this matter has now moved a long way up the tree. I've come here to keep you informed as a matter of courtesy, but I'm now taking my orders direct from the head of the Mossad. Finding that tablet has become my highest priority. All other considerations are secondary, and any level of collateral damage is acceptable. And it means that anyone who tries to prevent us from obtaining the relic will be considered expendable."

The shock clearly registered on Nahman's face. "Dear God," he muttered. "Is this really necessary?"

Barak nodded and glanced at the two men. "If you're right in your analysis of the pictures we've recovered, those four clay tablets could lead us to the ultimate key to Jewish sovereignty. We will do whatever it takes to recover that relic."

40

Ahmed grabbed a handful of Angela's hair and pulled her head firmly against the chair. He ran the back of the blade of the flick-knife down her cheeks, first one, then the other, playing with her, the tip of the cold steel leaving a transient white furrow on her lightly tanned skin, a mark that faded into invisibility almost as soon as the blade had passed.

"Which side first?" he muttered, leaning close to her ear. "It's your face, so you can choose."

Angela's eyes bulged as she choked behind the tape gag, a thin trickle of mucous running from her nose. Bronson had never seen such terror on any human face, and there was absolutely nothing he could do about it.

"I'll tell you anything I know," he said desperately.

"Tell me where the tablet is," the tall man replied, his voice rising almost to a shout at the end of the sentence.

"I don't know," Bronson said bitterly. "And I won't know, no matter what you do to me, or to Angela."

"Then she'll die here, and so will you. Get on with it, Ahmed," he added.

At that instant there was a sudden noise from the floor above the cellar. The tall man grimaced in annoyance, stood up and turned toward the door. Ahmed stopped moving, his blade resting on Angela's left cheek.

Bronson stared at the door. He heard another noise, raised voices, and the clatter of shoes on concrete. The tall man called out something in Arabic, his irritation obvious from the tone of his voice.

"Wait for me to come back," he instructed Ahmed, and headed for the stairs.

For two or three minutes there was a confusion of noise from above, shouts of alarm or perhaps anger, a succession of faint thuds, and then silence fell once more. Staring at the flight of concrete steps, Bronson saw a *jellaba*-clad figure walking down them. He felt a sudden stab of fear. The tall man was returning, and this time there would be no further delays.

But when the figure arrived at the entrance to the cellar, Bronson's brow creased in puzzlement. The man was holding a large piece of cardboard in front of him, which completely obscured his face and most of his upper body.

Bronson glanced at Ahmed, who looked equally puzzled.

"Yacoub?" Ahmed asked.

The answer and what happened next were both unexpected.

"No," the man said, and dropped the cardboard.

Immediately, Bronson recognized the familiar features

of Jalal Talabani, his face grim as he raised the pistol in his right hand, looking for a target.

Ahmed emitted a sudden curse, then swung the flick-knife downward, toward Angela's face, at the same instant as Talabani pulled the trigger. The semiautomatic pistol was fitted with a slim suppressor, and the noise of the shot was little more than a dull pop. The slide flew back, a brass cartridge case tumbled to the ground, and Talabani fired again, then once more.

On the other side of the cellar, Ahmed clutched at his chest and flew backward, the flick-knife falling from his hand. As he crashed against the wall, a sudden fountain of blood sprayed in a wide arc across the floor.

Talabani ran over to the fallen man, felt for a pulse and then stood up, sliding the pistol into a holster under his *jellaba*. He bent down again, grabbed the flick-knife and strode across to Bronson.

"Jesus, Jalal. Am I glad to see you," Bronson gasped.

"You've been lucky, my friend," the Moroccan police officer said, as the newly sharpened blade of the knife made short work of the cable ties, freeing Bronson from the chair.

"Here," Bronson said, and took the knife from Talabani. He swiftly cut Angela free, pulling the tape gently off her face.

"Thank God, thank God," she sobbed, clinging to Bronson with a strength born of pure desperation.

Still holding Angela, Bronson turned to Jalal. "How the hell did you manage to get here?" he demanded. "And where are the rest of your men?"

"Somebody telephoned in a report of your kidnapping on the street, and managed to get the number of the van," Talabani said. "That was broadcast immediately, and we've had teams out looking for it all night. I was driving past this house—it's on the outskirts of Rabat—when I saw it parked outside. I called for backup, obviously, but I decided to try to get in myself. There were only a couple of people upstairs, and I managed to take care of them, and that tall one-eyed man as well—his name was Yacoub and he was well known to us—when he came up to investigate, and the rest you saw."

Bronson shook his head. "Thank God you did," he said. "That bastard you shot down here was just about to start slicing up Angela."

She gave a sudden shiver as he said the words. "Let's get out of here," she muttered, tears streaming down her face.

"Go now, my friend," Talabani agreed. "This place will be swarming with police officers any minute now, and I'm quite sure neither of you wants to get involved in a circus like that. Why don't you take my car?" He produced a set of keys from his pocket. "Go back to your hotel. I can always get a statement from you later."

"Won't that cause you problems, Jalal?"

"Nothing that I can't handle. Go."

"Come on, Angela," Bronson said. "We're out of here. Thanks, Jalal. I owe you."

They climbed the stairs out of the cellar, Angela still clutching Bronson, and walked down the hall toward the wide-open door of the property. Angela shuddered at the sight of two unmoving figures sprawled on the floor of the passageway, their *jellabas* covered in crimson stains.

She stepped over them gingerly, trying to avoid any contact with the bodies. Bronson glanced through an open door into a side room, to see another silent shape lying motionless on the floor. Talabani had obviously been very thorough.

Outside the house, dawn had just broken. Angela stopped and gulped in several deep breaths of fresh air, then suddenly vomited onto the dusty ground.

"God, what a nightmare," she muttered, pulling a packet of tissues out of her pocket and wiping her mouth. "How quickly can we get to the airport?"

Two minutes later, Bronson steered Talabani's Renault away from the whitewashed house, back toward the center of Rabat, Angela sitting beside him, still tense and shaking from her ordeal.

Jalal Talabani stood in the doorway and watched as his car disappeared down the road, then turned back into the property. He strode through the entrance hall, stepping over the two motionless figures sprawled on the floor, and through the open door into a side room.

On a couple of large cushions against the opposite wall a man lay on his back, a large dark red stain marring the front of his *jellaba*.

"They've gone," Talabani announced. "Was that how you wanted it done?" he asked.

The tall man with the frozen face swung himself up into a sitting position on the cushions and leaned comfortably back against the wall. He looked across at Talabani and nodded. "That was exactly how I wanted it done. The two men outside gave you no trouble?"

Talabani shook his head. "They pulled their pistols when I came in, but they were a lifetime too slow. Why did you want me to kill them?" he asked. "And Ahmed as well?"

Yacoub stood up. "Because Bronson had to believe this was for real. He and Lewis had to believe they'd escaped and that I was dead. Only then would they feel safe enough to follow the trail and find the relics. The men—all of them—were expendable."

"What now?"

"My men are already in position. They'll follow Bronson and Lewis, and when they find what I'm looking for, I'll take it off them. And then I'll kill them."

41

Bronson paid the two room bills at the desk, carried their bags out to the hire car, then took the road heading south out of Rabat toward Casablanca and the airport. They'd barely left the outskirts of the city when his mobile rang.

"You want me to answer that?" Angela asked, as Bronson fished in his pocket for the phone. He'd insisted she down a glass of brandy at the hotel, and he was surprised at how quickly she seemed to have recovered from her ordeal.

"No, thanks. It's probably work," he said.

Bronson pulled the car in to the side of the road as soon as he saw an open space, then answered the call.

"I've been trying to reach you, Chris," DCI Byrd said. "Get on the first flight you can. There've been some developments in the case over here."

"In England?" Bronson asked. "What kind of developments?"

"Kirsty Philips has been found dead—murdered, in fact—at her parents' home in Canterbury."

"Dear God, that's awful. What about her husband?"

"He's pretty much fallen to pieces. I've got a team working on the murder, but I need you here to liaise with them, just in case there are any connections between her death and what happened to her parents out in Morocco. How soon can you get back?"

Bronson glanced at his watch. "I'm on the way to the airport right now," he said, "but I doubt if I'll be on the ground in London until late this afternoon. Do you want me to come in to the station tomorrow morning to check in with you, or go straight off to the crime scene?"

"You might as well go straight there to make your number with the inspector in charge—that's DI Dave Robbins. The SOCOs and forensic teams will probably still be at the house. I'll send you a text with the address. Come in and see me tomorrow afternoon." Byrd paused. "You sound a bit tense, Chris. Are you OK?"

"I've had a really traumatic night. I'll tell you about it when I see you."

Bronson snapped the phone shut and turned to Angela. "That was my boss," he said, his face grim, "and it wasn't good news. Kirsty Philips has been murdered."

"Oh, God. It's got to be linked to that clay tablet, hasn't it?"

Bronson started the car again and pulled back onto the road. "Yes," he said. "And we both know that the people who want it want it very badly indeed." He paused. "So what are you going to do now? I don't think you're in any danger now that the tall man—the one Talabani called Yacoub—is dead. But you can move into my house if you're worried about staying in your flat."

Angela looked at him for a long moment, then sighed, pushing her hair back from her eyes. "Thank you—I'd like to do that," she said simply. "But, you know, I've not finished with this hunt just yet. When his thug was getting ready to slice my face to ribbons, that man Yacoub said something to you that I simply can't ignore. He said that he believed the inscription on the tablets could provide the location of the Silver Scroll and the Mosaic Covenant."

"You remember that?"

"Trust me, Chris, I can recall every second I spent in that cellar, and everything anybody said."

"I've never even heard of the Silver Scroll," Bronson said. "And what the hell is the Mosaic Covenant?"

"OK. In 1952, archaeologists working at Qumran found a scroll made of copper, which was unusual enough. What made it simply astonishing was that, although almost every other Dead Sea Scroll contained religious texts, the Copper Scroll was simply a list of buried treasures. The trouble was that the locations didn't make any sense—they were just too vague. But one listing on it referred to a second scroll that had been hidden somewhere else, a scroll that provided more details of where the treasures were concealed. That document—which nobody's yet found—has become known as the Silver Scroll."

"And the Mosaic Covenant?"

Angela nodded. "The word 'mosaic,' with a small 'm,' has several different meanings, though they all include the concept of multiple colors or components. But when you spell the word with a capital letter, 'Mosaic,' it means only one thing: 'relating to Moses.'"

"That's 'Moses' as in 'Moses and the Ten Commandments,' you mean?"

"Exactly. The prophet Moses, the author of the Torah and leader of the Israelites. That Moses."

"And what about the Covenant?" Bronson asked. "You're not talking about the Ten Commandments?"

Angela nodded slowly. "That's exactly what's meant by the Mosaic Covenant. I mean, forget about the Ark of the Covenant. That was simply a wooden box covered in gold leaf that was used to carry the Covenant around. The Ark probably rotted away to nothing centuries ago. But this is a possible clue to the location of the Covenant itself—the tablets the Ark was built to house."

"You can't be serious, Angela. Is there any credible evidence that Moses even existed?"

"We've been down this route before, Chris," she said with a slight smile, "and I think you know my views. Like Jesus, there's no physical evidence that Moses was a real person but, unlike Jesus, he does appear in more than one ancient source, so he's got more credibility for that reason alone. He's mentioned in the writings of numerous Greek and Roman historians, as well as in the Torah, and even in the Qur'an.

"But whether or not there's any historical reality to Moses as a person rather misses the point. If that man Yacoub was right, the people who hid the relics and prepared the tablets two thousand years ago *did* believe they possessed something that had belonged to Moses. That means whatever the relic actually was, it was already ancient even then. And any kind of stone tablet dating from well over two millennia ago would be an extremely important archaeological find."

"So you're going to start looking for it?"

"Yes, I am. I simply can't pass up a chance like this. It's the opportunity of a lifetime."

Bronson looked at her face. No longer pale, it was flushed with excitement and her beautiful hazel eyes sparkled with anticipation. "Despite all you've gone through today? You nearly got killed in that cellar."

"You don't have to remind me. But Yacoub is dead, and whatever his gang gets up to now, I doubt if chasing us to try to recover that clay tablet is going to be high on their list of priorities. In any case, we'll be leaving the country within a couple of hours, and I don't think that either the Silver Scroll or the Mosaic Covenant is in Morocco. The reference to Qumran is clear enough, and I have a feeling that—whatever was hidden by the people who wrote these tablets—they were buried in Judea or somewhere in that general area. The clay tablet the O'Connors found must tell us their whereabouts."

Bronson nodded. "Well, if you want to do any more investigating, I'm afraid you'll have to do it by yourself. I've got to get back to Maidstone to write up my report, and I might even get sucked into the investigation into Kirsty Philips's murder. I certainly don't think I'll be able to convince Dickie Byrd that I suddenly need to head off to Israel. Are you sure that this is worth following up?"

Angela looked at him. "Definitely," she said. She opened her handbag, extracted a few folded sheets of paper and began looking at them.

"Is that the Aramaic text?" Bronson asked.

Angela nodded. "Yes. I still can't work out how the coding system could have worked. I was so sure there were four tablets in the set, but the position of those two Aramaic words *Ir-Tzadok* and *B'Succaca* screws up that idea."

Bronson glanced down at the sheets of paper, then looked back at the road ahead.

"Tell me again how you think they'd have prepared the tablets," he suggested.

"We've been through this, Chris."

"Humor me," Bronson said. "Tell me again."

Patiently, Angela explained her theory that the small diagonal line she'd observed on the pictures of each of the tablets meant there had originally been a single slab of clay that had then been cut into four quarters, and that each diagonal line was one part of a cross, cut into the clay at the center of the slab to indicate the original positions of those quarters.

"So you've got four tablets, each covered in Aramaic script that's always read from right to left, but on the bottom two the only way that *Ir-Tzadok* and *B'Succaca* appear in the right order is if you read the two words backward, from left to right?"

"Exactly," Angela replied, "which is why I must have got it wrong. The only thing that makes sense is that the tablets must be read in a line from right to left. But if that *is* the case, then what's the purpose of the diagonal lines?"

Bronson was silent for a couple of minutes, staring at the ribbon of tarmac unrolling in front of the car, while his brain considered and then rejected possibilities. Then he smiled slightly, and then laughed aloud.

"What?" Angela asked, looking irritated.

"It's obvious, blindingly obvious," he said. "There's one simple way that you could position the tablets in a square, as you've suggested, and still read those two words in the right order. In fact," Bronson added, "it's so obvious I'm really surprised you didn't see it yourself."

Angela stared at the paper and shook her head. Then she looked across at Bronson.

"OK, genius," she said, "tell me."

42

Angela spread out her notes on the table in front of her and bent forward, studying what she'd written. They were in the departure lounge of the Mohammed V airport waiting for their flight to London to be called.

"I think your solution to the puzzle of the clay tablets has to be right. I wrote out everything we'd deciphered, but in the order you suggested, and now it does seem to make more sense. I just wish we had better pictures of the Cairo museum and the O'Connor tablets—it would be a great help if we could read a few more words of the inscriptions on those two."

She looked down again at the papers in front of her. Bronson's idea was *so* simple that she, too, was amazed it hadn't occurred to her.

Aramaic, he'd said, was written from right to left, and they'd more or less agreed that there had originally been four tablets, arranged in a square. Why not, Bronson had proposed, read the text starting with the first word at the right-hand end of the top line of the top right tablet—which they didn't have, of course—and then read the word in the same position on the tablet at the top left of the square. Then move to the bottom left, then bottom right and back to the top right, and so on, in a kind of counterclockwise circle. That, at least, meant that the words *Ir'Tzadok* and *B'Succaca* could be read in the correct sequence.

But even that didn't produce anything that seemed totally coherent—it just formed very short and disjointed phrases—until they tried reading one word from each line and next the word from the line directly *below* it, instead of the next word on the *same* line. Then, and only then, did a kind of sense begin to emerge.

What they now had read:

----- *by* ----- *ben* ----- ----- *perform the* ----- *task* ----- *the*
----- ----- ----- *completed* ----- ----- ----- *now* ----- -----
----- *last* ----- *the* ----- *scroll* ----- ----- *took from* -----
----- ----- *have* ----- ----- ----- *cave* ----- ----- ----- *place*
----- ----- ----- *of* ----- ----- ----- *settlement* ----- -----
Ir-Tzadok B'Succaca ----- *scroll* ----- *silver* ----- -----
----- *we* ----- ----- ----- *cistern* ----- ----- *place of*
----- *end* ----- *days* ----- *the tablets of* ----- *temple* -----
Jerusalem ----- ----- ----- *the* ----- ----- ----- *concealed*
----- ----- ----- *of* ----- ----- ----- *a* ----- ----- *four stones*
----- *the* ----- *side* ----- *a* ----- *of* ----- ----- ----- *height*
----- ----- *cubit*   *to* ----- ----- ----- *within* ----- ----- *of*
our ----- *and* ----- *now* ----- ----- ----- *we* ----- ----- -----
our ----- ----- ----- *invaders* ----- *our* -----

"Have you tried filling in any of the blanks?" Bronson asked.

"Yes." Angela nodded. "It's not as easy as you might think, because you can easily end up tailoring the text to whatever it is you want it to say. I've tried, and a few of the missing words seem to be fairly obvious, like the end of the last line. The word 'invaders' seems to stand out as being different to the rest of the inscription, so I think that's possibly a part of a political statement, something like 'our fight against the invaders of our land.' That would be a justification of their opposition to, most probably, the Romans, who were all over Judea during the first century AD.

"The rest of it is more difficult, but there are a couple of things we can be certain about. These tablets *do* refer to Qumram: the words *Ir-Tzadok B'Succaca* make that quite definite. And in the same sentence, or possibly at the beginning of the next one, I'm fairly sure that those three words mean the 'scroll of silver,' the Silver Scroll. That's what really excites me. The problem is that, if the author of this text did possess the scroll and then hid it somewhere, presumably in a cistern, which is what I'm hoping, we still don't know exactly where to start looking, apart from Qumran, obviously. And the country, of course, was full of wells and cisterns at this period. Every settlement, from a single house right up to large villages and towns, had to have a source of water close by. I've no idea how many cisterns there were in first-century Judea, but I guess the numbers would run into the thousand, maybe even tens of thousands."

She looked down at the deciphered text, studying the few words they'd managed to translate. If only they could fill one or two more of the blanks, they'd have some idea where to begin their search.

Bronson's next question echoed her thoughts. "Assuming the museum will agree to let you go out to Israel, where do you think you should start looking?"

Angela sighed and rubbed her eyes. "I've no idea. But the reference we've managed to decode is the first tangible clue to a relic whose existence has been suspected for over fifty years. Half the archaeologists in the field that I've talked to have spent some time searching for the Silver Scroll, and the other half have dismissed it out of hand as a myth. But the O'Connors' clay tablet is almost certainly contemporary with the relic, and I think the reference is a strong enough piece of evidence to follow up. And there's something else."

"What?"

"I don't know that much about Israel and Jewish history, so I'm going to need some specialist help, from somebody who speaks Hebrew, somebody who knows the country and its history."

"You've got someone in mind?"

Angela nodded and smiled. "Oh, yes. I know exactly who to talk to. And he's actually based in Israel—in Jerusalem, in fact—so he's right on the spot."

43

Bronson felt drained. He seemed to have spent all the previous day sitting in an aircraft, and the damp, gray skies were an unpleasant reminder that he was back in Britain, in stark contrast to the few hot and sunny days he'd just spent down in Morocco. He punched the address Byrd had sent him by text into the unmarked car's satnav and headed toward Canterbury.

When he arrived at the house, there were two police vans parked in the driveway and a couple of cars on the road outside the property. The front door was standing slightly ajar, and he slipped under the "crime scene" tape and stepped into the hall.

"You're Chris Bronson, right?" A beefy, red-faced man wearing a somewhat grubby gray suit greeted him.

Bronson nodded and showed his warrant card.

"Right, I'm Dave Robbins. Come through into the dining room to keep out of the way of the SOCOs— they're just finishing up in the lounge, and then we're out of here. Now," he said, when they were both seated at the dining table, "I gather from Dickie Byrd that you've had some contact with the victim?"

"I met her and her husband a couple of times in Morocco," Bronson agreed, and explained what had happened to Kirsty Philips's parents.

"Do you think there's any connection between their deaths and her murder?" Robbins asked.

Bronson paused for a few moments before he replied. He was absolutely certain that the three deaths were connected, and that the missing clay tablet was at the heart of the matter, but he didn't see how explaining all that would help Robbins find Kirsty's killer.

"I don't know," he said finally. "It's a hell of a coincidence if they're unconnected, but I can't think what the connection could be. What actually happened here? How did she die?"

In a few short sentences, Robbins explained what the police had found when they arrived at the house.

As he listened, Bronson's mind span back to the hotel in Rabat, and to the way Kirsty had looked when he'd seen her there: bright and full of life, her natural vivacity subdued only because of the double tragedy that had decimated her family. Intellectually he accepted the truth of what Robbins had told him, but on an emotional level it was still difficult to believe what had happened.

"Who raised the alarm?" he asked.

"One of the neighbors thought she'd pop in and offer her condolences for the loss of her parents. She went to the side door, saw Kirsty lying dead on the floor, and ran screaming up the road to her own house to dial triple nine. We've already done a door-to-door but we haven't found anyone who saw Kirsty arriving, and only two people noticed the neighbor doing a four-minute mile and howling like a banshee."

"Right," Bronson said. "I can't think what connection this has to Morocco. My guess is she might have disturbed a burglar, one of those sick bastards who find out who's died and then target their houses. And because she was only hit once, he might not have intended to kill her. If he thought the house was empty and she suddenly stepped out in front of him, he might have just swung his jimmy as a kind of reflex action, and hit her harder than he meant to. In my opinion, I think it's most likely that you're looking at a totally unrelated crime."

Robbins nodded. "Makes sense to me. And this is probably another bugger we're never going to solve. We've found no useful forensic stuff here apart from a few fingerprints that might or might not belong to the intruder. As far as we can see the killer jimmied the door, walked in, hit Kirsty Philips on the side of the head and then walked out again. There might be some more trace evidence somewhere, but if there is, we haven't found it yet. There's no sign of anything having been taken, or disturbed in any way. No forensics, no witnesses, no suspects, no motives. And that means no nothing."

"Yep," Bronson agreed, "it's every cop's worst-case scenario. Look, unless there's anything else I can tell you or help you with, I'll get out of your way."

"OK, Chris, thanks for that," Robbins said and stood up. "Leave the front door open on your way out, would you?"

The two men shook hands and left the dining room,

turning in opposite directions—Robbins right toward the back of the house where the SOCOs were still working, and Bronson left. As he stepped into the hall, Bronson glanced down at the rug just inside the front door and saw a scatter of envelopes lying there. Obviously the post had been delivered while they had been talking in the dining room, and the postman had placed everything on the mat rather than sliding it through the mailbox, simply because the door was still ajar.

"The post's here," Bronson called out, and automatically bent down to pick it up.

He noticed the package immediately, one end protruding slightly from under a white junk-mail envelope. It was bulkier than everything else there, and the Moroccan stamps were extremely distinctive.

Suddenly, he knew exactly what had to be in the small parcel, and saw clearly what the "burglar" must have been doing in the house—he'd just broken in a couple of days too early.

Bronson knew it was wrong, knew he was tampering with evidence, and knew that what he was doing might easily be sufficient to get him kicked off the force, but he did it anyway. As DI Robbins turned round and walked back toward him, Bronson hunched down over the mat, reached out, seized the packet and slid it into his jacket pocket with his left hand. With his right, he collected the rest of the mail, then stood up and glanced behind him.

Robbins was approaching, his hand outstretched. Bronson gave him the post and turned to leave.

"Typical," the DI muttered, flicking through the envelopes. "All bloody junk mail, by the looks of it. OK, see you around, Chris."

When Bronson sat down in the driving seat of his car he found that, despite the chill in the air, there was a thin sheen of sweat on his forehead. For a few seconds he wondered if he should take the package back, leave it outside the door or maybe put it on the carpet. But he told himself that the presence or absence of a two-thousand-year-old clay tablet at a crime scene in Canterbury would have no impact whatsoever on Robbins' success or failure in solving the murder. He also knew Angela would be delighted to get her hands on it.

Feeling a sudden jolt of pure adrenaline, he turned the key in the ignition and drove quickly away.

44

"I've got something for you," Bronson said, walking into the lounge of his small house in Tunbridge Wells.

"What?" Angela asked, as he handed her the package.

She glanced at the unfamiliar stamps that plastered one end of it as she turned it over in her hands. "Morocco," she murmured, and ripped open the envelope. She peered inside it, shook out a small object covered in bubble-wrap and carefully unwrapped it.

"My God, Chris, you found it!" Angela said, her voice high with excitement. "This is the missing tablet."

"I should bloody well hope it is," Bronson said, sitting down opposite her and looking curiously at the relic. It was much less impressive than he had expected, just a small, grubby, grayish-brown lump of fired clay, one surface covered in marks and squiggles that were completely meaningless to him.

Angela pulled a pair of latex gloves from her handbag before she touched the tablet itself. Then she picked it up and examined it carefully, almost reverently, her eyes sparkling.

"You were right," she said, glancing at the address on the envelope. "The O'Connors *did* post it to themselves."

"Yes, and I've just nicked it from a crime scene."

"Well, I'm really glad you did, as long as you won't get into trouble over it."

"It should be OK," Bronson said, with a shrug of his shoulders. "Nobody saw me take it, and the only people who know it exists probably think it's still somewhere in Morocco. I'll bet my pension that, as far as the rest of the world is concerned, this object has simply disappeared. As long as nobody actually *knows* we've got it, I don't think we're in any danger—and my meager pension should be safe as well."

Angela spread a towel over the coffee table and gently laid the tablet on it.

"It doesn't look like much," Bronson said.

"Agreed," she replied, "but it's not the relic itself that's important—it's what the inscription means." Her latex-covered fingertips lightly traced the incised markings on the face of the tablet; then she looked up at her ex-husband. "Don't forget how many people have died already. The stall-holder, the O'Connors, probably Kirsty Philips, and even Yacoub and his thugs in Rabat—the reason they're all dead is *something* to do with this rather dull-looking lump of two-thousand-year-old fired clay."

Bronson nodded. "It's a bit different when you put it like that. So now what?"

Angela looked back at the tablet. "This could be the

biggest break of my career, Chris. If Yacoub was right, this inscription could lead us to the hiding place of the Silver Scroll and the Mosaic Covenant. If there's even the slightest chance of finding either relic, I'm determined to follow the trail, wherever it leads me."

"So what are you going to do? Suggest that the museum mounts an expedition?"

"No way," Angela said firmly. "Don't forget I'm still a very junior member of staff. If I walk in and tell Roger Halliwell what I've found, he'll be absolutely delighted and no doubt he'll congratulate me. Then he'll politely push me to one side and in a couple of weeks the Halliwell-Baverstock expedition will arrive in Israel to follow the trail of the lost relics. If I managed to get involved at all, they might let me examine any bits of pottery they find."

Bronson looked slightly quizzical. "I thought you were all brothers—and sisters—in arms in the halls of academe? All striving together for the advancement of knowledge and a better understanding of human history?"

"Don't you believe it. Whenever there's a whiff of a major discovery, it's every man for himself in the scramble to be the one whose name is linked to it. All that brotherly support vanishes and the event turns into a high-class catfight. I know—I've seen it happen. I'll just tell Roger I'm taking a short-notice holiday in Israel to study some Aramaic texts and leave it at that."

Angela gestured toward the clay tablet lying on the coffee table in front of her. "Now we've got this tablet, it means we can read more than half of the original text, and that has to give us a good chance of working out the meaning of the whole of the inscription. I've got about a week of holiday owing, and I don't see any reason why I shouldn't take it in Israel, do you?"

"No, I suppose not. Are you sure Israel's the right place to start looking?"

"Yes, because of the reference to Qumran. After that, who knows?"

"Right." Bronson. "I'll come with you."

"You can't, Chris. You're in the middle of a murder investigation."

"No, I'm not. I've finished the report about Morocco, I've got nothing to do with the investigation of Kirsty Philips's murder, and I'm owed at least ten days leave. Dickie Byrd probably won't like it, but that's not my problem." Bronson reached across the table and took Angela's hand. "Look, I don't want you running off to Israel by yourself. I want to be close enough to take care of you."

Angela gave his hand a squeeze. "Are you sure? That would be wonderful, Chris. I wasn't looking forward to forging on by myself. And we do make a pretty good team, don't we?"

Bronson smiled at her. "You bet," he said. And we *do*, he thought contentedly, and not just as a pair of enthusiastic relic-hunters. But he knew he couldn't rush things . . .

"Right," Angela said briskly. "I'll get on the Internet and try to sort out flights to Tel Aviv. Once I've done that, I'll do some more work on that tablet. With that

Aramaic text and the other bits of translations, I'm sure we can work out where the clues are pointing. We must have got more information about these hidden relics than anyone else, so we can be sure we'll be there at the kill."

"I hope that's just a figure of speech," Bronson said.

45

Tony Baverstock looked at yet another list of clay tablets on the screen of his desktop computer and wondered, not for the first time, if there was any real point in continuing with the search. He must have studied pictures of hundreds of the things, and none of them— at least, none so far—had borne even the slightest resemblance to the one he was looking for.

To complicate matters, there were some half a million clay tablets sitting in museum vaults and storerooms that had never been translated. The information about this huge repository of tablets was usually limited to just one or two poor-quality photographs and perhaps a very brief description of the provenance of each object—where it was found, its approximate date, that kind of thing.

There were two reasons for his urgent search. First, Charlie Hoxton had called him the day before and told him to do it, which was in itself an entirely adequate incentive; second, his task had suddenly become even more crucial the previous afternoon, when he'd run into Roger

Halliwell in the corridor outside his office. The head of department had looked more irritated that usual.

"Something wrong, Roger?" Baverstock had asked.

"It's Angela. She's gone off on another bloody wild-goose chase," Halliwell had snapped. "I've only just found out she's been in Morocco for the last couple of days, and now she's taken more leave to run off to Israel to study some Aramaic text. It's not her field, for God's sake. She should stick to what she's good at."

Baverstock hadn't commented, but suddenly felt sure that somehow Angela must have either found the missing clay tablet or at least got hold of a decent picture of the inscription on it. That had been enough for him to redouble his efforts.

But despite his exhaustive research, he hadn't got his first "hit" until the next morning. The picture of the tablet was of fairly poor quality, and he spent almost twenty minutes studying the Aramaic inscription before he finally realized that he was looking at the tablet Charlie Hoxton already owned, and which Dexter had "sourced" from a museum in Cairo.

With a snort of disgust, he closed the window on his computer screen and returned to his search. Two hours later, having changed his search parameters five times in an effort to reduce the sheer number of relics he was having to check out, he found himself looking at the Paris tablet. He printed all the images available in the database on the color laser in his office, and spent a few minutes studying each of them with his desk magnifier before finally closing the connection to the museum intranet.

Then he locked his office and left the building, telling his assistant he was going away for a few days unexpectedly. He walked down Great Russell Street, stopped at the same public phone he'd used before, and called Hoxton.

"I've spent the last twelve hours looking for these bloody tablets," he began.

"Did you find anything?" Hoxton demanded.

"I spent half an hour studying *your* tablet—the one you got me to translate—before I twigged what it was, the photographs were such poor quality. But eventually I got lucky. There's a clay tablet sitting in a storeroom in a museum in Paris that's definitely a part of the set. From the mark in one corner of it, it's the one that goes on the bottom right of the block."

"Can you translate the text from the pictures?" Hoxton asked.

"There's no need," Baverstock replied. "The French have helpfully already translated the Aramaic for us. They translated it into French, of course, but obviously that's not going to be much of a problem. It'll just take me a little while to work out the best equivalent English words."

"Good," Hoxton said. "You're packed, I hope?"

"Of course. I wouldn't miss this trip for the world. We're still booked on the flight this afternoon?"

"Yes. I'll see you at Heathrow as we agreed. Bring all the pictures of the Paris tablet, and the French translation of the Aramaic, as well as your English version. This is going to be the trip of your lifetime."

PART THREE

ISRAEL

46

The flight was no problem, but actually getting into Israel took Bronson and Angela several hours, and that was *after* they'd disembarked from the aircraft. The problem was the small blue square they each had stamped in their passports with the word "sortie" printed in a vertical line down the left-hand side, a date in the center and Arabic script across the top and down the right side—their exit stamps from Morocco.

The Israeli authorities are notably suspicious about travelers arriving at any of their borders who have recently left an Arab country, even one as distant as Morocco. The moment the immigration officer had seen the stamps, he'd pressed a hidden switch and minutes later Bronson and Angela were whisked away into separate interview rooms while their luggage was found and comprehensively searched.

Bronson had anticipated what their reception was likely to be, and they'd taken precautions to ensure that none of the photographs of the clay tablets, or of their translations of the Aramaic text, remained on Angela's laptop, just in case the Israelis wanted to inspect the contents of the hard disk. She had transferred all these files to a couple of high-capacity memory sticks, one of which was tucked away in the pocket of Bronson's jeans and the other hidden in Angela's makeup kit in her handbag. Back in London, they'd gone to Angela's bank, where she had a safety deposit box that held the deeds to her apartment and other important papers, and deposited the clay tablet there, because they didn't want to risk traveling with the relic.

The questioning was thorough, relentless and competent. What had they been doing in Morocco? How long had they been there? Had they been there before? If so, why? All repeated again and again, the questions the same, though the way they were asked changed frequently as the interrogators looked for any discrepancies or alterations in their answers. Bronson, who had considerable experience in sitting on the other side of the table, interviewing suspects, was impressed by their thoroughness. He hoped that his police warrant card and Angela's British Museum identification were helping to establish their bona fides.

Only toward the end of the interviews, when they were apparently satisfied with what they'd being doing in Morocco, did the officials begin asking why they'd come to Israel. Bronson had discussed this with Angela on the flight out, and they'd decided that the only right answer to this question had to be "holiday." Any other response would simply cause problems and certainly lead to more questioning.

It was midevening before they were finally allowed to leave the interview rooms by the unsmiling Israelis.

"I don't mind the security checks they do here," Angela said. "At least you can feel fairly safe on an El Al flight."

"We flew British Airways," Bronson pointed out.

"I know. I mean, when you're flying out of an Israeli airport, the chances of anyone being able to smuggle a weapon or a bomb onto a departing flight are almost nil. Did you know that all hold luggage is subjected to a pressure drop in a sealed bomb-proof chamber that simulates a high-altitude flight, just in case there's a bomb in a suitcase that's linked to a barometric switch? And that's in addition to everything being X-rayed and passing through explosive sniffers?"

"No," Bronson admitted, "I didn't. And that is comforting, especially when you compare it to somewhere as leaky and slapdash as Heathrow. The security there is a joke."

Angela looked at him with a quizzical expression. "I'm so glad you didn't tell me that *before* we took off."

Ben Gurion International airport is close to the city of Lod, about ten miles to the southeast of Tel Aviv, so the train journey only took a few minutes. The railway line followed the route of the main road into the city—in fact, for some of the distance it ran between the two highways—and they got off at HaShalom Station, at the edge of the industrial zone, and almost in the shadow of the hulking Azrieli Center.

Most of the hotels in Tel Aviv are unsurprisingly

strung along the Mediterranean coast, but their prices are fairly high, so Bronson had booked two rooms in a more modest establishment tucked away in the side-streets near Zina Square, not far from a tourist office.

They caught a cab from HaShalom to Zina Square, checked into the hotel and deposited their bags, then walked the short distance to the Lahat Promenade that borders Frishman Beach, found a restaurant and enjoyed a reasonable meal. Bronson wished fleetingly that they were going to return to the same room but he decided not to push this. They were in Israel, working together. This, for the time being, would have to be enough.

The BMI flight had landed at Tel Aviv on time late that afternoon; two of the three passengers traveling together on British passports cleared customs and immigration without any particular delays. The third man, Alexander Dexter, was pulled aside and subjected to about an hour of detailed questioning before he was allowed to proceed. But he'd expected that to happen because of the Morocco exit stamp in his passport, so it didn't bother him.

Outside the airport, he rejoined Hoxton and Baverstock, who'd already collected their prebooked Fiat Punto hire car, and the three men drove off together, heading for the center of Tel Aviv and their hotel.

Just over two hours after the BMI flight landed at Ben Gurion, a flight arrived from Paris. On board were four men of distinctly Arabic appearance. Their French passports, which lacked any signs of transit through Morocco, raised no suspicions at all, although their luggage was thoroughly checked by the Israeli customs officers.

Once they had left the airport in their Peugeot hire car, heading for a hotel they'd already booked on the outskirts of Jerusalem, the man in the passenger seat made a telephone call to a number in the city on a pay-as-you-go mobile that he'd bought just before they boarded the aircraft in Paris. Once he'd ended the call, he leaned back and looked incuriously through the windscreen.

"Everything OK?" the driver asked.

"Yes," the tall man known only as Yacoub said shortly. "I know exactly where they are."

47

The morning sun woke them both early—their rooms were side-by-side and faced east, toward the Haqirya district of Tel Aviv rather than toward the coast—and Bronson and Angela walked into the dining room just before eight to get some breakfast.

"So what do we do first?" Bronson asked, as they sat over coffee afterward.

"I'll need to call Yosef and see if we can see him today."

"Who?" Bronson asked.

"Yosef Ben Halevi. He works at the Israel Museum in Jerusalem. He was involved in a project at the British Museum a few years ago and I met him then."

"And why do we need him, exactly?"

"We need Yosef because he's an expert on Jewish history, and I'm not. I do know something about this area—about Qumran, for example—but not enough about the history of Israel to be able to interpret everything that's on that tablet. We need somebody like him, and he's the only authority I know over here."

Bronson looked doubtful. "Well, OK," he said, "but you don't really *know* this man, so don't let him see the pictures of the tablet or the translations. I think we should keep all that to ourselves, at least for the moment."

"I was planning to," Angela said. "I'll call him right now." She crossed to the reception desk.

She was back in a few minutes. "He's tied up all day, but he's agreed to drive over here to meet us this evening. Now, we'll need to try to translate the inscription on the tablet, obviously, but it might be useful if we visited Qumran as well, because it's the one location that we know is quite definitely mentioned in the combined inscriptions and so it's as good a place as any to start. I don't expect we'll find much of interest there, but at least it'll give us a feel for the kind of terrain we'll be searching here in Israel."

"Is it difficult to get to?"

"It shouldn't be. Like Masada, it's a renowned archaeological site, so I'd be surprised if there weren't regular trips out there."

"There's a tourist office about a hundred yards away," Bronson said. "We passed it last night when we walked over to the beach. Let's nip over there and see if we can buy tickets for an organized tour."

In fact, there were no tours to Qumran. Or rather, there were, but only on certain days of the week, and the next one that had availability wasn't scheduled for another three days.

"Not a problem," Bronson said, as they left the tourist office. "We'll hire a car. We'll need to be able to get around while we're out here. Do you want to go now?"

Angela shook her head. "No. I'd like to work on the inscription first. We'll drive over this afternoon."

"I don't want you to think I'm paranoid," Bronson said, "and I can't see any way that we could have been followed out here, but I still think we should keep out of sight. So I'd rather we didn't work in the hotel lounge or one of the public rooms."

Angela linked her arm through Bronson's. "I agree, especially after all we've been through. My room's a bit bigger; why don't we work in there?"

Back in her hotel room, Angela pulled a large paperback book out of her computer bag. "I found this fairly decent Aramaic dictionary in one of the specialist bookshops near the museum in London. With this and the on-line translation site, I think we'll manage."

"Anything I can do?"

"Yes. You can check the dictionary while I input the words into the on-line translator, so we have some form of cross-checking that we're doing it right. We need to do this slowly and carefully, because it's not just the language that's unfamiliar, it's the individual characters as well. Some of them are very similar, and we have to be certain that we're recognizing the correct symbols on the photographs. Let me show you what I mean."

She enlarged the image on the screen of her laptop and pointed at five symbols in turn that, to Bronson, looked remarkably similar. Then she copied them in a horizontal line onto a piece of paper. The line read: "ד ד ו ר ו."

"The first one," she said, "is *daleth*, which equates to

'd' or 'dh.' The second is *kaph* or 'k'; the third is *nun* or 'n'; the fourth *resh* or 'r'; and the last one is *waw*, meaning 'w.' I'm reasonably familiar with the appearance of the language, though I don't normally get involved in trying to translate it, and to me—and certainly to you—those characters probably look pretty much identical. But obviously the meanings of the words will be completely altered if you put the wrong letter or letters into it. And bearing in mind we also have to take account of the individual idiosyncrasies of the hand of the person who prepared this tablet, this is going to take some time."

Angela was right. It took them well over an hour to complete the translation of just the first line of the tablet. Eventually they developed a technique that seemed to work for them. They would look at each word and independently decide what each letter was. They wrote these down, then swapped notes to see if they agreed. If they'd come to different conclusions, they'd study that letter again, Angela magnifying the screen image—she had used an eight megapixel camera to ensure maximum definition—so they could look at each character in enormous detail. Only when both were satisfied that they'd got the letters themselves right did they turn their attention to the dictionaries.

But even after taking such care, they still couldn't translate the first three words of the top line of the tablet—at least, not to begin with. They went back over each letter in turn, choosing alternatives, and eventually managed to decipher the second and third words as "copper" and "the," but the first word, no matter what combination of different characters they tried inserting, didn't appear to be in either the printed Aramaic dictionary or any of the on-line versions.

"Right," Angela said, her frustration evident, "we'll come back to that later. Let's move on to the next line."

48

Hassan pulled the hire car to a stop in a parking lot—really little more than a dusty piece of waste ground—on the outskirts of Rām Allāh, a small settlement north of Jerusalem and deep in the territory of the West Bank. Almost as soon as he'd stopped the vehicle, two other cars nosed their way into the parking area and braked to a halt close by. As Hassan and Yacoub climbed out of their car, four men—all wearing jeans and T-shirts—emerged from the other vehicles and walked over to them.

"*Salam aleikom,*" Yacoub said formally. "Peace be upon you."

"And upon you," the apparent leader of the group replied, then asked: "You have the money?"

Yacoub turned to Hassan, who reached slowly into the outside pocket of his light jacket and pulled out a bundle of notes, then stepped forward. Yacoub raised his arm to stop him advancing any further.

"And you have the goods?" he asked. "Let me see them."

The man nodded and turned back toward one of the cars. As he and Yacoub reached it, one of his companions popped open the trunk, and all three men peered inside. On the trunk floor were two black briefcases, their leather scuffed and scratched. The man glanced round, then leaned inside, snapped open the catches and lifted the lids. Each case contained half a dozen semi-automatic pistols of various types, each with two or three magazines. All of the weapons looked well used, nicks and scrapes all over them, but they were all clean and oiled, which suggested they had been properly cared for.

Yacoub bent down and picked up several of the weapons for inspection.

"We'll take the two CZ-75s and two of the Brownings," he said, "and two magazines for each. You have plenty of shells?"

"Of course. How many boxes do you need?"

"Four will be enough," Yacoub said.

The man opened another, smaller case, took out three boxes of nine-millimeter Parabellum ammunition and handed them to Hassan, who passed over the money he was holding.

"Thank you, my friend," Yacoub said. "A pleasure dealing with you."

"The weapons," the man replied, as he checked the money and then slammed the trunk shut. "When you've finished with them, call me. If they're undamaged we'll buy them back at half the cost."

"Only half?"

"That's our normal rate. Take it or leave it. You have my numbers."

49

The longer Angela and Bronson worked at the translation, the easier it seemed to get, and although the first line had taken them over an hour to crack, they managed to get the entire inscription finished in just under three hours, which Angela didn't think was bad going, even though there were still three words that had stubbornly refused to yield their meanings.

They rewarded each other with a drink from the minibar and then started the most difficult phase of the entire operation—trying to decipher what the Aramaic text actually meant. As he'd done before, Bronson wrote out the words they'd translated, in the order they appeared on the clay tablet:

> *land cavity describes of the copper -----*
> *of four tablets Ir-Tzadok took perform*
> *belief south of of we of*
> *secure width ----- ----- the have*
> *to and we the the and*
> *the cubit altar place scrolls the*

Then he reversed the order to allow them to read the words in the correct sequence:

> *----- copper the of describes cavity land*
> *perform took Ir-Tzadok tablets four of*
> *of we of of south belief*
> *have the ----- ----- width secure*
> *and the the we and to*
> *the scrolls place altar cubit the*

Bronson looked at what he'd written, then flicked back through the other pages in front of him.

"Right," he said, "I'll incorporate these words in the full translation and then maybe we'll be able to see the wood rather than just the trees."

He worked for a few minutes, then passed over the final version—or at least the final version with the information they had to hand:

> *----- by ----- ben ----- ----- perform the ----- task of*
> *the ----- ----- have completed ----- ----- and now -----*
> *----- the last ----- the copper scroll ----- ----- took from*
> *----- ----- we have ----- ----- the cave ----- ----- the place*
> *----- ----- scrolls of ----- ----- the settlement ----- ----- Ir-*
> *Tzadok B'Succaca ----- scroll of silver ----- ----- ----- we*
> *----- ----- the cistern ----- ----- place of ----- end of days*
> *----- the tablets of ----- temple of Jerusalem ----- -----*
> *----- the ----- ----- we concealed ----- ----- altar of -----*
> *----- describes a ----- ----- four stones ----- the south side*
> *----- a width of ----- ----- and height ----- ----- cubit to*

----- ----- cavity within ----- ----- of our ----- ----- belief
now ----- ----- secure we ----- ----- to our ----- ----- the
invaders ----- our land

"I can probably fill in another couple of the words we haven't deciphered." Angela pointed at the third and fourth lines. "I think that section reads 'the settlement known as Ir-Tzadok B'Succaca.' I just wish we had a few more . . ."

Her voice died away as she stared at the page, and Bronson looked at her sharply. "What is it?" he asked.

"The lines just before it," she said. "From the tone of what you've read in this translation, how would you describe the person who wrote it?"

"I don't follow you."

"I mean, do you think that person was a priest, or a warrior, or what?"

Bronson read the text again and thought for a moment. "There's not a lot to go on apart from that last section, where it looks as if he could be justifying fighting the invaders. So if I had to guess I'd say he was probably a warrior, maybe a member of the Jewish resistance or whatever they had in those days."

"Exactly. Now look at this section, from where it says 'the copper scroll' to 'the cave.' Remember that around the beginning of the first millennium the Jews didn't have an army. They weren't organized in the way that the Romans were, into formalized fighting units. They were more like gangs of fighters that would band together against the common invader when it suited them.

The rest of the time they fought among themselves when they weren't raiding settlements to steal food and money and weapons."

"Like guerrillas?" Bronson suggested.

"Precisely. With that in mind, I think we can make a bit more sense of that section of the text. Put the words 'which we' in front of 'took from' and that could be a description of a raid. They hit some settlement, and one of the things they took from it was a copper scroll."

"So?"

"So they obviously realized it wasn't just any old copper scroll, because it then looks as if they hid it in a cave, and probably a cave at Qumran because the reference to *Ir-Tzadok B'Succaca* occurs very shortly afterward." Angela paused and looked at Bronson. "What do you know about Qumran?" she asked.

"Not a lot. I know the Dead Sea Scrolls were found there, and I think they were written by a tribe called the Essenes, and then they hid them in the nearby caves."

Angela nodded. "That's one view, but it's almost certainly wrong. There *was* a community at Qumran, and the Dead Sea Scrolls *were* discovered in eleven caves located just to the west of the settlement. The scrolls contain multiple copies of the books of the Old Testament, and include every book of the Hebrew Bible apart from the Book of Esther. About eighty percent were written on parchment, and the rest—with one exception—on papyrus. Those are the facts. Everything else is a matter of interpretation.

"One of the problems is that the archaeologist who first excavated at Qumran in 1949—he was a Dominican friar named Father Roland de Vaux of the École Biblique in Jerusalem—started with the caves and the scrolls, assumed that the Qumran community had prepared them, and used that as the basis for his deductions about the people of that community. That's a bit like somebody excavating the remains of the Bodleian Library in a thousand years' time, finding only some of the ancient Roman texts that are stored there and assuming that the people of Oxford were Latin-speaking and addicted to gladiatorial games."

"A lot of people at Oxford *do* speak Latin," Bronson pointed out, "and it wouldn't surprise me if some of them were into gladiators as well."

Angela smiled. "OK, but you can see what I'm driving at. The point is that Father de Vaux made the assumption that, because the scrolls had been hidden close to the Qumran community, they must have been written by members of that community, though there was actually no empirical evidence whatsoever to support this hypothesis. And if the Essenes did write the scrolls, why did they choose to hide them so close to where they were living? It would have been pointless as a means of concealment. But once de Vaux had got that idea set firmly in his mind, it slanted his view of every single piece of evidence that he looked at.

"He came to the conclusion that the people of Qumran were members of a Jewish sect called the Essenes, a very religious group. When he started looking at the settlement itself, he claimed to have identified a *scriptorium*—a place where monks or scribes would have copied or prepared manuscripts—based purely on his discovery of a bench, two inkwells and a handful of writing implements.

"But there are plenty of different possible interpretations: it could have been a schoolroom or a military or commercial office, for example. And not even the tiniest fragment of a scroll has ever been found in the so-called *scriptorium*, and that is just ridiculous—if it really had been a room used only for that purpose, it would have been full of the tools and materials used by the scribes. At the very least you would have expected to find some scraps of blank papyrus or the remains of scrolls in the ruins.

"To support his belief that the Essenes were devoutly religious, he also identified several cisterns on the site as Jewish ritual baths, or *miqva'ot*. If he'd looked at Qumran in isolation, without knowledge of the scrolls, he would probably have assumed that the cisterns were just receptacles for holding water, which would be the obvious and logical deduction. De Vaux also ignored numerous other significant items that were recovered from the site. Don't forget, archaeologists are very good at ignoring inconvenient facts—they've had a hell of a lot of practice."

"But I thought archaeology was a science," Bronson said. "Scientific method, the peer review process, carbon dating and all that?"

"Dream on. Just like everyone else, archaeologists have been known to fudge results and disregard things that don't fit. Now, if Father de Vaux's theory was correct, then the Qumran Essenes would have lived lives of abject poverty, but other excavations on the site recovered money, glassware, stoneware, metal implements and ornaments, and assorted other relics, all of which seemed to imply that the inhabitants had been both secular and fairly well-off."

"But if Qumran wasn't a religious site, what was it?"

"More likely suggestions are it could have been a wealthy manor house; a principal or second home for an important local family; a stopping-off point for pilgrims en route to Jerusalem; a pottery factory; even a fortress or a fortified trading station.

"The other thing de Vaux did was try to stop anyone outside his select group of researchers from gaining access to the scrolls, or even seeing photographs of them. At least, that applied to those found in Cave Four, which represented about forty percent of the total material recovered."

"But they did publish details of some of them, surely?"

"Yes, but only the less important stuff. The texts found in Cave One were released between 1950 and 1956. In 1963 the writings from eight other caves were published in a single volume, and two years later details of what was known as the Psalms Scroll, found in Cave Eleven, was released. And, of course, translations were quickly made of these texts by scholars all over the world.

"But the Cave Four material wasn't published until 1968, and then only a small amount of it. By that stage, Father de Vaux seemed to have decided that his lasting legacy would be to deny access to the scrolls to all other scholars, and he imposed a strict secrecy rule that allowed only members of his original team or their specific designates to work on them. De Vaux died in 1971, but his death changed nothing: scholars still had no access to the Cave Four material, or even to photographs of the scrolls. That lasted until 1991—almost half a century after their discovery—when a complete set of photographs of the Cave Four materials was found, almost by accident, in a library in San Marino, California, and subsequently published."

"But if the Essenes or whoever lived at Qumran didn't write the scrolls, who did?" Bronson asked.

"Nobody knows. The most probable explanation is that they originated with some devout religious sect in Jerusalem, and were hidden in the Qumran caves by a group of Jews fleeing from Roman troops during one of the regular periods of political unrest."

"And exactly what's in them?" Bronson asked.

"Most of them are scribal copies of known literary texts, mainly Old Testament biblical material, but obviously much earlier examples than had been previously available. There are thirty-odd copies of Deuteronomy, for example. There were also a lot of secular texts, most previously unknown, which shed new light on the form of Judaism that was practiced during what's known as the Second Temple period. That was when the Temple in Jerusalem had been reconstructed after the original—Solomon's Temple—was destroyed in 586 BC. The Second Temple period ran from 516 BC until AD 70, when the Romans sacked Jerusalem, destroyed the Temple and ended the Great Jewish Revolt that had started four years earlier.

"And the Copper Scroll," Angela finished, "is completely out of whack with everything else that was found at Qumran. In 1952, an expedition sponsored by the Jordanian Department of Antiquities was working in Cave Three and found a unique object designated 3Q15—that simply means it was the fifteenth relic found in Cave Three at Qumran. It was a thin sheet of almost pure copper, some seven feet in length, which had apparently snapped in two when it was being rolled up by whoever had prepared it. After two thousand years in the cave, the metal was badly oxidized, incredibly brittle and fragile, and clearly couldn't simply be unrolled. It was unlike anything anyone had seen before, at Qumran or anywhere else, because of both its size—it was the biggest piece of ancient text ever known to have been recorded on metal—and its contents.

"The problem the archaeologists had was deciding how to open it. They spent nearly five years looking at the scroll before they came to a decision, and then they did the wrong thing. They sent it to the Manchester College of Technology where it was sawn in half lengthways using a very thin blade. That opened up the scroll completely and gave the researchers a series of curved sections of copper that they could study. Unfortunately, the Manchester people—and almost everyone else—failed to notice two things about the scroll.

"When it was discovered, the spaces between the sheets of rolled copper were filled with a hard-packed material, almost like fired clay. This was assumed to be nothing more than an accumulation of dust and debris over the millennia, but it wasn't. Nobody thought to check the conditions in the cave at Qumran where it was found. If they had, they'd have discovered that the soil in those caves was a very fine dust, almost a powder, which contains no silicon that would allow it to solidify. Even if the soil is dampened, it simply returns to powder when it dries out. Whoever had written the scroll had covered one side with a layer of clay before rolling it. And then they had fired it in a kiln to turn the clay into something almost as hard as pottery."

"Why? To protect the copper?"

"Oddly enough, most likely exactly the opposite. Most researchers now believe that the authors of the Copper Scroll expected the metal to corrode away, and their intention was to leave the text of the scroll imprinted on the clay. That was the other thing the Manchester team failed to register.

"The scroll is primarily written in Mishnaic Hebrew with a handful of Greek letters whose purpose and meaning is still unknown. In fact, there are fourteen Greek letters on the scroll, and the first ten of them spell out the name 'Akhenaten.' He was a pharaoh who ruled Egypt in about 1350 BC, and his main claim to fame is that he founded what was probably the world's first monotheistic religion. But the Copper Scroll dates from at least a millennium later than this, so why his name is on it remains a complete mystery."

"Why did the authors of the scroll go to such trouble?"

"Probably," Angela said, "because of the contents. It looks as though they wanted to make certain that the record would survive for as long as possible, much longer than a papyrus scroll might, for example. And the reason for their determination was because almost all that's on the Copper Scroll is a list of treasure, possibly that of the First Temple in Jerusalem and, if the quantities listed are correct, today it would be worth in excess of two billion pounds."

50

"So the Copper Scroll's really a treasure map, then?" Bronson asked.

"No, not a map, exactly. It's a list of sixty-four locations, sixty-three of which are supposed to be where large amounts—sometimes tons—of gold and silver are hidden. The sixty-fourth listing gives the location of a duplicate document that apparently provides additional details of the treasure and where it's been hidden. Some people think this might be what's become known as the Silver Scroll.

"The only snag with that is that nobody has any idea if the Silver Scroll exists or, if it does, where it might be found. The location given in the Copper Scroll simply says that the supporting document is to be found 'In the pit, adjoining on the north, in a hole opening northwards, and buried at its mouth,' which is hardly what you'd call a precise location."

"So what happened to the Copper Scroll?" Bronson asked.

"When Father de Vaux found out about it, he realized immediately that it was a flat contradiction of everything that he and his team had been proposing. An ascetic religious community could hardly be the custodians of—if the figures have been translated correctly—some twenty-six tons of gold and sixty-five tons of silver. So he did what academics and scientists usually do when presented with hard evidence that conflicts with their own cozy little world view. He declared that the Copper Scroll was a hoax, a forgery or a joke.

"None of these suggestions was convincing. If it wasn't a genuine document, you have to ask why the creators of the scroll went to so much trouble when they made it—I mean, why would they bother? Though we don't know a hell of a lot about any of the communities that existed in Judea during this period, it's never been suggested that any of them were great practical jokers. Even if they had been, why would they go to so much trouble to produce the scroll, and then hide it away in a remote cave where nobody would be likely to find it for hundreds or maybe even thousands of years? Don't forget, the Dead Sea Scrolls were found entirely by accident.

"But the real point is that the listing on the Copper Scroll is just that—a listing. Each item is recorded, with its location, but without any embellishment. It reads just like an inventory of goods, nothing more, and that does give it a kind of authentic feeling."

"And these people in Manchester just cut the thing in two?" Bronson said.

"Exactly. They failed to appreciate that the clay was at least as important as the copper and removed it as the first step. I don't know how they did it, but whatever technique they used also damaged the copper, so it was a kind of double-whammy. They'd probably have done better to leave the clay alone and remove the metal piece by piece. Instead, they coated the outside of the scroll in a strong adhesive and cut lengthways down it with a very thin saw-blade. That resulted in a couple of dozen curved sections of copper that the researchers could then start translating, but of course the very act of cutting the metal partially destroyed some of the text."

"Has any of the treasure been found?" Bronson asked. "I mean, that would validate the scroll, wouldn't it? It would immediately prove that the listing was genuine."

Angela sighed. "If only it was that easy. The locations specified in the scroll probably meant something at the start of the first millennium, but they mean almost nothing now. The listing contains things like: 'In the cave next to the fountain owned by the House of Hakkoz, dig six cubits: six gold bars.' That's fine if you know who 'Hakkoz' was, and where his fountain was located, but after two thousand years the chances of finding the treasure with a description as vague as that are pretty slim. And in fact, we do know something about this particular family or house, which is more than can be said for most of the names recorded on the Copper Scroll, because 'Hakkoz' is in the historical record. A family with that name were the treasurers of the Second Temple in Jerusalem, but frankly that doesn't help much, because we don't know where they lived and, of course, it could have been a completely different Hakkoz family that was referred to in the scroll."

Bronson stood up, stretched his aching back and walked across to the mini-bar to get another drink.

"But what I don't understand is what this has to do with the Silver Scroll and Moses' tablets of stone."

Angela took the glass he was holding out for her. "Look what the inscription says next. The reference to the Silver Scroll implies they hid it in a cistern some-where, and later in the text it states that—somewhere—they concealed some tablets. But not just any old tablets. They were 'the tablets of the temple of Jerusalem,' and that's really exciting. It also means that Yacoub could have been right—there's at least a possibility that these tablets could be the Mosaic Covenant. So this piece of Aramaic script, some of which was on the clay tab-let Margaret O'Connor found, is a description of three separate relics being hidden away—a copper scroll, a sec-ond scroll made of silver, and these Mosaic tablets. And now I think I know why, and I think I know when. The importance of one single word in that text has only just dawned on me."

"Which word?" Bronson asked, leaning forward.

"This one," Angela said, pointing.

"'Ben'?" Bronson asked.

"Yes. There's a very famous fortress not too far from here called Masada, which finally fell to the Romans in AD 73 after a long siege. The rebels holed up there were known as the Sicarii, and their leader was a man named Elazar Ben Ya'ir. *Ben*," she emphasized. "Neither of the dictionaries we've been using list proper names, and that could explain why we haven't been able to translate this word here." She pointed at a series of Aramaic characters on the laptop's screen. "I think that this text could be an actual description of the Copper Scroll being hidden in a cave at Qumran by a bunch of Sicarii who'd escaped from Masada just before the citadel fell. That would also explain why the Copper Scroll is so completely different to all the other Dead Sea Scrolls—it was never meant to be a part of the same collection.

"Think it through, Chris." Angela's hazel eyes were sparkling with excitement. "The Copper Scroll is completely different to the rest of the Dead Sea Scrolls. It was an inventory of hidden treasure: the other scrolls dealt almost exclusively with religious matters, most of them actually biblical texts. Absolutely the only feature it shares with them is the language inscribed on it—Hebrew—though even that's odd. The script on the Copper Scroll is Mishnaic Hebrew, a form of the language used to express in writing the oral traditions of the Torah, the Five Books of Moses." She leaned back in her chair and thought for a few seconds. "The only explanation that makes sense is that this scroll—the Copper Scroll—came from a completely different source."

Bronson nodded. Angela's logic was, as usual, compelling. "I know what you said before, but isn't it at least possible that the other objects—the 'scroll of silver' and the 'tablets of the temple'—were also hidden somewhere at Qumran?"

Angela shook her head. "I don't think so. If they'd hidden everything in one place, I would expect the inscription to say something like 'and at Qumran we hid the two scrolls and the tablets,' but the text describes hiding the first scroll and then goes on to talk about concealing the other objects. That suggests they hid one relic there and went somewhere else to hide the others."

She looked at Bronson. Her determination to solve this mystery was almost palpable.

"It's up to us to find out where they put them," she finished.

51

"Got it," Tony Baverstock muttered, running his eyes over the sheet of paper in front of him again.

The three men were in his room at the Tel Aviv hotel. Ever since they'd arrived in Israel, Baverstock had been poring over the translations of the Aramaic text he'd copied from the clay tablets.

"You've cracked it?" Charlie Hoxton asked. He put down a bottle of local Dancing Camel beer he'd bought that afternoon and walked across to the table where Baverstock had been working.

"I wondered at first if there might be three missing tablets, not just one, but if that were the case, the lines in the corners made no sense. So I tried to reassemble the tablets into a square and looked again at the inscription. The answer was childishly easy. You read the first word at the right-hand end of the top line of the first tablet, which is the one we don't have, of course."

Baverstock gestured at the scatter of papers on the table. He'd prepared four sheets of A4, and written the

English versions of the Aramaic inscriptions he'd managed to translate on three of them, then slid them into position. The fourth sheet, the one at the top right, was blank apart from a short line in the bottom left-hand corner, that mated with similar lines drawn on the other three pages.

"Then," Baverstock went on, "you read the word in the same position on the next three tablets, reading counterclockwise, of course. That gives you: 'by Elazar Ben,' so the first word, the missing word, is probably 'selected' or 'ordered' or something similar. The next word on the tablet that we don't have is almost certainly 'Ya'ir,' to complete the proper name of the leader of the Sicarii at Masada. But that word doesn't occur on the top line of the inscription. Instead, you take the first word from the line *below*, and repeat that process for each tablet. It's a very simple but clever code."

"Right, got that, I think," Hoxton muttered impatiently. "All clever stuff. But all I want to know is what the bloody tablets *say*."

"I already know what they say," Baverstock snapped, and handed over another page.

Hoxton carefully read what the ancient-language specialist had written down in block capitals.

"Very impressive, Tony," Hoxton nodded. "Now tell me what all that lot means. What are we actually looking for?"

"I would have thought it was obvious *what* the inscriptions refer to," Baverstock replied sharply. "The decoded text explicitly mentions the 'copper scroll' and 'scroll blank silver.'"

"But unless there are *two* copper scrolls, that relic has already been found," Dexter said.

Baverstock snorted. "That's the point. Look at the inscription, and you'll see that the discovery of the Copper Scroll at Qumran actually validates what's written on these tablets. That relic was found in Cave Three in 1952; the people who prepared these clay tablets put it in there. Look at the text."

Baverstock underlined the relevant passage with a pencil. "Let me just fill in a few of these blanks with my best guesses," he said, scribbling on the sheet. "Right. That reads something like: 'The copper scroll that we took from Ein-Gedi we have hidden in the cave of Hammad the place of the scrolls of . . .' The next word's missing, because it's on the fourth tablet. Then the text continues: 'beside the settlement known as *Ir-Tzadok B'Succaca.*' That's as clear a statement as you'll ever find describing the hiding of the Copper Scroll.

"I don't know what this word is here, between 'of' and 'beside,' but it presumably refers to either a place or a person. It might be Jericho or Jerusalem, say, or possibly the name of the person or tribe that owned the other scrolls. It's a pity we don't know what it is," Baverstock mused, "because it might once and for all solve the mystery of who actually wrote the Dead Sea Scrolls. But it's interesting that the inscription specifically states that the Copper Scroll came from Ein-Gedi."

"Where's that?"

"Ein-Gedi was an important Jewish settlement built around an oasis not far from the west side of the Dead Sea, fairly close to Qumran, in fact. And that gives us another clue—or rather a confirmation—that the people who prepared these tablets were members of the Sicarii. About the only raid on Ein-Gedi of any significance, according to the references I've found on the Internet, was in either AD 72 or 73, and was carried out by a raiding party of Sicarii from Masada. That ties in quite nicely with the first few words of the inscription because at that time the Sicarii were led by Elazar Ben Ya'ir. About seven hundred inhabitants of Ein-Gedi were slaughtered, and the raiders made off with whatever they could lay their hands on. It looks like one of the objects they found was the Copper Scroll, and another was the Silver Scroll."

Hoxton and Dexter were both studying the inscription while Baverstock offered his explanation.

"What about these 'tablets of the temple,'" Hoxton asked. "Did they come from Ein-Gedi as well? And what are they?"

Baverstock shook his head. "The inscription doesn't say that the Sicarii looted them, so it's possible they already owned them. The complete phrase probably states 'the tablets of the temple of Jerusalem.' Maybe they were decorative stone slabs, or perhaps they were tablets with prayers or something engraved on them. Whatever they were, they're not important to us. What we're after is the Silver Scroll."

"And the big question, of course," Hoxton said, "is where we start looking. This inscription says that the Copper Scroll was hidden at Qumran. Does that mean that the Silver Scroll was put there as well?"

"No," Baverstock said. "The two relics are referred to quite separately. The Copper Scroll was left in the cave at

Qumran, but the other scroll was concealed in a cistern somewhere else. At the moment, I'm not sure what the author of this inscription meant by the expression 'the place of something end of days.' The simplest interpretation would be 'the place of *the* end of days,' but I'll need to do a lot more research before I can tell you what he was referring to. And while I'm doing that, you'd better sort out the hardware we need. When we move, we'll probably have to move fast."

52

Bronson and Angela were heading southeast toward Jerusalem and the Dead Sea beyond.

Bronson wasn't entirely sure what he'd been expecting, but he was surprised at how fertile most of the land they were driving through seemed to be, at least the strip along the Mediterranean coast. He supposed he'd been anticipating a much more arid and desert-like environment, but in fact the only bit of Israel that really qualified as a desert was the narrowing triangle of land that poked south from the widest point of the country to the Gulf of Aqaba. This area, bounded by Rafah on the Mediterranean coast, the southern end of the Dead Sea and the Israeli coastal resort of Elat, comprised the Negev Desert, a hot, desolate and largely uninhabited tract of land.

"According to this map," Angela announced, sitting in the passenger seat with the document in question spread out on her lap, "we should reach the boundary of the West Bank in about ten minutes."

"Is it going to be a problem, getting in there?"

"It shouldn't be, no. We'll just need to watch out for the roadblocks and checkpoints—we're bound to have to pass through a few of them."

They got held up in the Jerusalem traffic, which was hardly surprising, given that a population of nearly one million people was crammed into the comparatively small area occupied by the city. Once clear of the city limits, the road turned northeast and ran just to the south of Jericho—the oldest fortified city in the world—before veering east toward the Jordanian border. When they reached the northern tip of the Dead Sea, Angela directed Bronson to take a right-hand turn, and they drove south, down through the Israeli kibbutz of Nahal Kalya, and on to the western side of the Dead Sea itself, the lowest point on the land surface of the earth. A short distance beyond that was Qumran.

The traffic was still fairly heavy, even after they'd escaped the snarling jams that plagued Jerusalem's crowded streets, and there were several cars both ahead and behind them. What Bronson hadn't noticed was that one of these vehicles—a white Peugeot with two occupants—had been behind them ever since they'd left Tel Aviv, never approaching closer than about seventy meters, but never losing sight of them.

As they'd driven through the territories of the West Bank, the scenery had changed, the generally fertile land to the west of Jerusalem giving way to a more rugged and inhospitable landscape, and as they approached Qumran it changed yet again, becoming ranges of rocky hills punctuated by deep gullies.

Qumran itself was located partway up a hillside, on a

plateau about a mile to the west of the shore of the Dead Sea, offering spectacular views over the flat desert below. The ancient site was partially surrounded by beige-brown hills, banded with subtle shades that indicated different levels of strata. Some of them were pockmarked by dark, mainly irregular oval, openings. It was, Bronson thought, an extraordinarily forbidding place.

"The caves?" he asked, pointing to the west when they reached the plateau.

"The famous caves," Angela agreed. "There are around two hundred and eighty in all, and most are between about one hundred yards and a mile from the settlement. Ancient remains have been found in nearly sixty of them, but the bulk of the Dead Sea Scrolls came from just eleven.

"The closest cave is only about fifty yards from the edge of the plateau, which is probably one reason why Father Roland de Vaux believed the inhabitants of Qumran were the authors of the scrolls. He simply didn't believe that the Essenes—or whoever it was who lived here—wouldn't have known about the caves and what was inside them. What could have been the remains of a series of shelves was found in one cave, and that led to a theory that the caves might have been used by the inhabitants of Qumran as their library. But, as I said before, there are a lot of problems with the whole Qumran-Essene hypothesis." She took off her hat and mopped her forehead with a handkerchief that was already damp.

The heat was brutal. They were both sweating after the climb up from where they'd parked their car, and Bronson was glad they'd stopped at a shop near their hotel in Tel Aviv and bought wide-brimmed hats and several bottles of water. Dehydration would be a very real possibility if they weren't careful.

"If the caves are that close," Bronson said, "it would be surprising if the people who lived here didn't know what was in them."

"Agreed, but that doesn't mean they were responsible for writing them. At best, they might perhaps have seen themselves as the guardians of the scrolls."

Bronson looked down at the desolate landscape below the plateau, the featureless desert relieved only by occasional patches of green where small groups of trees of some kind barely clung to life. In the middle distance, the Dead Sea was a slash of brilliant blue, a vivid band of color that hid the desolate reality of the lifeless waters.

"Hell on earth," he muttered, mopping his brow. "Why would anyone want to live in a place like this?"

Angela smiled at him. "At the start of the first millennium, this was an extremely fertile and very prosperous area," she said. "You see those trees down there?" She pointed at the scattering of green patches on the desert floor that Bronson had already noticed. "Those few trees are all that's now left of the old date plantations. History records that in biblical times the entire area stretching from the shores of the Dead Sea all the way up to Jericho and beyond was carpeted with date plantations. Jericho itself was known as the 'town of dates,' and Judean dates were enormously coveted, both as a foodstuff and for their alleged medicinal properties. In fact, the tree became accepted as a kind of national symbol of Judea. You can see that very easily on the *Judea Capta* coins the Romans minted after the fall of Jerusalem and the conquest of the country. They all show a date palm as part of the design on the reverse. But it wasn't just dates. This area also produced balsam, apparently the best in the entire region."

"And balsam is what, exactly?"

"It can be a lot of things, actually, from a flower up to a tree, but in Judea the word referred to a large shrub. It produced a sweet-smelling resin that had numerous applications in the ancient world, everything from medicine to perfume. And the region was also a major source of naturally occurring bitumen. One of the ancient names for the Dead Sea was *Lacus Asphaltites*, or Lake Asphaltitus, the lake of asphalt. That's a pretty strange name for any body of water, and the reason it was called that was because large clumps of bitumen—also known as asphalt—could be recovered from its waters."

"You mean bitumen and asphalt as in road-building? The black sticky stuff that holds everything together? What on earth use was that two thousand years ago?"

"For a seafaring nation it was vital, because they could use it to caulk the bottoms of their boats to make them watertight, but the Egyptians were the main customers of Dead Sea bitumen, and they had a very different use for it."

"What?" Bronson asked.

"As part of the embalming process, the skull was filled with molten bitumen and aromatic resins. Bearing in mind that by about 300 BC the population of Egypt was nudging seven million, there was a lot of embalming going on and the bitumen trade was highly lucrative. Take my word for it, this was a really important part of Judea."

Bronson looked round at the alien landscape. He found this hard to believe. To his untrained eyes, Qumran looked like nothing more than a confused jumble of stones, only some of which appeared to form walls. He thought of the turbulent history of the region, of the terrible privations the Essenes must have suffered as they tried to cope with the extreme heat, the lack of fresh water, and what had to be one of the most implacably hostile environments on the planet. To him, and despite the brilliant sunshine, Qumran and the whole surrounding area seemed sinister, perhaps even dangerous, in some indefinable way. He shivered slightly despite the baking temperature.

"Well, I'm ready to leave here and get back to the comforts of civilization," he said.

Angela frowned and put her hand on his arm. "I know how you feel—I don't like this place very much either. But before we leave here, I would just like to take a quick look in one or two of the caves, if you don't mind."

"Do we really have to?"

"Look, you could go back to the car and get the air con started, if you like, but I'm going on up. I've read about the caves and the Dead Sea Scrolls, and so much of my work has involved this area, but it's the first time I've ever been able to visit an ancient Judean site. We've come all this way, and I'm desperate to have a look inside a couple of them, just to see what they're like. I won't be long, Chris, I promise."

Bronson sighed. "I'd forgotten how determined you can be," he said with a smile. "I'll come with you. It'll be good to get out of the sun, even if it is only inside a cave for a few minutes."

53

Yacoub held his mobile phone to his ear and listened as Hassan provided a running commentary while he shadowed Bronson and Angela around the old settlement. Although he was used to the high temperatures in Morocco, Yacoub was finding the heat oppressive, even though he was wearing the lightest jacket and trousers he'd been able to find. He would have preferred a *jellaba* and *keffiyah*, but that style of dress would have marked him as an Arab, and in Israel that was something he wanted to avoid, because of the attention he might have attracted.

"They're acting just like tourists," Hassan reported. "They've walked around the ruins, but now it looks like they're going to leave."

There was silence for a few seconds; then the man spoke again. "No, they're not heading for the parking lot. It looks as if they're walking up to the caves."

"Right," Yacoub said. "There was a reference to Qumran on my tablet, so it's possible they think the relics are hidden somewhere here. Follow them, and try to get close enough to hear what they're saying. If they go into a cave, follow them in unless it's really small. You're just another tourist, and they don't know your face, so there should be no danger."

"And if they find the relics?"

"That's obvious," Yacoub said. "You kill them and then you call me."

"It's not very deep," Bronson remarked, as they stood up cautiously just inside the entrance to one of the caves close to the Qumran plateau. "It's more like a crack in the rock than a cave."

The entrance was about three feet wide and five high, but the cave itself only extended a matter of perhaps fifteen feet into the rock, and was completely empty.

"No," Angela agreed, "but there are some here that are a whole lot bigger than this. Let's take a look in one more. Then we'll go."

"Fine by me," Bronson said, leading the way out again.

Once they were outside, he looked around, then pointed farther up the slope. "That looks like it could be bigger," he said, indicating a much wider oval opening in the rock face perhaps eighty yards away. "Do you want to try that one?"

Angela looked up the hillside, and nodded. They were both finding it hard to talk in the oppressive heat.

As they set off, picking their path slowly and carefully across the hillside, Bronson glanced behind him. A man was making his way up the slope toward them, apparently heading for the one of the caves. There were actually numerous people visible at Qumran and on the surrounding hillsides, and nothing in particular to distinguish this lone tourist from any of the others swarming over the site, but the figure still concerned him.

When they'd emerged from the first small cave, the man had been heading directly toward them, or toward the cave itself, but now he had changed direction and was walking toward the larger cave Bronson and Angela were aiming for. Either that, or he was on an intercept course with them. Whichever it was, Bronson decided to watch him.

Angela reached the cave entrance first and stepped inside, Bronson following a few seconds behind, after taking a last glance down the slope. The man was over fifty yards away, still ambling, apparently quite innocently, toward them.

Motioning Angela to keep quiet, Bronson stepped back to the entrance and peered out, being careful to keep himself in the shadows. The approaching figure paused about thirty yards away and, as Bronson watched, he slipped a mobile phone into his jacket pocket.

"Oh, shit," Bronson muttered, as the man pulled a semiautomatic pistol out of his belt, extracted the magazine from the butt to check it, then replaced it and cocked the weapon. "There's a man heading this way with a pistol."

"A policeman?" Angela asked hopefully.

"Not in a million years," Bronson said. "Not carrying a weapon like that."

He looked around the cave. There were two short side

passages, one on either side of the entrance, each one
partially blocked by fallen rocks. Either of them could
be a death-trap, but only if the approaching man knew
somebody was hiding in them.

"Quickly," Bronson said, pointing to his right. "Go
into that passage and hide behind the rock-pile."

"Where will you be?"

"Down there, deeper in the cave. I'll make some noise
and try to attract his attention. As soon as he's passed
you, get out and go back to the car."

"No, Chris." Bronson could hear the fear in her voice.
"I'm not leaving you here."

"Please, Angela, just do it. I'll feel happier knowing
you're safely out of the way. And I'll follow you down as
quickly as I can."

Bronson turned and strode deeper into the musty
darkness. He didn't have a gun, but he did have a flashlight, something he'd remembered to buy in case they
did go into any of the caves. Now he switched it on,
thankful that he had it with him. Behind him, he heard
Angela's quick footsteps and glanced back to see her vanishing into the side tunnel.

And then the brilliant oval of light that marked the
cave entrance was partially obscured as a figure stepped
inside.

54

Bronson moved further back into the darkness.

The cave seemed to extend some distance into the hill-side, maybe thirty or forty yards, the gap between the walls narrowing sharply as he retreated further from the entrance. The floor was a carpet of rutted and uneven rocks, loose stones and patches of sand, the walls cracked and fractured slabs of tortured stone, and with frequent blind-ended passages just a few feet long. And it was hot. Really hot, the air still and almost heavy with the heat.

He looked back toward the entrance. The figure seemed to be motionless, just inside the cave, possibly waiting for his eyes to adjust to the darkness. But as Bronson looked, the man turned and took a couple of steps toward the passage where Angela had taken refuge. Quickly, Bronson kicked out, sending a few stones tumbling across the rocky floor, and switched on his flashlight again.

"That's interesting," he said, deliberately raising his voice as he shone the beam of the flashlight deeper into the cave. "Let's just check that out."

At the sound of his voice, the figure paused and swung round, his attention clearly drawn by the beam of light and Bronson's voice, and took a few silent steps further inside the cave.

Bronson saw the figure drawing his pistol, the unmistakable black shape a sinister extension of his right arm. The good news was that the man had moved away from Angela's hiding place, but the bad news was equally obvious—he was heading straight toward him. Knowing that his options and freedom of movement were becoming more restricted, Bronson took another step deeper into the cave and the narrowing darkness ahead.

He shone the beam of his flashlight around the end of the cave, looking for inspiration and either somewhere to hide or some kind of a distraction. But there were few hiding places and none that he liked the look of.

"That could be it, you know," he said loudly, keeping up the pretense that Angela was with him. "Stand here and hold the flashlight steady."

Bronson placed the flashlight on a rock, illuminating a small group of rocks on one side of the cave that almost looked as if they'd been piled up like a cairn.

Then he walked across in front of the flashlight beam, closing his eyes as he did so to preserve his night-vision. His action cast a huge shadow across the rock walls at the end of the cave and would, he hoped, ensure that their unwelcome visitor believed he was on the far side of the flashlight, looking for something in the gloom beyond.

But that wasn't where he was going to be. The moment he was clear of the beam he ducked down and turned back toward the cave entrance. Pressing himself close to the rock wall, he watched the approaching figure, now perhaps only fifteen or twenty feet away from him.

The man's attention seemed fixed on the flashlight beam, still shining on the pile of rocks. He was moving slowly and carefully toward the light, keeping to the center of the cave, and obviously taking great care not to make any noise.

Bronson needed to keep his attention there, looking toward the far end of the cavern. He picked up a couple of small pebbles and gently lobbed them behind him—an old trick but effective. They bounced across the floor of the cave somewhere near the stationary flashlight.

The figure kept walking, approaching slowly, and Bronson could clearly see the pistol held ready in the man's right hand.

Then there was a sudden scraping and clattering sound from the cavern entrance as Angela came scrambling out of her hiding place, heading toward the mouth of the cave.

The man spun round, raised his pistol and pulled the trigger.

The sound of the shot was thunderously loud in the confined space, and Bronson had no time to check if Angela had been hit: he was already moving, fast.

Even as the unidentified figure fired his weapon, Bronson started running. He pushed himself off the wall of the cave and barreled straight across the rocky floor, smashing into the man's stomach with his shoulder. The man gasped in surprise and pain and crashed down to the ground, the pistol spinning from his hand and landing with a clatter somewhere beyond him.

Bronson gave him no chance to recover. As they struggled together on the rock-strewn floor of the cave, he pulled his right arm free and smashed his fist into the man's solar plexus, driving the remaining air from his lungs. Then he brought his knee up—hard—into his groin. That wasn't perhaps the best of ideas, as Bronson's kneecap scraped against the rocks as he did so, sending stabbing pains shooting up his right leg.

But the man he'd attacked tensed, his hands grasping between his legs, so Bronson knew he'd incapacitated him, at least for a few seconds.

He scrambled to his feet and looked down at the bent figure lying moaning on the floor. The pistol. He knew he should grab the man's weapon, seize the advantage, but he couldn't see it anywhere. Sprinting to the back of the cave, he grabbed his flashlight and walked back to the groaning figure. He shone the beam all around him, looking for the telltale gleam of metal. Nothing. Then something caught his eye, something glinting dully, and he crossed over to investigate.

It *was* the pistol, but it had fallen between two rocks, into a near-vertical crack that was little wider than the weapon itself, and he couldn't slide his hand in far enough to even touch it. To get it out he'd need to either move one of the rocks—which might not be possible—or find something like a length of wood he could use as a lever. And he didn't have time for that, because the man he'd attacked was already up on his knees.

As the man got to his feet, Bronson aimed a punch at

his jaw, but missed as his target swayed backward. Then he heard an ominous click and saw the flash of steel as a switchblade snapped open. Bronson backed away as the man stabbed the knife toward his stomach, then swung at his assailant with the only weapon he had—his flashlight.

When he'd looked in the shop that morning, he'd seen several different kinds, but Bronson had always believed in buying quality whenever he could, and the one he'd chosen was a heavy-duty aluminum tube that held three large batteries. And at that moment he was delighted he'd spent the extra money.

The flashlight crashed into the side of the man's head and he collapsed face-down on the ground. Amazingly, the flashlight still worked, although Bronson could feel that there was now an impressive dent in one side of it.

He looked at the unmoving figure for a few seconds, then reached down and seized his shoulder, rolling the man onto his back. He shone the flashlight beam at his face for a moment, then nodded slowly.

"Now why am I not surprised?" he muttered.

He made one more unsuccessful attempt to retrieve the man's pistol from the crevice in the rocks, then walked out of the cave.

Angela was waiting about twenty yards away, hidden behind a rocky outcrop, a cricket-ball-sized stone clutched in her right hand.

"Thank God," she said, standing up as Bronson appeared. "Are you OK?"

He put his hand on her shoulder, then brushed her cheek gently where it was streaked with dirt.

"I'm fine. The shot didn't hit you?"

Angela shook her head. "I thought he was firing at you," she said. "What happened in there?"

Bronson grinned. "We had a difference of opinion, but fortunately I had the element of surprise."

"He's dead?"

"No, just sleeping it off. Just as well I had this flashlight."

Bronson pointed at her improvised weapon, which she'd dropped and was now tumbling away down the hillside. "What were you going to do with that?" he asked.

"I've no idea, but I wasn't going to leave you up here."

"Thanks," he said, suddenly feeling a lot happier. "Now, let's go. Just because I've dealt with one man doesn't mean there aren't others watching for us. We need to hurry."

55

"So we carry on?" Bronson asked, as they drove back to Tel Aviv.

They'd made it down the hillside to the parking lot in record time, and he was driving as quickly as the road conditions allowed. He had to assume that somebody had followed them from their Tel Aviv hotel to Qumran, and he intended to get back to the city and find another place to stay as soon as they could.

"Yes," Angela replied. "If anything, I'm even keener to find the Silver Scroll and the Mosaic Covenant, especially now that it seems others are after them as well. I think we can assume that, can't we?"

Bronson nodded, his eyes on the road.

"But what I can't work out," Angela continued, "is who—besides us—is looking for these relics."

"I don't know, but when I looked at that man's face up there in the cave I knew I'd seen him before. I've got a good memory for faces, and I'm sure he was one of the people in the photographs Margaret O'Connor took in the *souk* in Rabat, which means he was one of the Moroccan gang. I guess he'd been told to follow us and try to recover the clay tablet that Yacoub thought we'd got."

"You should have killed him. And then taken his gun."

Bronson shook his head. "Killing him would have been a really bad idea," he said. "Leaving him with a sore head means the Israeli police probably won't get involved, and that suits me just fine. I would have grabbed his pistol, but it fell into a crevice in the rocks and I couldn't get it out." Bronson paused and looked at Angela. "If we carry on, this could get pretty dangerous for us both. Are you prepared for that?"

"Yes," Angela said firmly. "We have to find that scroll."

That evening, Bronson and Angela ate an early dinner in Angela's room in the small hotel they'd hastily moved to when they returned from Qumran. Bronson had chosen a place well away from the center of Tel Aviv, where he hoped they'd be less likely to be spotted by any watchers, and where surveillance might be a little easier for him to detect. When they'd finished their meal, they had over an hour before their appointment with Yosef Ben Halevi, so they took another look at the translated inscription.

Angela logged on to the Internet and the Aramaic translation site she'd found earlier, and started inputting all the Aramaic words they could read, including those from the tablet stored in the museum in Paris, just in case there had been any mistranslations there, while Bronson looked up the same words in the printed Aramaic dictionary.

After about half an hour she sat back in her chair. "There seem to be only a few possible changes," she said, "and none of them are important, as far as I can see. In the first line we had 'settlement,' and that could also mean 'village' or 'group of habitations.' In the third line, 'concealed' could be 'hidden' or 'secreted.' In the fourth line the Web site suggests 'cavern' instead of 'cave,' and in the fifth line 'well' rather than 'cistern.' But those are all just different words that have almost the same meaning—it's simply a matter of interpretation."

Bronson cracked two miniatures of gin from the minibar, added tonic and gave one of the glasses to Angela.

"Any luck with the words you couldn't translate before?" he asked.

"Some, yes. I'd be prepared to bet that the first word on the right-hand side of the top line is 'Elazar,' part of the name Elazar Ben Ya'ir. And I did finally translate this word."

She pointed at "Gedi," which she'd written on the fourth line of their translation of the Rabat tablet, replacing the blank that had been there previously.

"Where did that come from?" Bronson asked.

"Because I couldn't find that word in any of the dictionaries, I wondered if it could be another proper name, like 'Elazar,' so I started looking for Aramaic versions of family and place names, and I found that."

"'Gedi'?" Bronson asked, pronouncing it like "Jedi" from the *Star Wars* films.

"Yes. But I don't know of any locations near Qumran with that name that seemed relevant. I'm hoping that Yosef might have some ideas when we meet him."

"And what about the word next to it? Any luck with that?"

Angela nodded slowly. "Yes," she said. "That translates as 'Mosheh,' the Aramaic version of 'Moses.' And that means the sentence now reads '*the tablets of* ----- *temple of Jerusalem* ----- ----- *Moses the* ----- -----.' If we take an educated guess at the blanks, the original probably said 'the tablets of the temple of Jerusalem and of Moses the great leader,' or maybe 'famous prophet,' something like that."

Angela paused and glanced at Bronson. "But what's obvious," she said, "is that Yacoub was right—the 'tablets of the temple' almost certainly mean the Mosaic Covenant, the stones of the prophet Moses, the original covenant struck between God and the Israelites."

Bronson shook his head. "You can't be serious."

"I'm not," Angela said, "but whoever wrote this inscription obviously believed it."

"The Ten Commandments."

"No. Everybody thinks there were ten commandments, but actually there weren't. It all depends which bit of the Bible you look at, but the best two lists are probably in Exodus 20 and Deuteronomy 5, and both these sources state that Moses came down from Mount Sinai with fourteen commandments."

" 'The Fourteen Commandments' doesn't have quite the same ring to it, does it?"

Angela smiled at him. "No, not really. But if you study all of Exodus, you can find over *six hundred* commandments, including gems like 'you shall not suffer a witch to live' and 'you shall never vex a stranger.' "

"When did Moses live, assuming he was a real person?"

"Well, as always with this kind of thing, the answer depends on which source you prefer. According to the Talmud, he was born in about 1400 BC to a Jewish woman named Jochebed. When the Pharaoh Feraun ordered that all newborn Hebrew boys be killed, she placed him in a basket of bulrushes and set him adrift on the Nile. He was found by members of the Egyptian royal family and adopted by them. That's the story we're all familiar with, and it's pretty much the same story as that of King Sargon of Akkad in the twenty-fourth century BC, except that the river he floated down was the Euphrates.

"There are a lot of different versions of the myths and legends surrounding Moses, but most Christians and Jews believe he was the man who led the Israelites out of slavery in Egypt and delivered them to the Promised Land in what is now Israel. What's quite interesting is how often Moses appears in source books of different religions. In Judaism, for example, he appears in a whole host of stories to be found in the Jewish apocrypha, as well as in the Mishnah and the Talmud. In the Christian Bible he appears in both the Old and New Testaments, and he's the single most dominant character in the Qur'an. The Mormons include the Book of Moses—that's supposed to be his translated writings—in their scriptural canon. On a lighter note, the founder of Scientology, L. Ron Hubbard, claimed that Moses owned a disintegrator pistol which was useful in fighting off the aliens who had invaded ancient Egypt."

Bronson shook his head. "But do you mean Moses

did exist or didn't? And if he didn't exist, how can the Mosaic Covenant ever have existed?"

"Nobody knows if Moses was a real flesh-and-blood man," Angela replied, "but the historical validity of the Mosaic Covenant is quite difficult to dispute, simply because there are so many contemporary references to the Ark, the gilded box in which it was housed. The Jews carried something around in it, something that was of crucial importance to their religion."

She looked at her watch and stood up. "We need to leave right now to meet Yosef." She paused. "Listen, Chris, we don't mention the clay tablets, and certainly not the Mosaic Covenant. In fact, just let me do most of the talking."

56

Their new hotel was near Namal Tel Aviv—the port at the northern end of the city—in a maze of one-way streets, but close to Rokach Avenue, which Bronson hoped would offer them a fast route out of Tel Aviv if the need ever arose. Angela had arranged to meet Yosef Ben Halevi in a bar just off Jabotinsky, near the Ha'Azma'ut Garden and the Hilton Beach.

It was only a short walk in the relative cool of the evening, but Bronson decided they'd take the pretty route, simply so he could satisfy himself that they weren't being followed. So instead of walking straight down Hayark or Ben Yehuda, they followed the Havakook pedestrian walkway past the Sheraton Beach, and then cut through the Hilton Hotel itself.

The city was buzzing, elegantly dressed couples strolling beside the deep blue waters of the Mediterranean as the sun sank below the western horizon in a chaotic artist's palette of primary colors—reds and blues and yellows. But once they entered the tangle of narrow streets to the east of the Ha'Azma'ut Garden—many named after the world's major cities, like Basel, Frankfurt and Prague—the scene changed. The hotels were replaced by white-painted low-rise apartment buildings, four and five stories high, walls studded with air-conditioning units, their ground floors a scattering of bars and shops, emblazoned with unfamiliar and exotic signs in Hebrew. Every available parking space seemed to be occupied, frustrating drivers who were nudging their slow-moving vehicles through the crowds of pedestrians as they looked for somewhere to stop.

"There it is," Bronson said, leading Angela across the street toward the bar. He'd spotted nobody taking the slightest interest in them.

For some reason, Bronson had been expecting that Yosef Ben Halevi would be a venerable professor, bent, gray and stooped, and probably well on the wrong side of sixty. The man who stood up to greet them as they walked into the small and quiet bar was none of these things. About thirty, tall, slim and handsome, and with a mop of curly black hair, he cut an almost Byronic figure.

"Angela," he said, his smile revealing perfect teeth, their whiteness dazzling against his tanned face.

Bronson disliked him immediately.

"Hullo, Yosef," Angela said, raising her face to be kissed on both cheeks. "This is Chris Bronson—he used to be my husband. Chris, this is Yosef Ben Halevi."

Ben Halevi turned to Angela as they all sat down. "You were very mysterious on the phone," he said. "What are you doing out here, and how can I help you?"

"It's a little complicated—" Angela began.

"Isn't it always?" Ben Halevi interrupted, with another brilliant smile.

"We're here on holiday, but I've also been asked to do some research into certain aspects of first-century Jewish history, because of some inscriptions that have turned up back in London."

"A working holiday, then?" Ben Halevi suggested, with a glance at Bronson.

"Exactly. Specifically, I'm looking into events that took place in the vicinity of Qumran, toward the end of the first century AD."

Yosef Ben Halevi nodded. "The Essenes and the Sicarii, I suppose? With a side order of Roman legions and the Emperors Nero, Vespasian and Titus, probably."

The man clearly knew his subject, and Bronson was glad that Angela had chosen such a quiet place to meet him. There were only a handful of people in the bar, and they could talk freely at their corner table without any danger of being overheard.

Angela nodded. "One of the things that puzzles me is the word 'Gedi,' which seems to be a proper name, or perhaps part of one. Does that ring any bells with you?"

"Certainly. It depends on the context, obviously, but the most obvious answer is that it's a reference to Ein-Gedi. And, if it is, that's a probable link to the Sicarii. Where did you come across it?"

"It's part of an inscription we unearthed," Angela said smoothly.

"Right, Ein-Gedi," Ben Halevi said. "It's a very fertile oasis lying to the west of the Dead Sea, what the ancients used to call Lake Asphaltitus, not far from both Qumran and Masada."

"Only an oasis?" Bronson said. "That's not very exciting."

"It's not *only* an oasis. It's been mentioned numerous times in the Bible, particularly in Chronicles, Ezekiel and Joshua. It even gets a probable name-check in the Song of Solomon—Ein-Gedi is the most obvious interpretation of the word 'Engaddi' that occurs in one verse—and allegedly King David hid there when he was being pursued by Saul. It was a really important place throughout quite a long period of Jewish history."

"And the Sicarii?"

"I was just getting to that. According to Josephus— you've heard of him, I hope—while the Romans were actually besieging Masada, some of the garrison of Sicarii managed to slip out and launch a raid on the Jewish settlement at Ein-Gedi. It was a major attack, and they killed over seven hundred people. You have to remember that at this period in history Jews fighting other Jews wasn't that uncommon.

"Not much is known about the inhabitants of Ein-Gedi at the time, but the oasis must have been reasonably prosperous to have been able to support that many people. Presumably the Sicarii were looking for food or weapons, that kind of thing, to help them in their fight against the Roman forces encircling Masada. Of course," Ben Halevi finished, "it didn't do them any good, because the citadel fell not that long afterward, and all the Sicarii there perished."

"That's interesting, Yosef," Angela said, making a mental note, then changed the subject. "We're also interested in the background to the story of the Mosaic Covenant. For Chris's benefit, could you explain a bit about that as well?"

"The Mosaic Covenant?" Ben Halevi said, looking closely at Angela—too closely for Bronson's liking. "Right. Well, according to your Bible—the Old Testament, obviously—one of the most sacred objects owned by the Israelites was the Ark of the Covenant, which was stored in several different sanctuaries in Judea over the years, including Shiloh and Shechem. When Jerusalem was captured by King David, he decided to build a permanent resting place for the relic there, and the Temple Mount in the old part of the city was the obvious choice.

"Solomon was the second son of David, and ascended to the throne as King of Israel in 961 BC. He continued the work his father had started, and completed the temple in 957 BC. The building was not only the home of the Ark itself, which had its own special room there called the *devir*, or holy of holies, but also a place of worship for the people. According to legend, though the temple was fairly small, it had a courtyard large enough to accommodate a substantial number of worshippers. It was apparently constructed primarily of cedar, but with a lot of gold ornamentation inside. This became known as the Temple of Solomon, and later as the First Temple. It lasted for some three hundred and seventy years until Nebuchadnezzar, king of Chaldea, razed Jerusalem to the ground and completely destroyed the building. The

Ark of the Covenant vanished from the historical record some time during this period."

"What was the Ark made of?" Bronson asked. "Gold, I suppose?"

Ben Halevi shook his head. "Most accounts state that it appeared to be gold, but we believe it was actually made of acacia wood that was then covered in gold leaf. It was apparently very highly decorated, with an ornamented lid and rings on the sides that allowed it to be carried using poles thrust through them. If that description was correct, the chances are that the wood had rotted and the Ark itself might well have disintegrated by this time, so it may not have been stolen.

"Anyway," Ben Halevi continued, "about half a century later, work started on erecting the Second Temple, which was probably similar in design to the Temple of Solomon, but more modest in scale. It was destroyed in AD 70 by the Romans—and as you probably know there's been no Jewish temple on the Mount since then, and that's a problem for many Jews."

Ben Halevi gestured toward the waiter, who brought over a bottle of red wine and refilled their glasses.

"You mean because you don't have a place to worship?" Bronson asked.

Ben Halevi shook his head. "Not just that, though obviously it's an important point. No, to fully understand why the lack of a temple is so important, you have to delve into your Old Testament, into the Book of Revelation, in fact. You're familiar with it, I presume?" he asked, another smile slowly becoming visible.

Bronson and Angela both shook their heads.

"Shame on you," Ben Halevi said lightly. "Let me explain. The Book of Revelation was allegedly written by a man called John of Patmos, who was possibly also the Apostle John, because he was believed to have been exiled to the island of Patmos in the Aegean late in the first century AD. It's probably the most difficult book in your Bible to understand, because it's entirely apocalyptic, all to do with the Second Coming and the end of the world, which is why early versions of the book were known as 'The Apocalypse of John.' Now, the truth is that nobody knows if the author was the Apostle John or somebody completely different, just as nobody knows if the man who wrote it was a true visionary, a seer, who was accurately describing visions and images sent to him by God, or just a harmless loony who'd flipped from living on a sun-baked rock in the Aegean surrounded by goats.

"The trouble is that a lot of people have taken what's written in the Book of Revelation as the gospel truth, literally believing every word. Predictably enough, most of these fundamentalist believers live in America, a nice long distance away from us on the front line in Israel, but there are quite a lot of people here who share the same beliefs. And one of the crucial ideas culled from Revelation is that there will be a Second Coming, a day of Apocalypse, when Jesus will return to the earth, but this time as a warrior, not a messiah, and His arrival will herald the final battle between good and evil. After that battle, which the forces of good will win—obviously—Jesus will reign over a peaceful earth for a thousand years."

"Do you believe that stuff?" Bronson asked, his expression openly skeptical.

"I'm a Jew," Ben Halevi replied. "I'm just reminding you of what *your* Bible says. *My* beliefs are irrelevant."

"But do you?" Bronson persisted.

"Since you ask, no, but it's what the majority believes that's important, and you'd be surprised how many people do expect the world to end pretty much as Revelation foretells."

"And this revolves around the Third Temple?" Angela suggested.

"Exactly. According to one interpretation of Revelation—and not everyone agrees with this—Jesus will only return to earth when the Jews possess all of the Holy Land. The closest we came to that was in 1967 when our soldiers captured Jerusalem, and for the first time in almost two millennia we regained control of the Western Wall and the Temple Mount itself. But control of the Mount was almost immediately handed back to the Muslims by Moshe Dayan."

"Why on earth did he do that?"

"Well, Dayan was the Minister of Defense at the time, so the decision was his, and it's even possible to argue that it was the *right* decision. The Temple Mount was already occupied by the Dome of the Rock and the Al-Aqsa Mosque, two of the holiest sites in Islam. If Israel had retained control of the Mount, there would have been enormous pressure to destroy these buildings in order to erect the Third Temple, and if that had been done, we would almost certainly have found ourselves at war with the entire Muslim world, a war we probably wouldn't have been able to win. What Dayan did brought at least a measure of peace—or the hope of it, anyway."

He sighed, and Bronson knew that he was thinking of the recent terrible unrest and the continuing battles between the Palestinians and Israelis.

Angela leaned forward slightly and looked at Ben Halevi.

"Finally, Yosef, what's your opinion of the Copper Scroll? Do you think it's a genuine listing of some treasures, or just a hoax?"

The Israeli smiled slightly. "That's fairly easy to answer," he said. "I think most researchers are satisfied that the Copper Scroll is a real listing of real treasure. It's also been suggested that it was only ever intended to record the hiding places of the treasure for a short time, the idea being that the objects would be recovered within a matter of months or a few years at the latest after being hidden. But if that is the case, why didn't the authors of the scroll write it on papyrus instead? Why would they take such enormous time and trouble to prepare a document apparently intended to last for eternity, if the text they were going to produce would only be applicable for a few years?

"And if the Copper Scroll *is* a real listing, that suggests that the reference to another document—the so-called Silver Scroll—is also real, in which case the short-term hiding place argument takes another hit. Why produce the Copper Scroll *and* another, possibly silver, scroll, to record something so ephemeral? Nobody has so far offered a convincing reason for that discrepancy.

"The only believable suggestion I've heard was that the two scrolls would have to be read together to decipher what was meant. In other words, the Silver Scroll would positively identify the area where something was hidden, and then the detailed reference on the Copper Scroll would lead you to the exact hiding place. In that case, it would make sense to hide the two scrolls in separate locations, which we know was done, because there's nothing like the Silver Scroll concealed anywhere at Qumran."

Bronson and Angela exchanged glances. That was a sort of confirmation of what they had deduced from the inscription on the clay tablets.

"To some extent," Ben Halevi finished, "that argument is supported by the fact that the Copper Scroll wasn't really hidden—it was just placed in a cave with a lot of other scrolls. And it *does* refer to the Silver Scroll being properly concealed somewhere. So does it exist? I have no idea, but we know the Copper Scroll is real, and the consensus is that the record is genuine, so that makes me think that there could well be a second document, another scroll, hidden somewhere. Unfortunately, we've not the slightest idea where."

He glanced at his watch, got to his feet, shook Bronson's hand and kissed Angela. "It's late and I have to work tomorrow," he said. "Reading between the lines, it sounds to me as if you're on the track of something interesting, maybe even significant. Please keep in touch with me, and whatever you need, I'll do my very best to help you."

57

"Where are they?" Yacoub asked, his voice quiet and controlled.

"They've checked out of their hotel."

"I already know that, Musab," the man with the frozen face said, his voice still calm. "That wasn't what I asked you. Where are they now?"

Musab—one of the three men Yacoub had selected to accompany him to Israel for the operation—looked away, unable to hold his boss's gaze. "I don't know, Yacoub," he admitted. "I didn't expect them to leave their hotel, because they'd booked their rooms for a week."

"What are you doing about it?"

"I've got one of our contacts checking every hotel in Tel Aviv. We'll find them, I promise."

For a few seconds Yacoub didn't reply, just settled his lopsided gaze on his subordinate. "I know you will," he said finally. "What concerns me is how long it will take. If we don't know where they are, we can't know what they're doing, and we've come too far to lose them now."

"As soon as I hear, Yacoub, I'll tell you."

"And suppose they've moved to Jerusalem? Or Haifa? Or somewhere else in Israel? Or left the country and gone elsewhere in the Middle East? What then?"

Musab looked noticeably paler. Obviously not all of these possibilities had occurred to him.

"I want them found, Musab, and I want them found right now. And then we'll grab them, because they might already have found the relics. Even if they haven't, it's time they told us what they know. Do you understand?"

The other man nodded enthusiastically. "I'll get my man to start checking other locations straightaway."

Yacoub turned to the other man standing beside the door of their hotel room. "Go and get the car," he ordered. "We'll take a drive around the city and see if we can spot them. Most of the hotels are on the west side, near the sea."

"Do you want me to come as well?" Hassan asked. He was lying on the bed, an ice-pack pressed to the side of his head where Bronson had caught him with the heavy flashlight.

"No," Yacoub replied. "Stay where you are." He looked back at Musab. "When you track them down, call my mobile."

"I'll find them within the hour, I promise."

"I hope you do, because now your life depends on it. But I'll be generous. I'll give you ninety minutes."

As Musab turned away to reach for the telephone, his hands were trembling.

58

"Did that help?" Bronson asked.

They had left the small bar and were walking slowly back toward their hotel through the streets of Tel Aviv. The night was warm and the city busy, dozens of people still crowding the pavements, walking purposefully or standing in groups and talking outside the bars. Fleetingly, Bronson wished he was simply in Israel on holiday; that he and Angela were carelessly strolling back to their hotel after a romantic meal. Instead, he was watching the shadows for armed men while the two of them tried to work out where to start looking for a couple of almost mythical relics lost to the world for over two millennia.

"It's starting to make a bit more sense now," Angela told him. "I think that when the Sicarii raided Ein-Gedi, they found something more than just food and supplies, and that's what the inscription is telling us. It's at least possible that the Sicarii found *all* of the relics referred to in the clay tablets when they mounted that raid. There were contemporary accounts of important treasures being moved out of Jerusalem for safekeeping during the wars with the Romans. As Yosef said, Ein-Gedi was an important—perhaps even the most important—Jewish settlement close to the city during this period, so maybe it was chosen to hold various objects for safekeeping. But before they could be restored to the temple in Jerusalem or wherever they came from, the Sicarii stormed the oasis and stole everything they could lay their hands on. And according to the coded inscription we've deciphered on these clay tablets, that explicitly included the Copper Scroll as well as the Silver Scroll, and the tablets of the temple of Jerusalem."

"So we're on the right track?" Bronson asked.

"Definitely. All we have to do now is work out where to start looking."

For a minute or so they walked on in silence, Angela lost in thought while Bronson kept up his scan of the area, checking for any possible surveillance—or worse. But wherever he looked, the people appeared reassuringly normal and nonthreatening, and he slowly began to relax. Maybe their unannounced move to a different hotel had worked, and they'd thrown Yacoub's men—because Bronson was certain he'd recognized their attacker at Qumran—off the scent.

His comfortable feeling only lasted until they reached Nordau Avenue, the wide boulevard that runs eastwards from the northern end of the Ha'Azma'ut Garden.

They crossed to the tree-lined central reservation, and then had to stop at the edge of the highway to allow a number of cars to pass. The last one in the line was a white Peugeot, traveling quite slowly, the shapes of a driver and front-seat passenger dimly visible in the soft glow of the street lighting.

When the vehicle passed directly in front of them, Bronson glanced incuriously at the driver, a swarthy, black-haired man he knew he'd never seen before. Then the passenger leaned forward, talking animatedly on a mobile phone. Bronson saw his face quite clearly, at the same moment as the man in the car turned to stare at him, and for the briefest of instants their eyes locked. And then the car was past them.

"Christ," Bronson said, reeling backward and grabbing Angela's arm. "That's bloody Yacoub!"

"Oh, God, no," Angela moaned. "But he's dead. How could it be?"

Even as they turned and ran, Bronson heard the sudden squeal of tires from behind them as the Peugeot slewed to a stop. And then a burst of shouts in Arabic, and the sound of running feet pounding across the pavement toward them.

"Wait!" Angela shouted as they reached the south side of Nordau Avenue.

"What?" Bronson glanced at her, then stared back the way they'd come. Their pursuer—he could only see one figure, and he was sure it wasn't Yacoub—was no more than fifty yards away.

Angela grabbed his arm, kicked off one of her high heels, then bent down and ripped off the other.

As she did so, a shot rang out, the bullet smashing into the wall of the building just inches above their heads, then ricocheted away into the darkness. The flat crack of the shot echoed from the concrete canyons that surrounded them, seeming to still the noises of the night.

"Jesus," Bronson muttered.

"Let's go," Angela yelled, dropping the shoe onto the pavement.

A hundred yards behind them, Yacoub ran around the Peugeot and dropped down into the driver's seat. Slamming the door closed, he rammed the gear lever into first and accelerated hard down the road. At the first junction, he wrenched the steering wheel to the left, shooting out in front of an approaching car, whose driver sounded a long irritated blast on his horn. Yacoub ignored the noise as he powered along Dizengoff, his attention entirely focused on finding the next left turn so he could cut off the fleeing pair.

Musab had been as good as his word. His contact had identified the hotel Bronson and the woman had checked into, and he'd telephoned the information to Yacoub just before the hour was up. Bizarrely, Yacoub had actually been on his way to the hotel, talking to Musab on his mobile, when he'd glanced through the windscreen and seen Bronson and the woman standing at the side of the road right in front of him.

Yacoub didn't know the area, but he guessed that if he turned left three times, he should end up in front of his quarry. The first street he came to—Basel—was no-entry, with a line of cars waiting to come out of it, but the next was Jabotinsky, another wide boulevard. He turned left, going more slowly, then left again, entering the maze of narrow streets that lay behind the major roads.

He had to be in the right area now.

Screams and shouts of alarm greeted the sound of the shot and, as Bronson and Angela raced down Zangwill, people were yelling and starting to run. Confusion and panic spread through the crowd, which Bronson hoped might actually help them get away. Chasing two running figures through a busy street was one thing—doing the same thing when *everyone* in the street was running was an entirely different matter.

Zangwill is a one-way street, and three cars were heading down it, straight toward them, but slowing down rapidly as frightened pedestrians started spilling out into the road, trying to work out where the shot had come from.

"This way," Bronson said, pointing. They weaved around the front of the first car, which had now stopped, onto the pavement on the left-hand side of the street. A group of people spilled out of a bar right in front of them, attracted by the noise outside. Bronson cannoned into one of the men, knocking him to the ground, but he barely even paused, just glanced back to make sure Angela was keeping up, then ran on.

The man chasing them had a pistol, and had already shown that he wasn't afraid to use it. Bronson knew that their only hope of escape was to keep moving, to keep ahead of him. That wasn't much of a plan, he realized, but right then he hadn't got any better ideas. And he was worried about Angela. She was keeping up with him, but in bare feet it would only take a sharp stone or a piece of glass on the pavement to effectively cripple her. He had to do something to either get them away from Yacoub's man or somehow disarm him.

At least their pursuer hadn't fired at them again. Perhaps there was a measure of safety in numbers, in being a part of the crowd. Maybe he didn't want to risk hitting an innocent bystander—or more likely he'd hidden his weapon to avoid being identified as the gunman. There might be Israeli police or soldiers in the area who would have little compunction in gunning down an obviously armed man on a crowded street.

Bronson looked behind them, searching for their pursuer, but at that moment, in the mêlée of running figures in the street, he couldn't see him. That might work to their advantage, or at least give them a few moments' respite.

"In here," Bronson panted, his voice harsh and strained. He grabbed Angela's arm and pulled her into a bar.

About a dozen young Israelis, male and female, stared at them as they crashed in through the door.

Angela bent forward, hands on her thighs, panting and gasping for breath. Bronson span back, staring through the front windows of the bar as he scanned the street for any sign of the gunman. The scene outside was chaotic, figures running and moving in all directions, and for a few moments he thought they'd managed to evade the man.

Then he saw him, barely thirty yards away, heading straight toward the door of the bar, a slight smile crossing his face as he saw Bronson.

Bronson span round, grabbed Angela by the arm and ran, almost dragging her, to the back of the bar. There was an archway on the right-hand side, an enamel plaque screwed to the wall beside it bearing two words, one definitely Hebrew, the other what looked like Arabic. He couldn't read either of them, but directly below that plaque was another one, much smaller, that displayed two stick figures, one wearing a dress—the universal sign for a toilet.

"Get in there," he said urgently, "and lock the door."

Angela shook her head. "I'm coming with you," she panted.

"Don't argue. I can run faster without you. I'll go out the back door. Once it's quiet, get out of here and run to the Hilton. I'll meet you there."

He gave Angela a shove that sent her through the archway, then sprinted for the rear door of the bar. Bronson hit the safety bar with his foot as he reached the door. It crashed open, swinging back on squeaking hinges, and he dashed through and into the space behind the building. It was a small yard, discolored stone walls on three sides, crates of empty bottles stacked against them. To his right, a half-open door beckoned, an alleyway beyond it. He looked back into the bar as he turned for the door, ready to run.

The front door of the bar swung open and the black-haired man strode in, his hand already reaching inside his jacket.

Bronson instinctively ducked and dived to his right. Then the window in the door exploded outward as a bullet plowed through it, the sound of shattering glass completely inaudible against the crashing echo of the shot. Screams and yells of terror rang out from the bar. Bronson risked a single glance back to ensure the man was still running toward him, then took to his heels. At all costs he had to draw the thug away from Angela.

He raced through the door in the side wall and looked both ways. He had no choice. The alley was blind-ended, running down the side of the bar and ending in a ten-foot brick wall at the far end. Bronson ran right, back toward the street. Behind him, another shot rang out as his pursuer burst out of the rear door of the bar, the bullet hitting the wall so close to Bronson that he was showered with stone chips.

Crowds of people milled around on the street, but Bronson knew he couldn't risk trying to hide in some group. He had no doubt Yacoub's man would just shoot him down, and probably anyone else who got in his way.

He forced his way through the mass of humanity, dodging left and right, then broke free, running hard toward the end of the road.

Yacoub distinctly heard the sound of two shots, very close together, as he swung the Peugeot left into Basel to head back toward the coast. Ahead of him he saw running figures, men and women fleeing in panic into the street from the road on his right, dodging through the traffic as they desperately sought sanctuary.

In the distance he could hear the nerve-jangling wailing of sirens. Somebody—probably one of the bar or restaurant staff—had made a call, and Yacoub knew they had just minutes to finish this, before the whole area would be swarming with police.

This had to be where Bronson and the woman had fled. With any luck, his man would act as a beater, driving the prey toward the hunter. All he had to do was sit there and wait for them. Bronson was expendable—he'd told his man that—but he wanted the Lewis woman alive. He could, he was sure, persuade her to tell him whatever he wanted to know. A cruel, lopsided smile appeared on his face as he considered that pleasurable prospect, then vanished. First, they had to find and seize her.

He slowed down, like the drivers of the vehicles in front of him, and pulled in to the side of the road. But he stayed in the car. He knew what a distinctive figure he cut, how memorable; he would only show himself if there was no alternative.

Almost without conscious thought, while his eyes were still searching the running people around him, Yacoub lowered the driver's door window, then reached inside his jacket and took out his pistol. He pulled back the slide and then let it run forward, stripping the first cartridge from the magazine and chambering it. He clicked off the safety catch on the left side of the frame and then held the weapon loosely in his right hand, below the level of the side window, and just watched and waited.

Bronson reached the T-junction at the end of the street and broke right, heading toward Hayark, the road that ran parallel to the coast. All around him, people were running in panic, but he couldn't risk slowing down. He had no idea how close his pursuer was behind him, and daren't look round for fear he'd trip or stumble or simply crash into someone or something.

He skirted a group of teenagers who were standing and staring back down the road, reached the opposite pavement and ran harder.

Yacoub saw Bronson emerge from the street on his right and start running along the road. He raised the pistol, but then lowered it when he realized his target was much too far away to risk a shot.

He looked to the right, expecting to see Angela Lewis following Bronson, but there was no sign of her. Then he saw his man sprinting into view barely fifty yards away, pistol clutched in his right hand, and Yacoub guessed what must have happened. Lewis had given him the slip, and it was Lewis they wanted, not Bronson.

Yacoub leaned out of the car window and waved, simultaneously sounding the car horn and flashing the headlights. His man glanced to his left, saw the car and immediately changed direction, hiding his pistol as he ran. He stopped, panting, beside the car door and bent down.

"Where's the girl?" Yacoub demanded.

"I was chasing her. She was with Bronson."

"No, she wasn't, you idiot. I've just seen Bronson and he was definitely by himself. Go back the way you came. She must be hiding somewhere down that street."

"The bar. The last time I saw them both, she was running into a bar with Bronson."

"Right. Go back there," Yacoub ordered, "and find her."

"What about Bronson?"

"Leave him. Just find the woman."

Some seventy yards further along the road, Bronson was crouched down between two parked cars, staring back the way he'd come. He'd finally looked behind him, and for the first time since he'd started running, he couldn't see any sign of pursuit. There were people all over the road, but the man who'd been chasing him was nowhere in sight.

The thug had definitely been behind him when he ran out of the bar. Unless he'd managed to lose him in the crowds, there was only one explanation that made sense. They wanted to kill him, but they were trying to snatch Angela. The gunman must have seen she was no longer running with him, and had gone back to find her.

For a few seconds Bronson wrestled with indecision. He'd told Angela to get out of the bar and make for the Hilton Hotel, but suppose she hadn't managed to get away? Suppose Yacoub and his man were even then dragging her screaming out of the bar and into a car?

There was only one thing he could do.

Bronson took a final look round the street, then stood up and started running as hard as he could back down the road, back toward Zangwill and the bar where he'd left Angela.

Yacoub was looking the wrong way, watching his man run back the way he'd come; he never saw Bronson sprint past on the opposite side of the road.

The noise of the sirens was now much louder, and as

he glanced in his mirrors he saw the first police car swing into the street behind him, blue lights flashing, and accelerate down the road. He waited until it had passed and turned down the road opposite, then eased the Peugeot out from the curb and drove sedately along Basel to the end, where he swung left, away from the commotion.

Bronson slowed to a trot as he neared the bar. A few minutes had passed since the last shot had been fired, and the mood of the crowd seemed calmer now the immediate danger from the lone gunman appeared to have passed. Bronson didn't want to attract any unwelcome attention by running, though every fiber of his body was urging him to hurry.

Two police cars screeched to a halt, blocking the road. Blue-uniformed officers piled out, weapons in hand, to be immediately surrounded by gesticulating crowds of people. Bronson ignored them and walked calmly past, stopping a few yards from the bar.

The establishment appeared to be almost empty, just a couple of people standing near the door and peering out. But then Bronson suddenly spotted Yacoub's thug walking out of the alleyway, empty-handed. And at the same moment the Moroccan saw him, and then the armed police just a few yards away.

For a long moment, the two men held each other's gaze. Then, as somebody in the crowd raised a shout and pointed at the Moroccan, Bronson saw the man drawing his weapon, the black muzzle of the pistol swinging toward him.

People ran, terrified by the sight of the automatic pis-

tol. Bronson span round, ran a few steps and dodged behind a parked car—though he knew the thin steel would
offer little protection against a high-velocity round.
He dropped flat, making himself as small a target as he
could.

The Moroccan fired, the copper-jacketed bullet
smashing through the back window and the rear door. It
hit the tarmac less than a foot from Bronson's head and
whined away into the night.

Even before the sound of the shot had died away, the
man fired again, this time over the heads of the group
of people still crowded round the police cars. Everyone
ducked for cover, even the armed officers, and by the
time they recovered, the gunman was fifty yards away and
running hard down the road.

The police couldn't fire at him because of the number
of civilians still crowding the street, and he was in any
case already well out of pistol range. The Israeli police
cars were facing in the wrong direction, and the three
officers who gave chase were encumbered with bullet-
proof vests and heavy utility belts. It was going to be a
very one-sided race.

But as the Moroccan reached the end of the street, another police car swung round the corner and braked to a
stop. Bronson saw the gunman raise his weapon and snap
off a quick shot at the vehicle as he ran, but then two Israeli police officers stepped out of the car, pistols raised,
and a volley of shots rang out. The Moroccan appeared
to stumble, then fell forward heavily onto the unyielding
tarmac surface of the road and lay still.

The officers approached him cautiously, pistols aimed

at the unmoving figure. One kicked out at an object lying beside the Moroccan—presumably the man's pistol—then pressed his own weapon into the man's back as his companion snapped handcuffs onto his wrists. Then they stepped back and holstered their weapons. From their actions Bronson knew that the gunman was either dead or very badly wounded.

From the vantage point he'd selected, a hundred yards away at the eastern end of Basel, Yacoub sat in the driving seat of the Peugeot hire car and dispassionately watched the last act of the drama unfold. The moment his man pointed his weapon at the Israeli police car, Yacoub knew he was doomed. He should have just run on past the vehicle and kept his pistol out of sight. It was a stupid mistake, and he had paid for it with his life.

And no doubt now Bronson and the woman would change hotels once more. Musab and his contacts would just have to track them down yet again. But, Yacoub reflected, he seemed to be getting quite good at doing that.

Bronson didn't care about Yacoub or his gunman. All he was worried about was Angela.

He pushed his way into the bar. The two Israelis inside looked at him, but didn't try to stop him. Something in his face must have told them that trying to do so would be a very bad idea. He walked into the toilets and opened all the doors. There was nobody inside, but on the floor of one of the female cubicles he found a smear of blood.

Bronson turned around and walked out of the bar,

back into the street. Had she escaped? Was she even then waiting for him at the Hilton? Or had Yacoub's thug found her, dragged her out of the bar and then killed her, dumping her body in the yard at the rear? That appalling thought stayed with Bronson as he strode down the adjacent alleyway and stepped into the yard.

Shards of broken glass glittered like discarded jewels in the light from the bar, but otherwise the small open space looked exactly as it had before. Bronson heaved a sigh of relief. He'd seen Yacoub's man walking out of the alleyway, so if Angela's body wasn't in the bar or back there in the yard, she had to be still alive—somewhere.

He jogged back to the street and looked round again. He needed to get to the Hilton, and quickly.

He'd barely taken a dozen steps before he heard her calling his name.

"Chris!"

He turned and saw her. Her clothes were disheveled, her face smeared with dust and sweat and tears and her feet were bare, but he still thought she was the most beautiful thing he'd ever seen.

"My God, Angela." He stepped forward and pulled her to him. "You're safe."

"I am now," she muttered, burying her face in his shoulder. For a long moment they stood locked in embrace, oblivious to the crowds of people milling around them.

"The Hilton?" Bronson asked gently, as Angela eased back.

"I couldn't get there," she said. "I think I must

have trodden on a piece of glass somewhere. My foot's agony."

That explained the blood on the floor of the cubicle.

"Can you walk?" he asked.

"Not far, and not fast," Angela said.

Bronson glanced round. The street was full of people, and there were now four police vehicles and at least a dozen armed officers standing there. Angela would probably be as safe in that place as anywhere in Tel Aviv.

"Over there," Bronson said, pointing to a still-open bar with several vacant tables inside.

Angela wrapped her arm around his shoulders and hobbled over to the door. He pushed it open and pulled out a chair for her to sit on. A waiter walked over and Bronson ordered a brandy.

"You stay here," he said, standing up to leave. "I'll go and get the car."

"Good. I can't wait to climb into bed."

Bronson shook his head. "Sorry, but you won't be sleeping anywhere in Tel Aviv tonight. We have to get out of here, and quickly. It was no coincidence that Yacoub and his tame gunman pitched up here this evening. Somehow they knew which hotel we'd moved to. I'm going to get back there, grab our stuff and run." He stood up. "Stay right here. I'll be back as soon as I can, and then we'll hit the road."

59

"But how can Yacoub still be alive, Chris?" Angela demanded, returning to a theme she'd already visited several times during what had turned out to be a very long and uncomfortable night. "Are you absolutely sure it was him?"

They were sitting in their hire car in the parking lot of an all-day restaurant outside Jerusalem, waiting for the place to open so they could have breakfast.

Bronson had seen nobody in or near the hotel when he'd run there after leaving Angela in the bar. He'd checked around the building as thoroughly as he could, then gone in, packed their few belongings, paid the bill by shoving a handful of notes at the puzzled night clerk, and driven away. They'd been on the road more or less ever since, because trying to find a hotel open to new arrivals after midnight had proved fruitless. In the end, Bronson had given up and headed for Jerusalem, and the restaurant parking lot had seemed as good a place as any to wait out what remained of the night.

Once they'd stopped, he had gently washed the ragged cut on the bottom of Angela's left foot. It wasn't too deep, though it was certainly painful. He'd placed a thin pad over it and secured it with strips of plaster he'd bought from an all-night pharmacy in Tel Aviv. Angela had pulled on a pair of trainers and tried a few steps. The trainers weren't elegant, but with them on her feet she could at least walk again—she wouldn't be running anywhere for a while.

Bronson sighed. "Look," he said, "Yacoub doesn't have the kind of face it's easy to forget. And I didn't tell you this before, but what Jalal Talabani did when he rescued us back in Rabat just seemed too easy to me. One man—even with the element of surprise in his favor—would find it difficult to take out three armed men, especially if he was tackling them in a house he'd never set foot inside before. I think he had help, and the only reasonable explanation is that Yacoub must have set it up for him."

"But Talabani did kill those men, didn't he?" Angela asked.

"Definitely. I checked Ahmed's body myself."

Angela shivered. "So Yacoub must have been prepared to sacrifice at least three of his men—Ahmed and the two we saw upstairs—just for what?"

"To convince us that he—Yacoub, I mean—was dead so we would feel happy about following the trail he'd prepared. The word 'ruthless' barely covers what he's prepared to do. He wanted us—or rather *you*—to be so determined to find the Silver Scroll and the Mosaic Covenant that you'd come out here to Israel and lead him straight to the relics. And it wasn't a bad plan, really, because you've got the contacts and the knowledge to pull this off. All he would have to do was follow you, and that's what he's been doing."

"But that gunman tried to kill you, Chris."

Bronson nodded. "I know. I can only assume Yacoub's losing patience. He probably wanted me dead so that he could kidnap you. Then he'd try to persuade you to tell him where to look for the relics."

Angela's face looked pale in the early-morning light. "Dear God. I'm really glad you're out here with me, Chris. Yacoub simply terrifies me. He wouldn't even need to torture me—one look at his face and I'd just tell him everything."

Bronson shifted his gaze from the road beyond the parking lot—ever since they'd stopped, he'd been checking the passing vehicles, just in case they needed to make a quick getaway. Now he looked across at Angela. "Look," he said, "if you want to give this up right now, it's no problem. We can be sitting on a flight out of Ben Gurion back to Britain in a few hours, never come back to Israel, and forget all about these lost relics. It's your decision. I'm really just along for the ride."

Angela didn't reply for a few moments, just sat there with her head slightly bowed, her hands clasped in her lap, almost a Madonna figure. Then she shook her head and swung round to face Bronson. "No," she said firmly. "If I walk away now I know I'll always regret it. This is the biggest opportunity of my career—of any archaeologist's career, in fact—and I'm not prepared to give it up. We'll just have to make sure we stay one step ahead of

Yacoub and his band of pistol-toting thugs. And that's your job, Chris," she added, with a small smile.

"So no pressure, then," Bronson said, an answering smile on his face. "Right, if you're determined, let's decide where we go from here. Once this place finally opens and we've got some food inside us, I mean."

As he spoke, the illuminated signs of the restaurant suddenly flickered into life, and Bronson saw figures moving around inside the building.

"At last," he muttered. "Let's eat."

An hour later they walked back to their car.

"Any ideas?" Bronson asked, sitting down in the driver's seat. Angela had taken several pages of notes with her into the restaurant, and had read through them carefully while they had breakfast She had said little during the meal.

"Possibly, just give me a few minutes."

Bronson nodded as if he'd just made a decision, and leaned across to Angela. "Can I ask you something? Something personal?"

"Yes," she replied cautiously, drawing out the word. "What?"

"Yosef Ben Halevi? You worked with him, right?"

"Yes, about five years ago, I think it was. Why?"

"So you don't really know him that well?"

Angela shrugged. "No, not really, I suppose. He was just a colleague."

"Right. It's just—I don't know—there's something about him that I don't like. It's almost as if he's hiding something. And I didn't like the way he kept probing, trying to find out what we were really looking for."

Angela shook her head. "He's an expert on ancient languages and Jewish history. The kinds of questions we were asking were bound to intrigue him. He can probably sense that we're on the track of something, and he'd like to be a part of it. I'm sure that's all it is." She smiled slightly. "You're not jealous of him, are you?" she asked.

Bronson shook his head firmly. "No, definitely not. I'd just rather we didn't get involved with him any further. I really don't think I trust him."

Angela smiled again, wondering how much of Bronson's instant distrust of the man was due to Ben Halevi's undeniable physical attractiveness, and how much was just his policeman's instinct working overtime. Not that she suspected the Israeli of anything underhand, but she recognized that it would perhaps be better to keep him out of the loop from now on, now she hoped they were getting close to their goal.

"Right," she said, looking back at her notes. "I've been trying to put myself in the position the group of Sicarii would have found themselves in back in AD 73. They've got three important Jewish relics to hide. They put one in a cave at Qumran—which was not perhaps the most secure of locations, though as it turned out it kept the Copper Scroll hidden for two millennia—and went on somewhere else with the remaining two, the Silver Scroll and the Mosaic Covenant. Now, even then, Jerusalem was the most important city in the whole of Judea, and I don't think it's too wild a suggestion that they might have hidden the relics somewhere there."

"But if they had done that," Bronson objected, "surely they'd have been found by now. Jerusalem's been continuously occupied and fought over for at least two thousand years. How could anything like the Silver Scroll have stayed hidden?"

"Actually," Angela said, "the first settlement on the site dates from about 3500 BC; but I didn't really mean *in* Jerusalem. I meant it was more likely that they chose a hiding place *under* it. The whole of the city and the Temple Mount is like a honeycomb. There are tunnels everywhere. Back in 2007, a group of workmen in Jerusalem employed by archaeologists to search for the old main road out of the city discovered a small drainage channel, and that led directly to a huge unknown tunnel that might have run as far as the Qidron river, or possibly even to the Shiloah Pool at the southern end of Jerusalem, from the Temple Mount. There's a possibility that it might have been used by the inhabitants of the city to get out of Jerusalem during the Roman siege of AD 70, and it was a probable escape route for some of the treasures of the Temple. The Qidron river—Wadi Qidron—heads eastwards from the city, but about halfway to the Dead Sea it splits, one arm continuing to the Dead Sea while the other heads directly to Khirbet Qumran."

"Qumran again," Bronson observed.

"Yes," Angela said. "One interpretation is that when the Roman siege began, trusted Jewish priests and fighters gathered together all the scrolls of the Second Temple and escaped with them down that tunnel to Qumran, where they hid the scrolls in the caves near the settlement—those documents that became known as the Dead Sea Scrolls. It's as convincing a suggestion as any I've heard."

"But what about the relics we're looking for? Where do you think they could be?"

"I've got an idea. Obviously the people who buried the Silver Scroll would have had no idea of the tortuous history that would eventually unfold around the Temple Mount, but I think there's a good chance that they might have selected one of the existing tunnel systems under or near the rock as being a secure location for the relics. Now, in the present political climate in Jerusalem, there's no possible way we can get access to the tunnels under the Mount—not even bona fide Israeli archaeologists can manage that.

"But," she continued, "the inscription on the clay tablets refers explicitly to one very particular kind of underground space—a cistern. I think at the last count something like forty-five different cisterns have been identified in the various caves and chambers that run under the Temple Mount, so that does make sense. I think that the Sicarii who hid these relics deliberately chose a hiding place underneath what all three major religions—Christianity, Judaism and Islam—now believe to be the holiest site in Jerusalem, perhaps in the world."

"But which cistern?" Bronson asked. "If there are more than forty of them, and we can't get into the tunnels, that's it, isn't it? Even if we could work out exactly which cistern the relic is hidden in, there's no way we can recover the relic."

"Not necessarily," Angela replied, a smile playing over her lips. "I've been studying our translation of the inscription, and I've just spotted something. The inscription doesn't say 'a cistern,' it says 'the cistern,' and that suggests it's referring to a very specific cistern, one whose location would have been generally well known. And around the beginning of the first millennium, there was one obvious place close to the Temple Mount that everybody would have known was a cistern. The writer of the tablets would certainly have been familiar with it."

"Which was?"

"Hezekiah's Tunnel," Angela said. "I hope you like water."

60

"They're on the move." The young woman sitting in the lobby of the Tel Aviv hotel lowered her newspaper and bent her head forward slightly so that her lips were close to the tiny microphone clipped under the lapel of her jacket. "All three of them are just leaving the hotel. I'm right behind them."

The hotel had been under intense scrutiny by the Mossad team ever since Hoxton, Dexter and Baverstock had flown in from Heathrow.

"Copied. All mobile units, heads up and stand by. Acknowledge."

A chorus of radio calls confirmed that all the Mossad surveillance team members were on the net and ready.

Levi Barak, sitting in the passenger seat of a sedan parked about seventy yards down the road from the hotel entrance, focused a pair of compact binoculars on the target building. As he watched, three men emerged and began walking down the road in the opposite direction. A few seconds later, a short, dark-haired woman stepped onto the street behind them, a newspaper tucked under her arm, and began following them, perhaps thirty yards back.

"Right, you know what to do," Barak said. "Keep me informed," he added, as he stepped out of the car.

The three men seemed oblivious to the fact that they were under surveillance, and were just walking steadily toward a small parking lot—the hotel didn't have its own garage.

Barak stood on the pavement for a few moments, watching as his team of Mossad surveillance officers moved smoothly into position, covering the parking lot and all its possible exits.

Moments later, a white car drove out of the parking lot and turned into the road. Seconds after that a large motorcycle and a nondescript sedan drove slowly down the street behind it. As soon as all three vehicles had moved out of sight, Barak strode across to the hotel entrance.

Less than five minutes later a technician carrying a bulky briefcase walked into the hotel lobby. Barak nodded to him, then strode across to the reception desk where the manager was already waiting, a pass-key in his hand. The three men stepped into the elevator, and the manager pressed the button labeled "3."

The first thing Barak saw inside Tony Baverstock's room was a laptop computer sitting on the desk by the window. He gestured to the technician, who moved across to it and powered it up, but even before the operating system loaded, a password request appeared on the screen, and the man muttered in irritation. He knew they'd never be able to guess it, and there might be a logging system built into the laptop that would record anyone inputting the wrong password, so he pressed the start button and held it until the computer shut down. He had a simpler solution.

From one of the pockets at the back of his briefcase he took a CD-ROM, which he inserted in the computer's drive. This contained a boot program that would start the computer independently of the programs on the hard disk, and at the same time bypass the password screen. He sat down at the desk, switched on the laptop again and watched the screen. The boot program gave him access to all the folders on the hard disk, and as soon as the system had finished loading, he plugged a lead into one of the USB ports, attached a high-capacity external hard disk and copied all the datafiles he could find on the computer, as well as the e-mails and the list of Web sites the user of the machine had recently visited. While the copying process ran, he quickly scanned the folders he thought most likely to hold details or pictures of the tablet—principally the "Documents" and "Pictures" folders—but without finding anything useful or informative.

"Anything there?" Barak asked, several pieces of paper in his hand.

"Nothing obvious," the technician said, shrugging as he disconnected the external drive and replaced it in his briefcase. He knew that the techies at Glilot would find the information, if it was there.

Barak nodded to the man as he left the room, his work completed, and looked round. His search hadn't been particularly productive, but he had found a half-empty box of nine-millimeter Parabellum ammunition in a suitcase in the wardrobe, which had considerably elevated his level of concern about these three Englishmen. He'd also found several pages on which words had been scribbled—words that he knew from his conversations with Eli Nahman and Yosef Ben Halevi might have been a part of the inscription on the clay tablet they were desperately searching for.

And there were two words that had leaped out at him from one sheet. Somebody had scribbled "Hezekiah's Tunnel" on it, and that had prompted Barak to place an urgent call to the leader of the surveillance team following the Englishmen. That was one possibility he'd managed to cover.

Ben Halevi had called him that morning to report what the other two people involved—Christopher Bronson and Angela Lewis—had asked him when they met the previous evening. It looked as if there was a real possibility one of the two groups of searchers might be getting close to finding the relics. All the Mossad had to do was sit back and wait, then move in at the last moment. It was all, Barak thought, going as he'd hoped.

He ran a pocket-sized hand-held scanner over the pages he was interested in, then replaced the sheets of paper on the desk exactly as he'd found them. He took a final look round the room, nodded to the manager, and left.

61

"Is that it?" Bronson demanded, fanning his face with his hat. They'd done a bit of shopping, and Bronson was carrying a waterproof bag holding flashlights and spare batteries. Both he and Angela were now wearing shorts and T-shirts, and Crocs beach shoes.

They were standing close to the bottom of the V-shaped Qidron Valley, looking across toward the Palestinian village of Silwan. Below and to their right, the focus of Bronson's attention was a set of stone steps that descended steeply toward a masonry arch, beyond which all was black.

"This is one end of it, yes," Angela confirmed. "This is the entrance to the Gihon Spring. This tunnel was a significant feat of engineering, especially bearing in mind that it's nearly three thousand years old. Jerusalem is situated on a hill, and was fairly easy to defend against attackers because of its elevation. The one problem the defenders had was that their principal source of water, which is right in front of us, was located out here in the

Qidron Valley and lay some distance outside the walls of Jerusalem. So a siege, which was the commonest way of taking most military objectives in those days, would always result in the capture of the city because eventually the stored water supplies would run out.

"In the mid-nineteenth century an American scholar called Edward Robinson discovered what's now known as Hezekiah's Tunnel, named after the ruler of Judea who constructed it in about 700 BC. It's also called the Siloam Tunnel because it runs from the Gihon Spring to the Pool of Siloam. The tunnel was obviously intended to function as an aqueduct and channel water to the city. It's more or less S-shaped, about a third of a mile long, and there's a slope of a little under one degree all the way down, which would ensure that the water flowed in the right direction.

"Building it would have been a massive undertaking given the tools the inhabitants of the city were known to possess, and current theories suggest that the tunnel was actually partly formed from a cave that already ran most of the way. An inscription was found at one end of the tunnel stating that it was constructed by two teams of workmen, starting at opposite ends. The spring was then blocked and the diverted water allowed to flow to Jerusalem itself. That's basically the legend and more or less what the Bible claims.

"But in 1867, Charles Warren, a British army officer, was exploring Hezekiah's Tunnel and discovered another, much older, construction now called Warren's Shaft. This consisted of a short system of tunnels, which began inside the city walls and ended in a vertical shaft directly above Hezekiah's Tunnel near the Gihon Spring. It allowed the inhabitants to lower buckets into the water in the tunnel without exposing themselves outside the walls. Dating it accurately has proved difficult, but the consensus is that it was probably built in about the tenth century BC."

"Wow," Bronson said. "Three thousand years ago— that's pretty old. And I guess you're going to insist on exploring it thoroughly." He looked without enthusiasm at the gaping entrance to the spring. "Let's get on with it. You said it'll be wet?"

"That's why we're wearing what we're wearing. This isn't just your usual damp tunnel. This is actually an aqueduct. At best we'll have to wade, and if it's really deep we might even have to swim."

"Terrific," Bronson muttered, and started toward the steps.

They walked down the stone stairs and passed under the arch, then stopped for a few seconds to let their eyes grow accustomed to the dark.

"It looks deep," Bronson said, staring at the water, which appeared almost black in the gloomy interior. "And cold," he added.

He undid the waterproof bag and took out two flashlights. He checked that both worked properly, then handed one to Angela and resealed the bag, which still held the spare batteries.

"I hope the guy in the shop was right when he said these flashlights were waterproof as well," he said.

"As long as one of them works, we'll be fine. There

aren't any turnings, so all we have to do is keep walking until we get to the other end."

"Just remind me what you think we might find down here."

"Right. This tunnel was already almost eight hundred years old when the Sicarii were looking for a place to hide the Silver Scroll," Angela said. "I think the reference in the clay tablets to a cistern could mean they hid it down here. So we'll be looking for any cracks in the rock that could conceal something, or any cavities that could have been chipped out by them. If it is somewhere in this tunnel, I'm hoping that the archaeologists might have missed it, because everybody believes that this tunnel is just an aqueduct, nothing more. As far as I know, nobody has ever done a serious search for hidden relics down here, because nobody in their right mind would hide anything in a well or cistern."

"Except that we know they did."

"Precisely." Angela hesitated. "This was my idea, so do you want me to go first?"

Bronson put his hand on her shoulder, immediately remembering that she'd never been fond of dark and confined spaces. "No, I will," he said, switching on his flashlight and stepping forward into the dark water.

"Watch your head," Angela said, following close behind him. "The lowest roof height is under five feet."

Within a few steps they were both in water—cold water—up to their knees. Their flashlights illuminated walls and ceiling of gray-brown rock, peppered with thousands of small white spots.

"They're the marks left by the picks and other tools

when King Hezekiah's men dug this tunnel," Angela explained.

"You're right. This would have been a mammoth undertaking," Bronson said, his voice echoing slightly as they moved deeper into the darkness.

The light from his flashlight suddenly showed that the tunnel branched to the left, the ceiling height dropping steadily. He turned that way, crouching down and shining his flashlight upward. The short tunnel ended abruptly, but above them was an opening in the ceiling. Bronson stopped and moved slightly to one side so that Angela could crouch beside him.

"What's that?" he asked. "It looks like it could be a tunnel or shaft going vertically upward."

"That's exactly what it is. What you're looking at is the bottom of Warren's Shaft. Up there is where the inhabitants of Jerusalem would have come with their buckets to collect water. They'd have lowered them down that shaft."

Bronson could feel his heart thumping with anticipation as they shone their flashlights up at the stone walls above them. But there were no signs of any possible hiding places.

"I'd have been very surprised if there was anything up there," Angela said. "This area and that shaft have been thoroughly explored from both directions. If the scroll is somewhere in here, it won't be anywhere as obvious as that."

They backed out and moved on, the water level and the height and width of the tunnel varying considerably as they progressed. It was very cold and very dark, and both of them were already shivering, their clothes soaked through. Instead of the light shorts and T-shirts they were wearing, Bronson realized they'd have been better advised to bring wetsuits or even thigh waders. They walked on, the temperature dropping still further and the water becoming deeper. As his shivering increased, Bronson began to wonder just how long either of them would be able to continue.

62

"Are you sure this is the place?" Dexter asked, the beam of his flashlight playing over the walls of the tunnel.

All three men were standing in water up to their thighs, their shorts and the lower parts of their shirts soaked. So far they'd found nothing at all.

"I keep telling you that I don't know," Baverstock said, his voice angry. "This was my best guess, based on the mention of a cistern in the clay tablets. Hezekiah's Tunnel was the most important water source the people of Jerusalem had, so logically it was certainly somewhere we had to check. And it's close enough to the Temple Mount to match the 'end of days' reference as well."

"The trouble is that this is just a tunnel hacked out of the rock," Dexter said. "There are virtually no hiding places anywhere in it, as far as I can see."

"Well, we certainly won't find anything if we just stand here talking," Baverstock growled. "Keep moving, and keep looking. I only want to do this once."

*   *   *

Bronson and Angela had been walking for perhaps twenty-five minutes when their flashlights picked out an almost pagoda-shaped and fairly low section of the roof, the rock in the center forming a graceful downward curve while the edges extended slightly upward. That section of the tunnel was fairly wide.

"This is the meeting point," Angela said. "This is where the two tunneling crews met back in 701 BC."

"That's amazing," Bronson said, "especially when you think how easily they could have missed each other. Look at the technology they had to use in the Channel Tunnel to make sure both teams arrived at the same place at the same time."

They moved on, and a few moments later Bronson stopped again.

"There's another really short tunnel here," he said. "It's only a few feet long."

"There are two of these," Angela told him. "It looks as if they were started by the workmen who were digging toward the spring, but then they must have realized they were heading in the wrong direction and abandoned them."

They checked every inch of the false tunnel, above and below the water level, then carried on to the second one, where they repeated the process.

"The walls and roof are pretty rough in places, but I've not noticed anything that could be a hiding place for a box of matches, far less a two-foot-long scroll," Bronson said. "And I assume what we're looking for would be at least that sort of size?"

"Probably, maybe even bigger than that." Angela sounded fed up. "I still think this was the most likely place for them to have hidden it, but maybe I misread the clues. Anyway, we're here now, so let's keep looking."

A few minutes later, as they approached the Pool of Siloam and the ceiling height rose considerably, Bronson spotted a dark oval in the wall high above them.

"That's worth a look," he said, moving his flashlight around to try to illuminate the opening better. "I think that's a cavity."

Angela peered up as well. "You could be right," she said, sounding more hopeful.

Bronson found a small ledge and carefully placed his flashlight on that to provide some light. "I reckon it's about ten feet up," he said. "If you stand on my shoulders you should be able to reach inside it."

Angela switched off her own flashlight and tucked it inside the pocket of her shorts.

Bronson cupped his hands together. Angela put her foot in the stirrup he'd formed, rested her back against the wall of the tunnel and lifted herself up. As she placed her feet on his shoulders, Bronson moved slightly forward and braced his arms against both sides of the narrow tunnel.

"Can you reach it?" he asked.

"Yes. I'm just about to feel inside." There was a pause, and then Angela's voice, high and breathy with excitement, announced: "There's something here!"

63

"Can you hear voices in front of us?" Dexter asked.

Baverstock was dismissive. "Yes, but don't worry about it. A lot of tourists come here to do this walk. They think it gets them closer to God. Just keep looking."

"I won't be sorry to get out of here," Hoxton muttered. "This place gives me the creeps."

Bronson could feel Angela's feet moving slightly on his shoulders as she stretched up to reach into the cavity.

"What is it?" he asked.

"I don't know. Something round and solid. Hang on. I'll try to pull it out."

She reached up again and tugged at the object her fingers had found. There was a scraping sound, and then she lost her grip on it. Something tumbled down, clattering against the rock wall, and fell with a splash into the water.

"Oh, damn it."

*   *   *

Less than twenty yards behind them, Tony Baverstock stopped dead and stood in absolute silence, listening. Then he turned to Hoxton.

"I recognize that voice," he whispered. "That's Angela Lewis, which means the man with her is probably her ex-husband. These are the two I told you about. That means she's following the same trail we are. She's been looking at the same clues as I have, and she must have come to the same conclusion."

"But has she found the Silver Scroll?" Hoxton asked. "That's all that matters."

"I don't know," Baverstock said, "but we'd better get up there and find out."

Without a word, Hoxton and Dexter moved forward, heading down the tunnel toward the sound of the two voices, Hoxton pulling a small semi-automatic pistol from his pocket as he did so.

"Was that it, Angela?" Bronson asked.

"It was definitely something. Hang on—let me just check and see if there's anything else in the hole." She paused, then added: "No, and it isn't really a cavity, more like a small ledge."

Quickly, she climbed down off Bronson's shoulders and back onto the floor of the tunnel.

"It landed just about there," Bronson said, shining his flashlight at the water.

"Good," a new voice said, and two flashlights snapped into life, their beams instantly dazzling Bronson and Angela.

"Who the hell are you?" Angela demanded.

Nobody responded immediately, but Bronson heard the unmistakable snicking sound as the slide of an automatic pistol was pulled back to chamber a round.

"Get behind me, Angela," he said.

"Very noble," the voice mocked. "But if you don't get the hell out of here right now, you'll both be dead. You've got five seconds."

"We—" Angela said, then stopped talking as Bronson grabbed her arm and began pulling her down the tunnel.

"Come on, Angela," Bronson said. "We're out of here."

Hoxton waited until the splashing sounds had diminished almost to nothing as Bronson and Angela scrambled away down the tunnel, heading toward the Pool of Siloam.

"Right," he said, turning to Dexter and putting away his pistol. He aimed the beam of his flashlight at the dark surface of the water. "That's where they said it fell, so why don't you find out what it was?"

"Me?" Dexter asked.

"There's nobody else here, is there? I'll stand guard, make sure those two don't come back."

Dexter muttered something under his breath, then handed his flashlight to Hoxton, took a deep breath and reached down. His head went below the surface as his hands searched the floor of the tunnel, and a few seconds later he popped up again, holding a round object.

"What is it?" Baverstock demanded eagerly as he walked up to join his two companions.

Hoxton focused the beam of his flashlight on the object, then muttered in disappointment. What Dexter was holding was nothing more than a round rock, about four inches in diameter.

"Is that it?"

"It's all I could find down there on the floor," Dexter said, "but I'll take another look."

He handed the stone to Hoxton and submerged again.

"There's nothing else down there," Dexter said a few seconds later, standing upright and shaking the water out of his hair.

Hoxton shone his flashlight up and around them, then focused on the same ledge Bronson had spotted. "It had to have come from up there," he said, his voice sharp with bitterness. "Christ—what a letdown. I really thought that was it. I guess it's been sitting on that ledge for the last few million years. Right, let's move on."

Bronson and Angela stepped out of the dark archway and emerged blinking into bright sunlight at the Pool of Siloam. Their transit through Hezekiah's Tunnel had taken them well over an hour, but they'd covered the last section as quickly as they could, not knowing who the armed men behind them were, or what they wanted. And they were still empty-handed, apart from the small waterproof bag holding their flashlight batteries.

The Pool was at the bottom of an oblong space between some of Jerusalem's old stone buildings. Almost opposite the archway, a flight of concrete steps, the open side protected by a steel banister, led up to the street above. About half a dozen young children wearing tattered shorts played in the water, splashing about, laughing and calling to each other, their gaiety in stark contrast to Bronson's mood.

"Well, that was a complete waste of time," he grumbled, as he and Angela climbed the steps out of the pool. They were both dripping wet and still cold, though the heat of the sun was already starting to dry their light clothes.

"Not the most pleasant experience of my life," Angela agreed.

"But we're out and safe, that's the main thing. Are you sure that what you dislodged from that ledge was just a stone, not a cylinder or anything like that?"

"No, definitely not. It was round and heavy. To me, it felt just like a rock, and that's what it sounded like when it hit the wall of the tunnel. Now, who the hell were those two men?"

"I don't know, but I do know that we're in serious danger. This is the second time in two days that we've been threatened by a man with a gun. Both times we've been really lucky to get away, and I have no idea how long our luck's going to hold. I don't know who those two men were—they sounded too English to be part of Yacoub's gang—but they're obviously looking for the same thing as us. Look, why don't we call it a day? No ancient relic is worth dying for, surely?"

"I'm sorry, Chris, but if our deduction is right, many people have already died over the centuries, either looking for it or trying to protect it. I'm not about to give up, not when I think we're so close to finding it. I'm determined to see this through to the end, whatever the cost."

64

Bronson and Angela decided to spend the night in Jerusalem. Their choice of accommodation in Tel Aviv had proved too dangerous—or too easy for somebody dangerous to identify—so Bronson was determined to avoid the bigger places.

He drove around the outskirts of the city and finally selected a small hotel in the northwestern suburb of Giv'at Sha'ul. The district was set on mainly sloping ground up in the Judean Hills, and dominated by a huge cemetery. The hotel was down a narrow, steep and flagstoned side-street, barely wide enough for a small car to negotiate. Bronson didn't even bother trying, just parked the hire car round the corner, walked back to the building and took two rooms on the third floor.

Giv'at Sha'ul was a strange mix of building styles. In stark contrast to the ancient heart of Jerusalem, where you could actually touch stone walls that had been in place for millennia, most of the buildings in the suburb were small, single-story houses, many of them in poor condition, despite being well under half a century old. Interspersed with these were a number of featureless concrete apartment blocks, most of them low-rise, though a few boasted a dozen or more floors, and the occasional detached building that hinted at long-gone days of elegance and sophistication. A handful of hotels, cafés and restaurants completed the picture.

The predominantly square-edged concrete and stone architecture was relieved in just a few spots by tree-shaded open areas, but Giv'at Sha'ul had no pretensions—it was a district where people lived and worked and prayed. It was functional and basic, and Bronson hoped they could just vanish from sight there. His only worry was that the hotel receptionist had insisted on copying their passports, because Israeli hotels had to charge VAT to all non-tourists, and Bronson's offer to pay both the tax and the hotel bill in cash had been dismissed. The law, the receptionist explained somewhat stiffly in fractured English, was the law.

Once they'd checked in, Bronson and Angela walked out of the building. They were both starving, having eaten nothing since their very early breakfast, but the hotel's small dining room didn't open for another hour. They walked toward the center of Giv'at Sha'ul and quickly found a café that was already serving dinner. They took a table right at the back, allowing Bronson a clear view of the door, and ate their meals quickly and with a minimum of conversation.

When they stepped outside, the daylight was fading and another spectacular sunset decorated the western sky.

"Beautiful, isn't it?" Angela murmured, stopping on the cracked pavement for a few seconds to stare at the irregular bands and swirls of color that marked the position of the setting sun.

"Yes, it is," Bronson agreed simply, taking her hand as he stood beside her. Again he wished they were just tourists, two people taking a holiday, instead of being embroiled in a search that seemed to him to be getting more dangerous with every hour that passed.

"Right, let's get back to the hotel. We've got a lot to do."

Bronson smiled wryly as he turned to follow Angela. Five seconds to enjoy a sunset, then back to work. The search for the relics had really got to her.

There were no mini-bars in their rooms at the hotel so, as Angela headed up the stairs, Bronson picked up a couple of gins and a bottle of tonic from the bar as a nightcap.

When they were settled in her room, their drinks on the tiny round table in front of them, Bronson asked the obvious question.

"Well, Hezekiah's Tunnel was a complete wash-out, so what do we do now?"

"What I would expect any competent police officer to do," Angela said, looking across at him impatiently. "We look at the evidence. We reread the Aramaic text and assess it again."

She leaned back in her chair.

"As I see it, there are only three possibilities. First, and most obviously, we *have* been searching in the right place, but over the last two millennia somebody else went looking in Hezekiah's Tunnel, found the Silver Scroll and sold it, or melted it down or something, so it's simply no longer around to be found. Obviously, I hope that didn't happen."

"Could that be the case, though? Are we chasing something that isn't there any more?"

"It's possible, but I don't think it's likely. Something unique and robust like the Silver Scroll would almost certainly have survived intact. Anybody finding it would probably guess that the value of the metal itself was far outweighed by the historical importance of the inscription. And if it had been found, I think there'd be something in the historical record about it.

"The second possibility is that the relic is still hidden somewhere in the vicinity of the Temple Mount, but not in Hezekiah's Tunnel. If that is the case, we've got problems. There are a lot of tunnels known to exist under the Mount, but access to them is impossible because the entrances have been bricked up or are blocked by tons of rubble. And then there are the forty-odd cisterns on the Mount itself, on what's known as the Lower Platform, and some of those are huge.

"You have to remember that the Temple Mount is one of the oldest building sites in history; over the centuries dozens of architects and builders have left their mark on it." She paused, then reached for her laptop bag. "Look, it'll be easier if I can show you on a picture."

She pulled up a plan of the Temple Mount and began pointing out the salient features.

"The Mount is constructed from four walls that surround a natural hill and form a pretty big flat-topped structure. The walls to the east and south are visible, but the one supporting the northern side is completely hidden behind later houses and other buildings. The northern end of the Western Wall is also hidden by later construction, and a large section of it is actually under the ground. There's a further flat platform built on the top of the Mount, and this section also includes the bedrock of the original hill itself. The Dome of the Rock—that's the spectacular structure topped with a gold dome—is the holiest Muslim site in Jerusalem, and it's built on this platform.

"The bedrock—the Foundation Stone—forms the centerpiece of the building, because that was where Muslims believe that Mohammed started his journey to heaven. Below the Foundation Stone is a small cave known as the Well of Souls, where Muslims believe that the spirits of the dead will assemble for judgment by God when the world comes to an end."

"Right," Bronson said. "I'm with you so far."

"Good." Angela grinned, and Bronson had to stop himself from leaning forward to kiss her.

"Now, all that's on the upper platform, but it's the lower platform that covers the majority of the surface of the Temple Mount. At one end is the al-Aqsa Mosque— that's the building with the gray dome. There are gardens on the eastern and northern sides and an Islamic school right at the northern tip. There's a fountain known as al-Kas on the platform that originally obtained its water from what were known as Solomon's Pools up at Bethlehem, fed by another aqueduct. Today, it's connected to Jerusalem's main water supply."

Angela indicated a spot on the edge of the plan of the Mount.

"There are several gates in the walls, and probably the best known is the Golden Gate. According to tradition, that's the one the Jewish Messiah will use when he finally enters Jerusalem, but he'd better remember to bring a hammer and chisel with him, because that entrance is completely blocked with masonry at the moment. In fact, all the gates are sealed up. Others include the two Huldah Gates, known as the triple and double gates because one has three arches and the other two. These were the original entrance and exit to the Mount from the oldest part of Jerusalem, known as Ophel. Then there's Barclay's Gate—nothing to do with the bank, obviously—and Warren's Gate. That was named after Charles Warren. I've mentioned him a couple of times already, but *you* should definitely know who he was."

"Me? Why?"

"Ever heard of Jack the Ripper?"

"That Charles Warren? The Commissioner of Scotland Yard? What the hell was he doing in Jerusalem?"

Angela smiled again. "Before he failed to catch the most notorious mass-murderer in British history, he was an officer—a lieutenant—in the Royal Engineers. In 1867 he was tasked with exploring the Temple Mount in an expedition financed by the Palestine Exploration Fund. The investigation revealed several tunnels that ran underneath both Jerusalem itself and the Temple Mount, including some that passed directly under the old headquarters of the Knights Templar. Other tunnels ended in various cisterns, and so presumably were disused aqueducts.

"As well as these tunnels, he also explored inside the various blocked gates. The Golden Gate, Warren's Gate and Barclay's Gate opened onto passages and staircases that originally led up to the surface of the Temple Mount. Behind the Huldah Gates were tunnels that went some distance under the Mount before sets of stairs led to the surface north of the al-Aqsa Mosque.

"The interesting bit is that to the east of the passage leading from the triple gate is a large vaulted chamber, usually referred to as King Solomon's Stables, though there's definitely no connection with Solomon. That chamber was built by Herod when he was carrying out his extensive works, and there is evidence that the area was used as a stable, probably by the Crusaders. Warren established that one function of this section was to support the corner of the Temple Mount itself.

"Warren also discovered that there were numerous tunnels running underneath the triple gate passage, and below the base level of the Mount. They led in different directions, but he had no idea about their function or purpose. And, of course, since Warren's nineteenth-century investigation, nobody else has been allowed inside the Mount to check them out."

"And we can't get inside the gates or the tunnels?"

"No," Angela replied. "Back in 1910 there was a case of an Englishman named Montague Parker who bribed the Muslim guards on the Temple Mount and started digging at night near Warren's Shaft. There was a huge outcry when he was discovered, riots even, and he was lucky to escape with his life. It was a complicated story, involving a Finnish mystic who claimed that he'd found clues encoded in the Hebrew Bible—in Ezekiel, in fact—that indicated the hiding place of the Ark of the Covenant. Here," she added, "I'll show you on the Internet."

She input a search string into Google, selected one of the hits and double-clicked on the link. The page opened, and she scrolled part-way down.

"That's Montague Parker," she said, pointing to a photograph of a man, his features indistinct, who was wearing what appeared to be a Royal Navy officer's cap and standing on the terrace of a hotel, its name partially visible behind him.

She reached for the touchpad again, but Bronson stopped her with a gesture. "Did you read that?" he said, pointing at the text below the photograph.

"No," Angela said, looking more closely. After a couple of minutes she sat back. "Bugger! I wish I'd seen this Web site before we went to Gihon Spring. I didn't know they'd done that."

The text they were looking at explained in some detail how Montague Parker's expedition had spent almost three years digging and widening in Hezekiah's Tunnel in a desperate search to find the Ark of the Covenant.

"That's really irritating," Angela said, her features clouded with annoyance. "I should have done more research. Not only was it a waste of time, but we nearly got killed in the process."

"What about these other cisterns?" Bronson asked, tactfully changing the subject.

"Oh, yes. Right, mostly they're of very varied design

and construction, presumably because they were built by several different groups of people over the centuries. Some of them are just chambers roughly cut out of the rock, while others were constructed with more care and attention. A couple of them—the ones normally known as cisterns one and five—might possibly have had some kind of religious function connected with the Second Temple altar, because of their location on the Mount. Cistern five also contains a doorway blocked with earth, so there could well be a further chamber or chambers beyond what's known to exist now."

"How big are these cisterns? Do they just hold a few gallons of water, or are they really big?"

"Some of them are huge. Cistern eight can hold several hundred thousand gallons, and number eleven has the potential to store nearly a million gallons. Most of the others are smaller, but they were all designed as proper cisterns, with reasonably high capacities. Don't forget, in antiquity water conservation was absolutely essential, and these cisterns were intended to hold every drop of rainwater that fell."

"But from what you've said, they can't be accurately dated, so we have no idea which of them were already in existence when the Sicarii were looking for a hiding place for their relics?"

"Exactly."

"Let me have another look at the translation we did, please," Bronson asked.

Angela opened her handbag and pulled out half a dozen folded sheets of paper. Bronson riffled through them.

"I thought so," he said. "The text specifically states 'the cistern,' and that's followed by two words we haven't cracked, then 'place of,' another blank and then 'end of days.' Our interpretation of that was 'the cistern at the place of the end of days.' If there was more than one cistern in the place where the Sicarii hid the relic, wouldn't it make sense for them to have written 'the cistern at the northern edge of the Mount' or something like that? I think what they wrote implies that there was only a single cistern in the place they chose, and that it would be a cistern everybody would be aware of."

"That's why I thought Hezekiah's Tunnel was the right location. It was certainly in existence at the time, and it was the biggest and most famous of all the cisterns near Jerusalem. But this information destroys that theory."

"Then there's only really one conclusion we can draw," Bronson said.

"Which is what?"

"That we've been looking in completely the wrong place. Wherever the Sicarii hid the relics, it probably wasn't in Jerusalem." He yawned—it had been a very long day. "We need to look at the whole inscription again."

65

"I was so sure we were right," Angela said. "It all seemed to fit so well, especially as Hezekiah's Tunnel is the most obvious of all the cisterns."

It was early morning in the holiest of cities, a salmon-pink sky presaging yet another blisteringly hot day. They'd been woken by the electronically amplified cries of the muezzins summoning the faithful to worship, a discordant and unforgettable dawn chorus borne on the still air from the mosques of Jerusalem.

They were again sitting in Angela's room, drinking bad instant coffee made worse by powdered creamer. Bronson had slept like a log, but Angela's face was pale and she had dark shadows under her eyes. He guessed she'd stayed awake for much of the night puzzling over the meaning of the inscription and the location of the lost scroll.

Bronson picked up the sheets of paper on which they'd written out the translation of the inscription and glanced through the disjointed text, hoping for inspiration.

"This phrase about the 'end of days' would fit very neatly with the Well of Souls, the cave on the Temple Mount where Muslims believe that the dead will gather to wait for judgment when the world ends," he said, then paused for a few seconds. "No—hang on a minute. The Sicarii weren't Muslims. In fact, Islam as a religion didn't even exist until about half a millennium *after* the fall of Masada, so our premise about the location must be wrong."

Angela shook her head. "It's not that simple, Chris. I wasn't suggesting the hiding place had anything to do with the Well of Souls. My interpretation of the 'end of days' expression was that it referred to the Jewish beliefs about the Third Temple—they think the end of the world will come shortly after it's built. Yosef Ben Halevi talked to us about this, if you remember. Like the Muslims, the Jews also think that the 'place of the end of days,' the place where the world will end, is most likely to be the Temple Mount."

Bronson looked crestfallen. "Damn," he muttered, "I thought I'd spotted the fatal flaw in your argument. So if Armageddon is definitely going to take place here in Jerusalem, the Sicarii must have hidden the Silver Scroll somewhere here. All we can be certain of is that they didn't stick it in Hezekiah's Tunnel."

For a few seconds Angela just stared at him, an inscrutable expression on her face.

"What?" Bronson demanded.

"Did I ever tell you you were a genius?" Angela asked, her eyes shining.

"Nothing like often enough," Bronson said modestly. "What did I do this time?"

"You've just made the obvious connection that I missed. I was so sure about the Temple Mount that I completely forgot about Armageddon—and that's somewhere very different."

"But I thought Armageddon was an event, not a place?"

"When most people talk about it they assume it means the end of the world. But in fact it *is* an actual place. It's called Har Megiddo, the hill of Megiddo, and it's about fifty miles north of Jerusalem. That's where, according to the Bible, the 'battle of the end of days' will take place, when the forces of good and evil confront each other for the last time."

"The 'place of the end of days' would fit, then?"

"It would match the expression very well. I don't know too much about the site, so I'll need to do some more research."

"But how do you get 'Armageddon' from 'Har Megiddo'?" Bronson asked.

"Well, it's not exactly a mistranslation from the Bible," Angela said, "not like the camel passing through the eye of a needle."

"That's a mistranslation?" Bronson asked. "I didn't know that."

"Yes. Why on earth would a *camel* want to go through the eye of a needle? It's yet another biblical expression that doesn't make the slightest bit of sense, but which has been trotted out in pulpits by preachers for hundreds of years, none of whom stopped to wonder what the expression was supposed to mean. Of course it's a mistranslation."

"So what should it be?" Bronson asked.

"Most of the Old Testament was originally written in Hebrew, with a few chapters of Ezra and Daniel in Aramaic, but the New Testament was in Koine Greek. The first translation was started by a man named John Wycliffe and finally completed by John Purvey in 1388. For the King James Bible, a group of over fifty scholars worked on not only the original Hebrew and Greek versions of the two books, but also looked at all the extant translations that had been made.

"It was translation by committee, and not surprisingly mistakes were made. There are two very similar words in Greek: *camilos*, meaning 'rope,' and *camelos*, which translates as 'camel.' Whoever was doing that bit of the New Testament misread the 'i' in the Greek as an 'e,' and the Church has been stuck with his mistake ever since. Amazing, isn't it?"

Bronson shook his head. "Now I think about it, I suppose it is. So what about Armageddon?"

"Right. The name of the place is Megiddo, and it's normally prefixed by either 'tel,' meaning 'mound,' or more commonly 'har' or 'hill.' It's not too big a jump to see how the name 'Har Megiddo' could have been corrupted over the years into 'Armageddon.' Megiddo was one of the oldest and most important cities in this country, and the plain below it was the site of the first ever recorded pitched battle. In fact, there've been dozens of battles—over thirty in all, I think—at that location, and three 'Battles of Megiddo.' The last one took place in 1918 between British forces and troops of the Ottoman Empire. But the most famous was the first one, in the

James Becker

fifteenth century BC, between Egyptian forces under the Pharaoh Thutmose III and a Canaanite army led by the King of Kadesh, who'd joined forces with the ruler of Megiddo. Kadesh was in what's now Syria, not far from the modern city of Hims and, like Megiddo, it was an important fortified town. We know so much about this battle because a record of what happened was carved into the walls of the Temple of Amun at Karnak in Egypt."

"So it was the site of the first battle in recorded history, and will also be where the last one takes place?"

"If you believe what it says in the Book of Revelation, yes. According to that source, Har Megiddo, or Armageddon, will be the site of the 'Battle of the end of days,' the ultimate contest between the forces of good and evil. It really *is* the place at the end of the world."

66

Dexter swung the wheel of the hired Fiat to the right and accelerated along the street that ran behind the hotel in Giv'at Sha'ul where, according to one of Hoxton's contacts in Jerusalem, Angela Lewis and Chris Bronson had taken two rooms.

In the passenger seat beside him, Hoxton was carefully feeding nine-millimeter Parabellum shells into the magazine of a Browning Hi-Power semiautomatic pistol. On the floor in front of him, tucked out of sight, was another pistol—an old but serviceable Walther P38—that he'd already checked and loaded.

Two days earlier, he'd met with a former Israeli Army officer on the outskirts of Tel Aviv. The price the man had demanded for the weapons and ammunition—he'd bought three pistols from him—was, Hoxton knew, nothing short of extortionate, but the Israeli was the only person he knew in the country who could supply what he wanted and, just as important, not ask any questions.

"Stop somewhere here," Hoxton ordered.

Dexter found a vacant space on the right-hand side of the road and parked the car in the early-morning sunshine.

"Their hotel's just around the corner," Hoxton said, handing over the Walther.

"I'm not that good with guns," Dexter muttered, looking down at the blued steel of the pistol in his hand. "Do I really have to take this?".

"Damn right you do. I've come too far to let this pair beat me now. We're going to find the Silver Scroll, and the only way to guarantee we can do that is to grab all the information—photographs, translations, whatever—the two of them have got. If we have to kill Bronson and the woman to get their stuff, then that's what we'll do."

Dexter still looked unhappy.

"It's easy," Hoxton said. "You just point the pistol and pull the trigger. We'll kill Bronson first—he's the most dangerous—and Angela Lewis will be a lot more cooperative if she's just watched her former husband die."

The two men got out of the car, both tucking the weapons into the waistbands of their trousers, under their jackets. They walked around the corner, then down the street to the hotel, and straight in through the lobby.

67

"So where is Megiddo? I presume we'll be going there."

"Oh, we'll certainly be going there. It's in northern Israel, on the Plain of Esdraelon overlooking the Jezreel Valley."

Angela clicked the touchpad on her laptop and brought up a detailed map of Israel.

"This is Esdraelon," she said, indicating an area close to the northern frontier of the country. "The Jezreel Valley is shaped a bit like a triangle lying on its side, with the point at the Mediterranean coast and the base paralleling the River Jordan, just here. All that area was once under water. In fact, it was the waterway that linked the inland body of water that's now called the Dead Sea with the Mediterranean. About two million years ago, tectonic shift caused the land lying between the Great Rift Valley in Africa and this end of the Mediterranean to rise, and the waterway turned into dry land. Once the Dead Sea no longer had an outlet, its salinity started to increase, with the result we see today."

"So what's at Megiddo? A ruined castle or something?"

"More or less. The point about Megiddo was that it had enormous strategic importance. In ancient times there was a major trade and military route known in Latin as the *Via Maris* or "Road of the Sea" and as *Derekh HaYam* in Hebrew. This ran from Egypt and up the flat land beside the Mediterranean to Damascus and Mesopotamia. Now, whoever occupied Megiddo controlled the section of this route that was known as the *Nahal Iron*—the word *nahal* means a dry riverbed—and hence could control all the traffic along the route itself.

"Because of its location, Megiddo is one of the oldest known inhabited places in this part of the world. In fact, in any part of the world. The first settlement there dates from around seven thousand BC—over nine thousand years ago—and it was finally abandoned in the fifth century BC, so the site was continually occupied for about six thousand five hundred years."

"So when the Sicarii went there—assuming you're correct—the place would already have been a ruin?"

"Oh, yes," Angela agreed. "The site would have been deserted for well over half a millennium by that time."

"And you think that could be the place referred to in the inscriptions? I mean, you now think it's more likely than Hezekiah's Tunnel or somewhere on the Temple Mount?"

"Yes, I do." Angela looked apologetic. "I suppose with hindsight I should have thought about it a bit more, and I should certainly have checked on what had been done in Hezekiah's Tunnel in the past. And—as you pointed out—with all the activity on and inside the Temple Mount over the years, the chances of anything like the Silver Scroll remaining undiscovered there were pretty slim."

"So what about Megiddo, then? Has that had scores of archaeologists poring over it as well?" Bronson sounded uncertain.

"Oddly enough, no. It has been excavated, of course, but not as often, or as exhaustively, as you might expect, given its history. Virtually nobody dug there at all until 1903, when a man named Gottlieb Schumacher led an expedition, funded by the German Society for Oriental Research. Twenty years later John D. Rockefeller financed an expedition by the University of Chicago's Oriental Institute, and that continued until the start of the Second World War."

"Hang on, that's a dig lasting fourteen years," Bronson pointed out. "They must have pretty much covered the whole site."

"It was a long expedition, true, but Megiddo is simply huge. As I said, the city mound itself covers about fifteen acres, and most archaeological digs tend to be focused in one fairly small area and are vertical rather than horizontal. They're usually interested in digging down through the different layers that represent the various civilizations that have occupied the site, and that's certainly what the Chicago team did.

"Since then, not too much has happened at Megiddo. An Israeli archaeologist named Yigael Yadin did a bit of work there in the 1960s, and since then there have been excavations on the site every other year, funded by The

Megiddo Expedition based at the university here in Tel Aviv."

"That still sounds like quite a lot of activity," Bronson said doubtfully.

"Perhaps it is," Angela agreed, "but the point is that if any of these expeditions had found the Silver Scroll, the whole world would know about it already. And don't forget, none of these archaeologists were looking for what might be described as buried treasure. They were just trying to uncover the history of the site. We're not. We're going there to look for one very specific object, in one very specific place."

"So there *is* a cistern somewhere on the hill?" Bronson asked.

"In fact, there isn't," Angela said, with a slight smile, "and that's good news. A cistern is where you *store* water, but a well or a spring is a *source* of water. When we were checking our transcriptions using the on-line dictionary, it suggested that the Aramaic word I'd translated as 'cistern' more accurately meant a well. And what's at Har Megiddo is a well, not a cistern. That's another indicator that we're now on the right track."

"Right," Bronson said. "There's no time to lose. I'll just go and get my things together. We can look at the route once we're in the car and heading north." He looked at his watch. "Ready in five?"

68

"They're on the third floor," Hoxton muttered, as he pushed the button to call the lift. "Adjoining rooms, 305 and 307. This shouldn't take long."

They stepped out of the lift together, and walked down the narrow corridor. Outside number 305 they stopped. Hoxton leaned forward, pressing his ear against the door.

"I can hear movement inside," he whispered, stepping back and easing the Browning out of his waistband. "You cover the other door," he told Dexter. He watched as his companion moved a few feet down the corridor. "Ready?"

Dexter looked unhappy but took a firm grip of the pistol and nodded. Hoxton rapped sharply on the door.

"Who is it?" Bronson asked.

"Maintenance," an indistinct but clearly male voice replied. "There's a problem with one of the lights in your room that we need to fix."

Bronson stepped back. Two things bothered him about what he'd just heard. First, every member of hotel staff they'd talked to so far had spoken English to some extent, some of them haltingly, others quite fluently. But the man outside the door didn't just *speak* English: as far as Bronson could tell, he *was* English. Why would an Englishman be working as a maintenance man in a small hotel in Jerusalem?

The second thing was that all the lights in the bedroom and bathroom were working perfectly.

"I've just got out of the shower," Bronson said. "Let me put on some clothes."

Walking quickly across the room, he stuffed the rest of his possessions into the overnight bag he'd been packing, and then crossed to the connecting door with room 307 and knocked gently.

"I'll only be a few seconds," he said aloud, as the connecting door opened.

Swiftly, Bronson slipped through into Angela's room, pushed the door to behind him and locked it. "We've got company," he said. "Get your stuff together. We need to get out of here right now."

Quickly Angela shoved all her clothes into her carry-on bag. Bronson closed her laptop and slid it, with the papers and notes, into her leather computer case. As he did so, there was a splintering sound from the adjoining room.

Striding over to the door, Bronson transferred his bag to his left hand, and turned the handle gently with his right. But as he eased the door open, a figure on the other side kicked out, slamming the door back against the wall, just missing Bronson. And, as Bronson looked out into the corridor, he immediately registered the pistol the man was holding in his hand.

Bronson reacted instantly. He swung his overnight bag toward the man's face, then kicked out with his right foot. His blow caught the stranger's forearm and knocked the pistol off aim, and Bronson followed up the kick with a hard right-hand punch to the man's stomach. The gunman bent forward, retching, and the pistol clattered to the floor. Bronson brought his right knee up, hard, into the man's face.

The gunman yelled in pain, as spurts of blood from his broken nose splattered the carpet in the hallway.

"Run," Bronson shouted, pointing down the corridor, toward the fire escape.

As Angela sprinted down the corridor, Bronson reached down and tried to grab the fallen pistol, but the gunman was too quick for him and grabbed for it himself. Bronson kicked out, sending the weapon skittering across the floor and out of reach, then turned and then ran after Angela. Behind him, he heard cursing amid the cries of pain, and guessed that his attacker's companion was chasing after him.

There was a right-angle bend in the corridor, which Bronson took at speed, but then he slammed to a halt. The rest of the corridor was straight, and Angela was still only about halfway down it. Unless he could manage to slow down their pursuer, they'd both be sitting ducks as soon as the man rounded the corner.

He looked around for a weapon—any weapon. Absolutely the only thing there was a fire extinguisher mounted on the wall beside him. That would have to do. He dropped his bag and snatched it off the bracket.

Bronson moved slightly forward until he was right at the corner, and listened to the sound of running footsteps, trying to calculate just how close his pursuer was. Then he stepped forward, swinging the extinguisher in a vicious arc at waist height.

The man running toward him, an automatic pistol gripped in his right hand, had no chance to react. The extinguisher hit him full in the stomach and he fell backward, gasping for breath. But he held on to his pistol and, even as he tumbled to the floor, he pulled the trigger.

The crash of the shot in the confined space was deafening. The bullet missed Bronson by feet, ricocheting off the walls and ceiling. He knew the man would recover in seconds, and didn't hesitate, just threw the extinguisher at his attacker, grabbed his bag and ran for it.

At the end of the corridor the emergency exit doors beckoned. Bronson caught up with Angela just as she reached them, and pushed hard on the horizontal safety bar holding them closed. As the doors smashed open a siren began wailing. Bronson pushed Angela outside just as another shot echoed down the corridor, the flat slap of the bullet hitting the wall behind them clearly audible.

In front of them was a small square concrete platform, sections of steps descending from it in a zigzag pattern down to the street below, and another flight reaching up to the upper floors of the building.

"You first—quick," Bronson said. He glanced back down the hotel corridor. At the far end he saw the man he'd knocked down walking quickly toward him, holding his stomach with his left hand, the pistol in his right.

Then he fired another shot, and Bronson knew he couldn't wait any longer.

He shifted his bag to his left hand and jumped down the four steps to the first platform, grabbed the safety rail and swung himself round to go down the next set of steps.

Below him, Angela was already nearing the bottom.

"Run!" Bronson shouted. "Get round the side of the building." Seconds later, he saw her sprint away from the fire escape, her bags in hand.

He reached the bottom steps and looked up. His attacker had stepped onto the concrete platform and was leaning over the rail, taking aim with his pistol. Bronson knew the platforms and steps made hitting him virtually impossible. Once he moved away he would become an easier target.

But he had to move. The obvious route was to follow Angela—the corner of the building was a mere twenty feet away—but Bronson guessed that the man with the gun would expect him to run in that direction. Instead, he vaulted over the safety rail and ran for the other corner of the hotel, zigzagging from side to side.

He could heard movement as the gunman crossed to the other side of the platform; then two shots in quick succession smashed into the paving slabs close behind him. Then he reached the corner and dodged around it. He was safe—at least for the moment.

Sprinting round to the front of the hotel, he found

Angela standing by the wall, looking nervously back the way she'd come.

"Here," he called, taking her by the arm. "Quick. Follow me."

They ran away from the hotel, down the street and along to the spot where Bronson had parked the car. He unlocked it, tossed their bags onto the back seat, started the engine and drove away, watching his mirrors the whole time.

Angela was trembling slightly, from exertion or fear, or more likely both. "Don't say it," she muttered.

"I'm not going to. You know that I think what we're doing is dangerous, but I'm in it with you to the bitter end. Armageddon—here we come!"

"I think that bastard broke my nose," Dexter muttered as the two men walked quickly away from the hotel. "I can feel it."

"That's about the fifth time you've told me," Hoxton snapped, his breath still wheezing slightly. "Just shut up about it and walk."

"Where are we going?"

"We're going back to the hotel to see if Baverstock's got any further with the inscription."

"What about Bronson and Lewis?"

"We've lost them for the moment, but sooner or later my contacts will get a lead on them—they'll check into another hotel or something—and we'll get hold of the information they've got. We've come too far to stop now."

"And Bronson?" Dexter asked.

"He's a dead man walking," Hoxton said.

69

"We've been looking in the wrong place," Baverstock announced excitedly as he pulled open the door of his hotel room to let Hoxton inside. "What happened to you?" he asked, when he saw Dexter standing in the corridor, his shirt red with blood.

"He had a nosebleed," Hoxton said dismissively. "Are you saying that the scroll's not under the Temple Mount?"

"Yes. It suddenly dawned on me exactly where the 'place of the end of days' had to be, and it's *not* anywhere near Jerusalem."

Hoxton sat down. "So where is it?"

"Har Megiddo, or Armageddon. It's the place mentioned in the Book of Revelation as being where the final battle will be fought, the ultimate fight between good and evil, which will mark the end of the world as we know it."

"Don't get messianic with me, Baverstock. Just tell me where the hell it is."

"Here." Baverstock unfolded a detailed map of Israel and jabbed a stubby finger at a spot just to the southeast of Haifa. "That's where the Sicarii hid the Silver Scroll, I'm sure of it."

"You were also pretty sure they'd hidden it in Hezekiah's Tunnel," Hoxton observed. "So how certain are you this time?"

"Ninety percent," Baverstock said, "because of the reference to *the* cistern or well. I should have realized earlier. Jerusalem and the area around the city is full of water storage facilities. I thought the Sicarii had picked Hezekiah's Tunnel because it was the principal fresh water supply for the city, but when I looked at the inscription again I realized I was wrong. Hezekiah's Tunnel isn't really a cistern at all—it's an aqueduct that leads into the city from the Gihon Spring. A cistern is a water storage facility, often underground. If the Sicarii had hidden the relic there, I'd have expected them to use a different expression."

"And is there a cistern at this Megiddo place?"

Baverstock nodded. "Actually, it's another spring, but the important thing is the description of Har Megiddo itself. I'm quite sure that's where the author of the scroll was talking about."

Hoxton turned to Dexter. "Go and get yourself cleaned up," he said. "I don't want you dripping blood all over the car seats. And be quick about it. Then we'll get the hell out of here." He looked back at Baverstock. "Bronson and Lewis gave us the slip today, but I'd lay money they've already worked out that the Silver Scroll's hidden somewhere at Har Megiddo. We need to get up there as soon as we can."

Bronson and Angela's route had taken them northwest out of Jerusalem, skirting the West Bank and Tel Aviv, through Tiqwa and Ra'annana before joining the coast road at Netanya. The road paralleled the Mediterranean coast, along the edge of the Plain of Sharon, all the way up to Haifa.

But before driving on to Megiddo, there were a few things Bronson wanted to buy, so he turned the Renault west, toward the center of Haifa itself.

"Shopping time?" Angela asked.

"Exactly. I don't think I'll bother buying flippers because I doubt if I'll be swimming very far, but I'll certainly need a face-mask, and probably a rope."

Twenty minutes later they walked back to the car, Bronson carrying a small plastic bag and an empty rucksack, which he shoved into the trunk. Then they headed southeast out of Haifa toward Afula. The route they'd followed wasn't the most direct track to Har Megiddo, but it had saved them having to climb up and over the Mount Carmel ridge which separated the two areas of level ground that dominated the area—the plains of Sharon and Esdraelon—so it had been a much easier, and probably faster, drive.

"It's only midafternoon," Bronson said. "Why don't we go straight there and at least check it out? If you're right and what we're looking for is in an underground tunnel, it won't matter whether we go there in daylight or at night."

"That's true," Angela agreed, "but we'll have to be careful up on Har Megiddo at night, waving flashlights around. Any lights up there after closing time will attract attention."

"What do you mean—'closing time?'" Bronson asked.

"Well, the site is a major tourist attraction, you know. At this time of year it closes at five. And we'll have to pay to get inside."

70

Levi Barak looked with some satisfaction at the notes he'd scribbled during his exchanges on the radio with his various teams of watchers. Both groups of suspects seemed to be heading for exactly the same place in northern Israel. Bronson and Lewis were in the lead, having just reached the outskirts of Haifa after a brief stop in the city.

"Bronson's just turned southeast," one of the surveillance officers said, his voice crackling over the loudspeaker. "He's taken the road toward Afula, or maybe he's heading for Nazareth."

"Keep watching," Barak ordered, "and make sure they don't see you. I don't want them spooked now. I'll join you shortly."

"You're coming up here?" The man sounded surprised.

"Yes. Let me know the moment they stop again, even if it's just for a meal or a drink."

"Understood."

Barak leaned back from the radio microphone and picked up the internal telephone. "This is Barak," he said. "I want you to get me the number of the direct line for the commanding officer of the Sayeret Matkal. And when you've done that, I want a military helicopter on standby here within thirty minutes, fully fueled, with two pilots. If possible, get me one that's equipped with a For-ward-Looking Infra-Red scanner and a night-vision cam-era." He glanced at his watch, then looked out through the window, calculating times and distances. "And make sure it's here on time. The end-game is near."

71

The Plain of Esdraelon stretched out before them, a patchwork of green and fertile fields punctuated by small woods and clumps of trees. The road snaked away from Har Megiddo toward the lower slopes of a range of hills that rose in waves toward the distant horizon, gradually vanishing in the heat haze.

Bronson followed the road signs, written in Hebrew and English, and turned north from the Megiddo junction onto road number 66. After a couple of minutes, he made a left turn, and almost immediately swung left again. He slotted the Renault into a vacant space in the parking lot at the foot of the hill and switched off the engine.

For a few moments he and Angela just sat there in silence, staring up at the craggy slope that rose above them.

"It's big," Bronson said.

"I told you the area of the city extended to about fifteen acres."

"I know. Fifteen acres doesn't sound that huge when you just say it," Bronson replied, "but when you see something like this in the flesh it's a bit daunting. Are you sure you know where we should start looking?"

"Yes. There's only one source of water here, and the entrance to the tunnel that leads to it is now one of the biggest structures on the site. All the garrisons stationed here through the millennia had the same problem, just as they did at Jerusalem—the only reliable source of water lay outside the walls of the fortress. And in both cases, they did exactly the same thing: they dug an underground tunnel direct to the water source."

"Right," Bronson said. "We're not getting anywhere sitting down here in the car talking about it. Let's go and take a look."

Off to one side of the parking lot was a low building that housed the museum and visitors' center.

"Let's have a look around there first," Bronson suggested, glancing at his watch. "We've got plenty of time before the place closes."

The museum was quite informative, with numerous displays showing different sections of the site and an impressive model of how Megiddo would probably have looked in ancient times. By the time they walked out of the building, they both had a much better idea of the layout of the ruins, and Bronson had bought a guidebook in English that contained a detailed map of the entire site.

They followed the footpath that led to the entrance located on the northern side of the hill, and then started to climb, almost immediately surrounded by ancient masonry.

"According to this book," Bronson said, pointing to an ancient structure lying to the right of the path, "those are the ruins of a fifteenth-century-BC gate, and just around this corner we should see the main entrance to the fortress, what's called Solomon's Gate."

The gateway was in fairly good condition, built with massive stones and obviously designed to withstand not just attack by enemy forces, but also the ravages of time. There were three chambers located to the side of the gate, again in quite a good state of preservation.

"Each of these chambers," Bronson pointed out, again referring to the guidebook, "was designed to hold an armored chariot and two horses, presumably so that they could quickly sweep down onto the plain and sort out any trouble. A bit like a modern police squad car, I suppose."

They turned left, following a well-trodden path, and walked past the remains of Ahab's stables—though to Bronson the remains didn't look much like any kind of stables he'd ever seen, just a tumble-down collection of low walls and fallen masonry—and on to a viewpoint that offered a spectacular vista looking north over the Jezreel Plain toward the town of Nazareth, which nestled in the hills of Galilee.

They stopped near a large, almost circular, structure, approached by a flight of about half a dozen steps on one side. Angela took the guidebook from Bronson and pointed. "This is the circular altar that was renovated— not built, but *renovated*—over four thousand years ago," she said. "It was probably used for animal sacrifices. That temple"—she gestured toward another pile of tumbled masonry—"was built at about the same time. It's called the Eastern Temple, and when it was constructed it would have consisted of a vestibule, a main chamber and the Holy of Holies at the rear, which was the closest part of the building to the circular altar."

She paused. "It's phenomenal, isn't it? I can't quite believe it's all so ancient." She looked at him, her eyes shining, her face lit with excitement, and Bronson's heart gave a lurch. "It's different for you, I realize that. Your life and work are absolutely contemporary, but I live and breathe for this kind of thing, and I can't just walk past something as interesting as this."

She took his hand, and they walked together toward the southern section of the old city.

"Now that is really impressive," Bronson said, walking over to a circular metal railing that enclosed a huge pit and peering down into the shadowy depths. It looked as if it was some forty or fifty feet in diameter and about the same in depth, a huge hole dug into the hard ground and lined with stones. It must have been a massive undertaking. "Is this the cistern?" he asked.

"No. This is Jeroboam's Silo. It dates from the eighth century BC and was used to store grain. Apparently it held about thirteen thousand bushels."

"And a bushel is what?"

"It's a unit of dry volume—it's more or less equivalent to eight gallons. You see the double staircase?"

Bronson looked again, then saw what Angela was pointing at. Forming a part of the stone wall itself were two rough staircases, each apparently little more than a couple of feet wide, that spiraled from the top of the silo all the way down to the base, starting on opposite sides of the structure.

"I suppose they built two staircases so that workers carrying or collecting grain could walk down one and then up the other, all at the same time?" Bronson suggested.

Angela nodded, looking down into the silo.

"I wouldn't fancy walking down there myself. They're both pretty narrow, and it's quite a long drop to the bottom," Bronson added.

"Hence the steel fence." Angela stepped back.

The silo was the most complete section of the ruins they'd seen so far, and was surrounded by the shapes of ancient buildings, now reduced to dwarf walls little more than a foot or so high. Palm trees—date palms, Bronson guessed—grew from what would have originally been the floors of rooms or perhaps passageways. And everywhere, the tumble of light gray, almost white, masonry conveyed the unmistakable impression of age, of almost too many years to comprehend. He was aware of Angela shivering slightly, despite the heat. He put his arm lightly round her shoulders, and they moved on.

"Over here are what used to be thought of as Solomon's Stables," Angela said. "But the dating's been revised and it's now believed they were probably built at the time of Ahab, possibly on the site of the palace of Solomon. Ahab was the King of Israel in the ninth century BC, and it's been estimated that the stables could have held nearly five hundred horses, and accommodated the war chariots as well. At that time, Megiddo was known as the 'Chariot City,' and chariots would have been the decisive weapon in any skirmish or battle on the plains below. They were the armored shock troops of the day."

She looked around her. "OK, we follow this path down to the southwest. That should take us to the start of the tunnel that leads to the cistern."

"When does the tunnel date from?" Bronson asked, as they started walking.

"Originally it was thought it might have been built as long ago as the thirteenth century BC, but more recent research has dated it fairly conclusively to the ninth century BC, which makes it"—she paused while she did the math—"almost three thousand years old." She looked up and smiled at Bronson.

"So the water supply was outside the city walls?"

"Yes. The water source was a spring in a cave over there," Angela said, pointing ahead of them. "When Solomon ruled here, he ordered his men to cut a shaft through the walls of the cave to give easier access to the spring, but that wouldn't have helped if Megiddo was under siege. Ahab was a lot more ambitious. He had a wide shaft constructed, which meant digging down through all the underlying levels here at the top of the hill, and then further down into the bedrock itself. The shaft finished up at around two hundred feet deep, and then the real work started. His men dug a horizontal tunnel through the rock to the cave, a distance of almost four hundred feet, which provided them with hidden and impregnable access to the spring. As a finishing touch,

Ahab had the original mouth of the cave blocked by a massive stone wall, and then had the wall covered with earth, so that a potential enemy wouldn't even know there was a cave there."

While Angela had been talking, they'd reached the edge of the entrance shaft, a huge hole in the ground with sloping sides, so massive that it made the grain silo appear totally insignificant by comparison. Unlike the silo, this structure appeared never to have been completely stone-lined, simply because there was no need to do so, but the remains of various supporting walls and terraces were visible all the way down to the flat bottom. The crumbling remains of an old stone staircase descended the side of the pit where the slope was gentlest, though to Bronson it still looked as if it would have been an exhausting climb up for the defenders of the city, especially if they were burdened with pitchers of water.

There was a steel safety barrier fitted on the top of a low stone wall that ran around most of the perimeter. In one section there was a break allowing access to a new staircase, made of concrete and fitted with safety rails and a succession of level platforms to break up the descent, which allowed tourists to get safely down to the bottom.

"It's still quite a climb," Angela said, "nearly two hundred steps, but at least we only have to go down. They've created an exit at the other end, through the wall that Ahab built three millennia ago."

Bronson looked around them. It was now late afternoon and the last groups of tourists were beginning to make their way back to the exit.

"We're going to have to leave here and then lie low for a while," he said. "I'd better move the car out of the parking area, too, and hide it somewhere nearby. I don't want to advertise our presence here, and I think it's fair to say that the two men who tried to jump us in the hotel this morning are probably still out there looking for us."

Angela looked concerned. "I'm trying not to think about that," she said. "Let's just walk through the tunnel and see what the cistern looks like."

The tunnel, when they reached it, was a surprise. Bronson had been expecting something like Hezekiah's Tunnel, narrow and twisting with a low ceiling, but hopefully dry underfoot. But the Megiddo tunnel was arrow-straight, wide, tall—probably nine or ten feet in places—well-lit and with a planked walkway that allowed visitors to stroll easily from one end to the other.

There was nobody else in the tunnel as they walked its length. At the far end, steps led down to the well itself. Bronson and Angela stood on the lowest platform and peered over the edge at the water below.

"It looks deep," he said.

"It is," Angela agreed. "Most wells are."

"And cold," Bronson added with a sigh, knowing that it was he who was going to have to go down into it. "The trick is going to be getting out afterward. I'm glad I bought that rope." He was silent for a few seconds as he thought this through. "Right, we've seen what we needed to. Now let's go."

72

It was midevening and virtually dark when Bronson eased the Renault to the side of the road about a hundred yards beyond the Har Megiddo parking lot entrance, backed it into a patch of scrubland where it was hidden from view, and turned off the engine.

They'd left the site about four hours earlier, driven a couple of miles down the road, and found an open café where they'd had a light meal. Then Bronson had parked the car in the shade of a clump of trees on some waste ground just outside Afula, and he'd tried to sleep for a while, knowing that he'd need all his reserves of energy for what was to come that night. While he slept, Angela had gone over all her research yet again to make absolutely sure there was nothing she'd missed. When Bronson woke up, he made a final check of the equipment he'd bought in Haifa, and then they both changed into dark-colored tracksuits and trainers.

They'd driven back to Har Megiddo into the face of the setting sun, the green fields of the Plain of Esdraelon slipping quickly into shadow as the sun started to dip below the peaks of the Mount Carmel ridge. Barely eighteen hundred feet at its highest point, the ridge is some thirteen miles long, and runs southeast from the Mediterranean coast near Haifa.

Bronson turned to Angela. "Ready?" he asked.

"As ready as I'll ever be," she replied.

Bronson lifted the rucksack out of the trunk, opened it to make a swift check of its contents, then hefted it up onto his shoulders. He locked the car and they set off.

The main gate into the site would certainly be locked, but Bronson didn't think that would be a problem. A site as big as Har Megiddo was almost impossible to secure completely, and indeed parts of the site were protected only by low fences. In several places the steepness of the slope made any kind of a physical barrier pointless.

"This should do," Bronson said, leading the way up a reasonably steep slope to the end of one of the fences. Earlier that afternoon he'd noticed a gap that he reckoned they could both squeeze through.

They reached the end of the fence. Angela went through the gap first; then Bronson passed the rucksack to her before following her through.

"Go straight to the entrance to the water tunnel," he said, keeping his voice low, "and watch your step on these rocks. Some of them are pretty crumbly and loose."

He watched as she started making her way up the long and steep slope that rose to the top of the hill.

The site was deserted, and they walked quickly across to the open pit that marked the entrance to Ahab's Tunnel, and down the steps to the bottom of the shaft. The steel door was secured with a hefty padlock. Bronson put his rucksack on the ground and opened the flap at the top. Reaching inside, he pulled out a pair of collapsible bolt-croppers, extended the handles and fitted the jaws around the hasp of the lock. He squeezed the handles together, grimacing with the effort, the muscles of his arms bulging with the strain. With a sudden crack, the steel parted and the ruined padlock tumbled to the ground.

"We're in," he said. He replaced the bolt-croppers in his rucksack and opened the door.

"Creepy," Angela whispered, as they stepped into the darkness. "I hadn't imagined how much scarier an ancient place like this would be at night."

"We can't turn on the lights in case they alert a guard. We're going to have to rely on our flashlights."

The two narrow beams helped. At least with the flashlights switched on they could see where they were going, but Angela was right—it was creepy. They were both very conscious of the weight of rock and earth above, and of the weight of history that surrounded them.

There was no point in looking for anything in the tunnel itself—the deciphered inscription had specifically mentioned a well or cistern. If the relic was still in the ruins, they'd find it in the spring itself, and nowhere else.

At the end of the tunnel there was an arrangement of steps and platforms, allowing visitors to get close to the well. They climbed down to the lowest one, just a couple of feet above the surface of the water. Bronson opened the rucksack again and pulled out a coil of rope. Swiftly, he tied one end of it around the steel handrail attached to the last section of the staircase then, as a precaution, also lashed it around the wooden balustrade that bordered the platform directly above the water. This meant that he'd be able to climb up and down the rope from the platform itself. Before he tossed the rope over the side to dangle in the waters of the spring, Bronson tied a series of knots in it, about a foot apart.

"What are they for?" Angela asked, shining the flashlight on Bronson's hands so he could see what he was doing.

"When I come out of the water I'll be cold—I wasn't kidding when I said it would probably be freezing in there—and my hands will be numb. The knots should give me something more to grip on when I climb up the rope."

Swiftly, Bronson removed his shoes and socks, then stripped off his shirt, lightweight trousers and underwear.

Standing there naked in the gloom, he smiled briefly at Angela. Then, pulling a face-mask from his bag, he slipped the band around his head, then picked out a heavy black rubberized flashlight, bigger than the one he'd taken into Hezekiah's Tunnel.

"Can you pass me the flashlight once I get in the water? I daren't jump in because I don't know how deep it is or what rocks or other stuff there might be lurking under the surface."

Angela leaned forward suddenly and hugged him. "Be careful, Chris," she whispered.

Bronson swung his leg over the wooden balustrade, grabbed the dangling rope with both hands, and swiftly lowered himself down into the mouth of the cistern.

"Jesus, that's cold," he muttered as he slid feet-first into the water. Holding onto the rope with one hand he adjusted his face-mask, then reached up for the flashlight.

Bronson first shone the beam all around him, checking the walls of the cistern, but they appeared to be fairly smooth and featureless. He glanced up at Angela, gave her a reassuring smile, and then lifted his legs to dive down into the dark water.

About three or four feet below the surface, Bronson gripped a protruding piece of rock to give him some stability and to stop him rising straight back to the surface. The mouth of the spring was really too narrow to allow him to swim around, so he knew he'd have to keep on diving down and grabbing hold of something to keep him submerged while he searched the walls.

The good news was that the waterproof flashlight was working well, its beam illuminating the gray-brown rock that formed the walls of the spring. The bad news was that those walls appeared to be fairly smooth, with no convenient holes—natural or man-made—that could have been used to secrete anything.

He started searching carefully, holding the flashlight in his left hand as he circled the wall, moving from one handhold to another, then released his grip on the rock as he headed for the surface to take a breath.

"Anything?" Angela asked as he broke the surface.

Bronson shook his head, took another deep breath and dived down again. This time he went a little deeper, down to maybe six feet, but the result was the same. Solid gray-brown rocks surrounded him.

Back at the surface, he lifted the mask from his face.

"I've been down about six feet," he said, looking up at Angela, "and there's nothing there. The people who hid the relic can't have dived down much deeper than that, could they?"

"I've no idea, but you're assuming that the water level in the spring was the same then as it is now, and it probably wasn't. If the level was, say, ten feet lower when they hid the relic, and they dived to six feet, it'll be sixteen feet below the surface now."

"I never thought of that," Bronson admitted. He nodded, replaced his mask and vanished again.

For the next twenty minutes he repeated the process, diving down, grabbing hold of something to keep him in place, and searching in vain for any kind of a hole or crevice in the rock walls. And every time he surfaced, he felt colder and more tired.

"I can't do this for much longer," he said at last, his teeth chattering. "Another three or four dives and that's it."

"You've done your best, Chris. I never thought you'd have to go that deep to find it."

"Nor did I," Bronson said, replacing his mask. If it's here at all, he thought, as he plunged down again into the depths.

This time he powered down five or six feet below the depth he'd reached previously, grabbed another section of rock and looked around him. Far above he could see the dim circle of light that was the surface of the water in the spring, illuminated by the light from Angela's flashlight. And around him, the spring seemed to be opening up somewhat, the opposite wall barely visible in the light from his flashlight. It looked as if the spring was shaped like a bell, with a narrow throat at the top and widening considerably at his depth, which he guessed at about twenty or twenty-five feet.

Conscious that he could only stay submerged for perhaps another twenty seconds, Bronson turned his attention to the wall beside him. Unsurprisingly, it looked very much the same as all the other sections of wall he'd looked at so far. He changed position, pulling himself sideways to look at the next few feet, and then the next. Nothing.

His lungs starting to protest, Bronson released his grip on the rock and allowed himself to start drifting upward. And as he did so, the beam of his flashlight briefly illuminated something different, something he hadn't seen before. An object that seemed regular in shape, not rounded like the rocky protrusions he'd been using as handholds, but projecting horizontally from the stone wall of the spring.

And then he was past it, heading upward toward the light and the life-giving air.

"The padlock's been cut off," Hoxton muttered, shining his flashlight at the broken lock lying on the ground at his feet. "They've got here before us."

They'd driven up to Har Megiddo from Tel Aviv, a noisy journey with Dexter lying across the back seat and moaning about the pain from his broken nose. Baverstock had misread a couple of the road signs outside Haifa, which had delayed their arrival slightly, but they, like Bronson and Angela, had waited until the site closed before they entered it over the boundary fence. They were now standing beside the entrance gate to the water tunnel.

"Good," Dexter said. "I owe Bronson for what he did to my nose."

"If it is Bronson," Hoxton said, "we know how dangerous he can be. So we take it carefully and surprise him. No flashlights, no talking, no noise. It's three against two, and we're all armed, so it should be no contest. We'll make it look like a couple of tragic accidents, or maybe just weigh the bodies down and dump them in the cistern. Understood?"

Dexter and Baverstock nodded.

"We've all seen the pictures of the tunnel," Baverstock told them. "There's a wooden walkway with handrails either side, so once we're on that we can feel our way along. Bronson will probably be using a flashlight or lantern and we'll see the light from that long before we reach them."

Without another word, the three men moved slowly forward into the underground tunnel. When they stepped onto the wooden walkway, Baverstock stopped them for a few moments to let their eyes adjust to the almost total blackness.

"See that glow?" he whispered, pointing straight ahead. "They're already at the cistern. No more talking, just walk slowly and carefully, and stop well before the steps at the end."

Making barely a sound, the three men began moving cautiously toward the dim light at the end of the water tunnel.

*   *   *

Bronson surfaced again and grasped the dangling rope.

"Anything?" Angela asked, more in hope than expectation.

"I think I saw something. I'm going to have one last go."

Bronson inhaled and exhaled rapidly several times, hyperventilating to purge the carbon dioxide from his lungs, before gulping a huge lungful of air and diving under water again.

He forced himself down into the wider part of the spring, to the area that he'd been searching on his previous dive, trying to spot the object he'd seen before. But once again the stone walls all looked the same, with no obvious differences from one part of the cistern to another. He could feel the pressure to breathe increasing as he swam around, the beam of his flashlight roaming over the rocky walls.

Maybe he'd been mistaken. Maybe his eyes had deceived him, or perhaps he'd simply misinterpreted what he'd seen. He was about to give up when the light suddenly illuminated something a few feet above his head, something with squared edges that seemed to be sticking out of the wall. He'd dived too deep, and had been searching too far down.

Bronson kicked out and rose up, never allowing the beam of the flashlight to waver, keeping its light on the object. Then he was beside it, his lungs bursting, but determined to find out exactly what it was.

It looked almost like a log of wood, but the moment his hand closed around the end of it he knew it was some kind of metal. Bronson tugged at it, but it seemed to be jammed into a natural fissure in the rock. He changed his grip and pulled again, bracing himself against the wall of the cistern with his other hand, his fingers still awkwardly clutching the flashlight.

This time he felt the object move. He pulled again, and in a cloud of debris it suddenly came free.

Bronson kicked out, away from the wall and up toward the surface. As his head popped out of the water he sucked in a long breath, then another.

He passed the flashlight up to Angela and grabbed for the rope.

"What is it?" she asked, her voice high with anxiety.

"I don't know," Bronson said, still panting for air. "It was jammed into a crevice in the wall of the spring. I think it's metal. Here."

Angela got down on her knees and stretched out both hands to him. Taking the object from him, she placed it carefully on the platform beside her as he began hauling himself up the knotted rope.

The climb wasn't as bad as Bronson had feared, because he could use his feet on the side of the cistern as well as the rope, and in a few seconds he was standing shivering beside Angela on the platform.

She rummaged in the rucksack and pulled out a towel. Shivering and stamping his feet to get warm, Bronson dried himself and started to get dressed. Then she moved the beam of her flashlight to shine on whatever it was he'd found in the cistern.

"It looks like a sheet of metal, rolled into a cylinder,"

she said, her voice husky with emotion, and Bronson could see her beginning to shake too. "It's covered in algae, but I think I can see marks on it. God, Chris, I think this might be it. I think you've found the Silver Scroll."

73

"And so do I," said a new voice, somewhere above Bronson and Angela.

Suddenly the darkness was split by a trio of powerful flashlight beams that dazzled them. It was like Hezekiah's Tunnel all over again, except that this time there was nowhere for them to run to. They were trapped in a dead end, unarmed and helpless.

Bronson and Angela were pinned by the light, standing on the wooden platform and staring up at the men holding flashlights at the top of the final staircase.

Hoxton moved his flashlight backward slightly to illuminate the pistol he held in his right hand.

"As you can see, we're armed," he said, "so don't try anything stupid."

"What do you want?" Bronson demanded.

"I'd have thought that was obvious," Baverstock said. "We're here to take that scroll. Thanks for finding it for us. We didn't even need to get our feet wet."

Angela recognized his voice immediately. "Tony? I should have guessed. What are you doing here?"

"The same as you, Lewis. Looking for the treasure the Sicarii hid here two millennia ago. I'm so pleased you've found it. This is going to make me very rich."

"Nonsense," Angela objected, her tone sharp and angry. "If this is the Silver Scroll, it needs to be properly analyzed and conserved. It must go to a museum."

"Oh, it'll end up in a museum eventually, don't worry about that," Baverstock assured her. "What you've got there is probably the world's most famous treasure map. And when we've translated the text we'll have access to the greatest collection of buried treasure in history. We'll spend the next few years digging it all up and carefully selling a few of the best bits on the black market—Dexter here is an expert in that field—and then we can all retire on the proceeds. *Then* I'll trot back to the British Museum with the scroll. My name will be as famous as Howard Carter's."

"I always thought you were an academic, Tony," Angela said, her voice dripping scorn. "But you're really just a grubby little tomb-robber, aren't you?"

"I am an academic, but I've always been quite happy to do a bit of freelancing on the side. Rather like you, in fact."

"And if we give you the scroll, you'll let us go?" Angela asked.

"Don't be so naïve," Hoxton snapped. "If we let you live, you'll tell somebody about this scroll and the Middle East will be full of treasure hunters within a matter of days. Your career, and your life, are going to end right here."

"I'm a British police officer," Bronson warned him. "Kill me and you'll have every copper in Britain looking for you."

"If we were in a cellar in England, I'd agree with you, but we're standing underneath a deserted fortress in the middle of Israel. Nobody's going to know you're dead; no one will ever know you were even here. Both your bodies will simply vanish. That well behind you is deep enough to hold your bones for all eternity. Now, hand over that scroll." Hoxton pointed at Baverstock. "Get it, Tony."

Baverstock took a step toward the staircase leading down to the platform to take the relic, his pistol pointing at Angela, but Bronson had one desperate card left to play. He grabbed the scroll and jumped back, holding the relic directly above the dark water of the well.

"One more step and I'll drop this," he threatened. "I've no idea how far down this spring goes, but I can promise you it is deep. You'll need specialist diving equipment to recover it—if you ever do. As you said, this well could hold its secrets for all eternity."

For several seconds nobody spoke or moved, and then a single shot rang out, the echo crashing and reverberating around the cavern, shockingly loud in the confined space.

And then a man screamed in pain.

74

Dexter tumbled sideways, his pistol clattering to the floor as he grabbed at his leg, the shock of the bullet's impact momentarily stunning him. Then the pain hit him and he screamed.

Baverstock dived to the ground, trying to roll clear of the line of fire. Hoxton spun around, swinging his flashlight beam back up the tunnel, desperately searching for the origin of the shot as he brought his own pistol to bear. The light flashed over three motionless figures, standing barely twenty feet away.

The moment he heard the shot, Bronson dropped the scroll onto the wooden platform and pushed Angela bodily to one side and down into what cover there was behind the rocks that lined the chamber.

Before Hoxton could bring his weapon up to the aim, he was blinded by two beams of light and heard the sound of a second shot.

He felt a crashing impact in his chest at the same moment, and tumbled backward onto the wooden walkway. Then a numbing, crushing sensation spread across his torso as the lights around him seemed to fade into blackness. And then he felt nothing at all.

The beams of the flashlights shifted, the men holding them looking for new targets. They fixed on Baverstock, cowering at the side of the walkway and clutching a pistol. Two shots echoed round the chamber, so close together that they sounded like a single report, and Baverstock slumped backward, tumbling off the walkway and onto the rocky floor of the tunnel below.

An ominous silence fell as the echoes of the shots died away, and then again someone screamed in pain.

"Jesus, Chris! What the hell's happening up there?" Angela whispered.

"Keep down. I don't think anybody's shooting at us. Not yet, anyway."

Bronson grabbed the rucksack and reached inside it. He pulled out a crowbar and stood up, tucking the cold steel tool behind him, into the waistband of his trousers. It wasn't much of a weapon, but it was all he had. He'd managed with less before, he told himself. Far less.

"Like rats in a trap." The voice was soft, barely audible over Dexter's howls of pain.

The three men moved forward cautiously, their flashlight beams dancing on the floor.

One stopped beside Dexter and looked down at the

injured man, the beam from his flashlight playing over the widening pool of blood around his shattered thigh.

"Help me, please," Dexter sobbed, through the agony of his wound. "I need an ambulance or I'll bleed to death."

"No you won't," the softly spoken man told him, "and you won't need an ambulance either."

Almost casually, he aimed his pistol at Dexter's head and pulled the trigger.

One of the other men stepped to the opposite side of the walkway, shone his flashlight downward at Baverstock's crumpled and bloodstained form, and grunted in satisfaction. The third crossed to where Hoxton's body lay motionless. He swiftly searched the dead man's clothing, found something in one of the pockets and called out to his companion.

"You were right," he said. "He did have a tablet," and he held up the piece of fired clay he'd just recovered from Hoxton's pocket.

The other man walked across, took it from him, and studied it in the beam from his flashlight.

"It's a different one," he said. "Put it in your pocket while I finish up down there."

On the lower platform, Bronson and Angela could hear only the murmur of voices now that the shooting had stopped. Then there was a silence, followed by the sound of approaching footsteps.

Bronson looked up cautiously. He could see a tall man descending the staircase, a pistol in his hand and his face in shadow. Behind him, two other men stared down at them, their own weapons poised. There was absolutely nothing Bronson could do apart from put his hands in the air, at least until the man moved closer.

The figure reached the platform and stood there, staring at Bronson and Angela. The beam of the flashlight held by one of the figures above swept briefly across his face, and Bronson gave a smile when he saw the half-paralyzed face and single white eye.

"I can't say I'm surprised, Yacoub," he said. "After I saw you in Tel Aviv I expected you to turn up here. I suppose you've had people following us since we arrived in Israel?"

Yacoub nodded and smiled. The effect was chiling. "You're a clever man, Bronson, which is why I let you live back in Morocco. I knew then that you would go looking for the Silver Scroll, and I thought it likely that you might even find it." He gestured toward the greenish metal cylinder on the platform. "And you did. I'll take it now."

"It should go to a museum," Angela said, standing up.

For a few seconds, the Moroccan stared at her. "Everybody calls me Yacoub," he said conversationally, "but that's not my real name. Do you know *why* I'm called that?"

Angela shook her head.

"You must have heard of Jacob's Ladder?"

"It's a kind of rope ladder, used on ships," Bronson said.

"Quite right," Yacoub said, "and it's also a plant. But there's a third meaning. In the Christian Bible, Jacob had a vision of a ladder reaching to heaven. That's why people have called me 'Yacoub' since I was about fifteen, because I've shown a lot of people the way to heaven." He paused. "You will also no doubt be aware that I'm armed, and so are my colleagues. You are not. Hand over the scroll now, and you can walk out of here. Argue about it, and I'm quite prepared to shoot both of you and take the scroll anyway."

"You've just shot three men in cold blood," Bronson said, "and your men killed the O'Connors in Morocco. If you're prepared to do that just to retrieve a clay tablet, how do we know you won't kill us anyway?"

"You don't, Bronson. Now make up your minds. I'm not a patient man."

Bronson handed the scroll to Yacoub. The crowbar still hung uselessly from his trousers, but with two pistols pointing straight at him, he knew he'd be dead long before he could reach for it. "What will you do with it?" he asked.

"This scroll contains a list of the locations of Jewish treasure. I intend to find as many items as I can but, unlike those three pieces of garbage"—he gestured up the staircase, to where Bronson now knew the bodies of Dexter, Hoxton and Baverstock lay—"who were just going to loot the treasures for themselves, I intend to sell most of what I recover to museums and collectors in Israel. I'll just keep a few of the very best pieces for my own collection. And then I'll give the money the Jews pay me to the Palestinians, to help them rid this country of the Israeli vermin that infest it. It's a kind of justice, really, using Jewish money to help the enemies of the Jews."

He looked once more at Angela, who was still standing defiantly beside Bronson, then turned his back on both of them, walked up the staircase and motioned to his men to start the trek back up the tunnel. Behind him, Angela and Bronson stood alone in the dark, listening to the sound of footsteps on the wooden walkway.

75

As the footsteps of the three men receded down the tunnel, Bronson pulled on the rest of his clothes. He put his arms around Angela.

"At least we found the Silver Scroll and held it in our hands," he said to her. "That's something very few people will ever be able to say. It's just a shame we had to hand it over to Yacoub, but we had no choice. In the end, it was all for nothing."

"Maybe," Angela said, her voice low, "or maybe not." She didn't sound quite as disappointed as Bronson had expected.

"What do you mean?"

"The Sicarii claimed to have hidden something else here, something that was just as important to them. Perhaps even more important."

Bronson whistled. "Of course! The 'tablets of the temple of Jerusalem.' But do you know where to look?"

Angela grinned at him in the half-light of the flashlight. "I think so, yes. I'm not finished quite yet. Are you?"

*   *   *

Bronson picked up his rucksack and led the way up the staircase. At the top, they stepped around the bodies of Dexter and Hoxton, but the third corpse was nowhere to be seen.

"Where's Baverstock?" Bronson wondered aloud.

"Maybe he managed to get away."

"I doubt it. Yacoub shot the other two without hesitation, so why would he let Baverstock live?" Bronson glanced around the end of the tunnel, then strode across to one side of the platform, where there was a gap between the wood and the wall. He shone his flashlight beam downward. "Right, I can see his body down there. He must have fallen off the walkway when the bullets hit him."

"I don't care, Chris. They all got what was coming to them, and I'm not going to lose any sleep over their deaths, not even Tony Baverstock's. Let's get out of here."

As Bronson and Angela strode down the walkway toward the entrance to the water tunnel, there was a faint scuffling noise from the end by the cistern. A few moments later Baverstock hauled himself up and onto the walkway. He searched around in the dark for the pistol he'd dropped when he fell, and quickly found it.

One of the bullets fired at him had missed completely; the other had only nicked his shoulder, a wound that had bled quite a lot and stung like hell. When he'd fallen backward off the walkway, he'd decided to play dead, hoping that none of the attackers would think to put another bullet into him.

And it had worked. He was alive and almost fully mobile, and now he had a pistol in his pocket. More importantly, he'd heard every word Angela had said to Bronson about the tablets of the Temple, and he knew exactly what she was talking about. He even knew where they were going to start looking.

Baverstock bent down again and felt around the wooden walkway until he found a flashlight, checked that it worked, then headed off down the water tunnel to the entrance.

Angela and Bronson stepped out of the tunnel and emerged into the fresh night air in the middle of the fortress of Har Megiddo. They climbed up the steps and paused for a few moments at the top to catch their breath, then set off toward the remains of the temples.

"If you think about the way the inscription was written," Angela said, leading the way to the massive circular altar beside the temple ruins, "it suggests that the Sicarii hid both the Silver Scroll and these tablets at the same location, the scroll in the cistern and the tablets in an altar. And when they were here at Har Megiddo, the only altar on the site was the one we're looking at right now."

She stopped, reached into her pocket and pulled out the piece of paper she'd been studying that afternoon while Bronson slept beside her in the car. She shone the beam of the flashlight at the writing on it.

"Take another look at the inscription. It said '*the tablets of ----- temple of Jerusalem,*' which logically translates as 'the tablets of the temple of Jerusalem.' The next relevant phrase is '----- ----- *altar of ----- ----- describes a ----- .*' There are several blanks in that, but I think it probably originally read something like 'in the altar of stone that describes a circle.' The next section is a bit easier to guess. We translated that as '----- *four stones ----- the south side ----- a width of ----- ----- and height ----- ----- cubit to ----- ----- cavity within.*' I think that means 'removing four stones from the south side of a width of some cubits and height of one cubit to expose the cavity within.' "

" 'Some cubits'?" Bronson asked. "I can see why you think it's one cubit high, but the width is a bit bloody vague, isn't it?"

"Yes, but I don't think it matters. The important thing is that the inscription on the clay tablets claimed there's a cavity inside this altar, and they got access to it from the south side, by pulling out several stones. So that's what *we're* going to do."

They stepped closer to the altar, using their flashlights to ensure they didn't trip over anything because the area was treacherous, crisscrossed by low walls and a succession of quite deep square pits whose purpose Bronson could only guess at.

Deciding which part of the altar lay on the "south side" was easy. Bronson simply looked up at the sky, identified the Great Bear star formation and took Angela to the opposite side of the circular structure.

"That's north over there," he said, pointing up at the night sky, "so this is the south face of the altar." He bent down and used his flashlight to look at the stones that formed the side of the structure. "It doesn't look to me as if any of these have been touched for centuries."

He laughed shortly. "Which they haven't, of course. So where do we start?"

"The only dimension the inscription provides for the height of the stones the Sicarii removed was one cubit, assuming that my translation of the Aramaic word was right and meant 'cubit' rather than 'cubits.'"

"Remind me. How long was a cubit?" Bronson asked.

"Roughly eighteen inches," Angela said. "But they were removing stones to get access to a cavity inside this altar, and I think they would just have guessed at the size of the opening they created. From the looks of these stones, taking out almost any two of them *would* leave an opening with a vertical height of about eighteen inches, so that's not much of a clue."

Bronson looked again at the side of the ancient altar. "Well, I suppose we could just start more or less in the middle and see where that gets us."

"There's probably an easier way," Angela said. "There's no mortar between the stones, and one of the things I put in your rucksack was a wire coat-hanger. Untwist it and we've got a thin strong probe about three feet long. Slide it between the stones and see if you can locate the cavity that way."

"Brilliant." Bronson pulled out the hanger and a pair of pliers and began untwisting the steel. In a couple of minutes he'd got the whole thing straight apart from a "T" shape at one end that he could use as a handle.

"Start here," Angela said, gesturing to a large gap between two of the stones.

Bronson slid the probe into the space, but it penetrated for only about eight or ten inches before meeting a solid object, probably another course of stones behind the outermost ones. He pulled it out and tried again, but with the same result.

"This might take a while," he said, forcing the probe into another gap, "but it'll still be a lot quicker than pulling out stones at random."

After almost ten minutes, he had found no sign of any cavity behind the stones. Then, with a suddenness that surprised him, the improvised probe vanished deeper, much deeper, into one space. He pulled it out and tried again, with the same result. Instead of stopping after perhaps ten inches, the steel rod was penetrating well over two feet.

"There's definitely a space behind here," Bronson said. "Come on—let's start looking."

He opened his rucksack again and pulled out the steel crowbar. He slid the point of the tool between two of the stones and levered. Nothing happened, so he switched to the opposite side and heaved on the other end. This time, it moved a fraction. Bronson repeated the process on the top and bottom, and slowly the stone began to loosen. After a couple of minutes he'd freed it up enough to permit him to ram the jimmy deep into the gap at the top of the stone and lever it out of the wall. The stone crashed to the ground with a dull thud. Bronson moved it to one side and then he and Angela peered into the hole it had left.

Disappointingly, there was another stone directly behind the one Bronson had removed.

"I think that's the reason the probe went straight

through," he said, pointing into the hole. "That corner of the stone I've just shifted lined up almost exactly with the one directly behind it. Everywhere else I tried to run the wire through, it must have been hitting the face of one of the stones in the row behind."

"Try the probe again," Angela suggested.

This time, when Bronson slid the thin length of steel into the gaps around the stones of the inner course, it met almost no resistance and clearly entered some kind of a void.

"I'll move another stone from the outer layer," he said, "just to give me room to work, then take out a couple from the second course."

With one stone already removed, shifting a second one was easy. Bronson was concerned about the security of the stones above the hole he'd made in the side of the altar, but they showed no sign of falling out. The inner layers of stones were actually easier to move, because they were slightly smaller, and Bronson quickly pulled out three of them to reveal a small open space.

"Pass me that flashlight, please," he muttered, crouching down on his hands and knees to peer into the cavity.

"What can you see?" Angela demanded, her voice quavering with excitement. "What's in there?"

"It looks to me like it's empty. No, hang on—there's something lying flat on the floor of the cavity. Give me a hand. It looks as if it's quite heavy."

Bronson eased the thick tablet of stone out of the hole he'd made and with Angela's help rested it against the side of the altar. They both stood back and for a few seconds just looked at it.

"What the hell is it?" Bronson asked. "And there's another one in there, I think."

In less than a minute, they'd lifted out the second tablet and placed it gently beside the first one.

"That's it," he said, then looked back into the hole he'd made, using the beam of the flashlight to inspect it. "There's nothing else in the cavity," he reported, "except rubble and a lot of dust."

They both looked intently at the two stone tablets. They were roughly oblong with square bases and rounded tops, maybe an inch thick and perhaps fifteen inches high and nine or ten inches wide. Both surfaces of each slab had been carefully inscribed, and it looked to Bronson as if the two inscriptions were probably written in Aramaic—he'd seen enough of the language lately to be fairly certain he recognized it—and appeared to be identical.

"Dust?" Angela asked after a moment, glancing at him.

"Yes. The dust of two millennia, I suppose."

Angela pointed at the tablets. "But there's not a speck of dust on either of these."

Bronson looked more carefully. "Maybe I knocked it all off when I dragged them out," he suggested. "What are they? The Aramaic could almost be some kind of a list. It looks like a series of individual lines of writing rather than a solid block of text."

For a few seconds Angela didn't reply, just knelt down and stared at the two tablets, the tips of her fingers gently tracing the Aramaic characters. Then she looked up at him, her face pale.

"I never thought we'd find anything like this," she said softly. "I think these could be described as 'the tablets of the Temple of Jerusalem and of Moses.' It looks to me as if these could be early—really early—copies of the Decalogue."

"The what?" Bronson noticed that Angela seemed almost to be having difficulty breathing.

"I mean the Ten Commandments, the Mosaic Covenant. The tablets God gave to Moses on Mount Sinai. The covenant between God and man, the actual tablets that laid out the rules of the faith." She paused for a few seconds, then looked at Bronson, her eyes wide, almost scared. "Forget about the *Ark* of the Covenant. We could be looking at two copies of the *Covenant* itself."

"Who says they're copies?" asked Baverstock, stepping out from behind them, a pistol in his hand.

76

Angela and Bronson span round to stare at Baverstock, disbelief clouding their eyes. The light from their flashlights glinted off the barrel of the automatic he was pointing straight at them.

"I thought you were dead," Bronson muttered.

"That was the idea. I'm sorry about this," Baverstock said, the tone of his voice giving the lie to the words. "It might have been better if you'd both died down there in the tunnel. Don't try to dazzle me. Shine the flashlights at the tablets, or I'll shoot one of you right now."

Bronson and Angela obediently lowered their hands and aimed the flashlight beams downward to illuminate the slabs they'd just recovered from the cavity in the altar. The two ancient stones seemed almost to glow in the light.

"You can't be serious," Angela said. "Are you really suggesting these could be the original Covenant with God that Moses brought down from Mount Sinai? You actually believe these tablets were inscribed by the hand of God?"

"Of course not. Whatever hands carved these, they were made of flesh and blood, but otherwise I'm perfectly serious. There's no doubt that something known as the Mosaic Covenant existed, because the Israelites built the Ark to carry it around. The Ark vanished in about 600 BC when the First Temple in Jerusalem was destroyed by the Babylonians, but there are no traditions relating to the stones themselves. Most archaeologists assume that when the Babylonians looted the Temple they stole the Covenant as well as the Ark, but there's nothing in the historical record to confirm this."

Baverstock stopped talking and stared hungrily at the two slabs of stone that rested against the side of the ancient circular altar.

"So what happens now?" Angela asked. "We should take these to a museum and get them examined and authenticated."

Baverstock's chuckle was anything but humorous in the darkness. "I don't think so, Angela. I've no intention of sharing the glory. The Silver Scroll slipped through my fingers. That's not going to happen with these. I'm going to take them, and you're going to die."

"So you're prepared to kill the two of us just for your pathetic little fifteen minutes of fame? That's so sad, Tony."

"It won't just be fifteen minutes, Angela. It'll be a lifetime of glory. And your deaths will just add a little more blood to the thousand of gallons that have already been spilt in this place over the millennia."

The sudden beam from Baverstock's flashlight dazzled them both, and Bronson saw the pistol in the man's hand as he took aim.

Bronson reacted instantly. He threw his flashlight straight at Baverstock, the beam playing wildly across the rocky ground, a momentary distraction. Then he started to move. He stepped sideways, pushed Angela down onto the ground, and charged toward Baverstock.

Baverstock dodged to one side, avoiding the flying missile, and swung his weapon back to aim at his target—Angela.

Then Bronson hit him, knocking his right arm sideways just as Baverstock pulled the trigger. The bullet whined harmlessly across the ancient hilltop fort, far into the night. Bronson spun round, slightly off-balance. He reached out to grab the other man's arm, but Baverstock dodged, took a couple of steps backward and swung his pistol and flashlight toward him.

For less than a tenth of a second Bronson stared into oblivion, looking straight down the barrel of the other man's automatic; then he threw himself to one side, landing painfully among the sharp-edged rocks.

Baverstock started to turn, to alter his aim and fire again, but suddenly he stopped dead. His head slumped forward and he dropped his arms, the pistol and flashlight clattering to the ground. Then he clutched at his stomach, lifted his head and screamed, a high, wailing call of utter agony and despair that echoed from the surrounding rocks and stones.

Bronson grabbed his own flashlight, which had fallen nearby and was still working, and shone it at him. The pointed end of a slim steel blade was protruding grotesquely from Baverstock's midriff. As Bronson watched, horrified, the blade moved upward, blood pouring from the gaping wound. Baverstock's clutching fingers plucked ineffectively at the steel, more blood pouring from his hands as flesh was sliced off, and his howls of agony redoubled.

What he was seeing was so inexplicable that for perhaps two seconds Bronson simply stood there gaping. Then he ran toward the stricken man. But he never reached him.

Before Bronson had taken more than a couple of steps, the knife angled sharply upward. Baverstock's howls were suddenly cut short and he tumbled limply to the ground. He twitched once, then lay still. Directly behind him, the unpleasantly familiar figure of Yacoub was revealed, a long-bladed knife, still dripping blood, clutched in his right hand. And looming out of the darkness behind him were his two men, each pointing a pistol straight at Bronson.

"Unfinished business," Yacoub said shortly, kneeling to clean the blood off the blade on Baverstock's trousers. The knife vanished inside his jacket, and he shifted the pistol to his right hand. "I thought we'd killed him in the water tunnel. Get back over there," he said, gesturing to Bronson.

"Stay behind me, Angela," Bronson said, as he stopped next to her and turned to face Yacoub.

"Very noble," Yacoub chuckled. "You'll take a bullet for her? That won't be a problem. I've got plenty."

"You said you'd let us go," Bronson said. "Isn't it enough that you've got the Silver Scroll?"

"That was before you found those stones. I heard what that man Baverstock said about them. If those two slabs of rock really are the original Mosaic Covenant, they could change the whole course of the conflict here in Israel. My comrades in Gaza will know how to make the best use of them."

"They should be in a museum," Angela said, her voice angry. "You shouldn't be playing politics with relics as old and as important as these."

Yacoub gestured irritably with his automatic pistol. "Everything in this country is to do with politics, whether you like it or not. Old or new, it doesn't matter. Any weapon we can use, we will use. And now you can see why you're both expendable. Nobody must ever know that those stone tablets were found here in Israel. But I will be merciful. You'll both die quickly."

He lifted his pistol and pointed it at Bronson.

But before he could pull the trigger, there was a muffled bang from somewhere close by, and a faintly luminous object shot up into the sky. In seconds it ignited, burning with the brilliant white-hot light of magnesium, and the darkness was instantly turned into light.

For a moment, Yacoub and his two gunmen stood rigid, as if turned to stone, staring upward.

And then, in the pitiless white light cast by the descending flare, and like spectral creatures arising from the very earth, half a dozen black-clad shapes, their faces blackened with camouflage paint, appeared less than twenty yards away, emerging from behind the low stone walls that lay to one side of the altar. Each was carrying a Galil SAR compact assault rifle.

Yacoub yelled something in Arabic, and his two men dived for what cover they could find, then opened fire on their attackers. The momentary silence was shattered by a volley of shots as his two gunmen traded fire with the armed men, the booming of their nine-millimeter semi-automatic pistols a discordant counterpoint to the flat cracks of the 5.56 millimeter rounds fired from the Galils.

The moment the flare ignited, Bronson acted. He grabbed Angela by the arm and pulled her around to the side of the ancient stone altar. They ducked down, the solid stones acting as an effective shield against any bullets that came their way.

"Keep down," Bronson hissed, as a round cracked into one of the blocks of stone directly above their heads, sending a cascade of splinters and dust over them.

He risked a quick glance around the side of the altar. Yacoub's two men were pinned down behind another of the low stone walls that were the dominant feature of that part of the old fort. They were snapping off shots at their attackers, but they were outnumbered and out-gunned, and Bronson knew there was only ever going to be one outcome to this encounter.

Even as he watched, one of the black-clad figures moved to out-flank them, darting around the outside of the old ruined temple, taking advantage of every scrap of cover he could find. Within twenty seconds, he had reached a position where he could see both of Yacoub's gunmen clearly, and took careful aim with his Galil.

But he didn't fire. Instead, he called out something in Arabic.

Yacoub's men started at the sound of his voice, and both swung their pistols to point at him. It was their last mistake. His Galil cracked, the volley of half a dozen shots taking less than a second to fire, and the two Moroccans tumbled backward. They crashed to the rocky ground and lay still.

The figure ran forward, crouched down to check both the bodies, then stood up and looked around.

"Yacoub!" Angela said suddenly. "Where the hell's Yacoub?"

"I don't know. I didn't see where he went." Bronson looked cautiously over the circular stone altar to the area where the dark-clad men had appeared, then looked to his sides. But he saw no sign of the tall Moroccan.

Then a pistol shot rang out a few feet directly behind Bronson.

The man holding the Galil twenty feet away clutched at his chest and fell backward, the assault rifle falling from his hands. Almost immediately, a tall dark shape materialized beside him and seized his weapon, just as the flare guttered briefly and then went out, plunging the hilltop into sudden darkness.

Bronson stood up, and pulled Angela to her feet. "That was Yacoub," he muttered, "and now he's got an assault rifle. We've got to get out of here."

But as he stood, there came a noise like thunder, then a thudding sound and a tremendous wind, and the blackness of the night was suddenly banished by a brilliant blue-white beam of light from directly above.

Bronson and Angela turned to run, but instead they

found themselves staring into Yacoub's face, his milky-white eye and twisted mouth startlingly clear in the brilliant light from the Nightsun lamp on the helicopter hovering above.

"Stand still," Yacoub snarled, jamming the barrel of his pistol into Bronson's stomach. "You two are my ticket out of here." He gestured with the barrel of the Galil toward the area next to the circular altar. "Put your hands in the air and get over there. Both of you."

"Stay on my left, Angela," Bronson whispered as he turned to obey, "and walk a little in front."

Obediently, Angela moved forward, naked terror etched into her features.

"Quickly," Yacoub snapped, jabbing Bronson hard in the back, the barrel of his pistol pressed against his spine.

And that was just what Bronson had wanted, and why he'd told Angela to move in front of him.

He moved forward a couple of steps, took a deep breath, then swung his left arm, his fingers straightened into a blade, down and back as hard as he could. The side of his hand smashed into Yacoub's left forearm, the force of the blow driving the Moroccan's hand—and the pistol he was holding—to one side, away from Angela.

Then it was just a matter of speed. Bronson spun round, his left arm continuing to force Yacoub's pistol off aim, and drove his clenched right fist straight into the Moroccan's face. Yacoub staggered backward, desperately trying to bring his pistol to bear.

Bronson hadn't finished. He took a half-step closer to Yacoub and punched upward with his left hand as hard as he could. The heel of his hand smashed into the base of Yacoub's nose, splintering the fragile nasal bones and driving them deep into the Moroccan's brain. It was a killing blow. Yacoub fell backward, his limbs twitching and his body going into spasms as his brain began to die.

Bronson grabbed the pistol that the Moroccan had dropped as he fell, took aim and fired two shots directly into his chest. The twitching ceased. Yacoub gave a final convulsive shudder, then lay absolutely still.

For a few seconds, Angela and Bronson stared down at the body of the man who'd caused them so much grief.

Then they turned round. Three of the black-clad figures were standing about ten feet away, their Galils aimed straight at them. One of them gestured at Bronson. He looked down at the pistol he was still holding, and tossed the weapon away. Both he and Angela raised their hands in the air in surrender. Bronson didn't know who these men were, though he could make an educated guess, but they were clearly no friends of Yacoub, so it was at least possible they were on the same side. And with three assault rifles pointing at them, there was no choice anyway.

One of the figures issued an order in a language Bronson thought sounded like Hebrew, and another man stepped forward and briskly handcuffed their arms behind them, then checked they weren't carrying any concealed weapons. As soon as he'd done that, the air of tension eased noticeably.

With a roaring, clattering sound that was completely unmistakable, the helicopter landed on a patch of level ground about fifty yards away, the rotors kicking up a huge cloud of dust and debris that billowed out across the site. Bronson and Angela turned away and closed their eyes.

As soon as the chopper touched down, the roar of the jet engines diminished and the dust cloud dispersed. Bronson turned back to look across at the helicopter, a bulky black shape just visible against the deeper black of the night sky, its navigation and anticollision lights now switched on. In the light from the flashlights held by the men around them, he could see two figures walking slowly toward them.

The men stopped directly in front of them and, immediately they could see their faces, Angela gave a gasp of surprise. "Yosef!" she said. "Why are you here?"

Yosef Ben Halevi smiled slightly. "I could ask you the same question," he replied. "Why are you and your ex-husband digging around on one of Israel's most important ancient sites in the middle of the night?" He smiled again. "But I think I already know the answer to that one."

He turned to his companion and murmured something. The other man nodded, and at a gesture one of the men removed their handcuffs.

"Who are you?" Bronson asked the other man. "Shin Bet? Mossad?"

There was no reply, and after a couple of seconds Yosef Ben Halevi turned to his companion. "We've just watched Bronson kill a man in front of half a dozen witnesses. Whether or not he knows your name and who you work for really doesn't matter."

"Yes, I suppose you're right. OK, Bronson. My name's Levi Barak, and I'm a senior officer in the Mossad."

Bronson pointed to the black-clad figures standing a short distance away. "Are they IDF?"

Barak shook his head. "Not exactly. They're members of the Sayeret Matkal, a special operations unit that works for the Israeli Defense Forces Intelligence Command. It's a deep reconnaissance unit with counterterrorist responsibilities, something like your British SAS."

"I've heard of it," Bronson said. "Weren't they the people responsible for the Entebbe rescue? When PLO terrorists hijacked an Air France plane and flew it to Uganda?"

Barak nodded. "That was an outstanding piece of work. But we're not here to discuss past military operations. We need to decide what to do with you and Angela Lewis."

"And what to do with what you found," Ben Halevi interjected. "Where are the relics?"

"The stone tablets are resting against the side of the altar over there," Angela said, pointing, "but I have no idea where the Silver Scroll is. The man that Chris killed took it away from us in the water tunnel."

Barak issued an order, and two of the men walked around the circular altar, picked up the stone tablets and brought them over to where Ben Halevi was standing. They rested them carefully against a low wall.

The academic crouched down in front of them and, as Barak illuminated the tablets with the beam of his flashlight, he gently, almost lovingly, ran the tips of his fingers over them, caressing the ancient script. "Old Aramaic," he muttered, then stood up.

"Are they what you thought they were?" Levi Barak asked.

Ben Halevi shook his head. "It's far too early to say, but to me they look right."

"And to me," Angela said. "You do mean the Decalogue, don't you? The original Covenant? The second set of stones that Moses himself carried down from Mount Sinai?"

Yosef Ben Halevi nodded slowly, barely able to take his eyes off the ancient relics.

"Right," Barak said briskly. He looked back at Bronson. "You just killed a man," he stated flatly, "and as a police officer you know what that means."

"It was self-defense," Angela said hotly. "If you saw what happened, you'd know that."

"I did see it, but there's a problem. The Sayeret Matkal officers are properly authorized members of Israel's armed forces, able to carry weapons and use them. That man"—he pointed at Yacoub's body—"was killed by a pistol, and not the type we carry." Barak turned and beckoned one of the officers toward him. "Give me your weapon," he instructed.

The officer hesitated for a second, then undid the Velcro strap on his holster and handed over the pistol.

"This," Barak said, "is an Israeli Weapons Industries SP-21 nine-millimeter pistol. One of its characteristics is the polygonal rifling in the barrel. That pistol"—he pointed at the weapon Bronson had dropped on the ground—"is a Czechoslovakian CZ-75, with conventional rifling. When we carry out a post-mortem on the body, we'll find one or two deformed nine-millimeter slugs in the torso, and the rifling marks will clearly show the make and model of pistol that fired them. That will tell the pathologist that this man wasn't killed by any of the troops I ordered to come here. That's the problem."

Barak stepped across to where Yacoub's body lay, and with a single quick movement raised the pistol and fired a single round into the corpse's chest. The body twitched with the impact.

Then he walked back and returned the pistol to the Sayeret Matkal officer. "Now," he said, "the pathologist will find a bullet fired from an SP-21 in that man's body, and will come to the appropriate conclusion."

"What about the other two slugs?" Bronson asked.

"I think that the post-mortem will show that they passed straight through his body and were not recovered. And now," Barak said, "it's time for you to leave. We have to tidy up this place before the tourists start arriving tomorrow morning, and we've still got to find where that one-eyed bastard hid the Silver Scroll."

Three minutes later, Bronson and Angela stared down through the open side door of the helicopter as it lifted away from Har Megiddo. Below them, banks of floodlights were being set up to enable the search for the Silver Scroll to get under way, and the top of the old fortress seemed to be swarming with black-clad men.

77

The rays of the early-morning sun were just striking the roofs and upper levels of the buildings around them, turning the white stone to silver, when Bronson pulled the hire car to a stop in a parking space just off Sultan Suleiman, close to the bus station and at the very edge of the Muslim Quarter of the Old City of Jerusalem.

He and Angela got out and started walking southwest, toward the Damascus Gate. It was three days later, and they were booked on a flight back to London out of Ben Gurion late that afternoon, courtesy of the Mossad. They'd spent most of the time since the showdown at Har Megiddo in an interview room in an anonymous ministry building in Jerusalem, explaining precisely what had happened since Bronson had been briefed to fly out to Morocco what seemed like weeks earlier. Eventually, Levi Barak and Yosef Ben Halevi had decided that there was nothing else they could usefully tell them, and Barak had suggested it would be best for all concerned if they left Israel as soon as possible.

On this, their last day in the country, they'd decided to take a look around the Old City. As they crossed the street to walk along beside the massive city wall, Bronson glanced behind him.

"Are they still there?" Angela asked, taking his hand.

"Yes. Two gray men in two gray suits."

Levi Barak had made it clear that they could go where they liked before their flight, but insisted that they would be watched at all times, and they'd quickly got used to the sight of their two silent shadows.

There were no tourists anywhere, and precious few locals, and the day was pleasantly warm, but the pink and turquoise sky was redolent with the promise of baking heat later.

"It's like having the place to ourselves," Angela said.

The sense of quiet and calm lasted until they reached the open area in front of the Damascus Gate.

Despite the early hour, there were already crowds of people milling round the dozens of temporary stalls— many of them little more than small wheeled carts with umbrellas to shade the produce and the seller—that had been set up among the stately palm trees. Angela and Bronson walked past elderly women wearing traditional embroidered dresses selling snap peas from open sacks, and the air was heavy with the scent of fresh mint. In several places Bronson saw colorful posters, all depicting handsome young men, spread on the ground almost like prayer mats.

"Arab pop stars," Angela said, in answer to his unspoken question.

They walked down stone steps, worn smooth by the

passage of countless feet over numberless years, through an impressive archway topped by turrets and into the noisy, bustling and vibrant world of the Khan ez-Zeit *souk*. A world of narrow cobblestoned alleys; of coffee shops where men played cards and talked as they bubbled tobacco smoke through water pipes; of cobblers and tailors and spice sellers and stalls selling brilliantly colored fabrics; of boxes of vegetables and vendors surrounded by hanging meat; of men dropping balls of chickpeas into huge cauldrons of boiling oil to make falafel. Arab music—discordant to Bronson's ears—blasted from tinny transistor radios and the occasional ghetto-blaster, almost drowning out the cries of the vendors hawking their wares and the constant buzz of conversation, of haggling and arguing over the prices and quality of the goods on offer.

They turned left onto the Via Dolorosa, leaving the hubbub behind them. Bronson took Angela's hand as they walked.

"Well, I suppose you could say we achieved something," he said.

"Absolutely," Angela replied. "This has been a really good week for archaeology in general, and Jewish archaeology in particular. Without lifting a finger, apart from employing a bunch of special forces troops and a few surveillance officers, the Israelis have recovered the legendary Silver Scroll, which means that if there *are* any Jewish treasures left buried somewhere out in the desert they'll now be recovered by *Jewish* archaeologists, which has to be the right thing. Mind you, that will take years because of the time they'll have to spend just conserving the scroll and working out how best to open it to read the inscription."

"Let's hope they don't send it to the people in Manchester who cut open the Copper Scroll."

"I don't think that's likely. Silver—and I'm assuming the scroll *is* silver—is much more resilient than copper, and being immersed in fresh water for the last two millennia shouldn't have done much more than tarnish it. There's even a possibility they might be able to unroll it and read it just as it was written, though I think that's perhaps a bit optimistic."

Then Bronson asked the question that had been troubling him the most.

"Those stone tablets, Angela. Do you really think they were the Mosaic Covenant? Do you think Baverstock was right?"

Angela shook her head. "I'm an academic, and that means I'm paid to be cynical about anything like this. But I don't know," she said, "I really don't know. From what I've read of the biblical descriptions of the Decalogue, they were pretty similar, but that doesn't prove anything. Some scholars believe that the passages in the Bible accurately describe the stone tablets, but it could just as easily work the other way round. The stones could have been fashioned to match the biblical descriptions. In other words, they could have been manufactured specifically to validate the oral traditions of the Bible, to give the wandering Israelites something solid to believe in.

"But a part of me—just a small part—thinks that Baverstock might have been right. There was something spooky, almost otherworldly, about those two stones.

Like the fact that there didn't seem to be any dust on them, although the cavity we dragged them out of was full of the stuff. And the way they seemed almost to glow when we shone our flashlights at them." She gave a slight shiver. "This doesn't sound like me talking, Chris, does it?"

"What do you think the Israelis will do with them now?" Bronson asked, as they turned right to head toward the Kotel Plaza and the Wailing Wall.

"They'll keep them safe, obviously," Angela said. "I had a few words with Yosef Ben Halevi after they'd finished questioning us. I asked him the same thing, and his reply was interesting. He said they'd worked really quickly, and had already taken hundreds of pictures of them, and carried out a variety of other tests to check the patina of the stones, the way the Aramaic letters were formed, all that kind of thing, to try to establish their age. But then he told me that he'd been instructed—and the way he expressed it suggested the order came from the very highest level in the Knesset—that the tablets were not to be put on display, or their existence acknowledged, because of the possible political repercussions if they were."

"So what are they going to do with them?" Bronson asked again.

"Yosef said they'd be going back where they belonged."

"What—back to that altar at Har Megiddo?"

Angela shook her head, then pointed ahead of them, toward the Kotel Plaza. "That's the Wailing Wall," she said. "Do you know why it's called that?"

"No idea."

"The origin of the name is simple enough. After the Second Temple was destroyed by the Romans in 70 CE, no Jews were allowed to visit Jerusalem until the early Byzantine period. Then, they were permitted to visit the Western Wall just once each year, on the anniversary of the destruction of the Temple. The Jews that came here leaned against the Wall and wept over the loss of their holy temple, and that was how the 'Wailing Wall' name was coined."

Bronson looked again at the massive structure on the other side of the square. "But that wall was never actually a part of the Temple, was it?" he asked. "It was only a supporting wall for the ground on which the Temple had once stood. So why do the Jews revere it so much?"

"You're quite right—it was nothing directly to do with the Second Temple itself. But orthodox Jews believe that the divine presence, what they call the *Shechinah*, continues to reside in the place where the Temple used to stand. When the Temple was built, the Holy of Holies, the inner chamber where they would have kept the Ark of the Covenant, was at the western side of the building, and that was where the *Shechinah* would have remained. All Jews are forbidden by their own laws to go onto the Temple Mount itself, to the original Temple site, so that wall"—she pointed—"is the closest they can possibly get to that location. And *that's* why it's so important."

"So?"

"So I think you could argue that if the Ark of the Covenant was supposed to be kept somewhere on the other side of that wall, that would also be the logical place to keep the Covenant itself."

They walked toward the north side of the Kotel Plaza, to the entrance to the Western Wall Heritage, where tours of the tunnels that lay behind the Wailing Wall began.

"That's odd," Angela said. The gate was obviously locked, and there was a large sign across the entrance that stated the exhibition and tunnel were closed due to possible subsidence.

She walked forward and peered into the gloom beyond the gate. Then she turned round and walked back to Bronson, a small but satisfied smile on her face.

"What is it?"

"There are lights on inside, and I could see various people moving around. I'd be amazed if there was any subsidence in the Kotel Tunnel. The stones there are absolutely massive—the biggest one weighs about six hundred tons—and they're resting on solid bedrock. I had my suspicions when I saw that the place was closed, but seeing people inside there now is proof to me. The Israelis are going to put the Moses Stones right back where they belong, in some kind of a hidden shrine behind the Wailing Wall, and as close as they can get to the site of the Holy of Holies of the Second Temple. So now, when the devout Jews come to pray at the Wall, they'll be as close as anyone's been for the last two millennia to the Mosaic Covenant."

Bronson stared at the Western Wall Heritage entrance for a few seconds, then nodded. "Yes," he said. "That does make sense."

They turned away to head back toward the car, Bronson glancing behind at their two escorts.

"You know you never answered my question," he said.

"Which one?"

"The one I asked you in the helicopter as we flew away from Har Megiddo. I said we should form a partnership. We seem to be getting quite good at tracking down lost relics."

Angela nodded, then laughed. "But has it occurred to you that every time somebody's pulled out a gun, it seems to have been pointing straight at us?"

"Yes," Bronson said slowly, "but we've survived it all, haven't we?" He paused and looked at her. "Suppose I gave up being a copper and you stop working at the museum, and we just spent our time tracking down buried treasure?"

"Are you serious?" Angela demanded.

"Yes, I am. We *do* work well together."

"And would our partnership be more than just a working one?"

Bronson took a deep breath. "You already know the answer to that," he said. "I'd like that more than anything."

Angela looked at him for a few seconds before replying; then she smiled. "Why don't we talk about it over lunch? I spotted a decent-looking restaurant on the Via Dolorosa."

"Brilliant idea," Bronson said, linking arms as they walked down Chain Street toward the Church of John the Baptist and the ancient, tortured heart of that most ancient of cities.

AUTHOR'S NOTE

This is a work of fiction, but I've tried to ensure that the book is firmly grounded in fact wherever possible. The places I've described are real, and most of the events I've written about which occurred in the first century AD are also in the historical record.

Masada

The description of the fall of Masada is as accurate as it is possible to be, almost two millennia after the event. The siege ended precisely the way I described it, with the Sicarii defenders effectively committing mass suicide rather than surrender to the hated Roman army. Two women did survive the siege, and they later told the historian Josephus what had occurred. Their account is generally accepted as being an accurate and certainly contemporary description of the events of the last hours before the fortress fell.

Between 1963 and 1965 the Israeli archaeologist Yigael Yadin carried out excavations on the site, during which eleven *ostraca*—small pieces of pottery or stone—

were found in front of the northern palace. One of them bore the name "Ben Ya'ir," the leader of the Sicarii, and each of the others bore a single different name. It's not known for certain, but it seems at least likely that these were the names of the ten men who carried out the executions of the Sicarii defenders prior to the breaching of the wall of the citadel.

Hezekiah's Tunnel and the Pool of Siloam

Nearly three thousand years old, this tunnel remains a significant feat of engineering.

Jerusalem is situated on a hill, and was fairly easy to defend against attackers because of its elevation. The one problem the defenders had was that their principal source of water was located out in the Qidron Valley and lay some distance outside the walls of Jerusalem. So a prolonged and determined siege, which was the commonest way of taking most military objectives in those days, would always result in the capture of the city because eventually the stored water supplies would run out.

In about 700 BC, King Hezekiah was very concerned that the Assyrians led by Sennacherib would besiege Jerusalem and decided the water supply problem had to be solved, though there's now some doubt about whether he really deserves all the credit.

In 1838 an American scholar named Edward Robinson discovered what's now known as Hezekiah's Tunnel. It's also called the Siloam Tunnel because it runs from the Gihon Spring to the Pool of Siloam. The tunnel was obviously intended to function as an aqueduct and channel water to the city. It's more or less S-shaped, about a third of a mile long, and there's a slope of a little under one degree all the way down, which would ensure that the water would flow in the right direction.

Building it would have been a massive undertaking given the tools the inhabitants of the city were known to possess, and current theories suggest that the tunnel was actually partly formed from a cave that already ran most of the way. An inscription was found at one end of the tunnel which suggested that it was constructed by two teams of workmen, starting at opposite ends. The spring was then blocked and the diverted water allowed to flow to Jerusalem itself. That's basically the legend and more or less what the Bible claims.

But in 1867, Charles Warren, a British army officer, was exploring Hezekiah's Tunnel and discovered another, much older, shaft system now called Warren's Shaft. This consisted of a short system of tunnels which began inside the city walls and ended in a vertical shaft directly above Hezekiah's Tunnel near the Gihon Spring. It allowed the inhabitants to lower buckets into the water in the tunnel without exposing themselves outside the walls. Dating it accurately has proved difficult, but the consensus is that it was probably built in about the tenth century BC.

And if that wasn't enough, a few years later, in 1899, yet another and very much older tunnel was discovered that also ran directly from the Gihon Spring to the Siloam Pool. This is now known as the Middle Bronze Age Channel, and is estimated to date from about 1800 BC, almost four thousand years ago. It was a simple ditch dug deep into the ground, and was then covered with large slabs of rock, themselves hidden by foliage. Obviously the fact that it was a surface channel as opposed to an underground tunnel was a potential weak point in a siege.

So from today's research it looks as if Hezekiah simply looked at the existing water channels, saw their weaknesses and decided to improve on them, rather than having the inspiration himself to create the aqueduct and then organize the work. It could be argued that his tunnel was really just a bigger and better version of the Middle Bronze Age Channel.

Qumran and the Dead Sea Scrolls

The settlement of Qumran is located on a dry plateau, about a mile inland from the northwest bank of the Dead Sea and near the Israeli kibbutz of Kalia. It's probable that the first structures there were built during the early part of the first century BC, and the site was finally destroyed in AD 70 by Titus and troops of the X Fretensis Roman legion.

Most accounts agree that the Dead Sea Scrolls were discovered accidentally by a Bedu goat-herder named Mohammed Ahmad el-Hamed, who was nicknamed "edh-Dhib," meaning "the wolf." Early in 1947, he either went into one of the caves near Qumran looking for a lost animal or perhaps threw a stone into a cave to drive out one of his goats, and heard the sound of something shattering. The result was that he found a collection of very old pottery jars containing ancient scrolls wrapped in linen cloth.

Recognizing that the scrolls were old and perhaps valuable, el-Hamed and his fellow Bedu removed some—most accounts state only three scrolls were taken from the cave at first—and offered to sell them to an antiques dealer in Bethlehem, but this man declined to buy them, believing they might have been stolen from a synagogue. These scrolls passed through various hands, including those of a man named Khalil Eskander Shahin, colloquially known as "Kando," an antiques dealer. He apparently encouraged the Bedu to recover more of the scrolls, or possibly visited Qumran himself and removed some of them—whatever happened, Kando eventually personally possessed at least four of the scrolls.

While arrangements for the sale of the relics were being made, they were entrusted to a third party for safe-keeping, a man named George Isha'ya, who was a member of the Syrian Orthodox Church. Recognizing the importance of the scrolls, Isha'ya took some of them to St Mark's Monastery in Jerusalem—a Syrian Orthodox establishment—to try to have the texts appraised. Mar Athanasius Yeshue Samuel, the Metropolitan of Palestine and Transjordan—a "metropolitan" is a rank between a bishop and a patriarch, more or less equivalent to an archbishop—heard about the scrolls. He examined them and managed to buy four of them.

More of the scrolls started appearing in the murky Middle Eastern antiquities trade, and three were purchased by Professor Eleazer Sukenik, an Israeli archaeologist. Shortly afterward, Sukenik heard about the scrolls Mar Samuel had acquired, and tried to buy them from him, but couldn't reach an agreement.

Then a man called John Trever became involved. He

was employed at the American Schools of Oriental Research (ASOR), and was an enthusiastic photographer, which turned out to be a significant hobby. In February 1948 he met Mar Samuel and photographed all the scrolls the Metropolitan owned. Over the years, the scrolls have steadily deteriorated, but his album of pictures has since allowed scholars to see them as they were at that time, and has facilitated their study and permitted translations of the texts to be made.

The Arab-Israeli War of 1948 resulted in the removal of the scrolls to Beirut for safekeeping. At that time, no academic had any idea where the scrolls had been found, and because of the turmoil in the country, carrying out any kind of search for their source was not feasible. It wasn't until January 1949 that a United Nations observer finally discovered what then became known as Cave 1 at Qumran.

Once the first cave had been found, further searches were carried out and the other caves in the area were explored. The scrolls were found in eleven of these caves, but no scrolls or fragments were ever discovered at Qumran itself.

The first archaeological expedition to Qumran was led by Father Roland de Vaux of the Ecole Biblique in Jerusalem. He began his excavations in Cave 1 in 1949, and two years later started digging at Qumran as well. This approach was badly flawed, because de Vaux assumed that the inhabitants of Qumran had written the scrolls, and used the contents of them to deduce what Qumran must have been.

It was a classic circular argument, and the result was

entirely predictable: because the scrolls were mainly religious texts, de Vaux came to the conclusion that the inhabitants of Qumran were devoutly religious, a sect called the Essenes. Every artifact he and his team recovered from the site was interpreted in line with this assumption, despite the lack of any empirical evidence to support this conclusion. So a water cistern became a Jewish ritual bath, and so on, and any finding that disagreed with this hypothesis was simply ignored or assumed to be later contamination.

The Copper Scroll and its listing of tons of buried treasure, of course, flew directly in the face of de Vaux's interpretation of the site, and he dismissed it out of hand as either a hoax or some kind of joke.

The Copper Scroll

The Copper Scroll is still one of the more perplexing mysteries of Middle Eastern archaeology. Discovered by Henri de Contenson in 1952 in Cave 3 at Qumran, it was completely unlike any other relic found anywhere, before or since. Although generally regarded as one of the Dead Sea Scrolls, absolutely the only reason for this assumption is that it was found with other scrolls in one of the caves at Qumran. In every other respect—material, content, and language—it is entirely different.

Made from almost pure—99 percent—copper, the preparation of which would have been extremely difficult, and almost eight feet in length, the scroll is simply an inventory, a matter-of-fact listing of the whereabouts of an enormous hoard of treasure. The language used is unusual. It's an early form of Hebrew—what's known as a square-form script—which appears to have some linguistic affinity with pre-Mishnaic Hebrew and even Aramaic, but some of the expressions used are only completely comprehensible to readers familiar with both Arabic and Akkadian. In short, the palaeography (the style of writing) and the orthography (the spelling) used in the Copper Scroll are unlike any other known contemporary texts, from Qumran or anywhere else.

Another peculiarity is the presence of a handful of Greek letters that follow certain of the locations listed, and the first ten of which do, as stated in this novel, spell out the name of the Egyptian pharaoh Akhenaten. Theories abound, but nobody has so far produced any convincing reason why this should be.

It's been suggested that the Copper Scroll contains some thirty mistakes, of the kind that would be expected from a scribe copying a document written in a language with which he was unfamiliar, suggesting the possibility that the contents of the scroll had been copied from another, perhaps earlier, source. This, again, is pure conjecture.

The locations of the hidden treasure listed in the Copper Scroll are both highly specific and completely useless. The depth at which a cache of gold has been buried, for example, is described in detail, but discovering the actual location requires an exhaustive knowledge of town and street names, plus property ownership information, from first-century Judea, knowledge that has been lost for two millennia.

The general consensus among archaeologists is that

the Copper Scroll probably is genuine, and that the treasures listed were hidden in the Judean desert. It's even possible that one of them has been found: in 1988 a small earthenware vessel containing a dark, sweet-smelling oil was found in a cave not far from Qumran, and one interpretation of a listing on the Copper Scroll suggests that it could have been one of the items recorded.

The Silver Scroll

Perhaps the most intriguing entry of all on the Copper Scroll is the last one, which states that another document had been hidden that contained more detailed information about the location of the various treasures. One translation of this enigmatic section of the text reads: *A copy of this inventory list, its explanation and the measurements and details of every hidden item, is in the dry underground cavity that is in the smooth rock north of Kohlit. Its opening is toward the north with the tombs at its mouth.*

This other document—which has become known as the Silver Scroll—was one of several treasures claimed to be hidden in the city of Kohlit, but the exact location of this place is unknown. There is an area named Kohlit lying to the east of the Jordan River, but there's no evidence to suggest that this is the place referred to in the Copper Scroll, and the only other "Kohlit" in the Middle East is K'eley Kohlit in Ethiopia, much too far away to be a possibility. The other clue is the reference to the "tombs at its mouth." This could be interpreted to indicate a north-facing cave close to a burial ground, but is of little real help.

But the important point is that, if the Copper Scroll *is* an authentic listing of buried treasure, then the reference to the Silver Scroll must also be assumed to be authentic, which means that this legendary object did exist. The authors of the Copper Scroll presumably knew exactly where the Silver Scroll was secreted, because of their accurate—though meaningless to us—description of its location. But that doesn't mean the relic is still in the same location specified in the Copper Scroll.

The first century AD was a time of tremendous turmoil in Judea, with constant skirmishes between bands of Jewish rebels and the Roman legions, and it's certainly possible that important objects—which would have implicitly included both the Copper Scroll and the Silver Scroll—could have been removed from their hiding places and taken to locations that were more secure. The caves at Qumran were one such place, and proved to be a safe repository for the Dead Sea Scrolls for almost two millennia. It's quite possible that Ein-Gedi was thought to be another.

Ein-Gedi

As stated in *The Moses Stone*, the oasis at Ein-Gedi was one of the most important settlements outside Jerusalem during the first century AD, and was raided by the Sicarii during the siege of Masada, exactly as I described. It is certainly possible that the Jewish priests might have believed the Temple was under imminent threat from the advancing Roman army, and would have tried to remove their most important treasures to a place of safety. If so, Ein-Gedi would have been an obvious choice.

If the Temple of Jerusalem had been the custodian of the Copper Scroll, Silver Scroll and the Mosaic Covenant at this time, the presence of these relics at the oasis beside the Dead Sea would not have been unexpected. And during their raid, the Sicarii would probably have grabbed anything they could lay their hands on.

If these Zealots *did* unexpectedly find themselves in possession of three of the holiest treasures of the Jewish nation, they would have done everything in their power to ensure that the hated Romans wouldn't be able to seize them, hence my fictional account of the four Sicarii clambering down from the fortress at Masada.

The Temple Mount and the Wailing Wall

The Western Wall—of which the Wailing Wall is a part— is one of the four retaining walls of the Temple Mount, and its construction shows a distinct gradation from the bottom to top. The courses of masonry at the base, and extending to about two-thirds of the way up, are formed from large single blocks of light-colored stone, the biggest ones probably at least a meter cubed. Above them, significantly smaller stones have been used, all the way to the top.

The wall isn't a single structure, though the lower part looks as if it is. In fact, only the lowest seven courses of stones have indented borders, so they are all that date from Herod's time, when he strengthened the Temple Mount in 20 BC. Above them, the next four layers of stones are slightly smaller, and they were laid down during the Byzantine period, which ran from AD 330 to

640. The third section, above that, was built after the Muslim capture of Jerusalem in the seventh century, and the layer at the very top is the most recent, added in the nineteenth century. That was paid for by a British philanthropist named Sir Moses Montefiore. What isn't visible are the further seventeen courses of stones, all now underground because of the almost constant building and rebuilding that has taken place in that part of the city.

The origin of the name "Wailing Wall" is simple enough. After the Second Temple was destroyed by the Romans in AD 70, no Jews were allowed to visit Jerusalem until the early Byzantine period. Then, they were permitted to visit the Western Wall just once each year, on the anniversary of the destruction of the Temple. The Jews that came to the Wall leaned against it and wept over the loss of their holy temple, and that was how the name was coined.

The Jews were banned from visiting the Wall again between 1948 and 1967, when the city was controlled by the Jordanians, but during the Six Day War Israeli paratroopers seized the Temple Mount and this area of Jerusalem. They had no strategic objective in doing so, but the site had always been of immense religious and symbolic significance to the nation. Within weeks, over a quarter of a million Jews had visited the Wall. When the Israelis took control, most of what is now called the Kotel Plaza was already built on, and the only bit of the Western Wall that was accessible was about a hundred feet long, and the area in front of it was only some ten feet wide. The Israelis razed the area, and leveled and paved the square.

It's worth emphasizing that the Western Wall was never actually a part of the Temple—it was only a supporting wall for the ground on which the Second Temple had once stood. But orthodox Jews believe that the divine presence, what they call the *Shechinah*, continues to reside in the place where the Temple used to stand. When the Temple was built, the Holy of Holies, the inner chamber where they would have kept the Ark of the Covenant, was at the western side of the building, and that was where the *Shechinah* would have remained. All Jews are forbidden by their own laws to go onto the Temple Mount itself, to the original Temple site, so the Western Wall is the closest they can possibly get to that location. And that's why it's so important to them.

To the left of the Wailing Wall, beyond the wall of the adjoining building with its two massive buttresses, is the Kotel Tunnel, open to the public and a very popular tourist destination. The entrance is an archway set almost in the center of the building, with a curved line of Hebrew writing above it, following the shape of the arch. Below the Hebrew is the English translation: "The Western Wall Heritage."

The tour begins in a room known as the Donkey Stable, an epithet bestowed by the British explorer Charles Warren. It took workmen and archaeologists seventeen *years* to clear the accumulated rubble and rubbish from that room. From there, visitors walk into the Secret Passage. According to legend, the passage had been used by King David as a way of making his way unseen and underground from his citadel, which lay over to the west, to the Temple Mount. Unfortunately, the archaeological evidence suggests that the tunnel had actually been built by the Arabs in the late twelfth century AD. They had needed to raise the level of that section of the city and had built massive foundations to achieve that end. The tunnel had, in fact, been used to allow access to the Temple Mount, but for Muslim residents of Jerusalem, not Jewish worshippers. Later, the vaults had been sectioned off and used as cisterns, providing the citizens who lived directly above the tunnel with a constant supply of fresh water. This passage ends abruptly in a pile of rubble, a mute reminder of the state of the subterranean labyrinth before the Jewish archaeologists started work there.

In the Hall of the Hasmoneans, a large chamber that dates from the Second Temple period, is a Corinthian pillar more or less in the center. One of the indicators of the dating of the chamber is the way the stone is dressed, a mark of the way Herod's builders carried out their work, but the pillar itself dates from medieval times. It was brought in to support the roof, which was cracked and damaged and needed extra support.

In a narrow corridor later in the tour is an absolutely massive single stone. It's over forty feet long, nearly twelve feet high and between eleven and fifteen feet thick. The best estimates suggest it weighs around five hundred metric tons, which makes it one of the largest, perhaps even *the* largest, stone ever used in any building, anywhere in the world, bigger even than the stones in the pyramids. Most of the cranes available today can only lift about half that weight, so the obvious question is how Herod's builders managed to shift it. And not just move it, because although it's only about three or four feet above the level of the floor in the tunnel, the original street level was at least twenty feet below that, and the bedrock a further ten feet down.

That stone forms part of what's known as the Master Course, and research suggests that it was done for a very good reason. No mortar or cement of any kind was used when the wall was built, and the theory is that these huge stones served to stabilize it. Their massive weight kept the stones below them in place, and provided a firm base for the courses above. It's known that the wall has remained intact for some two thousand years and has survived several earthquakes, so Herod's builders were probably right.

Har Megiddo

The name of this historic place is Megiddo, and it's normally prefixed by either "tel," meaning "mound," or more commonly "har," or "hill," but sometimes it's also referred to as Tel-el-Mutesellim or the "Hill of the Ruler." Over the years, the name "Har Megiddo" has been corrupted into "Armageddon."

Megiddo was one of the oldest and most important cities in Judea, and the plain below it was the site of the first ever recorded pitched battle. In fact, there've been dozens of battles at that location, and three "Battles of Megiddo." The last one took place in 1918 between British forces and troops of the Ottoman Empire.

But the most famous was the first one, in the fifteenth century BC, between Egyptian forces under the Pharaoh Thutmose III and a Canaanite army led by the King of

Kadesh, who'd joined forces with the ruler of Megiddo. Kadesh was in what's now Syria, not far from the modern city of Hims and, like Megiddo, it was an important fortified town.

There were three possible routes the invading army could have taken as they headed north toward the Valley of Jezreel, where the enemy troops had assembled. The shortest was the middle route, a straight passage through Aruna, part of which would have meant the army marching through a very narrow ravine, or two longer but safer routes to the east and west.

Thutmose sent out scouts and discovered that his enemy had clearly assumed he wouldn't take the middle road. They'd split their forces to cover the other two approaches, but had left the ravine virtually unguarded, obviously assuming that the Egyptians wouldn't be stupid enough to send their troops into such an obvious killing ground. So the pharaoh himself led his men through the ravine. Aruna only had a few enemy troops stationed there and they were quickly scattered by the Egyptian forces, who then entered the valley unopposed. They did battle with the King of Kadesh's forces, defeated them, and ended up besieging Megiddo itself, which eventually fell. Unusually for the time, the Egyptians spared both the city and its inhabitants, and their victory marked the beginning of around five hundred years of Egyptian rule and influence in the area. We know so much about this battle because a record of what happened was carved into the walls of the Temple of Amun at Karnak in Egypt.

The Mosaic Covenant

It's been generally accepted that the Ark of the Covenant was a real object, probably a highly ornamented acacia-wood box covered in gold leaf, which was carried by the wandering Israelites. The logical assumption is that the Covenant itself was also a real, tangible object, and was kept inside it.

According to the Old Testament, in the third month after the Exodus, Moses gave the original so-called "Tablets of the Covenant," or more accurately the "Tablets of Testimony," to the people of Israel at the foot of Mount Sinai. This Covenant was a contract between God and His chosen people, the ten simple rules, the Ten Commandments, that later formed the basis of both the Jewish and the Christian faiths (though, as I state in the book, Exodus actually specifies that there were *fourteen* Commandments).

Moses then went back up to Mount Sinai before later returning to his people to find that they'd already deviated from the path he'd laid out for them. He found that they had ignored the second commandment, which forbade the construction of any kind of graven image for the purpose of worship. Moses' brother Aaron had made a Golden Calf and erected an altar in front of it. Moses flew into a violent rage and in his fury smashed both the tablets of the Covenant.

God then offered to personally carve a second, duplicate, set of tablets, and Moses went back up to Mount Sinai yet again to receive them, and it was these tablets that were placed in the Ark of the Covenant. In fact, the

Ark should have more correctly been called the "Ark of Testimony."

This Ark vanished in about 586 BC when the First Temple in Jerusalem was destroyed by the Babylonians, led by Nebuchadnezzar. But there are no traditions relating to the tablets themselves, only to the Ark, to the box they were kept in. It's been assumed that when the Babylonians looted the Temple they took away the Ark *and* the Tablets of the Covenant, but there's nothing in the historical record to confirm this.

But it *is* a fact that the Ark itself had become an object of worship and veneration by this time, so it's at least possible that when Nebuchadnezzar and his hordes descended on Jerusalem, the tablets had already been taken to a place of safekeeping, just leaving the Ark in the Temple. Whatever actually happened then, the truth is that the Tablets of Testimony, the original Mosaic Covenant, simply disappeared into oblivion over three thousand years ago.

What is almost certain is that, whatever happened to these tablets, they weren't lost. They were far too important to the Jewish religion to simply be mislaid. If they weren't seized by Nebuchadnezzar, then they were almost certainly hidden before the conflict began, and probably somewhere outside Jerusalem because the likelihood was that the city would be sacked and plundered by the invaders. Again, the oasis at Ein-Gedi would have been a possible, perhaps even a probable, hiding place for them.

At the end of the book I describe the Israelis hiding the Mosaic Covenant in a cavity behind the Wailing Wall.

If this relic was ever found, and the political situation prevented them from announcing they'd recovered the object, I think this is exactly where they'd want to put it, to return the Covenant to the place closest to where the Ark of the Covenant originally stood.

And in doing so, they'd effectively be reuniting the *Shechinah*, the divine presence, with the earliest record of the Covenant between man and God.

Read on for a special sneak peek
at the next pulse-pounding thriller
from James Becker

THE MESSIAH SECRET

Coming from Signet Select
in December 2010

Ldumra
AD 72

The nine men had made slow progress ever since they'd left the last village, the simple stone houses a distant ghostly monochrome in the gray light of predawn, and started the final stage of their long climb.

There was no road, barely even a track, leading to where they were going, though they knew exactly the route they needed to follow, a route that would take them high into the mountains and finish in a blind-ended valley. Each of them—bar one—also knew that they were making the last journey of their lives. Only one man in the group would ever leave that valley, or would want to. That journey—or, to be exact, the reason for that journey—was the culmination of everything they'd worked for throughout their adult lives.

They were well armed, each man carrying a dagger and a sword, and all but two of them also had a bow and a quiver of arrows over their shoulders. The whole area, and especially Ldumra, was well-known as a haunt of bandits and thieves. Their principal prey was the laden caravans traveling along what would later become known as the Silk Road, but they would show no compunction in attacking any group of travelers, especially if they believed those people were carrying valuables. And the nine men were accompanying a treasure that every member of the armed escort was fully prepared to die to protect. Only when they reached their destination would they be able to relax, when the treasure would at last be safe— safe, they hoped, for all eternity.

Two of the men rode slowly at the head of the group, each mounted on a woolly two-humped Bactrian camel, an animal surprisingly well-adapted to the harsh terrain. Following them, two yaks were hitched to a small and sturdy wooden cart, one man sitting on the bench at the front, whip in hand. Two other yaks followed, tied with short ropes to the rear of the cart, then half a dozen donkeys, each bearing a single rider and with a heavy pack on its rump.

In the flat loading area of the cart was a heavy wooden box, perhaps eight feet in length, four feet wide and two feet high. The box was invisible, being completely covered in piles of furs and other garments, baskets of food and pitchers of water and wine. The men hoped they looked like a group of simple travelers transporting nothing of value so they would be of no interest to any bandits.

And their appearance was unremarkable. With one exception, they all looked—and indeed were—indigenous to the area. Their skin was brown and heavily wrinkled from a lifetime's exposure to the sun in the thin air at high altitude, their eyes Mongoloid, their faces broad and flat, their hair black and worn long.

The odd one out was the youngest man, riding one of the donkeys near the center of the group. Perhaps twenty years old, less than half the age of the youngest of his companions, he had fair skin and an almost ruddy complexion. His eyes were a bright and startling blue and his hair—then invisible under his hooded cloak— was reddish-brown. He was known to his companions as "Sonam," the word translating as "the fortunate one," though that was not his given name.

The track from the village ran for less than a mile, and then crossed a mountain stream. The small caravan stopped by the bank and the travelers took the opportunity to drink and refill all their water containers. It would be the last stream they would cross before the steepest part of the ascent began, and although the valley was cold, with blankets of snow covering the peaks that surrounded them, an adequate supply of drinking water was essential.

The two men riding the camels remained mounted, alert for any signs of danger lurking behind the hills and within the scrubby vegetation that bordered the tumbling waters, but they saw nothing. In a few minutes all the members of the caravan had remounted and resumed their journey, fording the stream and climbing the bank on the opposite side.

The going became rougher the higher they ascended, the track—such as it was—barely wide enough to accommodate the wooden cart, and their progress was reduced to little more than a slow walking pace.

It was midmorning before they saw the first sign of anyone else on the mountainside. The leading camel walked around a bend in the track, and as the animal stepped forward, a shadowy figure dressed in gray melted back into the rocks, perhaps fifty yards in front, on the left-hand side.

Immediately, Je-tsun, the leading rider, reined in his mount and raised his hand to stop the caravan. He glanced behind him, checking that his companions had seen his signal, and at the same time grabbed his bow, removed an arrow from the quiver on his back and notched it, ready to fire.

"What is it?" the man riding the second camel asked, stopping beside him and readying his own bow. His name was Ketu, and their language was a local dialect that would, in time, become known as Old Tibetan.

"A man," Je-tsun said shortly. "In the rocks on the left."

The two men scanned the track that meandered along the side of the mountain in front of them. If the figure was a bandit, he and his fellow thieves hadn't picked a particularly good place for an ambush. The caravan—apart from the cart, obviously, which was unable to leave the track—could move well over to the right, away from the rock-strewn mountainside, which would give the riders space to maneuver, and to fire their arrows.

"Not where I'd have chosen to mount an attack," Ketu muttered.

As if in answer to his remark, a figure wearing a gray cloak appeared some distance further away from the track and, behind him, a handful of goats could be seen, moving erratically across the rough and rocky terrain towards a small level area studded with patches of green.

The two men sighed in relief.

"Was that who you saw?"

Je-tsun nodded. "I think so. It looks like him, anyway."

After a few minutes, the caravan resumed its slow but steady progress along the track and the increasingly uneven ground. Fallen rocks and trees frequently blocked their route, and several times three or four of the men had to dismount to drag and lever the obstacles to one side to create sufficient space for the cart to continue on its way.

Just after the sun reached its highest point in the sky, Je-tsun ordered the caravan to stop on a small level plateau that offered good visibility in all directions. They dismounted and clustered around the cart, where their supplies were stored. They chewed hunks of heavy unleavened bread and strips of dried meat, washed down with water—they wouldn't touch the wine until they reached their destination.

Less than fifteen minutes later, they were on the move again, and about half an hour after that, the bandits hit them.

The caravan rounded another bend to see a tree trunk lying across the track, completely blocking it. In itself, that wasn't a cause for concern—they'd had to shift half a dozen already on their journey—but when they reined in their mounts, the silence of the mountains was shattered by a sudden shouted command, and then a volley of arrows erupted from the rocks over to their left.

Most of them missed, but two hit Je-tsun squarely

in the chest, knocking him backwards in his saddle. He grunted with the double impact, but didn't fall.

Beside him, Ketu swiftly notched an arrow on his own bow and fired at one of the attackers they could now see clearly. A gang of about a dozen bandits, clothed in gray and brown cloaks, was standing among the rocks to the left of the ambush site, all armed with bows and arrows or throwing spears.

Behind the two men mounted on camels, the rest of the group surged forward, yelling defiance as they dismounted. They used the bodies of their animals for cover, unslung their bows and fired at the bandits. The exception was the blue-eyed younger man, who was quickly dragged behind the yak-drawn cart by one of his companions.

"Sonam, stay down!" the man hissed, seizing his own bow and pulling an arrow out of his quiver.

In seconds, the air filled again with arrows, the missiles clattering against the rocks and thudding into the wooden sides of the cart. The driver jumped off the vehicle and ducked into shelter—he had no bow—while his companions fought for their lives.

Three of the bandits fell screaming, tumbling back into the rocks, their bodies pierced by the well-aimed arrows of the travelers.

The driver of the cart suddenly howled with pain as an arrow slammed into his thigh. He fell backwards, both hands clutching at his injury, and the two other men dragged him behind the cart, desperately seeking shelter from the hail of missiles that still whistled across the mountainside.

One of the donkeys fell, three arrows striking it almost simultaneously and killing it instantly, and Je-tsun's camel roared in pain as a spear grazed its side. Two of the travelers collapsed to the ground, one with an arrow through his neck, the point glistening red in the weak sunlight, the other pierced by two spears.

Then another shout rang out, and for an instant the volley of arrows diminished as the bandits stared at the scene in front of them.

Both of the men mounted on the camels were still in their saddles, but each of them now sprouted a handful of arrows, their points embedded in their chests and stomachs. But neither Je-tsun nor Ketu appeared in any way affected by this—both were still aiming their bows and firing arrows without any obvious discomfort.

The sight was unsurprising to the travelers, but was clearly unnerving the bandits, who obviously believed both men should be dead or at least mortally wounded. The men pointed, shouting at one another in disbelief, then stopped the attack and simply took to their heels, vanishing into the jumble of rocks that covered the slope behind them.

For a few seconds, nobody on the track moved. They just stared at the hillside, making sure that their attackers really had gone, and weren't regrouping to launch another assault.

Behind the cart, Sonam and his companion stood up cautiously and looked round, then turned to give what assistance they could to the injured driver.

Je-tsun issued crisp orders. Two of his men drew their swords and ran across to the side of the track from which the attack had been launched, and from which a dull moaning sound could be heard, coming from one of the wounded bandits. Moments later, the moaning rose to a scream; then there was the sound of a blow and the noise stopped completely. Seconds afterwards, Je-tsun's men reappeared, one of them cleaning the blade of his weapon.

At the same time, two other men stepped forward to check on their companions who'd fallen, but it was immediately apparent that they were both dead. Swiftly, the bodies were stripped of their weapons and belts, and then the corpses were carried over to the opposite side of the track. There was no time to bury them, but Je-tsun ordered the two corpses to be laid out and covered with rocks, to try to keep away the vultures and other scavengers.

Only then, when he was sure the attack was over, did Je-tsun nudge his camel to make it kneel on the stony track, and dismounted. Behind him, Ketu did the same.

"It worked, my friend," Ketu said, stepping towards the other man and moving clumsily.

"It worked," Je-tsun agreed, and awkwardly pulled his cloak over his head, the front of it stuck fast to his chest by the handful of arrows. Underneath it, secured by wide leather straps over his shoulders, he wore two thick planks of wood, covering his chest and back, a rudimentary form of body armor.

Je-tsun placed the wood on the ground and plucked out the arrows, one by one, then donned the planks again and replaced his cloak.

He turned to look at the wound his camel had sustained, but it was little more than a graze. The spear had obviously struck the animal a glancing blow that had left a shallow cut on the skin. One donkey was dead, pierced by three arrows, and two others had minor wounds.

Je-tsun walked across to the yak-drawn cart and looked at the three men there, one injured, the other two ministering to him.

Sonam stood up as he approached, and Je-tsun bowed down in front of him. "You are unhurt, my lord?" he asked, standing erect again.

Sonam nodded. "Yes, but Akar is bleeding badly from his thigh. The arrow has cut through several blood vessels, I think."

Je-tsun nodded, clasped the younger man by the shoulders and then bent down to look at the injured man.

Akar looked up as Je-tsun knelt beside him. He was quivering with shock, and blood was pumping out of both sides of his thigh—the arrow had penetrated right through his leg, and was still lodged in the wound.

Je-tsun looked at the pain-racked face of the man he'd known for decades and shook his head. He knew that the injury was life-threatening simply because of the blood loss, but there was more to it than that. The bandits were known to smear the tips of their arrows with poison or excrement, and even if the wound wasn't fatal in itself, there was a good chance that infection would follow in the days to come, killing the victim more slowly but just as surely.

Akar stared at Je-tsun, knowledge of the reality of the situation written on his face. He nodded slowly, lifted his right hand and seized the other man's arm. "Make it quick, my friend," he said, leaned back on the rocky ground and closed his eyes.

Je-tsun nodded in his turn, drew a short dagger from the scabbard at his belt and swiftly drove it into Akar's chest, straight through his heart. The man on the ground shuddered once, then lay still, his features growing slack as the pain ebbed away for the last time.

About half an hour later, the small caravan—now three men down, their bodies already stiffening under a hastily built cairn of stones beside the track where the attack had taken place—moved off again. For the rest of the journey, the six men neither saw nor met anyone else, and they finally reached their destination, high up the valley, about an hour after sunset.

. Je-tsun ordered torches lit, then sent two of his men inside to check the structure thoroughly, and to ensure that nobody else had taken refuge there, though at that altitude it was unlikely. They emerged a few minutes later, to report that the place was exactly as it had been the previous year, when they'd found it for the first time, and when they'd spent almost six months preparing it, a task that had proved to be both physically demanding and had also required considerable ingenuity.

Je-tsun nodded in satisfaction. He ordered the yaks to be unhitched from the cart and had them turned loose, together with the remaining donkeys. They wouldn't need those animals again. But the two camels were tethered securely on a patch of level ground nearby, where scrubby bushes would provide them with something to eat.

The men removed all the furs and other goods from the cart to expose the heavy wooden crate underneath, lifted it between them and carried it into the entrance, where they laid it on the ground. Then they lit more torches to provide enough light to start their work. Balks of timber had been piled against the opposite wall, and it took over an hour to remove them all, and to reveal the inner chamber.

Before they entered, Je-tsun walked in and inspected it. The small room was almost square, and for obvious reasons devoid of windows or any other openings. At one end was what looked almost like an altar, an oblong shape made from hewn chunks of solid stone, the gaps between them filled with some kind of mortar, and the top covered with half a dozen slabs of stone.

The men picked up the heavy box again, carried it into the chamber and set it down beside the stone structure. Je-tsun issued another order, and his men began removing the slabs, leaning the heavy pieces of stone against the wall. Their actions revealed that the structure was completely empty, just an oblong cavity formed from shaped rocks. When they'd removed the last slab, Je-tsun peered inside, ran the tips of his fingers along the inner surfaces and nodded in satisfaction.

Building this cavity of stone had been one of the tasks he and his men had carried out the previous year, and his only concern had been the possibility of damp inside it, because their treasure was very fragile. But he could detect no signs of moisture on the cold stones that formed the cavity, the structure that would be the last resting place of the wooden box and its precious contents.

Getting the box inside the stone cavity was not going to be easy, just because of its size and weight, but they had foreseen the problem and Je-tsun had come up with a simple and effective solution.

One of his men laid three short lengths of wood in the base of the stone structure, to provide a platform on which the box could rest. Then, together, the six men lifted the box up to waist height, and then lowered it onto the top of the stone structure so that it lay across the opening. They slung heavy ropes underneath it, looped the ropes around their shoulders and, when Je-tsun gave the order, lifted the box again just using the ropes. They shuffled awkwardly around, maneuvering the wooden box until it lined up exactly with the opening, then lowered it carefully into the structure.

Once it was resting on the floor, they pulled out the ropes from underneath it. Then they carefully replaced each stone slab on the top of the stone structure, sealing the cavity again.

Once he was satisfied that it was properly sealed, Je-tsun took a hammer and chisel and, in the middle of the central slab, carved two symbols that, in the Tibetan dialect, equated to the letters "YA." Each of the men touched the carving once, then all but one filed slowly out of the chamber—that man had a single final task to perform. Then they closed the door for the last time.

It was too late to complete their task that night, so they ate some of their provisions and drank a little wine before wrapping themselves in the furs and sleeping as best they could on the cold and rocky floor.

The following morning they rose to finish their work. Concealing the entrance to the inner chamber took a couple of hours, but when they'd finished the result was impressive. Without knowledge of what was hidden there, nobody would have any idea that the inner chamber even existed.

Je-tsun inspected the result and expressed his satisfaction.

"We have done well," he told the men who'd followed him on this, their final mission. "Now it is time."

The men filed outside and followed Je-tsun up the valley floor to the edge of a cliff, where a deep gully split the rock.

As they approached the edge, the man known as Sonam moved a little to one side, his expression troubled.

"Is this necessary, Je-tsun?" he asked. "You have all been loyal to me and to our master. Such loyalty should not have to be rewarded in this way."

The older man shook his head. "We would not speak out willingly, my lord, but we know not what the future holds, and this is the only way we can be certain the secret will be preserved."

Sonam shook his head. "I cannot witness this," he muttered. "I will leave you now."

He stepped forward and clasped Je-tsun around the shoulders, then turned and walked away without a backward glance, down the slope to where the two camels were grazing contentedly.

Behind him, he heard the first cry of pain as Je-tsun began the willing slaughter of his faithful and trusting companions.